Praise for
My Hope Is F...

"A tender story, told with loving care, *My H... ...akes many a twist* and turn, as Lonnie must choose between two good men. Her struggle is genuine, and the outcome remains deliciously uncertain until the joy-filled ending."

—LIZ CURTIS HIGGS, *New York Times* best-selling author
of *Mine Is the Night*

"Joanne has hit a home run with her Cadence of Grace series, and this book wraps up the story nicely. But I was never sure of the ending—either man could have made her happy—until the end. With memorable characters and struggles aplenty, this is the kind of story that will have readers telling their friends, 'You've got to read these books.'"

—LAURAINE SNELLING, author of the Red River of the North
series, the Wild West Wind series, along with *Wake the Dawn*
and many other books

"In *My Hope is Found,* God's grace and tender mercies bloom in the rugged hills of early 1900s Appalachia. The familiar characters of the Cadence of Grace series live out the delicious tension of romance and reason, heartache and hope—discovering the true measure of love and lasting peace. If you need a healthy dose of hope for a pesky case of hopelessness, this one is a must-read."

—MESU ANDREWS, author of *Love Amid the Ashes* and winner
of the 2012 ECPA Book of the Year, New Author

"This deeply moving conclusion to the Cadence of Grace series will captivate your heart and keep you turning pages. Once again Joanne Bischof brings her well-drawn characters and beautiful setting to life in an intricately woven tale of faith and love that will leave you wanting more. I highly recommend it!"

—CARRIE TURANSKY, author of *The Governess of Highland Hall*

"Joanne has the rare talent of creating such compelling characters and story worlds that I wish her books would never end."

—SERENA B. MILLER, RITA Award–winning author of *The Measure of Katie Calloway*

"A soaring conclusion to the Cadence of Grace series! With lyrical phrasing, Joanne Bischof blends measures of faith, hope, and love into pitch-perfect, soul-stirring harmony sure to resonate in every reader's heart. Bravo!"

—JOCELYN GREEN, award-winning author of the Heroines Behind the Lines series

"In *My Hope is Found,* gifted storyteller Joanne Bischof writes of redemption and reconciliation. Her characters stepped off the page and into my heart as I held my breath over their heartbreaks, disappointed dreams, and ultimate choices, all skillfully woven through with spiritual truths. Bischof has found her calling as a writer."

—BETH K. VOGT, author of *Catch a Falling Star*

"Amid the beauty of the Appalachians, Lonnie Sawyer O'Riley finds herself in an impossible situation created by her beloved Gideon's wild past. Having no choice but to give him up and move on, she clings to stubborn hope that all will yet be well, somehow. Like a mountain trail, the story winds through sunlight and shadow, through love and despair, with glimpses of grace at every turn. *My Hope Is Found* is another keeper from Joanne Bischof."

—MEG MOSELEY, author of *Gone South*

BOOKS BY JOANNE BISCHOF

The Cadence of Grace Series
Be Still My Soul
Though My Heart Is Torn

MY
HOPE
IS
Found

A NOVEL

JOANNE
BISCHOF

MULTNOMAH
BOOKS

My Hope Is Found
Published by Multnomah Books
12265 Oracle Boulevard, Suite 200
Colorado Springs, Colorado 80921

Trade Paperback ISBN 978-1-60142-425-9
eBook ISBN 978-1-60142-426-6

Copyright © 2013 by Joanne Bischof

Cover design by Kristopher K. Orr; cover photography by Mike Heath, Magnus Creative

Published in the United States by WaterBrook Multnomah, an imprint of the Crown Publishing Group, a division of Random House LLC, New York, a Penguin Random House Company.

Multnomah and its mountain colophon are registered trademarks of Random House LLC.

Library of Congress Cataloging-in-Publication Data
Bischof, Joanne.
   My hope is found / Joanne Bischof.
      pages cm. — (The cadence of grace ; book 3)
      ISBN 978-1-60142-425-9 (pbk.) — ISBN 978-1-60142-426-6 (electronic) 1. Marital conflict—Fiction. 2. Life change events—Fiction. 3. Blue Ridge Mountains—Fiction. I. Title.
   PS3602.I75M9 2013
   813'.6—dc23
                                        2013019611

Printed in the United States of America
2013—First Edition

10 9 8 7 6 5 4 3 2 1

To Noah—my husband and best friend.
And to the moment our lives
became a celebration that God is mighty
and He is mighty to save.

My brethren, count it all joy when you fall
into various trials, knowing that the testing
of your faith produces patience.

JAMES 1:2–3

My name is Gideon O'Riley, but most folks called me Trouble. Perhaps they still do.

I never thought I'd end up with Lonnie, the shy girl—walk her home, steal a kiss. I swear I didn't think her pa would find out. I hear swearin's a sin, though.

Trouble. They say it for a reason.

A wedding and then a baby. I never deserved one bit of it. But because of her goodness, she showed me how to hang on. A wife. A son. Such joy—I can scarcely describe it. My heart suddenly lived outside my chest.

They were so innocent. And though I'd buried my sins in regret, I couldn't shake the thought that my family would be better off without me. Much better off. Because it didn't take long for my past to unearth itself; one man, two wives.

I really should've seen that one coming. I hate that I didn't. If only I'd known that I was still married to Cassie...

Lonnie, Jacob—my family. No longer mine, for the preachers wasted no time in taking them from me. I'd have given anything to shoulder their pain. I wanted to hate Cassie. I did for a while, to my shame. But through it all, she showed me love. More so when she gave me my freedom. Gave me hope.

Undeserved as it was.

A man can sell his soul for a whole lotta reasons. A lesson I learned too late. There's a way to regain your soul—I'm learning that as well. I don't know this kind of grace, and I sure don't know much about the God who gives it.

But something inside me wants to.

One

Rocky Knob, Virginia
January 1902

G*o home to them."*
With Cassie's words fresh in his heart, Gideon stepped from the woods. The sun hit his shoulders. Warm as a caress. His suspenders bounced around his legs. They'd been abandoned halfway through his trek. Overwhelmed by the reality of what the day would bring, he'd dressed in a hurry, hungry for the sanctuary of these woods. Gideon ran a hand over the back of his neck where the stiff muscles complained. A bachelor once more, he'd bunked out in his shop the night before, leaving Cassie alone in the house.

Though he'd had both pillow and blanket, sleep had been lost to him.

With his thoughts ricocheting between Lonnie and Cassie, his past and future seemed muddled. A coil of tangled wire. Rifle slung over his shoulder, Gideon circled his thumb over the smooth wood of the gunstock, the sound of birdsong paving the way to the cabin. Cassie's cabin—a place he would no longer call home. But it really never had been. He chewed the inside of his cheek. Where was home now? He knew the answer. There was only one place for him, and that was beside Lonnie.

His heart lurched.

Never would he have taken Lonnie's hand had he known he was still wed to Cassie. Never would he have taken Lonnie's hand had Cassie simply spoken up about what she knew. Secrets revealed too late. Much too late. Kneeling, Gideon checked his final trap.

Saying good-bye to Cassie should be simple. Especially since Lonnie and Jacob were waiting on the other side. So what was he doing out on a cold morning checking traps? Gideon straightened and gripped his catch, wishing with all his heart that it could be more for Cassie. That it could be better. Her words pressed against the edges of his mind.

"I want this chance to do something right. Go home to them."

And here he was, leaving. With a puff of his cheeks and a duck of his head, Gideon walked on. Surely God had been smiling down on him the night Cassie had spoken those words only days ago. She didn't have to let go. But she had. He chalked it up to grace and nothing less. Of her own free will, she was letting him go home. Return to the life he once had. The life with his young bride and son. Gideon's chest tightened at the thought of taking Lonnie and Jacob in his arms.

He prayed that someday he might extend the grace that Cassie had extended to him. The thought filled him with wonder. Wonder at what it would feel like to have the peace that Cassie felt when she stepped out in faith. In goodness. For in keeping her word, she'd given him his future. Which was why he'd slept fitfully until dawn, overwhelmed by it all.

He clutched the rabbits tighter. A warm spell had turned the snow to mush, making his steps easy, but the trail was no match for his attention compared to the truths that roiled in his mind.

He was leaving today. Though it could take weeks before he got word that all was finalized between Cassie and himself—just as it should have been long ago—he couldn't stay with a woman who was no longer his wife.

Gideon shook his head and strode toward the cabin. Soon he'd be on his way to Elsie and Jebediah Bennett's farm, to his family. In a week's time, he would stand before Lonnie. Pulse racing, he nearly lost his grip on the rabbits' feet. Gideon tilted his face to the sun, the joy of it all warming him as much now as it had then.

As he rounded the bend, the smell of coffee all but pulled his feet along, and he spotted the small cabin nestled against a stand of oaks. Gideon rolled his shoulder that ached in the cool weather and stomped up the steps, spying Cassie in the kitchen window. The house was bright and warm when he stepped in. His pack, filled with all that he owned, sat beside the door. Cassie was at the stove, her braid long and dark down her back.

She glanced at him, her face registering amusement. "I thought you'd be gone." She watched him as he sifted through her crock of knives. "You were going to leave at first light."

"I'd planned on it."

"But…" She glanced at the rabbits.

He found the knife he was looking for, grabbed her worn pan, and flicked his head toward the porch. He lifted the rabbits. "I'll be right back."

"Gideon." Her hand on his arm made him freeze. "I can do this on my own. All of it." Her expression drove her implications deeper.

Nodding slowly, he stepped onto the porch. Sitting, he nestled the pan between his feet on the lower step. She moved in beside him and sat. Her patched skirts swayed soundlessly over her small boots. He sensed a weariness in her flushed cheeks. Though the scarlet fever had long since left her body, her strength was slow in returning.

"You're only gonna have half a day of light."

He nodded. "I know. I'll be off in a bit."

Hands pressed together, she seemed unsure of what to do with them. "How did you sleep?"

"Well."

"Liar."

He glanced over in time to see her faint grin.

"That shack had to be freezing, and you scarcely had enough blankets." She touched the toes of her boots together.

"I'd say it was best that way." He peered across the farm to where her brothers' hammers could be heard over the quiet of late morning.

Cassie smirked, but her eyes seemed sad. "Is that so?" She gave him the look that had made him weak in the knees on more than one occasion. "After months of sleeping in the rocking chair, you would have suddenly had the notion to take me in your arms?" She elbowed him softly. "You do realize you never even kissed me proper."

Feeling a half grin form, Gideon ducked his head.

Her blue-eyed gaze shifted away, over the farm, as if the fallen petals of their lives were scattered about. "Well, the rumors will abound regardless."

That they would. He and Cassie had been married for months, and people would think what they wanted. It wouldn't help that his reputation around Rocky Knob was anything but saintly. Hands stilling in their work, he studied her, his heart aching afresh. "What will you do, Cassie?" How he wished he could shoulder this burden for her.

With a wave of her hand, she tossed his concerns aside. "There's more to this world than Rocky Knob. I've got a mind to start fresh. Maybe I'll head to Stuart. Farther, Lord willing."

That spark glinted in her eyes—fire and determination—and he knew she was going to be all right. The breeze lifted loose strands of her hair, sending the molasses-hued ribbons dancing.

Slowly he shook his head, overwhelmed. Through her grace, another burst of joy shot through him. He would see Lonnie again. He would hold his son. Watch him grow up. Memories of them had hung like dusty pictures in his mind, but soon he would add new memories. It was a gift he could never repay Cassie for.

"I'm going to miss you." Unshed tears glistened in Cassie's eyes.

Throat suddenly tight, Gideon could only nod in return. He rose and, setting the pan aside, dipped his hands in the wash bucket.

She motioned toward the open door and his pack just inside. "Will you be bringing nothing else? What about everything in your shop? all your tools?"

"Give them to Jack. He'll make good use of them." He scrubbed at the creases in his palms, thankful for the friend he'd found in Cassie's youngest brother. He ran the icy water up his forearms, then grabbed the tattered towel.

Her expression grew so soft, he warred with the urge to cup her cheek as he once had.

"He'll be grateful," she finally said.

"He's a good kid." He struggled to find more meaningful words, but his gratitude for the young man's kindness ran deep.

Eyes down, Cassie leaned against the railing. She crossed her ankles, then uncrossed them. Gideon dried his hands on the towel longer than need be.

She stomped her foot. "Off with you now. I can't take this." She waved him toward the steps as if to set him in motion. "You're like a stray dog that won't leave." She quick-swiped at her damp cheeks.

He laughed, the sensation filling the empty spaces of his heart.

She wiped her cheeks again. Gideon captured her hand as it fell. He squeezed it, letting his thumb trace a slow circle on her wrist.

Without meeting his gaze, she spoke, her voice as soft as he'd ever heard it. "Please don't say good-bye. I don't think I could handle it."

Gideon swallowed the lump in his throat. "Fine, then…" Cupping the back of her head, he pressed a kiss to her forehead. "You're *wonderful*," he whispered against her hair.

Cassie choked out a laugh. "And you're a *scoundrel*."

He stepped back, wishing there were some way to keep her from hurting. Keep her from taking her next steps alone. But she was no longer his wife.

She tucked both hands behind her skirts. "Off with you."

Gideon stepped inside the doorway and grabbed his pack. He slid it on, bedroll and mandolin strapped snugly against it, and glanced around the small cabin.

Ducking inside, Cassie returned with an envelope. "Your copy. Though it will take some time for everything to be confirmed once the circuit rider turns in our papers." Gideon took it, gripping it so hard that it puckered beneath his thumb. He couldn't lift his eyes. Couldn't move from the spot. It all seemed so unreal.

"I don't know what to say," he said softly.

They stood without speaking for several moments, and finally Cassie glanced toward the sun that hung low in the sky. Her voice was distant but strong. "This is what peace feels like."

Gideon looked at her.

She pressed her hand to the base of her throat. "I've always wondered." Slowly, she shook her head. "I've always wanted it. And I finally feel it. It's not something you can take. Or steal. Or beg or borrow… It just is. All my life, I've been fighting it." Her fingertips dented her flesh. "I can't explain it, but a burden has been lifted from my shoulders. For the first time in my life, I'm doing the right thing." She closed her eyes, driving her words like a wedge into his chest. "I'm so thankful for this, and I know God's gonna take good care of me." She smiled at him. "He's gonna take good care of you too."

The sweetness of her words pulled her name to his lips. Gideon clung to what she said, praying it was true. He'd disregarded God of late. Surely whoever it was that filled the heavens above would have a thing or two to say about his actions. Though he'd tried to push the guilt aside for months, he knew there'd be a reckoning. He just didn't know what it would look like.

"Go." She flung an arm around his neck, holding him tight. Then just as quickly, she pushed him away, eyes glossy. "Or you won't get far before nightfall."

With one last glance into the face he'd come to know so well, Gideon stepped into the yard, pleading with his legs to carry him down the path. Carry him to Lonnie. He prayed for a strength that he knew he didn't deserve. But he prayed anyway, hoping with all his might that God would see among the broken pieces of his heart the desire to be more. To be better.

If he could have but one more chance.

He walked until he reached the edge of the woods. Finally turning, Gideon waved overhead. Cassie waved back, then pressed her fingertips to her lips and held her hand out to him. Touching his own fingers to his lips, Gideon did the same. He turned, faced his future, and started up the trail. Hope twined itself around his fears, and for the first time in a long time, he took a deep breath of fresh air.

Even as his past filled him with bittersweet memories, his destination called to him.

Home.

Two

Toby's hand shook as he cradled the cold leather reins in his palm. "Easy now." His mount pranced sideways, her hooves striking the frozen ground with muted *thuds*. Blood pounded through his veins, and Toby willed his nerves to steady. *Easy now.* With a flick of her head, the brown mare followed his gentle urging toward the broken end of the fence, which she cleared in one smooth leap. Landing on the other side, Toby tugged the reins, and Gael slowed to a walk.

He glanced around the Bennett farm, hoping for a sign of Jebediah. The man was nowhere in sight. The barn-door latch was pressed firmly in place. A steady stream of smoke trickled from the stovepipe, and Toby knew they would all be inside. Jebediah, Elsie…

Lonnie.

His hand flexed around the reins. He'd hoped to find the older man alone.

After removing his black hat, he ran his fingers through his hair. He glanced toward the kitchen window, where Lonnie stood scrubbing at something in the washbasin. He could see her loose braid draped over her shoulder, and she laughed at something Elsie said in passing. Her lashes flicked up, and large brown eyes locked with his. Lonnie gave him a friendly wave. Toby slowly lifted a hand, feeling sick and more like a dumb oaf with each passing second. *You can do this.* He remembered the verses he had read in his Bible that morning. "Faith an' fear have no room t'gether," he murmured, then glanced at the windows, hoping she hadn't seen him talking to himself like an imbecile. He needed to find Jebediah and get this over with. *Faith. Not fear.*

Just one question.

The worst that could happen was that Jebediah would say no. His heart throbbed at the possibility. Jebediah was the closest man to a father Lonnie had, and Jebediah's refusal would cost him dearly. Toby gulped. Oh, that Jebediah would say yes. The back door swung open, and Elsie waved a dishtowel in his direction. He licked his dry lips.

"Good to see ya, Reverend McKee! We were just sittin' down for supper. Come and join us."

Toby glanced at the sky to gauge the location of the sun but saw only a thick quilt of charcoal clouds billowing toward the farm. Supper. Toby ran a hand down his face. How was he to sit beside Lonnie and make any sort of conversation when every word he'd rehearsed was colliding with his nerves? When he dismounted, his legs barely held him. Surely he could hide his distress better than this. He dropped the reins and rubbed his damp palms against his legs. "Pull it t'gether, man." It was just one meal. One meal and then he'd request a private audience with Jebediah.

One meal. One question.

He led the brown mare to the barn and with fumbling hands gave her a quick rubdown. He tied a feed sack over her long face, then left her to her supper in the only empty stall. As the light dimmed to a hazy gray, he strode across the yard and scaled the porch steps, his boots echoing hollowly through the quiet evening. The kitchen was warm inside. He shrugged out of his coat.

Lonnie turned and smiled at him.

Was that him breathing so hard?

"I was wondering if you'd gotten lost." She set a pan of golden biscuits on top of the stove and with quick fingers moved them one by one into a basket. She stuck the tip of her thumb in her mouth and wrinkled her nose that was dusted in faint freckles. "Hope you're hungry."

He was. But not for food. Toby watched Lonnie carry the basket to the table.

"Reverend McKee is here!" she called into the parlor.

Nearly stumbling beneath her load, Addie waddled into the kitchen with Jacob in her small arms. The pudgy baby was almost too heavy for the six-year-old girl. Jacob waved a small spoon in the air and babbled. His cheeks were round and rosy. When he squirmed, Addie set him down, and he crawled toward Toby, who scooped him up. Toby gave Lonnie's son a gentle squeeze. Boyhood was bright in Jacob's green eyes, the color a trait he hadn't gotten from Lonnie.

"I'm so happy you came!" Addie clung to his leg.

Toby patted her dark curls. "An' I'm glad you want me here," he laughed, his Scottish accent a stark contrast to the little girl's mountain drawl.

"Supper's ready." Lonnie gently urged her sister toward the table. She reached for Jacob, who squealed when she plucked him from Toby's grasp.

"He always does that," she said with a laugh in her voice. She lowered Jacob into his hickory highchair. Her gaze met Toby's for several seconds. He gulped, realizing he should sit. Several pairs of eyes studied him.

"You all right?" Jebediah tucked his napkin into his collar.

"Me?" Toby's voice sounded strange to his own ears. "Aye. Great." He took a shaky breath and held it until his body relaxed. "This looks good."

Clumsily, Toby tugged the chair across from Jebediah, the one he always sat in when he visited. Gideon's chair.

Really? He had to think about that now? A shake of his head, and Toby sat. When Lonnie settled beside him, he felt the warmth from her shoulder against his. Toby dropped his napkin and nearly knocked a glass over trying to grab it. When he straightened, Jebediah arched an eyebrow. Toby forced a smile.

"Would you like to bless the food?"

Toby tipped his head. "Sure. I mean, aye. I mean, it'd be a pleasure."

Lonnie laid her hand on the table, palm up. His breathing quickened, and he covered her hand with his. Her small, soft fingers felt right there. His mind went blank. Clearing his throat, he searched for words. Nothing came other than the verse he'd mulled over that morning. "Dinna worry about anything, but in every thing by prayer and supplication and thanksgiving let your requests be made known to God. Amen." His voice was pitifully weak.

He saw Elsie stifle a smile before moving the basket of biscuits in his direction. "Thank you, Toby. That was…lovely."

He sat in silent torture, doing his best to engage in conversation. He ate without tasting until the beeswax candles melted into ivory stubs. Jebediah ran a napkin across his gray mustache and tossed it on the table.

The older man leaned back and patted his stomach. "Best food I've ever had."

"Thank you." Elsie lifted the pan of stew to spoon the last of it onto Toby's plate.

Toby held up a hand. "That's plenty, thanks."

Jebediah scooted his chair back. "I should see to the chores before it gets any darker."

Toby stood, and when he knocked the table with his leg, it screeched against the floor. Cups rattled against plates. "I'll help you," he blurted.

Elsie held the pan over his plate, eyes wide and round.

Before he could think, Toby grabbed his coat and hoped he did not look as foolish as he felt as he burst past the kitchen door. He welcomed the cold air as he walked in stride with Jebediah to the barn. A wind traced against the skin of his neck and wrapped itself around his thick wrists. He pictured his hat hanging on the peg in the kitchen. His calfskin gloves on his bed at home, where he'd forgotten them.

"You all right?" Jebediah asked.

"Me?"

Jebediah chuckled.

After a slow breath, Toby stepped forward to tug the heavy barn door open. Inside was warm and dim. "I'm fine." The door creaked shut.

Without saying a word, Jebediah dumped hay into Sugar's feed trough. After filling a sack with oats, Toby secured it to the mule's nose.

"Actually," Toby began, trying to focus on the hungry animals, "I wanted to speak with you."

When the barn door rattled in the wind, their heads turned in unison. The metal hinges creaked and complained.

This was it. Rubbing numb fingertips against his palms, Toby tried to remember the words he had practiced over and over. "I wanted to ask you..."

Jebediah nodded slowly, patiently.

"What I'm trying to say is... I've been meaning to ask you..." With a sigh, Toby closed his eyes. "I'd like your permission to ask for Lonnie's hand in marriage." A single breath, then he looked at Jebediah.

Jebediah's eyes tightened for the briefest of moments.

Toby's heart thundered in his chest.

After a few moments' hesitation, Jebediah spoke. "Do you have any idea what that girl means to me and Elsie?"

With a slow nod, Toby answered, "Aye." He stepped forward, dry straw crinkling beneath his boots, and ran his hand across the back of his neck. "She means that much to me too, sir."

Jebediah's expression softened ever so slightly.

After setting the bucket down, Toby squared his shoulders. "I love her. More than anything." He hoped they'd be more than words to Jebediah. That the older man might have seen as much. "I'll take care of her, sir."

"I'm sure you will." Jebediah swept weathered knuckles across his forehead and over the bristles of his cheek. "You know I'm protective of her."

"As you should be."

Jebediah tugged on his beard. "I never thought this day would come." He folded his arms. "But here it is—and rightly so. Lonnie deserves to be happy." He squinted at Toby. "How much has she told you about Gideon?"

The name nearly clamped Toby's throat closed. "Not much."

After a slow sigh, Jebediah glanced toward the nearest window. "I found them, two autumns ago. The both of 'em. Wandering in the woods alone and lost. They had no home. No hope. And poor Lonnie…" Jebediah shook his head, memories deepening the creases of his forehead.

Toby nodded, but it killed him to think of Lonnie in that life. "And you brought them here."

"Gideon had a lot of growing up to do. Growing up that he was meant to do before he had a wife and child." Jebediah tugged his beard again, gray eyes distant. "Lonnie was much too good for the likes of him. But God had a plan for both of their lives. In the end, that boy broke his back every day trying to deserve her."

Toby struggled to make that image form. Yet he trusted Jebediah's judgment. He squared his shoulders again, feeling strangely unsettled. "Lonnie told me he's gone an' he's not coming back. If that's what worries you—"

"I'm not worried." Jebediah shook his head. "He's not coming back."

It was impossible to mistake the sorrow in Jebediah's voice.

"What I'm trying to say is that she's seen more heartache in her short life than I ever have."

Toby nodded.

"I don't want any more pain for her."

"No sir. I'll do everything I can—"

Jebediah held up a hand. "I know you will." His expression changed. A half smile tugged at the side of his mouth. "I won't keep you waitin' any longer, son. My answer is yes."

Toby's head lightened. "Yes?"

"You have my permission." The gray-haired man extended a hand. "Ask away. Her hand is for the taking by whomever she wants. And truth be told, I can't think of a better man I'd like to see her choose."

Dazed, Toby gripped Jebediah's hand and shook it.

Sleet pelted him like icy shot, and Gideon half expected to hear the echo of a shotgun as he tugged his floppy hat lower until it covered his frozen ears. At first the oilcloth coat kept him dry, but the slushy snow melted against his neck, trickling across his collarbone. Soaking him from the inside out. He stepped over a fallen log, the rotting wood blackened and covered in a layer of ice.

Still, he couldn't stop smiling. He was headed home. A few more days would lead him to the Bennetts' door. His feet slowed as he took that in. He would arrive unannounced. Unexpected. With nothing but his word. Nothing to his name. Pockets nearly empty, he suddenly wished he had more.

For he had nothing to offer Lonnie and Jacob, save himself.

Though she asked for so little, the yearning to be their provider—their protector—made him wish he had more than a few coins to his name. But there was little he could do about it now. He focused instead on the fact that in just a few days' time, he would hold Lonnie in his arms. He would pick Jacob up and never let him go. Even as Gideon's soggy boots squished through the slush, his pace quickened. Ignoring the drenched handkerchief in his back pocket, he smeared a hand over his eyes and down his unshaven jaw.

After another hour, the sleet slowed, then lightened as the storm moved past. Spears of sunlight struck the ground, sending up a sleepy fog wherever they touched.

Gideon tilted his face to the sky and closed his eyes. He'd been walking for two days now and had scarcely stopped to rest. Normally he would have made camp each night. But not this time. Never had he been in such a hurry. Never so eager to be home.

Still, the life that he'd lived the last few months trailed him like smoke.

A familiar pain pierced his chest, and Gideon rubbed his palm against the wet oilcloth as if that could soothe it away. He crouched against a tree and, with his pack in front of him, fumbled around until he found a piece of venison jerky. Sitting back on his heels, he took a bite of the dry meat. A blue jay darted down from the canopy of bare limbs, its wings fluttering against the wet air. Gideon watched it soar. He knew the feeling. The bird landed on a nest with a shiver of feathers.

Gideon wondered if he would be welcomed. They weren't expecting him. That much he knew. Why would they? All they knew was that he was married to another. He glanced over his shoulder and noted his footprints marking the way he had come.

How long ago it seemed that he and Lonnie had returned to Rocky Knob. Never did he anticipate that what should have been a short visit would forever change their lives. Remembering the moments that pulled Lonnie and Jacob away from him, Gideon hung his head. God had blessed him with a greater life than he deserved. But like the darkness that chases the day, the fruits of his reckless abandon had come looking for him. And he had lost everything. He had lost Lonnie. And now?

Gideon straightened. He pushed away from the tree, flung the pack onto his shoulder, and set off toward the only destination he could fathom. His family. Now that the sun had won its duel with the clouds, he took off his hat and let the rays warm him. Suddenly, it was as if the last four months had never happened. No one had pulled Lonnie from his grasp, forcing him to leave his family behind. Despite the muddy slush that clung to his worn-out boots, making each step a challenge, Gideon felt lighter as he pressed on. Nothing and no one stood in his way. Lonnie was only miles away. And he was a free man.

Three

As Lonnie strode from the kitchen, she tied her ticking-stripe apron into place, the fabric beneath as worn as her heart had felt that morning. She didn't know why, but a surprise wave of melancholy had hit her. Perhaps it was the weariness of a long winter. Perhaps it was the way Toby seemed distant the last few days. She tried to think of something she might have done or said, but nothing came to mind. Bucket in hand, she walked toward the far corner of the two-story house. Aside from Jebediah and Elsie, he was her one and only friend. She hated the thought of losing that. Of losing him.

The morning was crisp and damp, not the kind of day to be out in. But Lonnie couldn't sit still a moment longer. She picked her way through the slush to the edge of the house, where her leaching barrel sat a good foot off the ground on an old crate. Her thumb fiddled with her empty ring finger. A habit. Nothing more. Or so she told herself each time she thought of Gideon's ring lying in the box in her room upstairs. A wave of sadness threatened to slow her feet, but Lonnie forced herself to focus on the task at hand.

Crouching beside the barrel, she watched water trickle down the homemade trough and into her bucket. She sighed heavily, a thousand impossible hopes floating away on the breeze.

She'd woken to a slushy snow, and just as she had expected, the bucket was nearly full of hickory ash lye—the best, as her aunt had taught her. With nothing to do other than watch the dark liquid drain, Lonnie once again grazed her thumb where Gideon's ring had once rested. Then, just as quickly, forced her fingers to busy themselves with something. Anything. It was a habit she needed to break. For her hand had been bare for months now. Gideon's ring long since tucked out of sight. He had a new wife now. Lonnie rose.

Perhaps even a child on the way.

A flush slapped her cheeks, and she stumbled as she reached for her bucket. *Lord, give me the strength to get through this.* Lonnie grabbed the bucket and lugged it toward the kitchen. She tipped her chin up when it trembled and forced several slow breaths before opening the kitchen door.

"Whatcha got there?" Elsie asked when she walked in. The older woman sat at the table with Addie at her side. The little girl held a needle and thread while Elsie showed her how to work a seam. The room was warm with the scent of cinnamon and spice.

Lonnie set the bucket near the stove. "Lye." She moved to get Elsie's largest pot, glad her voice slipped out stronger than she felt.

"Did you not finish a batch of soap a few weeks ago?"

Allowing herself a moment before answering, Lonnie carried the pot to the stove, her braid swinging against her back. "These will be to sell in town."

"Ow!" Addie jumped and held her finger up to her face. Her eyes crossed as she studied it. "That hurt."

Elsie kissed the little girl's fingertips, then rose. She moved to the oven and gave Lonnie's arm a reassuring squeeze. "I don't want you to feel alone in all this. Jebediah and I are here for you." Elsie reached for her hot pad.

Lonnie stepped out of the way. "You've already done so much."

MY HOPE IS *Found* 19

The oven door creaked open, and Elsie pulled out a dark loaf of pumpkin bread.

"I want to help in any way I can." Lonnie motioned toward the pot of warming liquid. "It's not much. But it's what I know how to do." She tugged at her damp shawl, freeing it from her shoulders.

Elsie's smile was kind. "Well, when Jebediah takes this next batch in, you make sure and add a few extras to the supply list."

Nodding, Lonnie turned to the table and the gray-and-pink fabric that rested in a folded heap of pins and pattern cuttings. Waiting for the liquid to boil, Lonnie lifted up the makings of the small dress. She fingered the half-formed bodice, then opened the sewing basket. The lid tapped the table with a soft *thud*. She shuffled through its contents, finally holding out two spools of thread against the gray-and-pink plaid. "Which one, do you think?"

Addie twisted her mouth, then pointed to a light-gray thread that would nearly disappear with their tiny stitches. "That one's just right."

"I agree. Isn't it a pretty pattern?" She patted the folds of cloth that would soon be formed into the skirt.

Elsie stepped closer. "Send a man to town with a list of supplies and just pray that he knows what kind of fabric a girl would want for Christmas."

Addie dropped a handful of buttons with a soft clatter. She slipped from her chair and fell to her hands and knees, then crawled under the table. She bumped her head on the chair. "Ow. I never knew learning to sew would hurt so bad."

Lonnie chuckled. She pressed the soft flannel between her hands. "It's perfect."

"Of course it's perfect." Jebediah pushed the back door open and quietly lowered an armload of wood behind the stove. Addie scrambled from beneath the table and pranced toward him, her cheeks flushed.

Jebediah closed the door softly. He brushed his hands on his pants. "I have excellent taste." After tugging his pipe from his shirt pocket, he tapped it idly against his hand, then set it near the tin of tobacco on the shelf.

Elsie propped her fists on her hips, copper eyes narrowing.

His grin widened. "Oh, all right. The shopkeeper's wife helped me pick it out. I didn't know one fabric from another." He reached for a knife and sliced off a piece of bread. It steamed in his fingers when he broke it in half. "If it were up to me, y'all would be makin' a dress out of burlap."

Lonnie laughed as she rummaged for a needle in the sewing basket. "Well, thank goodness for female help." Needle in hand, she found her scissors and stepped to the parlor window, where the light was best. The rocker creaked as Jebediah sat nearby, brushing crumbs from his coat. Elsie followed close behind, a cup of coffee in her hands, which she handed to her husband.

"I saw Toby left his hat." Jebediah nodded back toward the kitchen. "Though I suppose he'll be by any day to fetch it."

Sewing lesson forgotten, Addie grabbed her picture book from the desk and crawled onto Jebediah's lap. After setting his steaming cup aside, Jebediah wrapped his arms around the little girl and creaked the binding open. He waited for Addie to find the story she wanted and settle her dark curls against his shoulder.

Lonnie lowered her scissors to the windowsill and looked out into the yard, where Toby appeared nearly every other day. He was one of the best men she'd ever known. She tried to focus on that truth, forcing any thought of a green-eyed man and what might have been into the deepest recesses of her heart, wishing with all her might that the yearning would fade. But it clung to her—an unwelcome visitor in the wee hours of the night when her determination waned under the longing for him to hold her. To hear his voice, tangle her fingers around his.

Her needle pierced the fabric, and she yanked the thread taut. After half a dozen tiny stitches, she took a deep breath, her thoughts far from the garment in hand.

Toby's a good man. She nearly said it out loud, so quick was she to remind herself. He would be a good father to her son. But did she love him? Lonnie fiddled with a corner of the little dress. She thought of his smile, of his kindness and goodness, and knew without a shadow of a doubt that she cared for him. Very much. The future would be bright. It had to be.

Leaning against the windowsill, she focused on the tidy row of stitches. The gray thread blended nicely, as she'd hoped. Elsie brushed past her, setting a plate of warm pumpkin bread at her side, followed by a cup and saucer. The dollop of butter melting on the bread made Lonnie set aside her chore long enough to have a taste. Brushing crumbs from her dress, she sipped the hot brew.

By the time Jebediah finished and Addie hopped up to put the book away, the sound of Jacob's cries came muffled from the bedroom. Lonnie's feet thrummed up the stairs, and she found him on her bed, his baby quilt tight in his grasp. A wide smile spread across his face, revealing several teeth he had worked hard to produce. He babbled at her and rubbed the back of his hand over his eyes.

She clapped and, reaching out, caught Jacob as he lunged into her grasp. They sank on the edge of the bed, and she buried her nose in his creamy neck.

She breathed in his scent and shut her eyes. "My boy," she whispered as they swayed side to side. Jacob nestled his face into her shoulder as if to rub away his sleepiness. Lonnie kissed his forehead and smoothed her palm over the silken skin and into curls the color of autumn.

Hair that mirrored his father's.

She battled against the ache. With a kiss to the top of Jacob's head, she closed her eyes, fighting off the memories of events that tore Gideon from her grasp. There was no sense in longing for what she could not have. No need to glance around to know that his drawer was empty. His scent long gone. And the echo of his laughter had long since faded from the walls.

The bed creaked when Lonnie stood. Pressing her son to her chest, she stepped toward the door.

Four

Gideon shook out his jacket and draped it over the shrubs. Shivering, he grabbed his only other shirt from his pack. He shook out the wrinkles, not really caring. Teeth nearly chattering, he yanked it on, followed by his jacket and pack. Without ceremony, he pressed on. As he fumbled the top shirt button into place, the breeze that tapped its chilly fingers against his chest made him wish for a patch of warm summer sun where he could lie down for a few hours and dry out proper.

An apple slipped from his pack and hit the damp and frosty bracken. He grabbed it up as his empty stomach rumbled. Judging by the light, he knew it had to be well past breakfast. He'd dawdled long enough trying to get dry. With only damp wood for a fire, the night had been a cold one. He'd tried to sleep but kept waking up shaking, so he finally forced himself to rise and keep moving, despite the dark. Another apple tumbled from his pack, and with a grunt, Gideon retraced a step and grabbed it, all the while thinking he'd forgotten to secure the flap of his pack. After sticking the small apple between his teeth, he pulled the pack off and tugged on the leather cord, cinching it tight.

"Hiya."

Pulling the apple from his mouth, Gideon glanced up to see an old woman standing in the path. "Mornin'." He wiped the back of his hand over his lips.

With a large walking stick in one bony fist and a basket in the other, the woman gestured toward him with her elbow. "You ain't from around these parts."

"No ma'am."

She studied him a moment. "Where ya headin', son?" An army of multicolored skirts swayed when she shifted her weight, the tattered hems brushing against her snowy boots.

"Fancy Gap," he answered.

The woman lifted her chin from the thick folds of scarf draped around her neck. Glancing southwest, she flashed a crown of silver braids. Turning her gaze back to Gideon, her eyes landed on the apple in his hand. "That all ya got to eat?"

"No ma'am." He took a bite.

"Hmm." Her gaze roved from his hat to his boots. "I've got a stew on."

By the look of her threadbare clothing and her bird-thin arms, that stew would cost her dearly. He shook his head and tried to swallow his bite so he could better speak.

She rested a knobby hand on the top of her walking stick. "Don't tell me a travelin' man in the middle of winter nibblin' on squirrel food is gonna turn down hot stew. You're half-frozen." She inched her basket higher up her arm. Several snowflakes floated down from the gray tempest above. A pair of honest eyes stared back at him.

Gideon scratched his head. "Then I'd say that's an offer I can't resist."

"Good." Her gaze sharpened and she glanced at his shirt.

He fiddled with a loose button absentmindedly, then suddenly remembered that, like a blockhead, he'd simply thrown it over his shoulders.

Her blue eyes held a hint of amusement. "You weren't expecting company, I see." She turned and headed toward the thickest part of the woods.

Gideon quickly thrust the buttons into place and tugged uselessly at the hem as he strode after her.

"Name's Adelaide," she said over her shoulder.

"Gideon O'Riley." His breath was frosty in front of his face. The snowflakes thickened around them.

"O'Riley," she repeated without slowing. She flicked a branch out of her way, and Gideon caught it before it smacked him in the face.

Even as he wiped his cold, wet fingertips on his sleeve, he spotted a small cabin tucked amongst the thick brambles, safely out of sight of pass-ersby. Adelaide pushed against the door and wiped her small boots on a mat just outside. "Kick yer feet."

Gideon did as he was told and carefully wiped the snowy mud from his boots until the smell of stew pulled him through the doorway. Heat stung his face. He dropped his pack. Adelaide set her things on the table and quickly went to work stoking the fire. Gideon glanced around the humble space. Dried herbs hung overhead and in every nook and cranny of the small cabin, it seemed. The air was musky and rich with their scents. Straightening, Adelaide rose on her tiptoes and reached for a basket above her head.

Gideon stepped closer, his eyes adjusting to the dim light of the tiny, one-room house. "Can I lend you a hand with that?"

"No." She grabbed a stick from beside the stove and hit the basket until it tumbled into her arms. She squinted at him, and despite the wrin-kles that framed them, her eyes held a childlike glow. "But it looks like *you* could use some help." She moved back to the fire and lifted the lid on a blackened copper pot. He stepped sideways, careful to keep out of her way.

"Well, ya just gonna stand there all mornin'?" Adelaide reached to a shelf and pulled down a jar of dried herbs. "Hang up that wet jacket by the fire before you catch cold."

He did as she said, his shirt taut across his shoulders as he knelt and held his frozen hands out to the flames. They tingled back to life. He spotted the woodpile that would hardly last the night. "Mind if I bring in some more firewood?"

With both hands clamped around the jar, her paper-thin skin did little to conceal the sinewy muscles of her small arms. "If it suits you." She grunted. "But you could start by opening this."

Taking the jar, he popped the metal lid and handed her both pieces.

"That was tighter than usual."

"Yes ma'am. It was."

She stared at him. "And like I told ya, name's Adelaide. Most folks call me that, so don't go callin' me nothin' fancy."

"Yes ma'am."

She thrust a twig of a finger toward him.

"Yes, Adelaide." He gulped.

With swift movements that did not match her age, Adelaide moved bowls to the table, followed by two cups and a pair of spoons.

Gideon stepped toward the door.

"Supper's ready. Firewood'll last." She glanced at him. "You sleepin' out there in this? There ain't an ordinary for miles and miles, and it'd be a shame to freeze that tail end of yours out there in the cold." She moved the heavy pot to the table, and when her arms shook, Gideon fought the urge to help her.

"I need to keep moving."

"Well, take a few hours and warm up, at least. Put yer bedroll right here in front of the fire."

"I will. Thank you." Not wanting to make a mess of her well-swept floor, Gideon sank into the chair beside the fire and unlaced his boots. His body settled in, exhaustion all but taking over. Yanking one boot off, he set it close to the flames to dry. As he worked on the second, his elbow bumped a little table, nearly sliding a pair of books to the floor. He straightened them and noticed a wrinkled newspaper. A glance at the date showed it was a month old, but what caught his eye was a Help Wanted advertisement. He touched his thumb to the page, noting the city of Stuart.

Gideon thought of the coins in his pocket. He glanced up at Adelaide as she placed a small loaf of dark-brown bread beside his plate. Though she'd never ask, the coins were hers. He moved to the washstand when she filled it with steaming water and, after scrubbing the grime from his hands and forearms, sat at the table at her bidding. Adelaide creaked into the chair across from him. She folded her hands together.

Her crown of silver braids tilted forward, and she closed her eyes. "For the bounty we are about to receive, may the Lord make us truly thankful. Amen."

"Amen." Gideon lifted his head.

She dunked her spoon into the pot and filled Gideon's bowl. "Well, don't stand on ceremony for me, young man. Dig in."

"Thank you." He poured cider into his cup from a chipped crock and filled her cup when she didn't object.

Leaning forward, he rested his elbows on the table, broke off a chunk of bread, and dipped it in the stew before sinking his teeth into the moistened crust. The hot bite all but melted in his mouth.

He glanced around. "Did you grow all this?" he asked, nodding toward the herbs hanging in the corner and along the window frame. Things grew in pots along the windowsill.

"Some of it. Others I gather. You can find just about anything." She took a sip of broth, her eyes finding Gideon's over her spoon. "If you know where to look." She slid a jar of pickles toward him.

He ate quickly, hungrier than he'd realized. When he'd finished a second bowl of stew, he leaned back in his chair. The fire was warm against his back. His feet were heavy, his head so light he had to run his hand over his face.

"Better lie down before you fall down." She stacked his bowl on top of hers.

Too tired to argue, he sat on his bedroll in front of the fire. Moments later he was lying down, and the quiet clatter of dishes being washed and stacked lulled him to sleep.

Overcome by exhaustion and soothed by the warmth, he felt his body become heavy. He let the day wash through him, out of him. A skirt brushed past his shoulder. Cassie. Gideon nearly spoke her name aloud. Or was it Lonnie? His head spun. The fire crackled and popped, bathing his senses in an orange glow. His dreams grew and just as quick seemed to fade. The memory of Jacob's laughter fading. Gideon felt his hands flex as if to capture it. But it was too late. Heat tore through his shirt, nearly burning his back, and Gideon shifted.

A shadow moved by, and he opened his eyes in time to see Adelaide's petticoat brush past his bedroll. Flames swallowed up a new log sacrificed to the roaring hearth. Boiling sap oozed from a splintered crack. Gideon sat up and rubbed at his eyes with the heels of his palms.

The soles of Adelaide's shoes tapped lightly on the floor. Gideon looked over to see her cram her burgundy sleeve up past her elbow before she snatched a skillet from the stove and shook a pair of fried eggs onto a plate. She grabbed the remainder of the morning's bread with her other hand. "I hope you slept well." She knelt and, using the hem of her skirt, moved a charred enamel coffeepot away from the flames. Her wrinkled face was the same level as his. "Hungry?"

Gideon ran his hand along his collarbone and felt glistens of sweat. "Yes ma'am. Thank you." Still dressed, he shook off his blanket and moved away from the fire. Remembering the wood he'd wanted to bring in, he ducked outdoors. The icy air hit him, and he grabbed as much wood as he could carry. Back in the house, he carefully stacked the load on her hearth. His arms finally empty, he brushed dust from his shirt and hands.

"Food's on," she said. "Have a seat."

"This smells"—he shook his head and tugged a chair away from the uneven table—"incredible."

"Nothing like travelin' the worn road to make a man want eggs and stale bread." She sat and filled his coffee. Gideon noticed there was no cream or sugar on the table. He took a sip, not caring either way. He'd take his coffee black any day as long as it was hot, and even that was optional at times.

Adelaide bowed her head. "Thank You, Lord." She hesitated and Gideon lifted his eyes. With a push of her lips, she shook her head. "Amen."

"Amen."

"Butter's fresh." She pushed an ivory crock toward him.

After smearing some on his slice, Gideon chewed the crust in silence. He ate his eggs in a few quick bites.

"More?" Adelaide asked, turning in her chair toward the stove.

Gideon waved her down. "I'm fine, thank you." He did not want to take any more of her provisions than necessary. "There's plenty of bread here. I hate to waste it."

"Spoken like a man who'd eat just about anything right now."

He nodded his agreement. His shoulder ached. From the cold or the journey, he didn't know. Probably both. He rubbed it gently.

Adelaide glanced toward the fire, her crown of braids catching the light. Gideon studied her hunched form and wondered how she survived all alone. He took in the small space, and though it was humble, it seemed to hold all a body could need.

"I'm afraid you won't get far in this weather."

"I've walked in a storm before."

Her eyelids, heavy with petal-thin skin, blinked twice. "I can tell."

Gideon shifted his boots.

"You comin' or goin'?"

"Little bit of both. Headin' back to my family. Wife and son." He'd spoken too soon. "Well, my son…and his mother." He cleared his throat.

Something flickered through her sharp eyes. "What took you away?"

It was a question he couldn't begin to answer. Not now, like this. Gideon rolled his sore shoulder.

She seemed to notice. Knife in hand, Adelaide smeared butter on a slice of bread, then set it gently in the center of her plate. Then she went to her bed and pulled a wooden box from underneath.

He wanted to change the subject. The less he talked about himself, the better. "What about you? Any family?"

She waved away the question as if it didn't exist. Snapping the case open, she returned with a small glass jar. From the jar she pulled a pinch of something and dropped it into a little pot, which she placed near the fire.

Returning, she tapped him on the shoulder. "Your shirt." She made the motion of him pulling it off to the side.

Uncertain, he slid the top buttons free.

She frowned.

Fine. He unbuttoned two more and pulled his arm from both his shirt and long underwear. With leathery fingers, she touched the muscle that always ached in the cold.

"What did you do?"

"I dislocated it. This past fall. Been botherin' me off and on ever since."

"Hmm." She pulled the small copper pot away from the fire and set it on the table. Scooping a finger full of moist, dark herbs, she pressed them against his shoulder. Almost too hot for comfort.

Gideon tightened his jaw, glad when the mixture began to cool.

She grabbed a rag and tore it into a strip. Gideon held his arm out as she wrapped his shoulder, sealing in the warm herbs.

"What is this?" he finally asked.

"It'll help the ache." She motioned for him to put his shirt back on.

With the tight bandage, his movements were slow, but he managed to slide his arm into the sleeve of his thermals.

"I've got a cure for anything that could ail a body." She watched as he slid his arm gingerly through the sleeve of his wrinkled work shirt. "But some things can't be cured with what you can gather from the earth."

Peering up at her, he started on the buttons.

"There ain't an herb on earth that'll cure what's ailin' *you*."

The fire crackled in the hearth, and Gideon lifted his eyes to the window. White flakes fell. The sky was growing darker, heavy clouds blanketing mountains that seemed to be holding their breath.

Holding a secret he wasn't privy to.

"Have you…have you ever wondered what it would be like to begin again?" He looked back at Adelaide. "Just start over. Have everything you've ever done wiped clean?"

She set the jar of herbs beside him, and by the look she gave him, it was a gift. Humbled, he studied her wrinkled face. She sat, and after a few moments, she spoke.

"I'm a good listener." An invitation.

Gideon focused on the last button, finally sliding it into place. He rested his hands on the table. "My whole life I've always worried about losing myself. I've always worried about missing out on what it was that I wanted."

"And now?"

"Now." He folded his fingers together. "Now, all I can think about is them. All I want is my family. Perhaps that's selfish in itself." They deserved to be cared for. Could he even do that?

Adelaide pursed her lips. "Letting go can be a harder way to love than holding on." Like rain on a river rock, her blue eyes glistened.

And he wondered what she'd lived through.

They sat in silence. Gideon rolled his shoulder gently, the soreness nearly a memory.

"S'pose you'll want to get on the road now. You've got a fair bit of ground to cover yet."

"Yes ma'am." Gideon stood and pushed in his chair. Adelaide rose and shuffled inside her cupboard as Gideon cinched his bedroll tight and fastened it to his pack. She slid the jar of herbs as well as a larger jar of pickles into his pack. In the corner of the room, she lifted the lid to an old chest and, after shuffling around, pulled out a dark knit cap.

She handed it to Gideon. "Keep warm out there."

"Thank you." When she turned away, Gideon slipped his coins on the windowsill beside her bed. After cramming the cap into his coat pocket, it took him but a minute to lace his boots.

Remembering the old newspaper, he asked if she still had need of it. Adelaide handed it to him along with a small bundle of bread. A thankyou on his lips, he slid both inside his pack.

"You take care now," she said.

"I will. You too."

Hands clasped in front of her, she stepped back.

Gideon nodded in farewell, then stuffed his hands in his coat pockets, ignoring his gloves. Snow fell gently all around. Beckoning him forward into a land of white and quiet. A purity that was filled with possibilities.

"Letting go can be a harder way to love than holding on."

But he'd already let go. He saw Lonnie's face in his mind. Something inside began to ache at the sight, and he swallowed hard.

How he missed her.

There was so much he wanted to say, but Gideon knew that the moment he saw her, words would fail him. Everything else would fade away. He'd fold her in his arms and not let go. The memory of her scent greeted him—a memory that had hidden itself for months. His blood surged, kindling a fire within him. It carried him forward. The feel of her hair, the sound of her voice against his neck.

His footsteps slowed. Would she push him away? Would she believe him? believe that he had loved no other but her?

Why should she? She had no reason to.

His breath quickened. Not after what he'd done. He'd left her to be with another. "But not by choice," he blurted aloud to himself, his voice so earnest he hung his head. Who was he fooling? He'd left all the same. For months, he and Cassie had lived beneath the same roof.

Husband and wife.

Chills crept across Gideon's shoulders at what Lonnie would think of him. Of what she must have imagined he'd done. His reputation would be hard to stand down. He'd spent all of his adult life with a woman at his side. On his arm. And then some. Lonnie knew that.

Oh, God.

What she must think of him? He hadn't loved Cassie—not in the way the law gave him freedom to these last few months. In the way it had to appear. But Lonnie had no way of knowing that. Even then, was she to simply take his word that he was no longer married? After all he'd done to break her trust, he didn't like the idea of having nothing but his promise to give her. He wanted to earn her trust, but he needed her to allow him into her life to do that.

He thought of the papers the circuit rider had slipped into his satchel. His and Cassie's wish to dissolve their marriage had surely reached the courthouse by now. Gideon had used the Bennetts' return address for his confirmation that all was settled. Had the letter arrived at the post office in Mount Airy?

It seemed too soon. Much too soon. Gideon's boots halted, and he glanced in the direction of the small town. He could go there and find out. It'd be a few days' journey, but even then, it could take *weeks* before he received confirmation from the courthouse. No. That would never do.

Or...

Gideon glanced southeast.

He could go directly to the Patrick County courthouse himself. A day or two would lead him to Stuart, where the courthouse was. A stop there for the proof he needed to show Lonnie that he was an unmarried man, and he would be on his way in no time. It took only a moment to decide, and Gideon picked up his pace.

It killed him to turn away from the path that would lead him home. He longed for his family, but he wanted to reach them as a free man.

And there was only one way to find out. Two more days and he would be in Stuart. One, if he walked fast. Lifting his eyes, he studied the darkening sky, then ducked his head and quickened his steps. One day. He would make it there in one.

Five

O ut you go." Lonnie shooed a speckled hen from her resting spot, and the chicken flapped out of the coop, into the open yard. She ushered out two more, taking care not to startle them. Rake in hand, Jebediah worked beside her, piling up old hay and feathers. Lonnie laid two green eggs in her bucket, a surprise considering the cold weather, and set the bucket aside. After blowing a lock of hair that fell across her forehead, she fiddled with the handkerchief knotted around her mess of a bun.

Jebediah lowered a shovelful of muck into the wheelbarrow that stood between them. Lonnie gripped the handles, and the wheels squeaked into motion.

"Lonnie, don't move that. I'll get it."

"I don't mind. Besides, it's only half full."

Jebediah's mustache lifted, and the skin around his eyes crinkled. "That's 'cause I knew you'd try and move it."

She pushed the wheelbarrow out of the coop, grateful the fresh snow scarcely rose past her toes. Tipping the load beside the garden just as Jebediah had done the time before, she watched the contents tumble out. A good shake, and the last of it freed from the rusted metal. Lonnie heaved the wheelbarrow to a stand and started back.

Scraping his shovel against the coop floor, Jebediah glanced up. "Let me move the next one."

"I don't mind. Honestly, it gets me out into the sunshine."

Jebediah looked toward the thick woods. Despite the late January temperature, he wiped his sleeve across his brow. "Toby should be here in a bit to lend a hand with the barn. I wanted to pay him, but he wouldn't hear of it."

Lonnie tugged at the flannel shirt hanging low over her muddy skirt. "He'll be here in a bit?" She tried to tuck loose strands of hair into her bun.

"He was supposed to be here just after breakfast." Jebediah's gray eyebrows fell. He lifted a shovelful of muck into the wheelbarrow and dug in for more. His breath came in spurts when he spoke. "Wonder what's keepin' him."

"I'm sure he'll be here soon."

"He will. That man's the hardest worker I know."

"Yeah?" Her voice sounded weak. Lonnie licked her lips to keep an unwelcome emotion from betraying her.

"Well." Jebediah glanced at the ground between them. He ran his palms together as if to wipe dust from memories meant to be forgotten. "You know what I mean." His tone was distant, apologetic. Gideon's name hung in the air.

Corralling her thoughts, Lonnie fiddled with the hem of the oversized shirt she'd put on that morning. They stood there several moments without speaking until finally Lonnie grabbed handfuls of clean straw and filled the empty nesting boxes. "Maybe I better go inside and get cleaned up."

"You don't want to wait around for Toby?"

She lifted a pinch of her skirt. "Not like this." Having spent the morning with Addie and the growing goats across the way, she was more than ready for a pass at the washstand and a change of clothes. Her heart sank when Toby rode Gael into view.

"Aw, come on. You look fine to me."

Lonnie laughed as she moved toward the house, all the while knowing it was too late to vanish out of sight. "Sure." She wiped her hands together, feeling the grit of dirt between them. "I think I look nice enough to give the mule a bath."

Hearing Toby approach, she forced herself to turn and face them.

As he walked toward the coop, Toby pulled a pair of work gloves from his back pocket. "Give the mule a bath, you say? Now that's a sight I'd verra much like to see." He slowed, finally standing closer to Jebediah than Lonnie.

But she had his gaze.

"Sorry I'm late. A man up the way just lamed his horse. Gael an' I spent the morning hauling wood from the forest to his door." He flicked his thumb over his shoulder toward the brown mare who was searching for something to graze on.

"How'd it go?" Jebediah asked.

Toby followed Jebediah's silent lead back into the coop, and Lonnie leaned against the doorway to keep from filling up the small space. "I think Gael was in a mood about getting up that early." He rubbed his forehead as if tired. "But she's young. She can handle it." His smile landed on Lonnie. "The good news is that with his horse out of service, he asked if I'd like to borrow his wagon for anything...so I thought I'd see if you might want to come with me to church this Sunday. I know it's too far on foot, but perhaps if I brought the wagon 'round..."

"Oh, really?" Lonnie straightened. "That would be such a treat."

"I thought you might enjoy a bit of an outing."

She nodded and suddenly remembered how desperately she needed to get inside and change. "Would you like some coffee, Toby?"

He rested a gloved hand on the end of his shovel. "That'd be nice, thank you." He seemed to study her.

"I'll be right back." Lonnie walked to the house. Inside, she scrubbed her hands in the kitchen washbasin, then snatched a tin mug from the cupboard and filled it with coffee. A splash of cream and a sprinkle of sugar later, she carried the steaming cup outside. As her fingers thawed from the heat, she watched Toby lower the wheelbarrow. Pulling off his work gloves, he met her halfway.

"Thank you." He tipped the cup to his lips.

Lonnie fiddled with the cuff of her plaid shirt. Gideon's shirt.

She thought she was rid of every trace. Every memory. But a few weeks ago, the shirt surfaced in Elsie's mending basket, and Lonnie couldn't bear to let it go. Why she'd worn it today of all days, she'd never know. It wasn't as if she really wanted to get it dirty. In fact, she had every intention of soaking out the stains and smudges from today. She peered up at Toby, who kept his eyes away, as if to give her time to speak.

"You're welcome," she hurried to say when she realized she was yet to answer. If she wasn't a mess from one end to the other today. She took a step back. "You'll stay for dinner, won't you? I can make that honey cornbread you liked last time."

"I think it was Jacob's favorite too." His voice warmed on the name of her son. "I think between the two of us, we ate most of the pan."

"I remember that." Another patch of peace seemed to cover her ever-mending heart. "He seems to like anything you do. Instead of trying to get *him* to eat his peas, I'm just going to give you an extra helping. That'll do the trick."

Tilting his face to the ground, Toby grinned as broad as she'd ever seen. He tugged at his hair, and when he finally glanced back at her, his eyes held a tenderness that made it nearly impossible to look away.

Jebediah leaned his shovel against the side of the coop and gripped the handles of the wheelbarrow. "It's a good thing I'm not payin' ya."

"I should get to work," Toby said. A friendly nod to Lonnie, and he strode back toward the coop.

Lonnie hurried into the house. She filled her washstand with hot water and crawled out of her clothes, tossing them to the side. As she scrubbed soap up her arms, she forced herself not to pick up Gideon's shirt, smooth out the wrinkles, and drape it over the chair. Once washed and dressed, Lonnie scurried downstairs to start the noon meal.

Struck with cabin fever, Elsie had taken the antsy children to a neighbor's house for the morning. The kitchen seemed to sigh an emptiness without her. Lonnie filled a bowl with cornmeal and leavening, cracked two eggs, then whisked in softened butter.

Through the window in the back door, she could see Jebediah and Toby working. Though she didn't want to let on, she knew Toby had spoken to Jebediah alone last week. The thought unsettled her, but not from anxiety. Lonnie stepped from the window. If her suspicions were correct, Toby would have a question for her soon.

And not just any question. She forced herself to take a steady breath.

After beating the batter until it was silky, she filled a greased cast-iron pan and slid it into the oven. She was gathering up broken eggshells when Toby shouldered the door open, an armload of wood pressed to his chest.

"Jeb and I just finished, and he sent me in to bring you wood." He dropped the split fir in the woodbox and brushed dust from his pants. "He might have mentioned something about wanting coffee too."

"Sounds like Jebediah." Lonnie filled a cup. "Would you like more for yourself?"

Toby placed his empty cup in the washtub. "No, thank you. I'm fine." He stood just behind her. Surely he wouldn't ask her *now*?

Hands atremble, Lonnie poured cream into Jebediah's coffee. *Oh dear.* Jebediah didn't take cream. Toby did. A shake of the pot showed it was nearly empty. Well, Jebediah was getting cream today.

"Okay." The word squeaked out. She set the pot down so hard the lid bounced off, hitting the floor in a splatter of coffee. Snatching a rag from the basket, Toby wiped it up. He replaced the lid and chuckled as he fiddled with the cloth between his hands. He spoke before she could.

"Elsie's not home, is she?"

Eyes down, cheeks aflame, Lonnie shook her head. She braved a glance up, knowing what a fool she must look.

A half grin lit his face. "I better get back out there then. Before Jebediah drags me out by my shirt collar."

She felt her neck warm. "Jebediah'd never do that to you."

His voice was soft. "He'd have every right."

His words were not helping her pulse.

She took a slow, steady breath, reminding herself that Toby was as good a friend as she'd ever had. Nerves or no nerves, she knew what the future held, and she was happy about it. "Well, don't go gettin' into any trouble over me."

"It'd be worth it." He stepped toward the door.

"And that coming from a reverend." She arched an eyebrow but wondered if her cheeks were as rosy as they felt.

"You're right. I apologize. I shouldna said that." His dimples deepened, voiding his apology. "S'pose I better do something to rectify the situation." His gaze touched hers before he stepped out. A cold burst of air swayed Lonnie's skirt, and the door closed behind him.

Six

G ideon heard the town of Stuart before he saw it. He crested a low, bare hill—the trees long gone—and spotted the buildings in the distance. He smelled smoke. Heard the clatter of horses and wagons and, somewhere far off, the ring of a hammer on an anvil. Yet the only sight to draw his attention was the large courthouse. The brick building stood out in its prominence, and for the first moment in days, doubt flitted through him.

Despising the feeling—the thought of losing Lonnie all over again—Gideon strode down the hillside all but talking aloud to convince himself not to be afraid. He crossed onto Main Street and headed straight for the courthouse that stood like a beacon in the center of town. He dodged a wagon and then a group of women, taking care to step over a dog sleeping across the wooden sidewalk.

Striding up the stone steps of the courthouse, he suddenly felt very small. Snow gathered along the bases of the massive columns, and Gideon shivered as he reached the broad porch. The tall doors were closed. A tug on one large handle and it opened more smoothly than he expected. He stepped into the warm building.

Greeted by the musky scent of perfume, he immediately spotted the source sitting behind a desk.

"Excuse me, ma'am." Gideon pulled his hat off as he approached the woman.

The receptionist looked up, a pair of spectacles pressed against her round face. The wiry bun mounded on her head was streaked in gray.

"I have a question, and I'm not sure where to begin."

Her smile was genuine. "What may I help you with?"

"I...uh... I sent an annulment request to the court through the circuit rider, and I'm curious as to its status."

He might as well have spoken in German for the look she gave him. "Annulment."

He nodded soberly.

"What is your name?" She slid a small pad of paper toward herself and picked up a stubby pencil. He spoke and she eyed him from head to toe. With an arch of her eyebrow, she scratched *Gideon O'Riley* in tiny script. "I will be right back. You may have a seat while you wait if you'd like." A gaudy ring on her finger caught the light when she waved her hand toward some benches.

Gideon turned his hat in his hand. "Thank you, ma'am."

Her boot heels echoed down the corridor, and he sat on a hard bench. A few people milled about, murmuring in hushed tones. Turning his hat nervously, Gideon looked out the window and tried to swallow, but his heart felt like it was in his throat. He all but jumped up from the bench when the woman returned. Her face was stony. Gideon drew in a heavy breath.

"Mr. O'Riley, I'm afraid that the judge has not gotten to your case yet." She pressed her hand to a broad belt that cinched the waist of her lacy blouse. "It could be a while yet. A few days...perhaps longer. *Most likely* longer."

"Longer?"

"Yes sir. These matters take time." She strode back to her desk with an invitation for him to follow.

"Is there a way I could speak to him? I need to get home, ma'am."

"I'm afraid not today. It's been a hectic day, and the judge has a hearing in several minutes." She glanced up at a massive clock on the wall above her. "And he's leaving today at five on the dot, as usual. Judge Monroe does not like his supper delayed. Perhaps you could return in a few days' time."

He didn't have a few days. But he was growing more certain that he couldn't return to Lonnie without proof that he was no longer married to Cassie. Gideon ducked his head. "Thank you."

As he stepped back, she eyed him. "You're not from around here?"

"No ma'am. I'm from Fancy Gap. I just came here to settle this."

"Ah." She drew in a slow breath and let it out as if she had all the time in the world. "Follow the main road downtown, and on your right, you'll see a yellow house. It's owned by Mr. and Mrs. Smith and is the ordinary in town. Unless you'd prefer one of the inns, though they are pricier."

A tug on his wrinkled shirt, and Gideon wondered what sort of hobo he must look like. "Thank you." After picking up his pack, he stepped out of the courthouse, where a faint snow fell softly. *Fantastic.* Just what he needed. There was no sun to gauge the time, but judging by the growl in his stomach, it had to be around noon. Gideon leaned against one of the massive pillars, pulled on his gloves, and made himself comfortable.

Folks strolled about in the street below, several climbing the steep steps into the courthouse, only to return an hour or so later. Gideon was half-frozen and nearly asleep when a man exited the brick building, his pristine black coat and glossy hat hinting that he was no mere citizen on courthouse business.

Gideon straightened so fast he nearly slipped and fell. Steadying his nerves, he strode toward him. "Sir."

The man looked at him as he pulled on a pair of shiny black gloves. Gideon nodded cordially, uncertain of how to begin, but all the while knowing this was his chance.

"Judge Monroe?"

The man glanced at him briefly. His nod was scarcely discernible.

"May I speak with you a moment, sir?"

The older man slid on a tall hat, taking care with his hair. "I've worked for nine hours straight today." His mustache twitched. "All I care about in this moment is the roast I know is sitting on my dining room table, and unless your name is Sally Monroe, I have no interest in what you have to say." Pulling a watch from his waistcoat, he started down the steps.

Gideon followed. "Sir, please. I just have a question." He hitched his pack higher up on his shoulder, and the mandolin hummed when he bumped it.

"And I'm afraid it will have to wait." The judge's silver eyebrows darkened his brow as he sized Gideon up in one blink. Snow flecked in brilliant specks on the man's black coat. "I do not conduct business outside of the court."

The judge walked on and wove through the evening crowd. A pair of men tipped their work hats to him as a dozen polished boots made prints in the freshly fallen snow. Gideon watched the judge go. He let out a heavy sigh, chagrined by the weariness that was beginning to wash over him. This was no time to come unhinged.

But he was cold. And mighty hungry.

Looking around, Gideon took note of the buildings up and down the main artery of town. He headed toward what he guessed was downtown, as the receptionist had advised. Glancing in the windows of the first inn, Gideon spotted a restaurant where happy patrons dined. He ran his hand over his mouth, forcing himself to say a thankful prayer for the bread in his pack. He walked on, slowly, having nowhere else to be.

Nowhere else except home. But that wasn't about to happen tonight.

Light pooled from business windows, and Gideon walked until the storefronts thinned to larger fenced yards. The sun must have set beyond the clouds, for the land was growing darker by the minute. He spotted the ordinary in the distance, lit by two cheery windows. The yellow building invited. Beckoned. But with nothing in his pockets, Gideon stopped before he got there and dropped his pack against the side of a building. The two-story clapboard would block the wind, and the overhang would keep the snow at bay. Though he would have lit a fire had he been in the woods, he was just going to have to live without one here.

With his bedroll folded in half, Gideon sat on the dry surface and sighed. He stared into the windows of the saloon, aglow with warmth and laughter. He stuffed his gloved hands against his sides and crossed one ankle over the other. A few hours, and it would be morning. A few hours, and he could be back at the courthouse. Gideon held his breath, if nothing else but to keep the cold out of his lungs. Finally, he drew in a shaky chest full of air, the iciness chilling him through. Closing his eyes, he settled his back against the side of the building as comfortably as he could.

He imagined Lonnie and Jacob preparing for bed. The thought of Lonnie reading their son a book by candlelight chased away his gloom, and he clung to the image as he fell asleep.

"I always feared you'd die young."

Shivering, Gideon opened one eye. A man stood over him, the voice familiar, but the blur of sleep fogged his mind. The morning sun over the broad shoulders of the man blinded him.

"I'm not dead," Gideon said, shifting his stiff muscles. He blinked, but the light was too bright.

"Nearly." The man had a kindness in his voice. A familiar drawl. Memories of working the apple farm flooded the front of Gideon's mind.

"Tal?"

"What on earth are you doing sleeping on the sidewalk? And in Stuart, of all places? Why didn't you stay at the inn? Or the ordinary?" Tal adjusted his weather-worn hat.

"Let's just say my funds are limited." Gideon groaned as he struggled to stand. "It's a long story."

Tal crouched and extended his hand. "You look plumb frozen, son."

Stumbling to his feet, Gideon forced his numb legs steady. But they were shaking something fierce. "I think I am." Gideon squinted at his friend, soaking in the joyous sight of a familiar face. Never had he expected to see his former boss standing before him. "What are you doing here?"

"Came on some business." Bending, Tal grabbed Gideon's pack and brushed at the icy layer of frost. "We'll talk over some breakfast, all right? Let's get you inside and some hot coffee into ya." Tal motioned uptown, and even as Gideon's stiff muscles complained, he followed Tal down the wooden sidewalk.

They strode in silence as if Tal was giving him a chance to wake up proper. Gideon's blood warmed as he moved. Tal didn't speak until they'd settled at a table in the inn restaurant and placed an order.

"So what brings you here?" Tal tossed his coat over the back of his chair, and in two breaths, a woman brought cups of steaming coffee.

Gideon wrapped his hands around the hot mug, pulling away only long enough to splash in a bit of cream and stir in sugar. A sip and he tightened his hands around the cup, feeling the warmth all the way to his toes. "I need to speak with the judge…if I can." The glass of the window was cool against his elbow.

When Tal's eyes widened, Gideon was glad the woman in the black apron brought two plates of biscuits and gravy, delaying the conversation. She set the plates down with a clatter and a smile.

"Thank you." Gideon turned his fork in his hand. He glanced at the clock, wondering what time Judge Monroe arrived at the courthouse each morning. "I'll tell you everything. But"—he glanced out the window, certain he must seem as distracted as he felt—"I'm not exactly sure what's going to happen just yet." Gideon turned back to his friend. "Listen, where ya headed next?"

"The merchant up on Fourth. It'll take me a few hours to stock up on the supplies I need. And then I've got to stop in at the saddler before I head back to the farm this evening."

Gideon took a bite of biscuit and then another. Conversation falling by the wayside from sheer hunger. Glancing out the window, he spotted a stout man in a dark coat stride past. His top hat glinted in the morning light. Gideon grabbed his coat. He downed a heavy gulp of coffee, all but scalding his tongue. Jumping to his feet, he gripped Tal's shoulder. "I will meet you at the merchant's as soon as I'm done."

"Sure thing, son." Tal glanced out the window toward the courthouse. He waved Gideon forward. "Don't worry none about me. You git!"

"See you in a little bit." Gideon squeezed Tal's shoulder, then darted out into the cold. Jacket in one hand, he barreled down the street, not caring about who stopped and stared. The wooden sidewalk thundered beneath his boots as he ran. Judge Monroe started up the steps of the courthouse as Gideon crossed the street.

"Sir." Gideon moved in his path, walking backwards. Panting. "Please, sir. I need to talk with you."

"Yes. You and half the people in this county."

"Please, sir." He gulped a breath of air. "Ten minutes."

The older man glanced up, and something registered in his eyes. "Not you again."

Still walking backwards, Gideon had to step out of the way of a pair of ladies in autumn-hued dresses.

Nearly to the massive doors, the judge adjusted the cuff of his shirt. He glanced at Gideon, his eyebrows so thick they shadowed his dark eyes. "Don't you have something better to do?"

"No." He didn't. "And I'll be back tomorrow if need be."

When the judge stopped walking, Gideon halted.

"And then I'll be back the next day. Until you talk to me. Ten minutes. It's all I'm asking for."

Shaking his head, Judge Monroe motioned toward the building. "I'll give you five. But this better be the end of it."

"Thank you, sir." Gideon followed him into the courthouse and past the wide-eyed receptionist he met the day before. Her perfume had changed, as had her hairstyle. Gideon nodded cordially, noting a twitch of amusement around her mouth. Uncertain as to how unusual this all was, he simply followed the judge down a corridor to a door with an etched-glass window.

Gideon stepped aside as the other man slid a key in the lock.

"This way."

The judge strode into his office and gruffly stuffed back the curtains on the windows. Gideon stood in the doorway.

"Sit." After working his way around the massive desk, the judge set a leather case beside his chair and sat with a sigh.

Gideon sank into the wooden chair across from him.

"What in tarnation can I do to get you out of my office so I can go on with my day?"

Gideon scratched his head. "I need to know if I'm married or not."

The man leaned back in his chair. "You're crazier than I thought."

"No, you see..." Gideon shifted his feet, and before he could give in to the heat rising up his neck, he explained his predicament. His past.

Judge Monroe stared at him blankly as he spoke. Slowly, he tipped his chin back. "I remember you." His face shadowed even as his thick hand rested lightly on the messy stack of papers beside him. "You caused a great deal of trouble for me. A *great* deal of trouble. Some months ago."

How he believed it. "Yes sir." Gideon scooted forward on the small chair. "I'm very sorry—"

The gray-haired man held up a hand before fiddling with one side of his mustache.

Gideon eyed the stack of papers on the desk. The judge followed his gaze to the mountain of cases beside him. Predicaments that were no doubt ahead of Gideon and Cassie's.

"When is your hearing date?"

"I don't have one."

"And the young lady? Your wife?"

"She's not here."

His eyebrows lifted. "You're not giving me much to work with. I'm a judge for the state of Virginia, Mr. O'Riley. Not a miracle worker."

"Please." Gideon said, chiding the tremor in his voice. "I need my son." He needed Lonnie.

Twisting his mustache between two fingers, the older man studied him. Gideon didn't blink.

"Do you have any idea how *unconventional* this is?"

He hadn't anticipated any problems, but now he knew what a fool he'd been to think this would be simple. "I'm sorry, sir." And he was. More than he could say.

After a knock on the door, the receptionist strode in with nary a sound. She set a steaming cup on the desk and then left just as quietly. Gideon glanced around at the shelves of law books. Some of the spines broader than his palm. The books that held his fate.

"Now you need to understand…this will require some time if you want me to give this any kind of attention. Rushing the matter will not help your case, Mr. O'Riley. As the state of Virginia sees things, you're still a married man."

Gideon hung his head.

"The wife who no longer wants to be married to you isn't here to state her case. Why is that?"

"She's too weak to travel. At least this far. Perhaps in time…"

Steepling his fingers, the man shifted in his chair. He sat a moment, staring at a spot on his desk. Gideon could all but see the wheels spinning in his mind.

Finally, the judge spoke. "There's most likely something to be done here, but I'll need a little time to resolve this satisfactorily for all parties involved." He waved a hand to the stack of papers. "But I'll need several weeks. A month. Possibly more."

Gideon fought to keep his distress from showing. Instead, he grabbed onto the only certain thing he could. "A month. I'll be back in a month." He was already on his feet before the judge could change his mind.

A curt nod. "Come back in thirty days, Mr. O'Riley. We'll get you back to your wife and son."

For the first time since entering the building, Gideon felt a burst of hope. "Thank you, sir." He reached for the judge's hand and shook it. "Thank you."

Seven

I s this ready to get loaded?" Gideon hoisted a crate off the merchant's counter. Tins of spices clanked together. Across the store, Tal was looking at a new pair of cutters with the shop owner's assistance.

"Yes, that one's ready to go." The clerk made a notation in his ledger as Gideon backed out the door.

He carried the crate out onto the sidewalk and slid it into the back of the wagon next to the rest of Tal's supplies. A tin of baking powder tumbled out and fell. Gideon picked it up, brushed it off, and set it back in its place.

The shop bell clanged as Tal stepped out.

"I better not break anything, or it'll come out of my pay."

"You got that right," Tal said with a laugh in his voice. "Which, if I remember correctly, was half of what I pay my other men." He slid his hat over graying hair.

"You know, I'm not sure if that offer still stands."

"Oh, is that so?" Tal clapped him on the back.

"I was a desperate man then."

Tal arched an eyebrow.

"All right, I'm still desperate. But have pity on a poor soul, will ya?"

Tal chuckled. "I'm sure we can work something out." He climbed onto the wagon seat, and Gideon lunged up the other side.

"Thank you," Gideon said seriously. "I appreciate you offering me the work. I need it."

"It's my pleasure. You're a good worker, and I'm glad to have ya. Besides"—he flicked the reins and the wagon lurched into motion—"couldn't very well leave you to sleep on the sidewalk in Stuart for a whole month."

Gideon nodded. "And I'm grateful for it."

The horses settled into an easy pace as Gideon and Tal rode out of town.

Hitching his boot up on the footrest, Tal relaxed into his seat. Gideon folded his arms over his chest and enjoyed the sunshine the day had to offer. Tilting his chin back, he let the rays hit his face. A moment later, he ran his hands down his face, realizing just how much he needed a bath and a shave.

"So tell me. What happened, Gideon?"

With the back of his hand, Gideon scratched his scruffy jaw. When he didn't answer right away, he felt Tal watching him. Finally, Gideon drew in a chest full of air. He let it out slowly. "I ran into a bit of trouble."

Tal twisted his mouth to the side. Waiting.

"It's a really long story."

"We've got the time."

With a puff of his cheeks, Gideon rubbed at a splinter in his palm. Before he could change his mind, he blurted out the words. "I was married before Lonnie." There was no sense pretending around Tal. No sense pretending around anyone.

Tal's eyebrows shot up.

Suddenly warm, Gideon shrugged out of his jacket. He dropped it on the seat and rolled back the cuffs of his shirt until his undershirt poked out against his forearms. "To a girl I grew up with. Lonnie didn't know about it. I didn't tell her because it was supposed to have been annulled. But it wasn't."

Tal's eyebrows shot higher. "How on earth…"

With a tug, Gideon pulled off his hat and tossed it between his boots. "This is why I needed to meet with the judge." He glanced sideways at his friend. "Like I said, it's a long story."

"And like I said"—Tal nodded toward the snowy lane ahead—"we've got the time."

Gideon wasn't sure how he would tell the story of a selfish man who followed his pleasures, but the words began to come. He told of how, at one time, his lusts had included Cassie. At another, they'd included Lonnie. Never once had he glanced over his shoulder to see what his actions might cost him.

What they would cost others.

And yet, he'd continued down the path of destruction. Of selfishness. The path that led a man to lose everything he'd ever loved, only to gain what he hoped to lose forever. In that moment, he understood heartache.

Gideon then spoke of the yearning to care for those he'd hurt. That and how grace unfolded in the unlikeliest of places. The rest of his story.

His life.

"I didn't deserve what Cassie gave me." Gideon pulled Jacob's knit cap from his coat pocket and turned it around in his hand. "She gave me my life back. She didn't need to…yet still she did." His shoulders felt burdened under the weight of that kind of goodness.

A goodness he would never come close to possessing. To repaying. Yet he was overwhelmed with the urge to try. Somehow. Someway. Chilled, Gideon leaned forward and rested his elbows on his knees, his son's cap still tight in his grip. They rode in silence for several minutes.

Finally, Tal squeezed his shoulder, holding tight as if understanding lived in his grip. "That's quite a story." He pulled away. "Quite a life you've lived already. It sounds like you've learned some mighty important lessons through it all."

"I sure hope so." Overcome with the urge to run his hand over Jacob's downy head, Gideon rubbed his palms together. "I keep thinking it ain't over, though."

"It never is," Tal said, his face kind. Sober. "It never is."

Gideon tugged his jacket into his lap and held it there, fiddling with a frayed cuff. "What if I can't get back to them?" Chin to chest, his voice sounded small. "What if something goes wrong?"

"It may." Tal nodded, as if aware of the possibility. "But…have you given any thought to the notion that maybe God has a plan? That maybe God already knows exactly how it's going to work out? That what you or I may see as wrong may just be another part of that plan? As perhaps these last few months have been for you."

Leaning back, Gideon slid his son's cap back into his pocket. "I sure wish He'd tell me what His plan is then."

Tal grinned. "Doesn't really work that way."

"I know."

"Though it'd be easier if it would. Sometimes life just takes faith."

"Faith."

"And hard work to keep your mind off the rest."

Chuckling, Gideon nodded. He was desperate for that kind of work. Anything to keep him from losing his mind at being so close to Lonnie and Jacob—yet still so far.

"So thirty days. Then it's back to town?" Tal asked.

"That's the plan."

Tal dipped his head in a soft nod.

Bouncing his heel, Gideon looked off into the distance. A month before he could know if he would ever be free to love Lonnie.

"Well, I'll see to it that you have plenty to keep you busy. Keep your mind off things." Tal gently flicked the reins.

"I'd say that sounds good. So where are you at in it all? Trees are dormant right now. What'll I be doing?"

"Well…" Tal cast him a sideways glance. "I've been working on a new variety that requires grafting. I had some success with it about five years ago. Produced a lovely apple. Back then I grafted just three trees. But now I'm working on increasing that, and I have what I need on hand to do a great deal more."

"I don't know anything about grafting trees. Do you think maybe it'd be better for me to work with something I couldn't ruin?"

"Maybe you'll be better at it than you think."

Gideon doubted it. But he appreciated Tal's faith in him.

"I'll show you. Owen too. You'll catch on quick, and the idea is to do it carefully and at just the right time. The young trees will need a bit of care. So you can help me tend to them during the cold weather until you leave."

Sticking up his bottom lip, Gideon nodded. "Sounds like a nice way to earn a living. I confess"—he rubbed his palms together—"I'm looking forward to getting back out in the orchard. I enjoyed that work."

"It suited you. It suited you real nice. And it's not that way with everybody." Tal smiled. "I think apple farming may flow in your veins."

Gideon chuckled. "Just maybe."

Eight

Lonnie folded her hands and tucked them beneath the heavy plaid blanket Toby had brought for her. With her hair pinned up in a crown of braids, she was glad she'd brought her ivory scarf to wrap around her bare neck this cold Sunday morning. Elsie had offered her a pair of earrings with the sweetest painted glass beads Lonnie had ever seen, but without pierced ears, she had settled instead for a comb with a delicate engraving to tuck into the plaits of her brown hair.

"This outing is such a treat, Toby. Thank you for going to all this trouble."

Leaning against the wagon seat, Toby flicked the reins with a dramatic air. "If you only knew how much this inconveniences me, you'd feel verra sorry indeed."

She elbowed him, and his eyes sparkled. Sliding her hand through the crook of his arm, she savored his warmth and his company. With Jacob content in her lap, she settled in for the five-mile ride to the church.

"Addie would have liked this. I'm just sorry that they all couldn't come."

"A bit of a cold, you said?"

"Yes. Addie wasn't feeling well, and Jebediah's snug in bed, though he fought it something fierce. And Elsie's so sweet to stay home and tend to them. Someday I hope to have s—" She fell silent and her cheeks warmed. Toby gave her arm the tiniest of squeezes.

Lonnie chattered away most of the ride, delighted by the new sights and sounds of the community as Toby pointed out houses and talked about the families they belonged to.

"I'm curious now… Of all the places you could have chosen to live. Why here?"

He lifted one shoulder in a shrug.

Half smiling, Lonnie elbowed him gently. "There's gotta be an answer."

"Not a very good one." His eyes were suddenly distant. "My folks had dreamed of this wilderness. We left Scotland when I was thirteen."

"And how…how long ago was that?"

He circled two fingers around a thick wrist, the reins resting easy in his grip. "Are you wonderin' how old I am, lass?"

She nodded sheepishly.

"Twenty-eight." He turned his eyes to the road as if not wanting to see what she thought of that. "We made it as far as New York, then lost my mother shortly after. To my father, the dream died with her. 'Twas just the two of us for a long time, then he passed a few years ago. With them both gone, I couldna just sit around." He glanced at her. "This seemed as good a place as any to settle. One can only search for so long before you realize there are just some things you canna outrun."

Gently, she squeezed his arm. "I'm so sorry."

Lifting her hand, he kissed it. "Dinna be sorry. I should have told you sooner."

They passed a handful of people walking the busy country road, a flurry of colorful coats and smiles.

"And there's the church." Toby squinted and pointed in the distance.

Lonnie craned her neck. She'd been there once or twice before, and each time the sight of the quaint building lifted her spirits. "It's just charming. To think someday soon it will be yours."

"Well, I'll preach there, if that's what you mean." He winked and she laughed.

He parked the wagon beside dozens of others. After hopping down, he spoke softly to Gael as he fastened her feed sack to her long nose. The horse flicked her tail and crunched oats. Lonnie straightened Jacob's sweater and tugged her shawl tighter over her pink eyelet blouse as Toby strode around to help them down.

Feeling dozens of eyes on them, Lonnie was glad when he simply took her hand instead of gripping her waist as he'd done when helping her up. It wouldn't have been seemly for the young reverend to hoist her down as she'd seen other men do for their wives. For she certainly wasn't his wife. Though a sparkle in his eye made her wonder if he didn't have something up his sleeve. He grinned, flashing those dimples.

Mercy, her nerves were unsteady when she was around him.

His mouth was near her ear. "There's a few folks I need to speak with before the service begins," he whispered. "But I'll only be a minute. Sit wherever you like, and I'll come find you."

"So you're not preaching this morning?"

"No, thankfully." He half grinned. "Not with a bonnie lass here to make me nervous."

She nearly swatted at him, then seeing a pair of young women watching their exchange, retained a careful composure. She was suddenly aware of how fetching Toby was to the young ladies of Fancy Gap. "Take your time," Lonnie said as they parted ways on the church steps. With Jacob in her arms, she stepped inside and walked along the narrow aisle, unfamiliar with the surroundings.

Quickly spotting Gus, the Bennetts' neighbor, who left every Sunday morning on horseback, Lonnie bade him good morning. He updated her on his young goats and told how the little nanny that would soon be hers was growing. Lonnie promised to bring him a batch of the soap she had curing in the cellar, and Gus said hers was the finest he'd ever used.

With church beginning in a few minutes, Lonnie turned to find a seat and spotted another familiar face. She nearly bumped into the dark coat.

"Good morning, Reverend Gardner."

The stout reverend glanced up from something he'd been reading, a slight surprise in his pale eyes. "Good morning, Lonnie. A pleasure to see you again."

"And you as well. It seems it's been ages." Yet not long enough, she realized, when the heart-wrenching memories struck her afresh. The man who had married her and Gideon was the same man who'd overseen their parting. And here she stood beside him.

He patted Jacob's head. "My, look how this little one's grown since last I saw him."

"I wish the Bennetts and I were able to attend church more. Today is a treat courtesy of Reverend McKee."

"Ah." Reverend Gardner nodded amiably.

When a thin silence fell, Lonnie spoke. "And how long will you be in Fancy Gap?"

"I'll be here another few weeks. And then it's back to Rocky Knob for me. Your mother will be very pleased to know that I saw you. I'll be sure to tell her hello for you."

"Thank you." Lonnie's heart filled with warmth. "I would appreciate that so much."

"I'll spend a month there, during which time Reverend McKee will take over the Sunday services here for a spell."

"Oh, wonderful." Lonnie whittled the toe of her boot into the floor. She cleared her throat. "And how is… I mean, do you often see…"

Reverend Gardner's face was kind. Knowing. "Gideon? No, not often."

With her free hand, Lonnie fiddled with her son's tiny fingers, fighting a swell of emotion at the sheer mention of Gideon.

"Rarely is he in church. Though there was one Sunday rather recently that he and Miss Allan—I mean that he and his…"

Lonnie's face flushed with heat. She prayed it didn't show.

Reverend Gardner cleared his throat. "That *they* were in church. It was a pleasure to see him there. After his lengthy absence…" His voice trailed off awkwardly.

"And were they…were they well?" Lonnie pursed her lips when her voice betrayed her.

"Both well. Though the young lady had recently been ill, it seemed. However, it looked as if she was recovering nicely."

"Ill?"

"I'm not sure what it is that had her under the weather, but when they were in church, she was thinner than I had remembered. And a bit pale. Poor thing seemed quite out of sorts."

Something struck Lonnie. An understanding she couldn't quite place. Or that she didn't want to. Before she could put her thoughts together, a woman spoke behind them.

"There'll be a baby by year's end for that one."

Shattering the shield before Lonnie could put it up.

Heart plummeting to her stomach, Lonnie turned to see the woman speak to another at her side. "I felt the exact same way each time I was expectin'. Mark my words. Those are the signs of a mother."

Turning, Lonnie suddenly felt lightheaded. "Oh," she blurted, her voice small, so tight was her throat. "W-well, thank you for your time, Reverend Gardner. I won't keep you any longer." She forced the words out dizzily and nodded an awkward farewell. Turning quickly, she found a seat and sank onto the hard pew before her knees gave way.

She was shaking.

Gideon. Her sweet, sweet Gideon. And Cassie. She wanted to scream.

The two women continued to whisper. "I got wind that that man was nothing shy of a heathen." Disapproval was thick in the glance they exchanged.

Lonnie was going to be sick. She stood and strode down the aisle. Spotting Gus, she hurried toward him. "May Jacob sit with you a moment? I'll be right back."

"Certainly!"

She settled Jacob in his arms, and Gus bounced the little boy on his knee. Lonnie darted from the church. Her shawl forgotten in a black puddle on the pew, the icy air engulfed her. She brushed at the moisture along her forehead and down her temple. Her heart clamored in her chest, and she pressed a hand to her throat, where her pulse thundered. Her head lighter than the snow falling around her, she sank onto a fallen log behind the church building, certain no one could see her.

Covering her face in her hands, Lonnie forced herself to take long, slow breaths. But still the nausea rose. She fought back tears. Fought them back with all her might, but despite her resolve, her shoulders shook, and she let out a sob. Clamping a hand over her mouth, Lonnie squeezed her eyes shut, sending a hot tear to her cheek.

A baby for Gideon. And Cassie was its mama.

Her darling Gideon. When her shoulders shook with sobs, she was thankful that the first hymn began within the chapel—drowning out the sound of her sorrow. The tiny inkling of hope that he had remained faithful to her severed. And why should she cling to such things? Why should Gideon have hung on to their love when there was no hope?

He had moved on. He had forgotten her.

"Lonnie."

She opened her eyes with a start.

Toby crouched in front of her. His face was filled with worry. He wrapped a hand around hers. It was then she realized how much she was actually trembling.

"What's happened?" he asked.

She clenched her jaw, refusing to let one more tear fall. Not in front of Toby. Quickly, she wiped her cheeks.

"I… It's just…" Oh, how could she tell him? A glance into his kind eyes, and she knew he deserved to know. He deserved to know all that ran through her and in her. He was her dearest of friends. And someday he would be more.

She took his broad hand in both of hers and held it close.

His eyes widened in surprise.

"This." She squeezed his warm hand tighter. "This life"—she freed one hand to beat her fingertips against where her heart seemed scarred beyond repair—"is bittersweet. Everything is tainted. I don't know if I'll ever be the same again. The hurt won't go away."

His face softened further. "Oh, Lonnie." He cupped her cheek. "I'm so sorry."

She tipped her chin up and drew in a deep breath, hoping it would wash away the tremor in her voice. But it was no use. "I need to stop loving him."

His expression tender, he covered both of her hands with his other.

"I've known ever since he left. But it hasn't made it any easier." Bending forward, she pressed her cheek to Toby's knuckles. "I'm sorry to have to say this to you. But it's not fair to you for me not to be honest."

"I'm glad you told me."

"God will make me stronger. I know He will ease this pain. It just takes time, doesn't it? I don't want to ask you to walk with me through this—"

"May I? May I be by your side through this?"

Sweet Toby.

"As your friend?"

Though another tear slid down her cheek, she smiled.

Then that's what he would be. Her friend.

His thoughts flew to Jebediah and their conversation in the barn. The moment he'd asked permission for Lonnie's hand. But now, with her cold fingers inside his, and the honest confession she just poured out so graciously, Toby couldn't imagine speaking the words. Confessing his desires. Not anytime soon.

Though he'd intended to ask her on the ride home.

To ask her to be his bride.

He'd rehearsed how he would say it over and over. Scarcely sleeping a wink last night. Toby fought the urge to run a hand through his hair. Fighting his own desires. Lonnie needed people in her life who loved her. Who cared about her. Who would walk with her through the pain. Was he not willing to put his dreams on the shelf if it meant doing just that?

He yearned for the future he'd imagined. *Perhaps someday.* That would be his constant prayer. But until that day, he wanted to be there for Lonnie. Wanted to help ease her pain. Even if in some small way.

Something twisted within at the thought of her never being his. But he knew how selfish that was. He didn't want Lonnie if it meant a life of sorrow for her. He wanted only to bring her joy. How he prayed that day would come.

Nine

Lonnie popped the lid on a jar of stewed pumpkin specked with cinnamon and nutmeg, and spooned the aromatic gooiness into her bowl atop a pair of eggs and a splash of cream. At her side, Elsie rolled out a round of piecrust. Lonnie had always known this recipe by heart, but with her mind a whir, she paused and shoved back her sleeves, then realized she'd counted the eggs wrong. Lonnie muttered to herself.

She felt Elsie watching her.

Lonnie focused on what she was doing, careful not to slosh her apron as she stirred.

"You've been mighty quiet since your outing with Toby the other day. Is everything all right?"

Nodding slowly, Lonnie stirred the pie filling with all the care she would have given to threading a needle. She cracked a third egg and mixed it in gently.

"Lonnie."

At Elsie's tender tone, Lonnie stilled. She glanced up, and Elsie's copper eyes met hers.

But the words would not come.

A gentle squeeze on her arm, and Elsie pulled Lonnie into a side hug. "Sweet girl, something is the matter. Lonnie, what's happened? Did Toby... Did he finally..."

"No." She let go of the bowl. "Toby didn't ask me to marry him." Feigning interest in a smear of flour on her apron, she brushed at it. "If that's what you mean."

Elsie nodded and released her.

"It's..." Lonnie reached for the salt and sprinkled in a pinch. It sat where it fell when she made no move to stir. "It's Gideon."

"Gideon?"

Pressing her hands to the chopping-block surface, Lonnie circled her thumb over the silken wood. She bounced her heel. Suddenly hot, she wanted to open a window. "He's... They're..." She dropped her head, closed her eyes for a breath, and then forced herself to look at Elsie. "It sounds like they're going to have a baby."

Elsie's rolling pin hit the board with a clatter. "Oh, Lonnie. No." Her eyes rounded, mouth working as if to speak. Lonnie had to look away from the pity in her face. She crouched, reaching for the sack of flour where it was wedged onto a shelf.

She didn't want pity. She wanted Gideon. Fighting the desire, she tugged on the sack again.

"I'm so sorry."

"It happens." Lonnie stood, the flour forgotten.

"What—"

"It's life and it happens and Gideon is Gideon and he's gone." She yanked the bowl toward herself. "He's gone, and he's not coming back. I don't know what on earth I was holding on to. He's married to Cassie, and I—" Words failed her. Chin trembling, she reached for another egg, then realized she'd already added one. "And I—"

Elsie's arms were around her in a heartbeat. "Oh, my sweet girl." She released one hand to smooth the hair from Lonnie's face, squeezing her so tight with the other that Lonnie closed her eyes to keep from crying. Elsie's words were soft. "God is with you for each step of this. And we are too. And we're not going to let you go." She gripped Lonnie's shoulders, her copper eyes searching. "This ain't gonna beat you. It's not."

"There's days that I just don't know how to keep my head up."

"Oh, sweetie. I know. This makes me so sad. I can only imagine what you're feeling." She kissed Lonnie's forehead. "But you've been keepin' your head up, and you'll keep doing it. I know in this moment it seems so hard. But for Jacob. For yourself. You keep your chin up. There is a whole life ahead of you worth livin'." Elsie's grip tightened. "And good things will be in it. Love and life and laughter. It may not feel that way right now. But good things lie in the days ahead. You just keep *fightin'* for it."

Furiously, Lonnie nodded. "I know," she gasped. "I know. I'm just so...so tired. So very tired, Elsie."

Pulling her tight again, Elsie rocked from side to side, the pie forgotten.

Light from the setting sun pierced through the window, hitting Lonnie's hair in a puddle of warmth. She wanted to stand that way forever—in the precious pocket of Elsie's arms, where the trials of life stood at bay and where peace floated along the hymn Elsie hummed ever so softly.

But at the sound of laughter coming from the yard, Lonnie opened her eyes and forced herself to straighten. Using the edge of her apron, she wiped at her cheeks.

"It sounds like Jebediah is back with the children." She gave Elsie's hand a firm squeeze, knowing there was more to say. But at the sound of Jebediah calling for them, she pushed her way past the door and onto the porch. In the little sled, Addie held Jacob snug in her lap. A mound of blankets covered the smiling pair. Jebediah's chest was heaving, and his cheeks were rosy.

"How was your walk?" Lonnie asked.

"It was wonderful!" Addie declared.

Jacob bounced his shoulders as if to ask for more. The older man laughed. "I think I've discovered his favorite thing to do." He gripped the rope with his gloved hands. "Why don't you two join me for the evening chores? Mind if I keep them out a bit longer, Lonnie?"

"Not at all," she said, shielding her eyes from the setting sun.

With a grunt, Jebediah tugged the little sled toward the barn, his steps slow, but his cheery words to the children carried along the breeze.

Lonnie turned to see Elsie standing in the doorway. Folding her arms, Lonnie shivered in the cold. The setting sun glinted orange on the windows, and an icy breeze stirred her apron and twirled her petticoats.

"Elsie, I want to get through this." She climbed the steps and leaned against the banister, staring out into the yard where Gideon used to work. "I'm *going* to get through this. I just wish it were easier. I want to stop loving him, and I know I must." But part of her hated having to kill off the love she had for him. A part of her was certain that just wasn't going to be possible.

Elsie moved in beside her and rested her plump arms on the railing. "He was worth loving." She squeezed Lonnie's hand. "That's what makes it so hard. He was worth loving. And he loved you in return. So very much."

"I know," Lonnie said, her voice unsteady. "I know he did." She could still feel his arms around her. Hear his laughter, see the impish light in his eyes that was so Gideon. Lifting her chest, Lonnie let the sorrow out, freeing it as if the setting sun could cover it, tuck it away for good. For tomorrow was a new day. Gideon was gone, but how she loved him. Lonnie felt

Elsie watching her. "I want to be thankful for that time and to remember it with fondness. The future can be bright, can't it, Elsie?" She leaned on the railing and watched the orange glow in the distance blink at her through the treetops. "It can be bright."

"So...just like I showed you yesterday. Ready?"

Gideon felt Tal watching over his shoulder. "All right." He let out a quick breath. Kneeling, Gideon held on to the base of a small apple tree. "I take the stock and notch it like this. Into a point with flat sides."

"With...a..."

"Sharp, clean knife. Keep it clean. Keep it sharp."

"That's right. And then?"

Pressing his tongue inside his cheek, Gideon picked up a delicate branch. "On the scion...slit it just like this." He moved the knife with slow, careful strokes. "Notched to fit flesh to flesh." Holding his breath, he carefully slid the two pieces together. They fit perfectly. With quick hands, he grabbed a piece of twine and began wrapping the union, securing the pieces in place. "Snug at first, then wrap tighter as you go. Last comes the wax, locking out any air. Ensuring a good fit."

"Spoken like a man who's done this a hundred times."

"Actually it's spoken like a man who has his boss leaning over his shoulder."

Tal clapped him on the back. "Well done. Now to do a few hundred more."

"Nothin' to it," Gideon said in jest. "But honestly. Is this all right?" He fingered his handiwork. "Will it take?" The breeze tousled his hair and flapped the open edges of his coat.

"Only time will tell. You did it as right as anyone else would have."

Gideon had been there less than a week, and already Tal had shown him all they would be doing over the course of the month as they grafted trees. The work had intimidated him at first, and while he still feared failing Tal, something about bonding the two branches together filled him with the satisfaction of this work. Gideon put his knife away and rolled up the twine, all the while praying the two separate trees might grow into one. Mold into a flesh that wouldn't know where it began or where it ended. It would just be.

It would grow. Produce. He nearly smiled at the thought. "What should I do with these things?"

"Just pack it all in that crate. It'll keep 'til morning. We'll come back and begin the real work." Tal slid his knife into a sheath. "Now that I know you aren't going to single-handedly take down my orchard."

Gideon scratched his head but grinned. "Let's hope not."

In the distance, Mrs. Jemson rang the supper bell.

Tal pushed the crate out of the way. He once again fingered the tree Gideon had just grafted. "We'll label as we go. That's the key. Otherwise we'll run into trouble without knowing what's what."

Gideon picked up a spray of cuttings and pieces of twine, then tossed them into the crate. He rested his forearm on his raised knee as he glanced out over the acres upon acres of leafless trees. Some tall and broad, having withstood the test of time. Others young, untried. The small branches in his hand offered so much possibility. So much of what could be. And here he was, able to be a part of it. Gideon drew in a contented breath, wishing Lonnie were here to share it with him.

The desire to bring it home to her sparked within. Yet it was over-shadowed by his greater desire. The longing he had to call out across the miles, to tell her that he was coming and that she was all he could think about.

Tell her not to be afraid. For he was returning to her.

Gideon stood, brushed the dust from his pants, and prayed this month would pass quickly.

Ten

Be sure to always use a capital letter at the beginning of the sentence." At the desk in the parlor, Lonnie leaned over her little sister's work.

"Every time?" Addie asked.

"Every time." Lonnie gave Addie's braid a playful tug. "And what goes at the end?"

Using her chalk, Addie scribbled a messy dot after the last word of her sentence.

"Very good." Lonnie knelt at her side. Jacob would be asleep upstairs for at least an hour, and Lonnie was thankful for the time to work with Addie on her lessons. "Soon, you'll be able to write a letter to Ma. Now—"

At a knock on the door, Lonnie lifted her head.

With Elsie upstairs dusting, Lonnie rose before Elsie might bother coming down. "Just a moment," she said to Addie. "I'll be right back."

Her stockinged feet made nary a sound as she crossed into the kitchen and peeked through the window. She spotted Toby on the porch, a package in his hands. He wore no hat, and his dark hair was slicked off to one side. He spotted her, and a single dimple appeared.

One hand pressed to the bodice of her blouse and the other on the knob, she took a quick, steadying breath before opening the door and letting in a burst of cold air. "Hello, Toby."

"Good afternoon." He switched the package from one hand to the other. He glanced into the quiet house. "Is this a bad time?"

"No, no. Come on in." She held the door open wider. "Please. Elsie's just upstairs and Jebediah's out in the barn."

"Thank you." He stepped in and yanked off his coat before draping it over the chair. His shoulder brushed hers in the tight space. "I need a bit o' help and was wond'rin' if you might be able to..." He set the poorly wrapped package on the table and worked on the tangled string. It knotted worse under his oversized fingers. "Och."

"Here," Lonnie said with a smile. She gently pushed his hands aside. "Let me see." She made quick work of the knot and unfolded the paper. "Fabric."

"Yes."

"You brought me white fabric."

"Yes. No. Well, it's not for you." He scratched the back of his head. "But now I feel guilty about that."

Lonnie pulled out the soft folds. "I'm sorry. I didn't mean it like that." They shared a laugh. "Let's start again, shall we?"

"Please." Toby motioned to what he'd brought. "You see, I ordered a new shirt from Mount Airy, and Mrs. Krause said she was heading into town and that she would pick it up for me."

"And this is what they sent you."

"Aye. Four yards of fabric." He lifted his hands, his dimples deep. "I dinna ken what to do with it."

Still laughing, Lonnie unfolded it. "So you need a shirt?"

"'Twould appear that way." His eyes sparkled with mischief.

"Well then, you came to the right place."

"You'll help me?"

She patted his sturdy forearm. "I'd be happy to."

"Och. I thank you."

"First, though, I'll need to take your measurements."

"All right."

"Follow me into the parlor."

"Now?"

"Unless you'd rather do it another time?"

"No. I mean…I dinna want to interrupt you."

She waved him forward. "I was just working with Addie on her spelling, and Jacob's napping. Please, stay."

Toby ducked his head.

Lonnie gathered up the fabric and carried it into the parlor. "Mr. McKee is here," she called to Addie.

The little girl smiled a toothy grin at the tall Scotsman.

"But I want you to finish your schoolwork," Lonnie added.

Nodding quickly, Addie turned to her slate and began scribbling away as if her life depended on it. Toby flashed Lonnie an amused glance.

"Just stand right here in the center of the room." Crouching, Lonnie pulled Elsie's sewing basket from beside the sofa. "And it'll only take a moment. We'll want everything to fit you just right." The measuring tape unraveled when she pulled it out, landing in a coil between them. "If you'll hold your arm out like this."

She gently touched his wrist, showing him how. "That's it. Now just a moment." Pinching the end of the measuring tape, Lonnie pressed it to the top of Toby's broad shoulder, then slid the tape down the length of his arm, her hands brushing the inside of his wrist. The skin soft and warm. Standing so close to him, she caught the sweet scent of evergreen. Her heart nearly tripped over itself. Pressing the tape firmly on both ends, she made sure it was taut. "Thirty-seven," she mumbled.

Toby stared at the empty space between them. Standing so close, the space suddenly seemed nonexistent.

Thirty-seven. Or was it thirty-six? Fighting a blush, Lonnie quickly measured him again. "I should write that down before I forget it," she said weakly. She moved to the desk and pulled out a scrap of paper. She found a stubby pencil in the drawer and jotted down the number. "Now I just need to measure your shoulders."

"Lonnie."

"Yes." She stilled long enough to look him in the eye, and it was then she realized she'd been avoiding it the last few minutes.

"I want to apologize for what happened the other day."

"Oh, Toby, it wasn't your—"

"Please. Let me say this. I shouldna have invited you there and then vanished, leaving you all alone in an unfamiliar place. 'Twas daft of me."

"You have no need to apologize." She lifted her chin. None of it was Toby's fault. Life just worked that way sometimes. She had to learn to keep going. No matter how much it hurt. She had to make the best of it.

"Look who's awake," Elsie called from the hallway. Lonnie turned toward the stairs just as Elsie appeared, a still-waking Jacob in her arms. He rubbed a tiny fist over his eyes. "I think someone wants his mama."

Lonnie took Jacob, so soft and warm, into her arms and held him close. "Oh, my wee boy. How was your nap?" She kissed his rosy cheek, still sticky with tears. She squeezed him tight.

Dust rag still in hand, Elsie marched back upstairs. Jacob rubbed his face against Lonnie's shoulder, then seemed to notice Toby for the first time. The baby stuck out his hands and reached for the man, all but lunging out of Lonnie's grasp.

Loosening her grip, she let Jacob crawl into Toby's embrace.

Brown eyes wide, Toby looked at the baby and awe unfolded in his expression. He glanced from Jacob to Lonnie then back again. The little boy pressed his cheek to Toby's chest, and his small back rose and fell in a single sigh.

Something twisted within Lonnie's chest. "He's taken with you." She smoothed her hand down Jacob's back.

"I—" Toby fell silent. But he held the baby with all the love a father might.

Her throat thick, Lonnie blinked at the tape in her hands. "What was I doing?" she asked softly, more to herself than Toby.

"My measurements." His voice was gentle.

Glancing into his face, Lonnie saw an expression so earnest she could scarcely look away.

A quick intake of breath, and she smiled up at him. "That's right."

It was impossible not to touch him as she ran the measuring tape from one shoulder to the other, measuring the width. He held Jacob still against one side of his chest, making it easy for Lonnie to get the measurement. She jotted the number down quickly, certain she'd never keep anything straight with her heart hammering so. Jacob still hadn't moved, and from the corner of her eye, Lonnie watched Toby kiss her son's hair.

Her steps were soft when she walked back to the center of the room. "Almost done."

Toby held still as Lonnie rose on her tiptoes and laced the measuring tape around his neck. Her fingers grazed the base of his hair. "Just one moment." She wrapped it around gently and felt him swallow against her hand. A glance up and she realized he was watching her. Quickly, she read the number. "Nineteen." She sank back down. "Good grief!"

"Is that bad?"

"No," she nearly squeaked and clamped a hand over her mouth, having not meant to say that aloud. "It's fine," she mumbled. She jotted the number down. "What did your mother raise you on?"

Toby laughed and rubbed his thick neck. His cheeks colored. "Is that all?"

"Just one more." Lonnie held one end of the tape near his collarbone and slid the other down to his hip so quickly Toby scarcely had time to hold still. She wrote down the final number and then turned. Her braid slipped from her shoulder.

"That's all I need. That and the fabric." She rolled the measuring tape around her hand. "I could have it to you by next week." She took Jacob from him.

Toby seemed to search for his hat.

Lonnie pointed toward the kitchen. "In there."

"You are a dear." He gazed at the pair of them. "But dinna rush."

"I won't…but even so, it'll be a pleasure to make it for you." She patted his forearm. "I will do my best to make it Sunday worthy."

"It will be perfect."

She could tell he meant every word.

Nodding his thanks, Toby turned to go. Seeing Addie, he knelt down. He whispered a promise to take her for a ride on Gael the next time he came. Eyes bright, Addie nodded eagerly. He tousled her curls, then rose.

Lonnie motioned toward the kitchen. "And may I send you home with some pie? Elsie and I made it just yesterday."

"That'd be lovely. Thank you."

Setting Jacob on the chopping-block surface to watch, Lonnie drew out a knife and cut a thick wedge. Then she searched in the cupboard for a small tin plate. "This should do it." She slid the pie onto the plate and wrapped it with a bit of cheesecloth. She turned with her offering. "It was my grandmother's recipe. I've been making it ever since I could walk."

"It looks mighty fine." His gaze drifted up from the pie. "Thank you. And I can't thank you enough for helping me with the shirt. You saved me a trip into town." He hesitated, and she sensed he wanted to say more.

"It's my pleasure." Truly it was. "There'll be enough fabric to make two, I'd imagine. So you're better off in the end."

Broad hand pressed to his heart, he smiled down at her. "You are too good to me." He half grinned. "How can I repay you? And I willna take no for an answer."

"You've already done so much. This"—she tipped her head toward the parlor, where they'd left the fabric—"is a joy." She lifted Jacob back onto her hip.

They stood a moment without speaking. Toby turned the plate in his hands. "It was good to see you." He nodded gently, then peered at her with dark eyes. "Shall I come and pick you up on Sunday again? Perhaps the Bennetts will be able to join us this time?"

"That would be lovely."

"And what about you, Lonnie? You're always thinking of others. Are you sure it'd be something that you'd enjoy?"

Lonnie glanced at his hands, where her tears had fallen the last time. "I'm sure." She drew in a deep breath. "One day at a time…"

He touched her cheek. "One day at a time."

She needed to keep taking those steps—even when they were hard.

His thumb grazed her skin.

She *wanted* to keep taking those steps. Even when she didn't know where they would lead.

Eleven

Standing in the woodshed, Gideon kept his hands steady as he wrapped the scion and the stock together. Owen and Tal worked quietly nearby, each man silent, focused. Despite the gray mist that blew past the open door, they were warm enough inside the old shed. The air inside hung heavy with the scent of ripe apples and old leaves, as if the shed had held a hundred harvests in its crates and barrels. Glancing around at the faded and weathered boards, Gideon could only guess that it had. Crates were piled high, some filled with the hardiest of apples, others empty, waiting. In the far corner stood countless bare-root trees just waiting for a home. A piece of earth to take root in.

Gideon shifted on his stool. An hour ago, he'd tossed his jacket on the worktable beside him, but now, with the sun sinking behind the tree line, he reached for it. He tugged his suspenders back up over his shoulders, then slid his jacket on, not bothering to button it. The air seemed to grow colder by the minute, and while he longed to go indoors, he had a handful more trees he wanted to finish. Gideon shifted his feet, stomping them to keep feeling in his legs.

"You boys 'bout ready for supper?" Tal asked, breaking the settled silence.

"Yes sir," Owen chimed in. He set his tool down with a clatter and turned on his stool.

Wrapping the two grafted pieces with thin twine, Gideon nodded his agreement, deciding to make this his last one. Finished, he clipped the twine and carefully set the fused portion on his workbench in the tidy pile, out of the way. Gideon tugged his knit cap low over his ears.

Using the edge of his hand, he pushed small branch cuttings into his other palm and carried them to the bin to be taken to the compost pile when it was full. He sat back down and straightened his tools, then bundled the twine into a tidy ball off to the side.

"Gideon."

"Huh?" Gideon glanced up at the sound of Owen's voice.

"Did you hear what I said?"

"No."

The young man grinned. "You've been here two weeks, and still you're humming that same song."

"I wasn't humming." Gideon stood. He tossed his cutters on the workbench, then stretched his arms overhead.

"Tell him he was humming." Owen glanced over his shoulder at his pa.

"You were humming." Tal cut a length of twine. "Same song. Two weeks."

Chuckling, Gideon shoved his stool under the workbench. "Great. Now I'm crazy." He moved toward the open doorway of the shed and leaned against the jamb. "Are you serious?"

Tal glanced up from his work, a smile in his eyes. "Does this look like the face of someone who's joking?"

Gideon folded his arms.

Owen shoved his tools back haphazardly and turned in his stool. "So why that one?"

"I don't know." Gideon scratched his jaw. But he did. It was the song he'd written for Lonnie, starting with the first notes he'd plucked on his mandolin all that time ago. The one he could never seem to get out of his mind. With two ornery mountain men staring at him—humor in their matching eyes—he wasn't about to confess as much. "Say, can we talk about something else?"

"Don't get embarrassed. You can't help being a lovesick fool."

"And what would you know about it?" Gideon tousled Owen's hair. Owen smacked his hand away, but not before Gideon had mussed his slicked-down curls. "You'll find out soon enough."

Tal slapped his palms on his thighs and stood. "All right. I'd say that's more than enough for one day. Let's get inside." He stepped out last, then Gideon and Own shut the two doors to the apple shed. Using his fist, Tal tamped the rusty latch into place. They walked toward the house.

"Say, Tal. I've been meaning to ask you." Gideon stuffed his hands in his pockets. "What are the chances I could take some trees with me? Could I cash in part of my earnings for some of those bare roots you've been storing?" He wanted to bring Lonnie something of lasting worth. Something he could one day leave his son. For they deserved all he could give them and more. "Would that be all right?"

"Sure thing. We'll get you set up real nice." He motioned for Gideon to take the lead up the steps. "Life's gonna make an apple farmer of you yet."

Inside the warm house the air was rich with the smell of seasonings and broth. Mrs. Jemson moved a loaf of brown bread from the stove. Little Jimmy and Carl were busy setting the table. Having grown taller, the boys were lankier than when Gideon first met them. Their freckles darker.

Gideon sat at Mrs. Jemson's urging. The family circled around, benches and chairs scraping out of place as they sat. Wedged between the two youngest boys, Gideon felt them watching him with wide, curious eyes as they often did.

At a soft nod from his father, Owen blessed the food. His voice sure. As if he'd done it a hundred times. Gideon tugged his knit cap off and stuffed it between his knees, all the while wondering what it would have been like to have been raised that way. What it would be like to have a faith that stemmed from some deep spring, that could simply pour forth. At the murmured amens, Gideon lifted his napkin and glanced around at the Jemsons.

How he wished it were Jacob's hand he could hold in prayer. Lonnie's cheery face across the table from him. Swallowing hard, Gideon stared at his food. He wanted Lonnie. He wanted to ask her the countless questions that roiled inside his mind. He wanted to hear her voice. Her faith. He wanted everything about her.

"Dig in." Mrs. Jemson popped the lid on the jam jar as her husband cut thick slices of dark, steaming bread.

As Gideon stirred his soup—a mixture of white beans and beef—the aroma of herbs and spices stirred memories of Elsie's kitchen. Slicing a tender chunk of carrot in half with his spoon, Gideon ducked it under the broth, his appetite forgotten. It took all his strength not to rise from the chair. Rise up and go get his family. He couldn't.

For they weren't his for the taking. At least not yet. He blew his breath out quick and ran a hand over his face. *Soon,* he told himself. *Soon.* A lift of his shoulder and he sighed. *Lord, let it be so.* Gideon fingered his glass, turning it in his hands. He wondered what he would say to her. What he would do the first time he saw her, saw Jacob.

"Gideon. Everything all right with the food?"

Lifting his head with a start, Gideon realized he'd been lost in thought. "Yes ma'am." He sipped from his spoon. "It's very fine. Thank you." He took the slice of bread little Carl offered. Suddenly realizing how hungry he was, he ate his supper and accepted a second ladleful of soup. When the bowls had been emptied and stacked, Tal rose and reached for his pipe. Owen and the boys carried the dishes to the washbasin as Mrs. Jemson wrapped the remainder of the bread.

Kneeling in front of the stove, Tal stoked the fire, then turned to carry the heavy stockpot from the table for his wife.

Not wanting to stand idle, Gideon snatched up the broom and swept the floor, then brought in an armful of firewood, stacking it carefully.

Tal settled down in the parlor, newspaper in hand, a curl of smoke rising from his pipe. Owen sat by the dark window. At his brothers' urging, he pulled out a whistle he'd been whittling for them. Soft shavings fell beneath his sharp knife. Hands in his pocket, Gideon studied the books on the tall, slender case beside the window.

Mrs. Jemson slid the kettle onto the stove and waved Gideon into the parlor. "Why don't you go sit?"

"No, thank you. You folks enjoy your evening together. I think I'll turn in early." Gideon glanced once more at the bookshelf. "Ma'am, may I borrow one of these?"

"Take any that you want." She stepped closer and shook out her damp apron.

Gideon lifted a heavy gray volume and flipped it open. The text was so small and the pages so many, his brain hurt.

Mrs. Jemson smiled knowingly when he put it back.

"Which would you recommend?" he asked, lifting up a smaller book. Inside were pictures of pencil-drawn flowers. He put it back, careful to stick it in the same place. Next he found a dusty Bible, a smaller volume than the one that rested on the mantel. His fingers grazed the worn and tattered spine. Gideon slid it back.

"Well…maybe a good adventure." She tapped her finger against her chin. *"Moby Dick."* She tugged out the thick novel.

"What's that one about?"

"It's about a seaman who goes on a great voyage, hunting a whale."

Gideon wrinkled his nose and shook his head apologetically. Laughing, Mrs. Jemson slid it back into place. She named several others. Gideon flipped through some of them.

"I didn't know you enjoyed reading," she said, wiping dust from a leather-bound book with the edge of her apron.

Pulling out another, Gideon shrugged one shoulder. He ran his thumb over the brown binding. "I don't. But I figured I might as well try and like it. Especially since I don't have anything else to do." He smiled down on Mrs. Jemson. "Maybe something that takes place on dry land."

From his bench, Owen snorted.

Eyes bright, Mrs. Jemson put the one in her hand away. "Then you might like this one." She tapped the book already in his hand. "It takes place during the French and Indian War. A great classic. And an adventure."

Gideon dipped his head in a nod and turned the book over. "All right, I'll try it." He raised it in soft salute. "Thank you." He eyed the small Bible, gently pulling it from its place. "May I borrow this as well?"

"You may. And keep them. They're our gift to you."

"No, I couldn't—"

She pressed the books toward his chest. "I insist."

Tal shook out his paper and mumbled around his pipe. "She won't take no for an answer."

"All right then. See you in the morning." With a nod and a thanks to Mrs. Jemson, Gideon stepped out into the cold night.

Twelve

With afternoon light streaming in through the parlor window, Lonnie settled down on the sofa and reached for her sewing. It had taken her nearly a week to finish the first shirt, but now that she had the pattern cut, she hoped to have the second one done in shorter time.

"You've made good progress," Elsie said, bustling in from the kitchen.

"Thank you." Lonnie slipped her needle quickly through the fabric and eyed her seam to make sure it was straight. She'd had to triple check Toby's measurements when she cut the pattern. Even still, she held the shirt up to the light and with a shake of her head couldn't figure out how a reverend managed to fill out such a thing. "I hope they fit Toby all right."

Elsie lifted Jacob from the rug and headed back into the kitchen. "A gunnysack would fit that man all right."

Smiling, Lonnie shook her head. At the sound of the washtub clanging into place on the kitchen floor, Lonnie gathered up her sewing and wandered toward the noise. Kneeling on the floor, Elsie was busy tugging Jacob's brown pants from his chubby legs. His feet kicked in anticipation of his bath. Lonnie tested the kettle, added the hot water, and then watched as Elsie checked the temperature with her fingertips. Jacob all but lunged in. Laughing, Elsie unpinned his diaper and lowered him into the galvanized basin. He tucked his hands into the water. Bending, Lonnie kissed a bare, creamy shoulder.

"That's my boy." Setting Toby's shirt on the table, she reached for her apron, knowing she'd be damp by bath's end. "I'll fetch the soap and his towel."

She hurried upstairs and found the soap on the washstand. Tugging open the wardrobe, she grabbed a fresh towel. Her fingers grazed the hair-cutting scissors. Snatching them up, she had a mind to give Jacob's hair a bit of a trim. The red and gold locks had curled around his ears, and she thought a little trim before church in the morning might do him good. Lonnie bundled the things in the crook of her arm and started for the kitchen. This would be the third week in a row she'd be able to attend church with Toby, and last week the Bennetts had been up for making the trip.

"You'll be coming to church again tomorrow?" she asked Elsie when she stepped into the kitchen.

"Wouldn't miss it for the world. It's so good of Toby to have orches-trated it all for us. Last Sunday was such a treat." She drizzled water down the back of Jacob's hair, and Lonnie handed her the soap. She set the towel near the stove to warm. Crouching beside the galvanized tub, Lonnie ran a comb through Jacob's thin hair and snipped it around his head. Elsie watched quietly.

Lonnie let the tiny, autumn-hued curls fall into her cupped hand. "I'm glad you'll be coming. It's always so nice for us all to go together. All the ladies were talking about that buttermilk pie you brought for the church dinner last week."

Elsie smiled. "The recipe is quite a secret. There's only one woman in the world I'll be passing it along to."

At her heartfelt words, Lonnie smiled. "They say there's going to be a wedding next month. I thought it might be nice to go. It's been so long since we've been to one. Could you imagine…" She squeezed Elsie's hand. "The music. The dancing."

"You must wear something very fine."

Lonnie nodded quickly, but only to chase away the emotions that crept in at the memory of the wedding she and Gideon attended last year, Gideon so solemn at her side. She'd loved him then more deeply than she had thought possible. More deeply than he'd even known.

"That blue chambray of yours is awful pretty. You could trim it with that bit of lace we found."

As Jacob played in the water beside Elsie, Lonnie sat in a chair and picked up Toby's shirt. A tug on the needle, and her thread snagged, puckering the fabric. "Yes. I need to look my best because this shirt is going to be mighty fine." The thread tangled worse. Chuckling, she snipped it to begin again.

"You two will make a fetching pair. Folk might wonder if it were the two of you gettin' hitched…" Elsie's voice trailed off, and she glanced at Lonnie, apologetically. "I'm sorry. I didn't mean to blurt that out like that."

"No need to be sorry."

"All in good time," Elsie said softly. "All in good time—if it's the Lord's will, of course."

"If it's the Lord's will." But Lonnie felt certain it was. Toby was a wonderful man. She counted herself truly blessed indeed to have him in her life. To hopefully one day be his wife.

As if their thoughts had wandered the same path, Elsie rose. "I just want…I just want to see you happy again." She reached for the towel.

"I'm happy, Elsie." Lonnie squeezed the older woman's hand. "A little more so each day." Lonnie lifted Jacob from the tub and set him in the toweled cradle of Elsie's arms. A little more each day. Peace and melancholy seemed to battle within. But only one could take the upper hand. One must overcome the other if she wanted a joyous life for her and Jacob. She didn't mind being happy. It was a heavenly feeling. It was *allowing* herself to be happy that she struggled with. Allowing herself to be happy despite all she had lost.

Despite the fact that Gideon had let her go.

Opened his hands. And let her go.

Overwrought, Lonnie stared at the sewing in her lap. *A little happier each day, Lord willing.* God promised He would see her through any tempest. Any storm. He wasn't giving up on her now.

Gloved hands resting on the top of the pitchfork handle, Gideon stared at the graying sky. His mother had used black walnuts to dye her yarn gray. The same hue tinted the rising tempest above. He wondered what the night might hold, and not wanting to dawdle, Gideon gripped the pitchfork and thrust it into the mound of compost to turn the dark, moist earth.

Tal and Owen worked nearby in the woodshed, their voices floating out as they picked over the apples that needed to be tossed. Each time they walked over with a bucketful, Gideon mixed it all together. Though muddy snow covered most of the yard, the bare patches making it possible to work the compost pile, he sensed another storm was on the way.

Mrs. Jemson walked by with a basket of laundry on her hip. She stopped in front of the woodshed and exchanged a few words with Tal. He planted a kiss on her cheek, and smiling, she strode toward the house. Passing Gideon, she slowed.

"How are you enjoying that book?"

"Fine, ma'am. Thank you." Gideon stopped working and took the opportunity to grab his jacket from where he'd tossed it aside. The temperature was dropping. Fast. "I gotta admit, though, I'm not really sure what's going on yet." He shrugged into his coat.

Setting down her basket, Mrs. Jemson rolled down the sleeves on her striped blouse. "Sometimes it takes a while to get into a story."

"I'm enjoying it, though."

Her eyes crinkled kindly. "I'm glad. It's one of my favorite books. Hang in there. I think you might like it in the end." Picking up her basket, she walked toward the house, her dry laundry safe from what loomed on the horizon.

"Better not let my wife lend you any more books. She'll make a reader of you yet." Work gloves under his arm, Tal slid on his hat. The dim light caught the silver stubble along his jaw. "She's all but ruined Owen and me. Got us quotin' poetry and all that nonsense."

Owen carried over a pair of shovels and handed one to his pa. The young man got busy working beside Gideon, turning the compost so the air and sun could break it down in time for spring planting.

"It's not as bad as I once thought. Once you get used to it." Gideon jammed the pitchfork into the compost pile and, with a grunt, lifted the heavy load to the other side. "I'm slower than molasses, mind you. I can't read more than a page or two a night." At Owen's taunting expression, Gideon pointed a finger. "You watch it."

Owen held up his hands and got back to work.

Shaking his head, Gideon turned another forkful of compost. "But what I really *don't* understand is the Bible. I flipped it open the other night and read about that man named Zacchaeus—"

"It's not *Zatch*-eus," Owen blurted. "It's *Zack*-eus."

Halting, Gideon straightened. "That's not how you say it."

The young man lifted a palm in a truce. "I'm serious. That's how you pronounce it."

Gideon glanced at Tal, who nodded his vote toward his son.

"Really?"

"Really."

Gideon said the name softly to himself, then shook his head. Now he was even more confused. "But the point is...Jesus says that He's going to that guy's house." Gideon felt his brows tug together. "Why would He do that? I don't understand. Even the other people in the story didn't understand. They said that man was a sinner." He yanked the pitchfork loose, then stabbed it back in. Using his boot, he jammed it in farther. "It seems Jesus would have other things to do. *Better* things to do."

Gideon watched as a pair of white flakes floated down in front of him; a glance at the sky confirmed that the clouds had thickened. The air was so still and cold, he shivered.

"I think you're missing the point of the story." Tal settled his shovel into the snowy mud and rested his boot on top of the spade. His eyes drifted to the trees at the edge of the farm. "The point of the story is that the man *was* a sinner, but Jesus wanted to go *anyway*." He glanced at Gideon, then at his son, then back again. "Those are the people He came to save. All of us. Each and every one."

Softly, Gideon shook his head, but his mind whirled as he stabbed his pitchfork back into the compost pile.

"Read it again," Tal said. "Read it again, and this time...look for it."

With a half shrug, Gideon nodded. "All right. I will." He turned another forkful of compost, still feeling Tal's gaze. Gideon glanced over as the snow picked up, a cold, lacy curtain across the land. "I promise."

Thirteen

T hat seems like too many." Standing in the apple shed, Gideon leaned back on his heels and studied the pile of trees Tal was assembling.

"I assure you, it's not." The man glanced up. "We agreed on half cash, half trees, right?"

Gideon crouched down. "Right. But this just seems like too many. I don't want to take more than my share."

"Hush up about your share and trust me, will ya? It's called wholesale. Besides, they're in my way."

Only half believing him, Gideon counted the spindly trees. "Thirty-two."

"All good strong stock. Husky roots." Tal touched the dry roots. "Set them to soak in water before planting, and if you do it just as I told you, they'll take like a dream." He added one more to the pile. "The cold weather'll keep them dormant. Just get them in the ground by the end of March, all right?"

"I can do that." Gideon stood back as Tal began wrapping the bundle with twine. "And you're sure they'll transport fine? I mean…I won't kill the lot trying to get them home?"

"They should be just fine. Be gentle with them. But they're hardy. They'll get home."

Standing, Gideon interlocked his fingers and gripped the back of his neck. He couldn't believe he was leaving in the morning. He couldn't help but smile at where he was headed.

"Come back in thirty days." Judge Monroe's words echoed in his mind. *"We'll see if we can get you back to your wife and son."*

"Smells like supper's ready."

Gideon followed Tal to the house, and when everyone gathered around the table, he sat on the bench between the boys. With the lantern flooding the table in warm, golden light, Tal bowed his head, and the Jemsons followed suit. Gideon closed his eyes.

Sure and strong as a mighty river, Tal's voice filled the room. "Lord, we thank You for this food and for the hands that have prepared it. And we thank You for the time we've had with this young man here…" Reaching around his youngest son, he gripped Gideon's shoulder, and Gideon closed his eyes tighter, struck with an unexpected emotion. "Still his fears, Lord. Still his fears. Guide him." His voice fell soft, no more than a throaty whisper. His grip tightened.

Gideon pulled his hands into fists on his knees.

"Be the strength he needs as he takes these next steps. Be his wisdom. Be his comfort. Prepare his family for his return. Prepare their hearts."

Gideon hung his head lower. Prepare their hearts. *May it be so.*

"We thank You for Your grace and Your mercy. Gifts we could never deserve—yet freely You give. Lord, we are thankful. Amen."

Lifting his head, Gideon whispered an amen. He glanced at Tal. "Thank you."

"And may the Lord be with you wherever you go."

Wherever he went.

Might it be so? He swallowed hard at the thought. They ate supper slowly, as if no one was in a hurry to turn in for the night. Thankful for Mrs. Jemson's hearty stew, Gideon stood and bid his farewell to the family. Tal followed him out onto the porch.

Gideon held out his hand, and Tal gripped it firmly. Gideon closed his other hand around his friend's. "I can't thank you enough. You've saved me twice now."

Tal shook his head but tightened his grip.

Gideon would be forever grateful for all the man had done. The first time he'd met Tal, after wandering onto his farm, Gideon's face had been bruised, his body battered. A poor choice had tangled him with the wrong crowd, breaking Lonnie's trust in him. Gideon knew that few men would have welcomed him into their lives that day. Few men would have invited him into their homes. Allowed him to break bread with their families.

Yet Tal had done it. Twice now.

At the realization, Gideon ran a hand through his hair. Although he wasn't the beaten man he'd been then, his spirit was bruised. His mind and heart weary. And once again, refuge had been offered. Gideon's throat suddenly felt tight. He wished with all his might that he could understand why. And how. How a man could show that kind of compassion to a stranger. A vagabond.

"Thank you." Gideon backed away and, with a clear night sky overhead, started for the bunkhouse. He glanced around the quiet, snowy farm, wondering what tomorrow would hold. A thrill of excitement shot through him, but reality quickly knocked, and Gideon blew out his cheeks. Before he could give in to his fears of what could transpire, he tried to remember what Tal had said.

Words of promise. Words of peace. That the Lord had a plan.

Still feeling the warmth of the prayer in his spirit, Gideon lay on top of his blankets and closed his eyes. But his sleep was restless. The bunk-house empty. As were his hands. His life.

He yearned for home. With his future hanging in the balance, Gideon tossed and turned until he could take it no longer.

Rising long before the sun, he dressed and set his pack on the bunk. After he stuffed his things into it, he slid the books Mrs. Jemson had given him on top and cinched the pack tight. Stepping out of the bunkhouse, he saw his breath fog in front of his face. Gideon knelt beside the stack of bare-root trees and, using the length of twine Tal had given him, fastened the spindly bundle to the oilcloth. Gideon tested the pack to see how it would hold. It was heavier, but secure. A light snow had begun falling, scarcely dusting the land in the white powder.

At his feet sat a small loaf of brown bread wrapped tight. A wedge of cheese and a pair of hardy apples were tucked into an old flour sack. With a silent thanks to the Jemsons, Gideon added the food to his pack. Shivering, he glanced toward the tree line, where the first gray light was beginning to appear. The sun would be up before he knew it, and he hoped to be halfway to Stuart by then. Hoped to be on the courthouse steps when the judge arrived. Tal had offered to drive him, but the thought of waiting around one more minute nearly drove Gideon mad.

His heart leaped with unbridled anticipation. A few days and he would see Lonnie. He would see how Jacob had grown. Gideon yanked the bunk-house door closed and, with nothing separating him from what lay ahead, took his first steps down the path. Toward Stuart. And then home.

Fourteen

Holding out his hand, Gideon squinted one eye closed and used the width of his four fingers to measure how high the sun had risen. Adding up the hours, he knew he was making good time—proved further when he came around a bend of trees and saw smoke rising in the distance from too many places to count. Stuart.

Knowing he couldn't very well march into the courthouse with his pack and bundle of trees, nor could he leave his things unattended, Gideon glanced around for a place to stash it all. He found a stand of shrubs that would keep everything concealed, though he doubted there would be many folks passing by.

He scaled the bare slope toward town, delighting in the sensation of the sun on his shoulders. He all but jogged up the courthouse steps, but a tug on the door proved it was locked. Gideon settled down on the steps and clasped his hands. He glanced down Main Street, taking in the sights and sounds of a sleepy town rising. A few folk milled about, some opening business doors, others hurrying in one direction or the other. It seemed few people wanted to be out early on a cold morning, and though Gideon longed for a fire and a hot cup of coffee, he stayed on the frosty steps and watched the road.

He spotted the receptionist first, coming up the wooden sidewalk. Her dark green coat scarcely brushed the tops of her shiny shoes. She climbed the steps, a set of keys in her hand. Gideon stood so as not to startle her. He'd left his hat on his pack, so he gave her a cordial nod. She glanced at him a moment, uncertainty lining the wrinkles around her mouth. Then recognition registered in her face. Was that a smile? She turned and slid the key into the lock.

"If you're waiting to speak with the judge, you might as well come in out of the cold."

With a tug on his coat and then his plaid shirt, Gideon followed her in. He wished he had something finer to put on, and he ran his fingers through his hair, doing what he could to set it in the right direction. He tried to not even *think* about a razor.

"You look fine, Mr. O'Riley," the woman said without glancing up from the ledger she was scribbling in. "We've seen much worse."

Gideon sat on the bench. Eyes on the clock, he shifted his boots.

The door opened in a burst, and the judge barreled past, his black coat flapping open in his wake. Stunned, Gideon straightened. A jam of the key in the lock, and the judge pushed his way into his office, closing the door with a solid *thud*. Gideon and the receptionist exchanged a glance.

"It's normal. Working Saturdays often puts him in a bit of a mood."

Gideon half stood. "May I?"

"Off you go."

He walked down the corridor as quietly as he could, then using the back of his hand, gently rapped his knuckles on the door.

"Come in." The man all but barked.

A quick swallow, and Gideon turned the knob. "Excuse me, sir."

The judge tugged off his spectacles with a snap and glanced up. He stared at Gideon blankly a moment, just as the receptionist had. Then the same clarity must have unfolded, for his frosty demeanor thawed. "Come in." His shoulder sank and his expression softened. He waved him to the chair.

Gideon sat.

Judge Monroe sifted through several files on his desk, finally pulled one out, and opened it across the messy surface. Leaning back in his chair, he propped his elbows on the armrests and pressed his hands together. "Have I told you yet how unorthodox this is?"

Gideon's heart hammered against the chair. No words would come. He glanced at the nameplate that rested on one corner of the desk that read *Judge of the County Court,* and beneath that, *Commonwealth Attorney.*

The man studied him, his expression sober. Finally, his face softened. "I've done some reading, and there are several options for settling this." He glanced at the clock. "I have a hearing first thing this morning, so I'll be quick. What do you know of the law?"

"Um…"

Hand raised, the man pulled down a book thicker than any Gideon had ever seen. In a matter of a few minutes, he explained what needed to be done. Gideon's ears pricked at the word *consummation,* but he was beyond any embarrassment there. At least there wasn't a roomful of people standing behind him this time. He'd been abstinent with Cassie all these months for no other reason than his love for Lonnie. Never once had he thought it would come to his aid in a court of law. Never once had he thought he'd be sitting here with a second chance at a life with Lonnie on the horizon.

"Are you saying what I think you're saying?"

The judge nodded slowly.

"You've figured it out?"

"Yes, but it's out of my hands now, so you can wipe that silly grin off your face. I still haven't received the affidavit from Miss Allan. I sent it three weeks ago. More than enough time for her to have received it. It should return here soon. Very soon, I hope. As I can only imagine you do as well." The judge pointed to a paragraph in the book and read it aloud.

Gideon tried to wrap his mind around the legal phrasings. As if sensing it, the judge leaned forward. "Basically, the affidavit that I sent to Miss Allan, confirming that her testimony matches your own, simply needs to be signed and returned."

"That's it?" Hope rose within him.

For the first time, the judge smiled. "That's it. I'm leaving out the messy bits, of course." He arched a silver eyebrow. "All the reading that's kept me up late at night on more than one occasion. But"—he studied Gideon a moment—"for some reason, I've decided to see this through. I'm not normally this willing to take on cases of this nature. But occasionally, I do one for the *good of the public*. And I'll have no peace from my wife and Mrs. Peterson"—he flapped a hand toward the hallway—"if I don't see this through. Your case is a rare one, Mr. O'Riley. And these women have it in their silly heads that…" He grumbled something about true love.

Gideon grinned.

"And, well, frankly"—the judge rose and dropped the file back on the stack—"I want you and this mess out of my life once and for all." Despite his words, the bite in his tone had vanished.

"So what do I do? What now?" Gideon rose.

"Go home. Consider the annulment pending, and as soon as it's final, I will send word." He lifted the file and held up a document with Jebediah's return address, the post office in Mount Airy. "This will be the best place to reach you?"

"Yes sir."

"You should receive confirmation shortly. Go home, Gideon O'Riley, and"—he tossed the file aside—"try and take a deep breath." Pulling out his gold watch, he held it idly in his hand and glanced out the window. "Start now. Young man like you'll be home in time for Sunday supper."

Tomorrow night. Was it truly possible?

"Thank you, sir." Gideon shook his hand. "I will. And I can't thank you enough." He backed out of the office and strode down the corridor. The receptionist's head was down in deep concentration. "Thank you, Mrs. Peterson." She glanced up, and he pressed a hand to his heart, when really he wanted to grab her and kiss her cheek for all she'd done. But he was in enough trouble as it was, so he simply smiled and tipped an imaginary hat. He wished he could thank Mrs. Monroe as well.

Gideon stepped from the courthouse, his heart near to bursting. The land lay in a thin blanket of snow, but the sky overhead was bright and clear. Without hesitating—without taking time to allow what was happening to sink in—he started up the road. Within minutes he had all he owned on his back, and the road toward home called to him.

Fifteen

Toby held the hymnal in one broad palm, and Lonnie turned the page as they sang along. She marveled in the pleasantness of his deep and earthy voice as he formed each word in his handsome Scots. Lonnie sang along, enjoying every moment of this Sunday. Jacob was asleep in Elsie's arms, and Jebediah looked finer than she'd ever seen him, with his gray beard brushing the dark dress coat she'd seen him wear only once or twice before. Addie stood straight and still, her coffee-colored curls bundled in a pretty ribbon. She lent an enthusiastic off-key voice that was nothing but joyful.

The congregation sang, some tittering toward the rafters, others belting out a baritone Lonnie could feel right down to her toes. She kept a close eye on the words, having sung this hymn only a couple of times as a girl.

Feeling joy in the moment, she looped her hand through the crook of Toby's arm. Savoring his strength. His presence. The smooth, new fabric of his shirt was soft to her hand. She felt his eyes on her and, glancing up, confirmed that she'd captured his attention. Still singing, she turned the page in the hymnal. His arm beneath her hand seemed unsteady, the pages of the hymnal suddenly trembling. Toby's voice grew quiet. Uncertain,

Lonnie let her hand fall free and strengthened her attention on the last words as they fell from her lips.

Reverend Gardner rose and stepped to the pulpit. His Bible in hand, he offered a brief benediction, then bowed his head. Lonnie closed her eyes. Toby's shoulder was warm against hers. He took the smallest of steps away from her.

Whispering an amen, Lonnie couldn't bring herself to look at Toby when she opened her eyes. Instead, she slid the hymnal in its place and brushed at an imaginary streak of dust on her sleeve. With Jacob still in her arms, Elsie rose and spoke to a woman across the aisle. Without so much as a word, Toby stepped toward a hunched man who waved him over with his cane. Wishing she knew what she'd done, Lonnie moistened her lips. Her heart in her toes, she glanced over her shoulder as she reached for her shawl. A pair of pretty girls sat behind her. Two pairs of blue eyes followed Toby's movements. It took only a moment for Lonnie to guess that the girls were sisters.

They glanced at her in unison, and she felt a coolness that made her toss her shawl over her shoulders. Still feeling their scrutiny on her, Lonnie swallowed her uneasiness and extended a hand.

"I'm Lonnie Sawyer. I don't know that we've met proper."

"Lydia McGuire." The girl shook Lonnie's hand gently. Her curls pinned back in a bun, she seemed the elder one. "This is my sister Doris."

"Oh." The last name sounded familiar. "Are you the one getting married soon?"

"No, that's our older brother." She hitched a thumb over her shoulder, but Lonnie couldn't make out who was who in the thick crowd. "You'll be coming to the wedding, though, I hope." She had to speak louder as the murmur of mingling voices grew.

"I believe we will."

The girl glanced back at Toby, distracted. "I noticed you comin' with the Reverend McKee to church this last month."

"Yes. He's a good friend." Lonnie explained about the wagon and how far off she and the Bennetts lived.

The other sister leaned in closer, her pale braid, trimmed with a white ribbon, nearly brushing the seat of the pew. "That's awful nice. Reverend McKee is such a kind man." Her voice held something that reminded Lonnie of the admirers Toby must certainly have among the congregation.

Distracted, Lonnie shrugged one shoulder, yearning to join Elsie. "That's Toby." Oh, why did she use his Christian name? At the sharp glance they exchanged, Lonnie suddenly wished she'd called him Reverend McKee.

Turning, she searched for Toby's broad back, finally finding him beneath one of the tall windows speaking to an older couple. She wondered what it would be like for him to find one of these young ladies. Someone who didn't have a shadowed past. Didn't carry such scars.

Knowing she oughtn't just sit there like a dunce, Lonnie searched for something to say, but words didn't come. Then, seeing Elsie talking to a couple near the back of the church, Lonnie rose to help her with Jacob. "I'll see you Friday at the wedding," she said to the sisters. "Thank you." She found the Bennetts nearing the door, and with Jacob still rubbing a hand across his eyes, Lonnie knew it was time to get home. She lifted him from Elsie's grasp. Side by side, they walked toward the wagon.

Suddenly, Toby was beside her. "I saw you speaking with the McGuire girls." His voice was tight.

"I thought I'd say hello. I—" She glanced at him. "Why?"

"No reason." He walked on, his eyes on the path in front of him. A hundred troubles seemed to float around his shoulders.

"Toby." Her hand on his arm made him halt. "Is something the matter?"

Finally he looked at her, his eyes pained. "I...I..." He stared at her for several heartbeats, then swallowed hard. "Elsie invited me to dinner," he blurted. Then winced.

"That's wonderful. It'll be so nice to have you." She said the words slowly, trying to help him along.

"I had to decline, Lonnie." His eyes on her were deep and dark. "I'd already accepted an invitation from the McGuires."

Lonnie thought of the sisters. "The McGuires," she repeated.

"Aye, but..." He ran a hand over his mouth, then formed it into a fist at his side. "Och. Would ye mind, Lonnie, if I came to call on ye this evening?" His Scots grew more lush as the color on his neck rose.

"Of...of course."

But he didn't smile. Lonnie glanced up to see that they stood beside the wagon. Uneasy, she lowered Jacob into the back and was about to climb in when Toby's hands gripped her waist, lifting her up. He released her just as quickly, as if he'd been singed by a flame. Warm chills covered her skin, but at his stony expression, her heart was suddenly in her throat.

Sinking at Jacob's side, her skirt billowed around them. Toby hesitated a moment before turning his attention to Gael's feed sack. Shaking her head softly, Lonnie scarcely noticed Jebediah help Elsie onto the wagon seat. Addie crawled over on her own, and Jebediah climbed into the wagon bed beside the little girl.

The ride home seemed to last a lifetime, with Toby gripping the reins as if it required every ounce of his attention.

Finally, Elsie settled a basket on the seat between herself and Toby. "Is that the shirt Lonnie just made?"

"Sorry?"

"The shirt you're wearing. It looks very fine."

"Aye. A fine seamstress, our Lonnie."

Our Lonnie. She folded her hands over her knees, wishing she could make sense of the way his words seemed to collide with his stormy tone. Toby guided the wagon onto the Bennetts' farm. Lonnie watched the snowy road behind them, remembering the pretty blue eyes of the McGuire sisters.

As if sensing her unease, Jebediah patted a worn and weathered hand on her boot. He gave it a gentle squeeze, a tender smile in his steel-gray eyes.

There was once a time—when she was just a wee thing—that Lonnie thought the world to be a perfect place. The next day, after draining a bottle of whiskey, her pa showed her otherwise. That same morning, her mother had knelt in front of her, the tears scarcely dried on Lonnie's little cheeks. Lonnie could still remember the feel of her mother's hands, damp and chapped from the dishes as she reached for her own. With love and sadness shining through her brown eyes, Maggie Sawyer had told her something. That if ever Lonnie were to marry, to choose wisely.

Lonnie hadn't thought about that moment when she stood in front of the church with Gideon. But suddenly, with afternoon shadows growing long across the Bennetts' parlor, it all came back to her. Perhaps it was because this time around, she had a choice.

And her choice was Toby. She prayed that didn't take away from all Gideon had been to her.

Lonnie pulled Jacob into her lap, her soiled apron testament to the tarts she and Elsie had made after church. She held her son close. Nestled snug in her lap, he pointed a chubby finger to a picture of a sheep in the book she held. He neighed like a horse, drawing her mind back to the story they were reading. Lonnie kissed his ear.

"No...see?" She turned the page. "Horse." She pointed to the animal. Jacob neighed again.

"That's my boy." She squeezed him tighter, thankful for all he was in her life, all the while pleading that God would show her the right steps so that her son could have a life so unlike her own. A life of love and laughter.

Knowing she should get up and put on coffee to go with the tarts, Lonnie slowly closed the book. "That's all for now. We can look at it more before bedtime."

Jacob kicked his feet and squealed. He tried to pry the book back open.

"No, Jacob. We're all done for now. You can come help me in the kitchen." She started to rise, but his fussing continued. Settling him on her hip, Lonnie looked him square in the eye. "Mama said no. You can't have everything you want when you want it." She kissed his hand and smeared away a tear. "You're just like your father," she whispered, then smiled despite herself. "Just like your father." Kissing his temple, she swayed slowly and tried not to think of the boy with the mandolin. The boy who'd become a man and stolen her heart.

But it was too late. For in a rush of emotion, his face filled her mind. Lonnie closed her eyes. Jacob settled his head against her shoulder as they swayed. Melancholy rose within her. Perhaps it was the memories. Perhaps it was the events of the morning.

She knew she should fight it back, but for just one moment—one heartbreaking moment—she wanted to remember him. Remember the love they'd shared. Remember his smile. His eyes. For he had been real. Their love had been real. Every bit of it. She would be thankful for what it was and what it had been.

And she would continue to say good-bye.

Lonnie opened her eyes. A lift of her shoulders, and she blew out a slow sigh, her heartache carrying on it like leaves on a breeze. She gave Jacob a squeeze as they walked into the kitchen. She sent up a prayer of thanks for God's goodness. His mercy through it all. He was seeing her through, and each day would get easier.

She set Jacob on the chopping-block surface, and he watched as she pulled the coffee grinder down from its shelf, filled it with dark beans, and cranked the handle. He reached out to help, and she let him try to turn it. "Almost." Settling her hand around his, she helped him crank the handle. "Thatta boy." It took her just a minute to get the coffee onto the stove, and then she carried Jacob to the porch. Addie was playing in the yard, doing what she could to form the last of the snow into a ball.

Lonnie tried not to think of Gideon. And she tried not to think of Toby eating at the McGuires'. Failing at both, Lonnie moved back into the kitchen and lifted the lid on the percolator. *You can do this, Lonnie.* She would think about coffee. That was simple enough.

Suddenly Addie ran up the steps and darted into the kitchen. Her dress was damp from her play. "Toby's here!" She ran back onto the porch, then skidded to a halt. Turning, she was breathless. "Oops! I mean *Reverend McKee* is here!"

Hearing the sound of a horse and rider, Lonnie carried Jacob onto the porch.

Jebediah stepped from the barn, rag in hand. Toby rode Gael over as she strode across the yard.

"Evenin'." Jebediah tugged on his beard. "Glad to see ya."

Toby dismounted. "Evening." His jacket was draped over the front of the saddle. Sharply dressed in his waistcoat and crisp white shirt, he pulled the jacket down, folding it over his arm. A bit out of breath, he swallowed hard and glanced from Jebediah to Lonnie, as if she held some unseen magnet.

"Come on in." Jebediah waved him toward the house. "The ladies have been doin' some mighty fine baking this afternoon."

"Actually, sir, I wanted to speak with Lonnie, if I may."

Lonnie's heart quickened.

Jebediah stared at the young man for several breaths before shaking his head. "S-sure. That'd be fine."

"I should get Jacob's sweater." Was that her who had just spoken?

But then Jebediah was lifting Jacob from her arms, his eyes kind. Knowing. Lonnie's heart thundered.

"I'll take him inside," he said softly. "He'll be waitin' for you when you're done."

Lonnie stared into his face. "Thank you, Jebediah." For more than she could ever say.

She owed him and Elsie so much thanks. For loving her and Jacob when she and her son had no one else. The gray-haired man walked toward the house, the sunset glinting golden on his plaid coat. Lonnie captured Jacob's green-eyed gaze, and her chest tightened something fierce.

"Lonnie." Toby's voice was gentle.

Quickly, she searched for words. "How was your dinner? At the McGuires?" She held her breath, then forced herself to let it out.

Folding his jacket up tight, Toby gripped it in one hand. His eyes found hers. "Let's just say I'm glad to see you."

A strange mixture of hope and nervousness bubbled up inside her.

She glanced up at the tall Scotsman. Suddenly wanting this bend in the road. This bend that would take her farther from what was. Because she knew what he had come here for. She felt it in the way he was watching her.

The fact that they were alone.

"I'm a mess," she blurted, realizing she still had on her stained apron. Was one supposed to wear an apron at a time like this? She swallowed hard. She'd never done this before. Never with Gideon. Because Toby was so different from Gideon.

Gently, he reached for her hand. "You look"—he blinked quickly after studying her longer than a reverend should—"verra fine."

She wanted to smile, truly she did, but she didn't expect these sudden nerves.

They walked toward the woodpile. With trembling hands, Lonnie sat on the chopping block. "How was your afternoon?" she blurted.

"Verra well." But his tone said otherwise. He rubbed his hands up and down his thighs, and Lonnie followed the movement, suddenly unable to look into his face. "I-I brought Jacob a new wooden spoon. I know how much he likes to dig." A smile carried on his voice.

"I'm sure he'll love it," she whispered.

"He's a good lad."

"He is."

Large brown eyes captured hers. "He's like his mother."

She shook her head and blurted out the first response that came to mind. "He's like his father." Her mouth parted with a small gasp.

Toby's gaze wavered.

"I'm sorry. I mean—"

He held up a large hand, his face soft. "I know what you mean." Stepping closer, he crouched in front of her. "Please don't feel bad. It's who Jacob is...and I love the lad for it."

A tangle of emotions filled her heart.

"Do you believe me?"

The answer came easy. Honestly. "I do."

He let out his breath as if he'd been holding it. "That wee one means so much to me. I hope you know that."

"Thank you." She pressed her hands to her cheeks, wishing they didn't tremble so, and tried not to think of Gideon. She fought it with every ounce of her strength. Yet she failed. Miserably.

"Lonnie, there's something I want to ask you." Moistening his lips, Toby reached for her hand, his fingers surprisingly warm.

"Wait!" she blurted.

He straightened, her hand still resting safely in his.

"I don't think you want to do this." She slammed her eyes closed. "Toby." A slow breath in and she let it out. "You deserve better than me. You deserve someone who's known only your love." Would he understand what she was saying? "If you only knew how many ladies have their hopes set on you. Girls who haven't been through the mess that I have. If you knew"—she tipped her head to the side—"if you knew the shadows I fight against, I think you'd change your mind."

"I'm afraid that's not possible."

Lonnie felt him move, and when he took both her hands in his, she finally opened her eyes. He was before her. Kneeling. Mud staining his pants. His face was earnest with unhidden longing.

Her heart dipped when he looked at her like that, and her fingers were warming inside his. Everything inside her, every part of her heart, mind, and soul, the parts that made up who she was, battled. "May I say one more thing?"

"Whatever you need." He lowered his face until his forehead rested against the back of her hand, and the tender sensation sent a bolt of lightning through her arm. Her heart tripped.

"I'm Jacob's mother. That's all you know of me. But I used to be...I used to be Gideon's wife. And that did not change because I *wanted* it to."

His shoulders rose and fell.

"It had to. Do you understand what I'm saying?"

He nodded, his head still bowed. "You're saying you still love him." His words muffled between their interlocked hands.

"Toby." Freeing one hand, she touched his cheek. "I won't lie to you. In many ways, I do." She touched her fingers to the bodice of her blouse. "But little by little, God is taking hold of those feelings, healing what's broken, tending to changes still to come. It's a journey, and it has been *anything* but easy. I just don't know how long I still have to go, before I'm wholly...wholly yours. But I want to trust that that day can come. I want that day to come. I want to be yours."

His eyelids nearly slid closed.

"But it will take time."

"Oh, Lonnie."

Despite her resolve, a tear puddled and fell.

"Will you let me?" He started to reach for her hand.

Her chest burned with a swell of all that had passed and all that could be. She nodded.

With soft movements, Toby lifted her hand and kissed her fingers.

She blinked away more tears.

"Lonnie?" His voice was soft, the thick accent chasing a world of sorrows away. "Will ye do me the honor of becoming my wife?"

For an instant, her heart searched. It searched the hidden places inside her. The places that clung to Gideon's memory. His love. And like sand over a river rock, the jagged pieces of her hope were being rubbed smooth. Healing was being found. And Toby's dark, earnest eyes all but pulled the answer to her lips. "I will."

Sixteen

Elsie kissed her on both cheeks. Jebediah hugged her tightly, and Addie jumped up and down, clapping her little hands. Lonnie smiled, sharing in their joy.

"He is a good man," Elsie whispered in her ear when she enveloped her in another hug. "This calls for a celebration." Elsie nabbed her apron from its hook and flung the laces around thick hips. "Toby, you must stay for supper now."

Lonnie rinsed her hands in the washtub and shook suds from her fingers before reaching for the towel. Toby draped his coat over a chair. Returning to Lonnie's side, he stood closer than he ever had, and she felt his warmth coming through his shirt. When Jacob's cries sounded from above, Addie pleaded to go and fetch him. She returned with Jacob in her arms and set him down in the center of the kitchen.

Holding onto Toby's pants, he pulled himself to a stand, and Toby lifted the boy into his arms. "Did you sleep good?" He tickled Jacob's tummy with a broad hand. Jacob laughed, and when he tried to squirm away, Toby quickly nuzzled the boy's neck, then lowered him back to the floor.

The sight sent Lonnie's heart fluttering. "What can I do?" she asked Elsie.

At Elsie's bidding, she slipped into the parlor and pulled the finest glasses from the cupboard. She carried a few to the kitchen, where she set them in place and went back for the rest. Returning, Lonnie nudged a pile of forks out of the way with her elbow.

Addie stooped to the baby's level and pinched her hands between her knees. Her brown curls bobbed as she bounced. "Guess what, Jacob? Toby's gonna be your new papa!"

A glass slipped from Lonnie's fingers, shattering against the floor. The room fell silent. Lonnie stared at the glass. Her cheeks burned.

Elsie clanged her wooden spoon against the pot. "Addie, why don't you fetch the nice napkins from the cupboard in the parlor? They're the white ones."

Addie nodded.

"Count out five, please." She guided Addie around the glass, then lifted Jacob to her hip before returning to her pot.

Lonnie reached for a large shard, but Toby was already at her side. "I can get this," she whispered and crouched.

He gave her wrist a gentle squeeze, his thumb lingering. "Let me help you."

She fought a tremble in her chin when she glanced up at him. "I'm so sorry."

He shook his head, his eyes kind.

"Elsie, I'm so sorry about your beautiful glass."

Spoon in hand, Elsie waved off the apology. "Accidents happen."

Lonnie filled her palm with the largest shards, then rose for the broom.

"Ow!" Toby dropped the glass even as the first drop of blood fell to the floor.

Lonnie snatched a rag from the basket and knelt beside him. She wrapped his hand and, when he winced, softened her touch. "Oh, Toby."

"I don't think it's verra bad." He lifted the edge of the rag to peer at the cut.

Lonnie shook her head. "You have a bad cut." His blood had already smeared against his palm, and with her hands still wrapped around his, they stood in unison. "Sit down and let me look at it." She gently pushed him toward the chair nearest the window.

Running in from the parlor, Addie stood with her mouth open and watched Lonnie tear the rag into a thin strip. Elsie brought over a moist cloth. As Lonnie dabbed at the blood, Toby winced.

"I'm sorry." She draped the bandage around his cut with gentle hands. "Does this hurt?"

"No," he breathed.

"Oh, Toby." Addie leaned her head against his broad shoulder. "Your poor hand."

Toby touched his cheek to her hair. "I'll mend. Your sister's a good nurse." He glanced up.

Lonnie knotted the bandage and folded the loose ends underneath, holding his hand in both of hers when she finished. "Let's hope so." She wiped a smear of blood from the crease of his palm.

"It's better already." Then he made a show of feeling the bandage with his other hand. For Addie's sake, she sensed.

From the parlor, Jacob laughed. Lonnie spotted Jebediah reading him a story on the sofa as she cleaned up the rest of the glass.

"Would you like to go for a little walk?" she asked Toby.

"It's snowing." But his voice was laced with adventure.

Lonnie freed her coat from the hook. "Not verra hard," she said, attempting his accent.

He chuckled, his dimples appearing. Toby grabbed his coat from the back of the chair. He slipped his bandaged hand slowly through the first sleeve, then shrugged it over wide shoulders. He caught the handle of the door before she could and, leaning past her, pushed it open.

Though the snow scarcely fell, Lonnie lowered her shawl over her hair and tucked the ends beneath her coat collar. When Toby offered her his arm, she looped her hand over his elbow, savoring how safe he made her feel. A thick mass of gray clouds blocked out the sky, casting shadows over the thin layer of fog that curved through the holler.

"Which way?" Toby asked.

Lonnie pointed to where Gael stood tied up beneath a tree, the ground under the mare's hooves dark where the branches above her head caught the snow. As they stepped into the yard, the snow fell feather light. Toby asked Lonnie if she'd like to go riding sometime, and Lonnie eagerly said yes.

"Day after t'morrow?"

"It's a date." Reaching into her pocket, she pulled out a nub of carrot. She motioned toward Gael. "Why didn't you take her to the barn?"

Toby drew in a slow breath, his words hesitant. "I wasn't sure if I'd be staying that long."

It struck her that he hadn't been certain she'd say yes.

His eyes sparkled, and he glanced at her hand. "Elsie's stew is missing somethin', I see." He spoke softly to the horse and gripped Gael's lead rope beside her neck. He brushed his hand against the mare's hindquarters, and Gael turned for him as if she could read his mind. Toby smiled down at Lonnie. "You have a cannie way of taking things unnoticed."

With the carrot in her palm, Lonnie stepped closer to the horse. She held it out, and Gael's velvet mouth nibbled. "It's a special talent."

"So I see." He patted Gael's dark coat, and the horse sniffed his broad hand as if searching for another treat. "I have nothing for you, lass." He glanced at Lonnie, his smile widening. "Are you trying to be her favorite?" The wind played with his dark hair.

Upon seeing that Toby had nothing to offer her, Gael dropped her head and sniffed Lonnie's hand, then nudged her arm.

Toby scratched his head. "Well, you're off to a good start."

She grinned, proudly. "I suppose I am. But it's only fair since I think Jacob just about prefers you over me."

He let out a throaty chuckle. "It's not my fault that I'm so much fun." He kicked at a clump of snow, still grinning.

"Is that what it is?"

He shrugged smugly.

"I think you bring him too many treats." Narrowing her eyes, she wiped her palm on her skirt. "*And* I think I have the messier job."

"Someone's gotta spoil 'im."

"Yeah, well, that's what Jebediah's for. Besides"—Lonnie sniffed— "that will all change soon. You won't be the spoiler anymore."

Toby looked at her.

She knew it was time to apologize. "About what happened inside, when Addie said—"

He touched her arm and stepped closer. "Dinna be too hard on yerself. One day at a time. Please don't be afraid that your past...your pain... will trample my joy." His hand slid up her arm, squeezing it gently. "'Tis not possible. You've already made me the happiest man alive. As you take the steps you need to take, I'd be honored to be by your side."

Speechless, Lonnie tilted her head to the side and peered up at him. She did not deserve his kindness. His patience.

"Supper's ready!" Elsie called from the porch.

"Come on." His hand found the small of her back, and he gently led her forward. "It's too cold out here without gloves."

Lonnie wiggled her bare fingers, teasingly. "And where might your gloves be, if I may ask?"

"I dinna need gloves." Toby mimicked her motion, only with more dramatic flair. "I have a bandage the size of a dishcloth."

She pushed against him, in no hurry to be anywhere but by his side.

Spotting one of the Bennetts' neighbors, Gideon waved to Mrs. Krause, and a broom stilled in the old woman's weathered hands. As if she'd just seen a ghost, her mouth hung ajar.

"Good to see ya." Without slowing, he tucked his hands in his pockets as the snow picked up its speed.

A few more farms to pass. He'd be home within the hour.

His wet boots marched to the beat of a softly falling snow. His stomach reminded him that he hadn't eaten since the evening before, but he was too eager to stop for it now. He tilted his face to the sky and let the icy flakes touch his skin. He blinked into the fading light of evening, but there would be no stopping to make camp this night. No, he welcomed the darkness. For it would bring him to Jebediah's door.

Glancing around, he savored the familiarity of these woods. He'd set traps in these woods. He'd taken Jacob for walks in these woods. Held Lonnie's hand. Kissed her smile.

This was his home. The place he longed to raise Jacob and love Lonnie for the rest of his life. Joy lifted his chest and quickened his pace.

Tugging his hands from his pockets, he pressed his warm palms together, overcome with the notion that by night's end, he'd cradle Lonnie's face between them. It killed him to think of not being able to kiss her. He wouldn't.

"And what will you do?" he asked himself aloud.

He would tell her the truth.

His legs were weary and his feet cold, but he scarcely felt either. It was impossible to feel the pain. Not with knowing that Lonnie and Jacob were no doubt settling in for the evening. His arms tingled at the thought of holding them. He'd hold them and never let go. His daydreaming must have carried him farther than he realized, for suddenly he halted.

The air nearly left his lungs at the sight of the Bennetts' house. Candlelight flickered in the windows. It took all his strength to keep from breaking into a run. Running up the stairs, bursting past the door, and kissing Lonnie the way he longed to.

But he could never do that. And his heart was pounding something fierce. Yanking off his pack, Gideon dropped it at his feet. He pressed his hands to his thighs and bent over, forcing himself to take slow breaths. His head was light. Dizzy.

Oh, God.

He could do this. He could do this.

Closing his eyes, he prayed. Prayed that she would understand. Prayed for grace. For mercy. For the time to be the man she deserved. He prayed for all that and more. His heart thundered. At the sound of a baby's laugh, his heart nearly tore in two, and snatching up his pack, he jogged across the farmyard.

Seventeen

Elsie waved everyone to the table. "Let's all sit and eat while it's hot." Lonnie sat beside Toby and fingered a loose pin in her hair. She tucked it back out if sight and was lowering her hand when she heard a knock at the door.

"Wonder who that could be," Jebediah said as he pressed his napkin beneath the collar of his shirt. He began to rise.

Lonnie waved him down. "I'll get it." The pin slipped free again, and popping it between her lips, she straightened her bun as she walked toward the door. Lonnie took a moment to slide the pin into place. She opened the door a smidge and peered out into the hollow night. She stepped onto the porch. Strange. Not a soul in sight.

Not wanting cold air to flood the kitchen, she cracked the door. The snow had slowed to a few silvery flecks here and there. A glance around the white yard, and she wished she hadn't taken so long. Whoever it was had perhaps gone to try the front door. She turned to head back inside when a man walked from the side of the house, not quite into the light.

Lonnie glanced over, unable to make out his face.

"May I help you?"

"Lonnie? Who is it?" Elsie called.

The man pulled off his hat and ran a hand through his hair before stepping closer. A brilliant pain bubbled in her chest, stretching into every sleeping corner.

Gideon.

"No—no one." Lonnie's voice faltered. "I'll be right there. Just a moment." Pulling the door closed, she stared into the dark night. Gideon stared back. Dawn broke within her at the sight of him standing before her.

He breathed her name. The sound so soft and perfect she took a single step toward him.

"Gideon." She marveled at the sound of it. At the sight of the man she thought she'd never see again.

His eyes didn't move from her face. His boots didn't move from where he was standing. With slow steps, Lonnie descended the porch and stood close. Too close. For he stepped back. Guarded.

"Gideon. It's you," she breathed. Even as she spoke the words, every impossibility pricked her heart. A thousand reasons he couldn't be here. But she quieted each one of them, grasping hold of this impossible moment.

One side of his mouth lifted. "It's me." His green eyes caught the candlelight streaming from the window.

Reaching up, Lonnie grazed her fingers against his hair, down his neck. "It's you." Tears stung her eyes. She brushed the side of her face against his coat, savoring his scent of smoke and cedar. Gideon captured her hand and, closing his eyes, turned his head to kiss her palm. A jolt of lightning surged through her arm, and Lonnie pulled it away, tucking it in the folds of her skirt.

He took a step back, and she was glad. Lest she forget he was not her husband.

"Where...where's..."

"Cassie?"

She nodded fiercely, dreading his answer.

"She's not here."

"No?" The word came out weak. Her chest heaved.

"She's back in Rocky Knob."

That's right. She wouldn't be able to travel in her condition. Lonnie's knees nearly buckled. Why was he doing this to her?

"Lonnie, there's something you need to know—"

Voices murmured from within. Then a chair scraped back, and footsteps crossed the floor.

The door opened. "Everything all right, Lonnie?" Jebediah called.

"Coming." She forced out a cheery tone. Standing in the shadows with Gideon, she wasn't ready to leave this moment. Not yet. But Jebediah's face was lit with worry. She couldn't blame him. "Coming," she said again, more softly this time. As a question—an invitation—to Gideon.

Lonnie turned and started up the steps, feeling him right behind. His fingertips brushed her arm, but before she could turn, Jebediah spotted him.

"Well, I'll be." He tugged his napkin from his shirt. "Gid!" He reached out, and they shook hands heartily.

"It's good to see ya, Jeb. So good to see ya."

The warmth of the kitchen was crushing as Lonnie ducked around Jebediah. The older man ushered Gideon in.

Elsie rose, and in an instant, she wrapped Gideon in a hug. "Oh, never thought we'd see the day!" Gripping his shoulders, she held him back and peered up. "What brings you here?"

"I, uh…" He glanced at Lonnie, then back at Elsie. "Needed to come home."

"Home?" Elsie asked. "But…Cassie…"

"It didn't work out."

As if his words were footsteps in the sand, Lonnie retraced them. But they didn't make sense.

Gideon stuffed his hands in his pockets and seemed about to say more, but as he glanced past them, his brows tugged together.

Elsie closed the door. "Come sit by the fire."

"Thank you, Elsie." His voice was distant because he wasn't looking at her.

He was looking at Toby, who stood only feet away.

Toby simply stared back. The kitchen seemed to shrink. Gideon looked from Lonnie to Toby then back again. His expression changing with every breath that lifted his shoulders. Gideon studied Toby from his heavy boots to his dark eyes. As if sensing what was brewing, Elsie stepped toward the parlor and motioned for Addie to follow her out of the kitchen. Jebediah leaned back in his chair and rested a hand on his stomach, eyes keen. Alert.

Lonnie motioned toward Toby. "Gideon, this is the Reverend McKee. We call him Toby." Her mouth suddenly felt dry. "He's a good friend of ours."

With a cordial nod, Toby stepped forward. "Pleased to meet ye," he said, a storm cloud thickening his Scots.

"And you." Gideon held out a hand, and Toby gripped it. Gideon's coat drew taut across his back as his shoulders tensed. She could see Toby's arm tighten through his shirt. Finally, they let go. Toby stepped back.

"Toby," Lonnie said softly. She motioned toward Gideon, who was standing so close that her arm bumped his. Much too close. "This is Jacob's father."

Toby nodded once, expression stony. "Aye. I ken the resemblance."

Neither one moved. Neither one spoke.

"Are you hungry?" Lonnie asked, needing to break their stares. "Have you eaten today?"

Gideon shook his head, gaze shifting from her to Toby and back.

"There's food on the table. Sit down." She hoped her voice sounded steadier than it felt. She waved them both over.

His troubled eyes on her as he passed by, Gideon turned toward the table.

Then he froze. His lips parted.

Sitting in his highchair, Jacob waved a tin cup over his head, finally lowering the cup onto his hair like a hat. He looked at Gideon with curious eyes. He set the cup on his wooden tray and, staring up at Gideon, sat more still than Lonnie had ever seen him.

Gideon didn't move. "Jacob." The name came out thick with yearning.

The little boy glanced around at the familiar faces he knew and did not seem to acknowledge significance in the man before him. Lonnie reached out to pull her son from his highchair. "Look who's here."

Jacob lunged to the side, just out of reach. Lonnie moved closer, and when she caught him beneath the arms, he let out a squeal, his features frightened. His eyes locked on the man whose face mirrored his own.

"It's your papa," she assured him.

Jacob shook his head and threw his spoon at the ground. He kicked his feet and squealed again when Lonnie tried to lift him.

"Jacob," she scolded.

Gideon stepped back. "Just leave him."

Mortified, Lonnie looked up at him.

He ran a hand over his mouth.

"I'm sorry," she whispered.

"Don't be." Gideon swallowed. "He doesn't remember me. I don't blame him." He rubbed his hands together and blinked quickly.

Elsie walked Addie back into the kitchen, and the girl watched with wide eyes.

Finally, Elsie drew in a loud breath. "Shall we sit and eat?" Like a calming force, she motioned them all to the table, where they crowded around the small space. Gideon and Toby reached for the same chair.

Gideon pulled his hand back. "Sorry."

"No." Toby motioned toward the chair. "My fault. You go ahead."

"I'll fetch another." Jebediah stepped around the table, his boots loud in the silence.

"Are they still in the same spot?" Gideon asked in a strained voice, as he hurried toward the door. "I'll get one." His hand found the knob, and in a burst of cold air, he stepped into the night.

A cold breeze hit Gideon's face, and before he could draw another breath, he closed the door behind him.

This wasn't happening.

Trudging into the yard, he ducked his head under the curtain of snowflakes that had picked up. It took all his strength to keep from looking behind him. He knew what he would see in the window. All of them but one his family.

The man watched Lonnie with a protectiveness that made Gideon's blood run cold.

He bit a growl off before it could reach his throat.

Lifting the collar of his coat and his eyes at the same time, he faced a darkness that seemed ready to swallow him up. Shivering, Gideon ducked his head and walked on.

In the barn, he moved a stack of crates full of dusty bottles, finally finding a pair of chairs. He grabbed a rag from the worktable and smeared away dust and cobwebs, then paused long enough to look around. The scent of wood and animals surrounded him. This was his home. Everything about it was familiar, and he wanted nothing more than to close his eyes and imagine that man away. What right did he have to think of himself as Lonnie's protector? What right—

Gideon froze. His shoulders stiffened. He hadn't seen Lonnie's left hand. Gideon looked at the house, an ache burning through him. *Oh, Lord. Please, no.*

Hauling the chair to the house, he shouldered the door open and brushed snow from his hair. He slid the chair where Elsie had set another plate. Lonnie's back was straight as a church steeple. Gideon wondered if her heart hammered as much as his did. Without ceremony, he sat and rested his fists on the table in front of him.

Lonnie's perfect scent wafted against him when she moved to tuck her hands beneath the table, pressed between her knees, Gideon assumed. He did not need to peek to know that her habits had not changed. Was she trying to torture him? Toby sat on her other side, and Gideon looked at him before stuffing his napkin in his lap. Fear burned in his mouth, and he tried to swallow it away.

When they were all crowded around, Elsie clasped his hand and bowed her head. Holding his breath, Gideon lifted his other hand, and Lonnie slid her palm over his.

He bit the inside of his cheek and slammed his eyelids shut. Did she feel him trembling?

Jebediah blessed the food and added his thanks for Gideon's presence.

Gideon nodded with each word, thankful to hear in the older man's voice that, although his arrival was unexpected, he was welcome. Lonnie's hand was warming inside his, and it took all his strength not to circle his thumb across her silken skin.

She was like a sister to him now. It had to be. Could he do this?

When the prayer ended, he had to force himself to let go. Elsie used the edge of her apron to slide the heavy lid off the dutch oven. "Everyone help yourselves." She moved the lid to the stove, where iron clanged against iron.

His appetite gone, Gideon tried to harness his thoughts, say something. Anything. "Do you ever sit, Elsie?"

Elsie blushed. "I sit all the time. Just not during meals."

Jebediah chuckled. "Tell us what's happened. What brings you here, Gid?" The older man took a sip of cider and lowered his glass, his fingers still clutching the rim, waiting for a reply.

Gideon felt Lonnie beside him as if she were the only person in the room. He cleared his throat. "I, uh…" Gideon smoothed his napkin in his lap and rested his wrists on the edge of the table. "I, um, I wanted to come home."

Beside his, Lonnie's foot was bouncing something fierce. He looked at her. She stared at the bread as if her life depended on it.

"You still haven't"—Lonnie seemed to have paled—"told us about Cassie." She glanced up at him, her face tormented. He hated what he was doing to her. He struggled for the words that would bring her peace. *God, help me.*

Gideon sat back against his chair, his gaze glued to the table. "She's in Rocky Knob." He nodded slowly to himself, searching for the words. They weren't coming. "I…I…"

Lonnie turned toward him ever so slightly. "Let's start at the beginning,

Gideon." Her voice was smooth and soft—but pained. "How was your wedding?"

He looked down at her. Her pointed gaze faltered.

"That's not fair, Lonnie." The words rumbled low, meant for her ears alone.

Chin quivering, Lonnie rose and stepped from the table. Chairs scraped when Toby and Gideon stood in unison. Lonnie hurried through the parlor and up the stairs. When Toby stepped to follow her, Gideon glared at him and hurried after Lonnie.

Darting up the steps, he found her in their room. Hands clasped together beneath her chin, she looked up when he walked in.

"Lonnie." He motioned down the hall. "Are you married?"

She tipped her chin up. "What difference does it make?"

"Please, Lonnie. I need to know."

"I'll give answers when *you* do." She stepped closer.

He couldn't think straight. Not in this room. With her so near. "Give me a question, Lonnie," he said, his voice pitifully weak. "Give me a question, and I'll answer it."

"Why are you here?"

"Because I want to be with you. I love you and I can't stop. Cassie—"

"Cassie."

"Yes." He motioned between them. "She allowed me to come home."

"Permanently?" Doubt tiptoed along the tremor in her voice.

"Yes, permanently."

"So you're…" Lonnie hesitated, then reached for him. "You're not married?"

Gideon ran a hand over his face. "Soon, no, I won't be. But right now…"

A shadow passed through her large eyes.

"Right now, Cassie is still my wife."

"Your wife."

Gideon nodded and, suddenly feeling hot, he loosened the top button of his collar. "Lonnie."

He felt her retreating. He was losing her.

"How could you come back like this?"

"I've spent a month in Stuart. I've visited with the judge twice now. He's working on my case." Gideon stepped closer and cupped her face in his hands. "Lonnie." He moistened his lips, overcome with the urge to kiss her forehead. "Any day now I'll get word that it's finalized." He forced his hands to fall away when his resolve wavered. "Any day now I'll be free...to marry you."

"But I don't understand. You and Cassie—"

Lonnie straightened, and Gideon turned to see Jebediah leaning in the doorway casually.

"Wanna get yourself shot, son?" His words were hard, but his tone seemed amused.

Gideon moved back. It struck him that he had no right to be in this room. It was Lonnie's. He had no right at all. He glanced around the familiar place, his eyes roving every surface. Every memory.

"Then I suggest you head on back downstairs."

Lonnie pinched the bridge of her nose. "Good night, Gideon."

Gideon strode down the stairs. Each step deliberate, grinding into his reality what was at stake—everything he'd ever loved. At the sight of the Scotsman sitting on the bottom steps, forearms on his knees, head bowed between them, Gideon halted. It pained him to have the man so close to Lonnie. In more ways than one.

Running fingers through his hair, Gideon gripped the back of his neck. "Excuse me." Not caring how sharp his words were, he waited for the reverend to stand and move out of his way. Gideon walked off the last step, their eyes nearly level.

"S'pose it's time to call it a night," Toby said.

"S'pose so." Gideon stared at him, and the man stared back for the briefest of moments, then grabbed his hat from the bottom step and moved through the parlor. Gideon listened as he bid farewell to Elsie and the children, and then he was gone.

Eighteen

With Jebediah holding the lantern, Gideon carried his pack, an extra blanket, and a pillow as they walked to the barn. It had finally stopped snowing. At least something was going right.

"You sure you won't sleep on the parlor sofa? Be a whole lot warmer."

"I'm used to the cold. Besides"—Gideon tucked the blanket beneath his arm, nearly dropping the pillow—"it's better this way." It was hard enough having Lonnie so near. He wasn't about to sleep a few steps from her door.

They stopped in front of the barn, and Jebediah set the lantern down.

Tossing his head toward the direction what's-his-name had gone, Gideon spoke. "Who's the chump?"

Jebediah arched an eyebrow as he opened the barn door. "If you *mean* Toby...he's a good man." At Gideon's expression, Jebediah waved him in. "I'm not saying you have to like him. Just be civil. All right?"

"I'll try," Gideon muttered.

"He's a good man. A friend to all of us." Jebediah set the lantern on the work surface.

Gideon set the bedding beside the lantern and, dropping his pack, leaned on the workbench. He lowered his head between his forearms. "And Lonnie?"

"What of her?"

"Don't make this difficult, Jeb."

The older man's mustache tilted up on one side. "All right. What do you want to know?"

"Is she... Are they?" The words slipped out pitifully. "I didn't see a ring...but, Jeb, I gotta know."

Jebediah opened a stall gate. "No. They're not married. But you sure as shootin' got here in the nick of time."

Relief coursed through him, but it was short lived. Before he could dwell on what could have been, Jebediah called him. He thumbed for Gideon to carry his bedding inside the empty stall. Gideon stepped around him.

"They're not married...but they're engaged."

Gideon's heart plummeted. He moistened his lips. "Engaged?"

"Just this evening."

Gideon forced himself to breathe as Jebediah's words sank in. He tilted his face to the rafters. "Are you serious?"

"I'm afraid so."

"How long have you known him?"

"Toby's been comin' around to help with the farm ever since you left." Jebediah hung the lantern overhead. His steel-gray eyes bore into Gideon's. "But we don't need as much help as he's willing to give, if you catch my meaning."

"Yes. I'll thank you to spare me the details."

"There's nothin' else. Reverend McKee is the best of men. If anyone was gonna court your Lonnie, he's the one to do it."

Gideon rolled his eyes. "That's not as comforting as you think it is."

Jebediah chuckled as he carried over an armful of straw. "This used to hold a donkey. Seems fitting."

Following suit, Gideon brought more straw and then spread it in a thin layer over the dirt. "I'm really glad you find this funny." Finished spreading out the straw, Gideon laid his bedroll crookedly on top and threw his pillow haphazardly at the other end. He stared at it. Not the homecoming he'd dreamed of. "And Jacob?" he asked softly.

"Hang in there. In a few days, he'll be back to his old self, and you'll see… That boy loves you very much."

Gideon flexed his hands, yearning to run them through his son's downy curls. Holding a stone to prop open the stall gate, Gideon pushed it open as far as it would go. He went back for his pack and set it beside the makeshift bed. It wasn't much. But it was dry. And sorta warm.

With a tug on his beard, Jebediah stood quietly several moments. "Gid. There's somethin' I need to ask you. Man to man." He shifted his boots, his gazed fixed on the ground between them.

Uneasy, Gideon turned to face him.

"I feel a bit protective of Lonnie. She'll make her own decisions, of course. But she's like a daughter to me, and I aim to look out for her. In any way that I can."

Gideon folded his arms and stared at his boots. "Yes sir." He sensed where this was heading.

"It has to do with Cassie. And you two being married folk."

Slowly, Gideon nodded. They stood for several moments without speaking.

"Goodness' sake, Gid, don't make me come out and ask you, son. This is hard enough." Jebediah tugged on his beard again, cheeks rosy.

Running the pad of his thumb over his lips, Gideon cleared his throat. "I'm glad you're looking out for Lonnie." He stared at his friend.

"She deserves all that and more." He kicked at a piece of straw. And then another. "Nothing...nothing *happened* between me and Cassie."

Jebediah twisted his mouth to the side. "You mean that?"

"I wouldn't lie to you."

Jebediah dipped his head in a nod and then squeezed Gideon's shoulder. "Lonnie'll be glad to know that." Glancing up with kind eyes, he patted Gideon on the back and stepped toward the barn door. "Maybe you deserve her after all."

Nineteen

rash. Lonnie's eyes flew open.

Thunk. Thunk. She sat up in bed. Another *crash.* She slid from the warm covers, her bare feet arguing with her even as she tiptoed across the freezing floor to the window. The back of her hand grazed the lace curtains. Just enough to peek through unseen.

Thunk. Thunk. Two pieces of wood joined the pile. Gideon placed another hunk of wood on the block. He picked up his ax and, in one smooth motion, brought it down.

Crash. The halves spiraled away.

His breath fogged, and Lonnie's hands involuntarily rubbed up and down her nightgown sleeves. She shivered but did not hurry back to bed, where Addie tossed in her sleep.

Setting his ax on its blade, Gideon bent and gathered the wood. Lonnie squinted as she watched him. Split, stack. It was not the most efficient method, but she recognized the rhythm and knew he was lost in thought. She watched him work, wishing his thoughts could be displayed like words on a page. But that was never Gideon's way.

She pulled her nightgown over her head and tossed it aside, then splashed ice-cold water on her face. Unraveling her braid, she loosened the kinks and gnarls, twisting it into a low bun at the nape of her neck. She snagged her dress from the back of the rocking chair and was still buttoning it up even as she searched for her shoes. Lonnie stepped quietly down the stairs. She grabbed her coat and threw it over her shoulders before opening the back door. Gideon looked up, then stood motionless. Lonnie slipped her hands through the sleeves.

Although the sky was still a dusky gray, there wasn't a cloud in sight. Her shoes crunched across the frost that had gathered on yesterday's thin layer of snow.

Gideon lifted his chin when she approached, any thoughts of chopping wood clearly forgotten. "It's too cold for you to be out this early."

Lonnie slid her hands into her coat pockets. "Then neither should you." But she knew he'd slept on the ground in weather colder than this.

Gideon moved a hunk of wood to the block. He gripped the ax handle.

Lonnie flinched when the splitting of wood shattered the silence.

"I know that coat." Turning, he stacked the pieces.

Running her thumb against the edge of the sleeve, she spoke the truth. "I couldn't part with it."

As if her face told more of the story, he studied her.

She searched for a way to change the subject. "I see you're busy at work already. You don't waste any time, do you?" She circled around him. His eyes followed.

"I couldn't sleep. Besides"—he motioned toward the woodpile—"it needed to be done."

Her finger poked out of the oversized sleeve toward the woodpile. "Toby helped Jebediah keep it going this winter—"

"Toby."

"Reverend McKee," she added softly.

"I know who you meant."

Her eyebrows pinched together. "Don't be like this."

Gideon turned back to his task and split another piece of wood, ignoring the fragments. He immediately split another, and his breathing picked up. "Sorry." He tapped the side of the ax blade against his boot before leaning the handle against the block. Crouching, he gathered up the pieces.

It seemed impossible to be speaking to him in this moment.

Her heart ached. Torn, she pressed her hand to her forehead. Every moment that he should have been by her side tallied up to a mound of heartache. A grief she'd forced into the attic of her heart, where it could not torture her every waking moment.

Because every moment that he hadn't spent with her...he had been with another.

Lonnie wasn't prepared to face that. She'd always planned on tucking it out of sight. Burying it. But here he stood.

Wood thudded onto the pile. His eyebrows tilted back, the same sad expression returning. "Reverend McKee... He seems like a good man. He stepped in when I couldn't." Gideon glanced toward the trees, and Lonnie wondered where his thoughts traveled. "I owe him my thanks."

She shifted her numb feet. "Really?"

"Absolutely."

"He'd be pleased to know you felt that way."

"I'd be happy to tell him." Gideon rested his ax on the toe of his boot and turned the handle from side to side. "Right before I tell him that I'll take it from here."

"You'll what?"

"That Jebediah won't need his help anymore. No sense in the poor man coming all this way to do farm work that I can do now."

"Gideon, that's not your decision."

He picked at a splinter in his palm. A pretend one from what Lonnie could see.

"So what is the decision, Lonnie?" His voice was soft against his chest.

She folded her arms and moved closer. "At the moment, nothing. Unless I understood wrong…you're still married." The ache burned so fresh it throbbed.

They stood a touch away. His eyes unmasked pain. "That's going to change, Lonnie. And please"—he brushed her hair back with his broad hand—"tell me you'll marry me when that time comes." His thumb grazed her chin, and she quickly pulled away.

"I don't know. I don't know what to think about you. This is all so new."

"What do you mean?"

"You and Cassie. I—" She squinted up at him. "I don't know what to think about that. For you to be with her and then just come back here like nothing ever changed." She tugged at a loose thread, turning it between her fingers, her throat so tight she feared the words wouldn't come. She swallowed hard, fighting the lump. "You're not the same man who left me. You're not mine anymore." She motioned between them. "I can't tell you what that does to me. You *loved* her."

"I don't love Cassie. I only love you."

"But…"

"No. Lonnie." He pressed a hand to his abdomen. "I never… Cassie and I were never…"

The words slipped out thin. "But a baby?"

"Baby?" He swallowed visibly, his eyes so wide she couldn't look away. "No baby, Lonnie." He motioned toward Rocky Knob. "There's no baby."

"What?"

Urgently, he spoke. "There's not even a *chance* of there being a baby."

Not even a chance. Her head spun. Knees shaking, she crouched. Her bun came loose, and her hair fell in a curtain when she lowered her head in her hands. "Gideon, I don't understand." The words came out slowly, her voice muffled. Finally, she peered up at him. "Reverend Gardner and I were talking, and he said she'd been ill, and I thought...I thought she was expecting."

"Oh, Lonnie." He knelt in front of her. "No. It's *impossible*. I need you to know that. I need you to understand. I never loved Cassie."

Lonnie studied his face.

"I fear that makes me a bad person, that I failed Cassie as a husband. But I only wanted you."

A single sob escaped her, and Lonnie slammed her eyes shut. His hands were around hers, his skin so rough and perfect. Her Gideon. Her sweet, sweet Gideon. Was it truly possible? The dying pieces of her heart tingled back to life.

"You're it, Lonnie. You're all I ever want. All I'll ever need."

She thought he was going to kiss her, so close was his face, but he pulled back quickly, deliberately. She looked at him as he pressed the back of his hand to his mouth. His eyes were troubled. Then he glanced past her, and his expression changed. Hardened.

She was about to turn when he spoke.

"Please say you'll wait for me."

Lonnie settled deeper, not caring that the snow was soaking her stockings. A horse whinnied at the far end of the yard. She didn't need to glance behind her to know who it was.

The back of Gideon's neck burned. The muscles in his shoulders tightened.

Toby tugged his mount to a halt and jumped down. Leading the horse behind him, he blinked several times as if stunned to see Gideon standing there.

Probably a nervous tic. Gideon strode toward him, feeling guilty that he'd left Lonnie behind. But his frustration tamped down any clear thinking. "What do you want?" he asked as coolly as he could.

"I've come to see Lonnie."

"What if she doesn't want to see you?" He crossed his arms over his chest.

Without answering, Toby led his horse forward. Gideon mimicked his steps until they were shoulder to shoulder, almost touching.

"Can I help you with something?"

"Yes. Leave."

Glancing sideways, Toby looked at him. Almost through him.

Gideon forced his gaze to remain steady.

"I've come to tell her I won't be able to take her riding tomorrow as I'd promised."

"Good, because you won't be welcome tomorrow." Lonnie was his wife. Or so she had been. Gideon ran a hand up his forearm. Sick because of all that was at stake.

"I don't expect you to like me."

"Right." Suspenders limp around his knees, Gideon itched for a fight.

"And I canna say I blame you. But I'm going to talk about this with Lonnie. It's only fair for this to be her decision."

"I don't know what you think *this* is, but—"

"Stop it, Gideon!" Lonnie was at his side.

They looked at her in unison. Toby's eyes danced over her face. Gideon wanted to slug him.

"Gideon." She grabbed him by the sleeve and pulled him away.

Stunned, Gideon simply followed.

"What are you doing?" she asked.

Toby strode to the porch and sat down.

Gideon scratched the back of his head. "I was just…"

"Just what?"

"I just…don't see why he had to come here. Now. This moment."

The breeze stirred her hair against her cheek, and she let out a slow breath. "I *do* need to talk to him. Hopefully without your trying to punch him." Disappointment clear in the set of her mouth, her hand moved to his chest, gently pushing him back a step, in the opposite direction of Toby. "But first"—she looked up at Gideon—"is what you said really true?"

"It is, Lonnie. I promise." How he wished he had some proof to give her, but he had only his word. He prayed it was enough. "We'll talk about it more. We've got all the time in the world, right?"

The man who had her promise of marriage sat stone still, and Lonnie turned to look at him. Gideon forced himself to breathe. She glanced back at Gideon. He sensed her distress. As if she wanted to be in two places at once.

Suddenly feeling like he didn't belong, Gideon stepped back. "I won't keep you."

"I'm sorry, Lonnie." Toby slid over on the step when she neared. She sat down beside him. "I shouldna have come here today. I came to talk to you about t'morrow. And Gideon thought… He thought he and I should talk." Toby's voice was calm, but an edge tainted it. "Canna say I disagree."

"I'm so sorry for this. Yesterday was a special day. And now…" Now it was all a mess. What would have been their celebration made so different by Gideon's return. Lonnie didn't know where to begin.

Then Toby spoke. "I thought a lot last night. About us."

"You did?"

Eyes dark, he ran a hand over his face. "What else would I have thought about, Lonnie?" His tone was raw. "I decided something and just wanted you to know." He motioned toward Gideon. "I won't try and take you from him. I know that's what he fears…but it wouldna be right." Slowly, he shook his head, then peered sideways at her. "Doesn't mean I wouldna like to try." He winked, surprising her.

For the briefest of moments, she pressed her head to his shoulder as she once had so freely. Now she didn't know what to do. Everything was tangled. All her hopes and dreams knotted with the past. All that had been and could have been suddenly wasn't water under the bridge.

Toby sighed.

Straightening, Lonnie wrapped her hands around her knees, tucking her skirt in. "Gideon is still married to Cassie."

"He is?"

She nodded. "He's been to the courthouse, and things are unsettled with it all. I'm not sure what's gonna happen."

"What is your hope?"

"*My* hope?" Tears stung her eyes. "I'm not sure. It's all happening so fast."

"All the more reason for me to take a step back. I dinna want you to feel any more pressure in all of this. You have much to sort through, and I dinna want to make that more difficult on you."

"Thank you, Toby. But"—she smiled at him—"don't think I'm going to just let you up and walk away."

A dimple appeared. "Wasn't planning on it. I said I dinna want to make *your* life difficult." He pointed to where Gideon had gone into the barn. "Now it would be just a wee bit fun making—"

Her elbow in his side silenced him. "You two!"

Toby held his hands up, the picture of innocence. Then his expression sobered. "Thank you."

"For what?"

"For letting me be here. As your friend."

She chose her words carefully, wanting to speak nothing but the truth. "You're more than my friend, Toby. I hope you know that."

Twenty

Sliding a crate toward himself, Gideon wiped the dust from his pants and gripped his hammer. The wood creaked, complaining against the movement after sitting untouched for so many years. The nails pulled loose, and the crate opened. Another box of books. He replaced the lid, pulled two nails from his lips, and pounded them into place. The lid groaned and squeaked. He slid the crate out of his way and reached for another.

Now that Lonnie had hired herself a new wood splitter, Gideon had sought out Elsie, seeing what he could do to make himself useful. Elsie had been eager to put him to work and asked him to find a crate of baby clothes in the barn. So here he was. Gideon steadied his grip on the hammer handle before flipping it over. The old wood popped and splintered, and then the nail hit the floor in a series of clinks. The lid slid off with a puff of dust. Gideon's shoulders slumped. Stacks of tiny, earth-colored garments lay neatly piled in rows. The clothes Elsie and Jebediah's little girl had worn.

Gideon did not have to guess what kind of pain the Bennetts had endured, for their ache mirrored his own. Two daughters lost. Both too young. Gideon swallowed. *Sarah.* His sweet girl. The child he'd never had the chance to hold.

He rubbed his palm against his forehead, then lifted a tiny wool sweater. He held it to the weak morning sunshine that filtered through the grimy window. A swirl of dust motes and light. With tiny sleeves and a snug collar, the green sweater was just the size to fit Jacob. The little boy had outgrown nearly all his infant clothes. Gideon set the sweater aside. Lonnie would be pleased.

He lifted another item and, shaking it loose from its folds, held up a tiny dress. He fingered the lace collar that had yellowed with age. Heartache struck him again as he thought of what Jebediah must have felt packing these things away all those years ago.

This would have fit Sarah by now. It would crush Lonnie to see this dress. He folded the garment with more care than he'd ever folded anything in his life and set it on his knee. He cleared his throat. Shuffling through the crate, he pulled out the items that would work for Jacob, while leaving the dresses and bows tucked safely out of sight. Replacing the lid, he understood why Elsie had given the task to no one else.

His knees were stiff when he rose. He strode toward the door, then stopped short. Dangling from a peg on the wall was a small chair he'd begun for Jacob. All those months ago. Gideon fingered one of the thin, spindly legs. He'd spent hours shaping it, thinking of his son the entire time. And now...

Gideon glanced toward the house. How many morning cuddles had he missed? How many good-night stories? No wonder his son didn't know him. Would that God but grant him the chance to change that. He felt sick at the thought of Toby tucking Jacob in at night. Lying down beside Lonnie.

Quickly shaking off the thought, he clutched the clothes to his chest and stepped out. With his boot, he pushed the door closed. He heard fabric rip and felt a burn against his side. Lifting his arm, he saw that a nail had torn through his shirt, scraping all the way to his skin. Perfect. Gideon pressed the latch into place and started for the house beneath a rising sun.

He found Elsie elbow deep in dishwater. He set the clothes on the table, and her eyes followed the movement.

"Thank you, Elsie." He nodded toward the small stack.

"Lonnie'll be down in a little while." Elsie scrubbed at a pan. "She's upstairs reading to Jacob."

Gideon shut the kitchen door softly, yearning to join them. But Jacob would probably hurl the book at his head, and Lonnie would probably remind him what a great reader Toby was.

Elsie arched an eyebrow. "Everything all right?"

He realized he was scowling. "Yeah, I'm fine."

"She won't be long. May I get you some coffee or something to eat?"

"No, thank you. Oh. But"—he stuck his thumb through the tear on the side of his ribs—"would you mind fetching me another shirt? This is the only other shirt I have right now. My good one's hanging on the line. There should be a few in the wardrobe."

Elsie clamped her bottom lip between her teeth.

"What's wrong?"

"They're gone."

"Gone?" A half smile lit his face, uninvited. "She didn't waste much time getting rid of me."

"She was a mess, Gid. I think of all people, you'd understand."

He stared at the wooden floor. "I kept the only thing I had of her."

"She didn't have a choice, and you know it." Elsie glanced upstairs. "It doesn't mean she wanted to." Her copper eyes searched his. "So don't you go thinking otherwise."

He doubted that. She seemed to have moved on quite nicely. She'd cleared him out of her life and nearly secured a new husband. What else needed to be done? Dig his grave?

"Give her time." Elsie tugged on his sleeve, her voice soft. "And in the meantime, give me that shirt. I'll fetch one of Jebediah's and have this mended for you as soon as I can."

"Thanks, Elsie." He watched her disappear.

In the parlor, he worked the buttons of his shirt loose and draped it over the banister. Settling down on the steps to wait for Elsie, he leaned forward and clasped his hands. The soft sounds of Lonnie lulling their son to sleep floated down. A lullaby. Running his hands together, Gideon closed his eyes.

Twenty-One

Lonnie dropped the dishes in the empty washtub and pulled her hands back so Elsie could fill it. "Thank you." Using a wooden spoon, Lonnie scrubbed at the roast pan, sticky from the remainder of caramelized onions. When her elbow burned, she smeared the back of her hand over her forehead. Voices filtered in from the parlor, but Lonnie was too busy with her thoughts to listen.

She scrubbed at a spoon until Elsie finally plucked the sparkling piece from her fingers, and it was then she realized she'd polished the same utensil for the last several minutes. Elsie's eyebrows lifted, creasing her forehead. Lonnie turned back to her work and, even as her cheeks blushed, knew she could sooner catch a sky full of fireflies than she could contain her thoughts.

"Gideon." Elsie said the single word softly, watching her.

Lonnie drew in a shaky breath. "I spent all these months trying to move on."

"And how did it go?"

Lonnie gave her a look and knew it was enough when Elsie smiled. Lonnie dipped her rag into the warm water. After a few moments, she finally spoke. "He's changed, Elsie." She cleaned a cup inside and out.

"In ways." Elsie said thoughtfully, stacking cups in a high cupboard.

The tuning of a mandolin drifted into the kitchen. Lonnie and Elsie lifted their heads in unison. Gideon strummed a quick lick, only a few chords long, then tuned again, the bitter notes becoming sweeter. Several moments of silence, and Lonnie heard Jebediah put in a request.

The song began.

"You go on, Elsie. We can finish this up later."

Nodding softly, Elsie tossed her dishtowel aside.

"I'll be in in just a moment."

After watching her leave, Lonnie stood for several minutes, cup in hand, water dripping down her elbow. Then she placed the dish in the tub and grabbed a towel. She shook out the damp folds of her apron and stepped into the parlor. Gideon sat on the edge of the fireplace, knees jutted up. His fingers slowed when she walked in.

"Don't mind me." She slid into the desk chair. Addie sat on the floor with Jacob in her lap, where the boy chewed on a piece of bread from supper. Crumbs caught on his rounded tummy.

Gideon plucked skillfully in soft rhythm, betraying the likelihood of only one instrument bringing the music to life. Jebediah and Elsie exchanged glances. Lonnie understood the look they shared—this was a treat. *And you?* Lonnie pressed her hand to her collarbone. With his head bowed, Gideon seemed in a world of his own. She couldn't help but watch him. His fingers moved effortlessly; the music he created formed in perfect harmonies. It was her song. But it had grown, matured. She had never heard anything like it.

His hair seemed darker than she remembered, ruddier, less golden. The way it looked in the winter, when the summer sun could not lighten it as if God had laced it with golden straw. The freckles on his nose had faded as well. Lonnie pressed her hands in her lap. She had missed it all.

She'd said good-bye to him in the fall, and here he was, months later, before her again.

What have you been doing, Gideon? Every day, every hour that he was gone, he was with another. She'd lost a part of his life. *And Cassie?* Cassie had gained memories—moments—with the man Lonnie, no matter how desperately she wished it were so, could not steal back. She felt the surge of jealousy afresh and pushed it away, knowing full well it would not heal her pain. As Elsie had told her long ago, jealousy only hurts the one who feels it.

Jacob slid from Addie's embrace, and when his small hand found the hem of Lonnie's skirt, she hoisted him onto her lap. She buried her nose in his soft curls and savored his sweet scent, slightly soapy from a recent bath. His feet kicked, then stilled. As his head pressed against her shoulder, she felt him sigh. His hand fell limp on her leg, his half-eaten bread forgotten.

Rarely did he sit so still. He stared at his father, his chubby fingers in his mouth. Lonnie kissed the top of Jacob's head. When Gideon looked up, his eyes first found hers, then drifted to their son. He smiled. A wholeness lived in his expression. A yearning in his eyes. He longed for his son. In ways she would never understand. For she had not been forced away.

As if hearing her thoughts, he lowered his face, seeming to turn his attention back to the music. But when his eyebrows lifted and his eyes locked with hers once more, she knew otherwise.

Leaning against the door frame of the darkened room, Gideon tucked his hands in his pockets and nearly held his breath. Lonnie smoothed her hand over Jacob's forehead and, kneeling in front of the large cradle Gideon made, placed the sleeping child in his bed. Jacob stirred but did not wake. Lonnie lifted his quilt over him and tucked it securely on both sides.

The glass panes rattled softly. She turned her face to the window. Gideon stood frozen in place, knowing he should make his presence known but finding it impossible to do so. He lifted a corner of his plaid shirt and tugged his undershirt free of his pants, letting the fabric fall loose around his hips. The end of another day.

Lonnie pulled the curtains closed.

"Will he be warm enough?" Gideon kept his voice low so as not to startle her.

Without turning, she nodded softly. He wanted to wrap his arms around her and lower his chin to her shoulder as he once had. But he didn't move. When Lonnie faced him, she seemed to sense as much and folded her hands in front of her skirt.

"I should leave," he said.

She squinted, as if frustrated it had to be this way. "Would you like to kiss him good night?"

Gideon sucked in a breath. "I don't know if that's a—"

"Please." She stepped toward the door, brushing past him without looking up. "Take your time."

He watched her stroll through the hall and quietly pad down the stairs.

Gideon straightened and his eyes roved the familiar room. Memories flooded him, and knowing it would be unwise to let them linger, he knelt beside Jacob's cradle and traced his thumb over his son's velvet cheek. Like black fringe, the little boy's lashes rested on plump cheeks, white nightshirt not fully buttoned. With fumbling, oversized fingers, Gideon pushed the last two buttons into place.

"It's me," he whispered, sliding his knees forward until they knocked against the bottom of the low cradle. Gideon leaned forward. He kissed Jacob's forehead, finally his nose. The boy shifted and rolled to his side, a relaxed sigh escaping him. Draping an arm on each side of the small child, Gideon pressed his ear to Jacob's chest and closed his eyes.

Careful not to place any weight on his son, Gideon listened to the rhythm of the boy's heartbeat, which brought a sting of tears to his eyes. He thought this day would never come. Lifting his head, he stared down at his son. "I love you," he whispered, unable to keep the longing from his voice.

After rising, Gideon stepped softly from the room. At the base of the stairs, he found Jebediah and Elsie reading by the firelight. Addie was curled up on the sofa beside Elsie, her head in the older woman's lap. Gideon nodded when they looked up, but he was too interested in the quiet movement coming from the kitchen to linger anywhere else.

He found Lonnie sitting at the table, one leg pulled beneath her. His shirt in her hands.

Stuffing his fists in his pockets, he leaned against the jamb. "Elsie was going to do that."

Lantern light fell golden across her skin when she looked up. "Elsie spent the afternoon at a quiltin' bee. They made a wedding quilt for the McGuire couple. So I just offered."

A tug on the nearest chair, and he sat opposite her. "I appreciate it."

"Oh…and Elsie said when the family heard you were back in town, they asked if you'd play."

"I can do that."

"It's next Friday."

He nodded. "I'll remember to take a bath then."

He could tell she was trying not to smile. In no hurry to be anywhere but beside her, he clasped his hands in front of him and rested his forearms on the table.

"What did you do?" she asked, holding up the tear.

"Caught it on a nail." He let out a low chuckle. "I suppose some things never change."

She shook her head, but her lips suggested she agreed. "Didn't you bring any other clothes?"

Gideon flicked his collar. "You'd think so. But I didn't have much."

Lonnie moved her hand beneath the fabric, then her needle spliced through. "Did you just leave everything you owned in Rocky Knob?"

"I didn't have much," he repeated.

"No?"

"Just what we brought to visit your family. Everything in that little sack." He held his hands in front of him, close enough to mirror the size of his pack. He tipped his chin. "I didn't exactly want to stay."

Her mouth fell open, then clamped shut. "Of course you didn't. I'm sorry." She lowered her hand to the table, the needle idle between her fingers.

"I didn't expect you to, uh—" He tugged at Jebediah's shirt, and his eyes lifted upstairs.

"I'm so sorry."

He could tell she meant it. "You couldn't have kept anything?" He knew the answer would pain him, but he needed to know.

"There was no point." Then her voice turned thoughtful. "There were some things I kept."

"My coat." He let a confident smile surface.

"Don't be smug." She turned her attention back to her sewing. Her stitch went wide, and she tried to yank it loose but the thread knotted in several loops. With a click of her tongue, she freed her needle and tried to save the thread.

"Am I making you nervous?"

"Not in the slightest."

Her foot bounced, voiding her words. The scissors spliced, and she discarded the gnarled bit. Snatching up the spool of white thread, she unwound a long piece and used her teeth to break it off.

Gideon had to stifle another smile. He crossed his boots, one over the other, and slid them forward. When his feet bumped hers, he pulled back and straightened. "So, what have you been up to? I mean, *aside* from finding a new husband."

She plunked her sewing onto the table. "You can be really difficult."

He tipped his chin, his heartbeat rising. "How long did you wait?"

"What?"

He spoke again, this time emphasizing each individual word. "How long did you wait?"

"You mean…meeting Toby?"

He nodded.

"I don't know if that's your business." Color rose into her cheeks.

"You said we could talk."

She closed her eyes as if to gain control of her irritation. Gideon shifted in his seat. When she finally looked at him, her gaze was sharp, and he knew he was walking a thin line.

"The Bennetts invited him for supper. He was a friend to them. It was…oh, I don't know…a handful of weeks after I came back. A little longer, perhaps." She shook her head as if she didn't want to think back to those days.

"That's it? A few weeks?" He regretted the words the moment they slipped out.

Her mouth twisted to the side. With slow movements, she pressed her needle into the fabric and stood. "And how long did you wait?" Her voice held a thousand hurts. "How many weeks…or was it just *days* that you waited after Cassie before you kissed me that night outside my house? I could scarcely stop you."

He swallowed. "Lonnie, I'm so sorry."

She pushed away from the table, her sewing forgotten in a heap on the chair. He heard her say good night to Jebediah and Elsie before her footsteps sounded on the stairs.

Twenty-Two

Gideon watched as Jebediah walked the length of the field, counting his paces as he did. The man's husky voice grew distant as his figure faded away, becoming smaller with each step, until the trees cast him in early-morning shadows. As he returned, Gideon shifted his weight, anxious to know if his plan would work.

"I'd say it's a quarter acre of *usable* land. The rest would have to be cleared." Jebediah stroked his beard.

Gideon pointed over the older man's shoulder. "That portion there could be cleared easy enough. Half the trees are dead, and the wood that's still green is small enough to manage. With a little work, I could add another quarter acre."

"I take it you'll be needing help. A lot of work for one person." His eyes sparkled as he studied his unused land.

"You up for it, Jeb?"

"It would be a lot of work." But he grinned.

Using his elbow, Gideon nudged him. "You know you're gonna help me. It's for the good of the farm."

"Good of the farm, huh?" His smile widened.

"I need to get the bare roots in the ground while they're still dormant. Less than a month."

When Jebediah nodded, his aged face, lit by the rising sun, was somber. "Have you talked it over with Lonnie?"

"Should I?" Gideon hitched his thumb in his belt. "She's not my wife. Doesn't seem interested in the notion of *becoming* my wife, even if that were possible, so I didn't really see the point." When Jebediah let out a low chuckle, Gideon felt his irritation heighten. "It's not funny."

"It's very funny. She's bein' stubborn. So are you. And you're in a heap of trouble. And poor Reverend McKee—"

"Needs to keep to himself." Gideon folded his arms. "I'll talk to Lonnie about it."

"I'd say that's wise."

"It still won't make her think any different of me," Gideon said softly. "I don't think anything I do will."

"I'd say so far you've consistently annoyed the socks off her."

Gideon struck Jebediah's arm with the side of his fist. "Thanks."

"Just bein' truthful."

"I know. That's why it hurts. You mean everything you say, you old goat. And it usually has to do with pointing out how much I screw up in life."

The lines around Jebediah's eyes deepened. He turned and Gideon followed. They walked in silence for several steps before Jebediah spoke up. "You screw up less than you think."

Gideon glanced at him. "That's not true and you know it."

"I'm being honest. Look back to where you started, Gid." He squeezed Gideon's shoulder. "The first day we met."

Gideon blinked, knowing Jebediah was right. But still, he did not feel the relief it should have given him. He was changed in many ways, yes, but in some, he was still the same man. The man with the short fuse and sharp tongue. Those traits—though he despised them—were laced through him. He did not know if he would ever be rid of them. Gideon held on to his thoughts as they crossed the yard. Just as the sun burst over the treetops, warming his back, they reached the house and ducked into the kitchen.

Lonnie did not look at him while she stirred the porridge. And she did not look at him when she placed a steaming bowl near his hand. Sitting at the table beside Jebediah, Gideon nodded his thanks and knew better than to try to talk to her. Not here. But he would as soon as he got the chance.

When Jebediah handed him the small pitcher of cream, Gideon drizzled it over his breakfast. Without bothering to stir, he dipped his spoon into the thick oats. Soft, small voices filtering from upstairs told him the children were just waking up. Lonnie disappeared, and by the time Gideon had nearly finished his food, she lowered Jacob into his seat. Addie climbed onto a chair much too big for her and yawned.

With Jacob's hair standing on end and his small eyes squinty, Gideon could not help but rustle his son's curls.

"Would you like to feed him?" Lonnie scooped porridge into a small, chipped bowl.

"I'd love to. You think he'd let me?"

"Worth a try." She set the bowl on the table and dipped a teaspoon into the mush. Taking a small amount, Gideon pulled Jacob's highchair around to his side, then lifted the porridge to Jacob's lips, and he took it. Cream dribbled down the boy's chin, and snatching his napkin from his lap, Gideon carefully wiped it away. "He likes it."

Lonnie slid in beside him. "He loves to eat. Like someone else I know." She stirred honey into her oats.

"I can't believe he's letting me feed him."

"Quickest way to the boy's heart." Elsie placed a cup of coffee in front of Jebediah. "He's getting used to you again. He's beginning to trust you." She placed a second cup in front of him.

"You think so?" Gideon offered Jacob another bite, which the boy gobbled down. His small feet kicked beneath his tray. When he showed Gideon his tongue, Gideon lifted another spoonful of oats that slid off, hitting the wooden tray with a *plop*. He scraped it up with the spoon, and Elsie, passing by with a rag, wiped it away. "Sorry, Elsie. I've never fed a baby before."

Lonnie looked at him. "Not even your younger brothers and sisters?"

Gideon shrugged. "I wasn't exactly the most useful person." He glanced at her in time to see her expression grow soft, knowing.

"Well, you're doin' a good job." She offered him a warm smile.

"Thanks." He wanted to say more but knew he'd better think through any words that came out of his mouth from now on. He'd be a fool to keep hurting her. By the time Lonnie had finished her breakfast and dropped her bowl in the washtub, Gideon was scraping the remainder of Jacob's oats into one final bite.

With the rag, Elsie stepped forward and reached for Jacob's fist.

"I'll do that." Gideon took the damp cloth and wiped the boy's sticky fingers. Jacob was soft in his hands when Gideon lifted him out of his highchair. Gideon took his son and carried the boy into the parlor, overjoyed when he did not protest. Sinking to his knees, Gideon placed Jacob on the floor in front of him.

"His toys are in the basket." Lonnie stood in the entryway and pointed beneath the desk.

Before Gideon could pull the basket out, Jacob crawled toward it. He plucked both baby and basket from beneath the desk and moved the whole operation to the center of the rug. Silently, Addie slid in beside him. Gideon looked down on the head of dark curls. She glanced up with large eyes and studied him for a moment before ducking her head sheepishly and pulling out a pair of blocks.

"These are his favorite." She set them in Jacob's reach.

Jacob lunged toward a block and, using two small hands, lifted a corner to his mouth. Drool followed.

"He chews on everything," Addie said with a grin.

"Does he?" Gideon was secretly grateful for Addie's knowledge. The only child he ever paid attention to in his life was Jacob, and in the months he was gone, the boy had blossomed from infancy. He knew which end was up, but not much beyond that. Gideon nudged Addie with his elbow and spoke quietly. "What do you think of this kid here?"

Addie flashed him a toothy grin. "He's a lot of fun. We play all the time." She rose to her knees and bounced up and down. "His favorite game is peekaboo."

"Is that so?"

She demonstrated how the game worked, and when Jacob started laughing, Gideon joined in by placing a nearby throw over his head. Every time he yanked it off, flashing Addie and Jacob a cockeyed grin, the children burst into laughter. He threw the blanket over his head and growled. When the children giggled, he pulled it free, his eyes crossed, a goofy smirk on his face.

Suddenly standing in front of him, Lonnie folded her arms over her chest, amusement bright in her expression.

"Oh." Gideon dropped the blanket and smoothed his hair. "Hi there."

"Hello." She bent to lift Jacob, who had been busy playing for nearly an hour. "I ought to get him dressed." She smiled at him.

Gideon watched her go, her skirts swaying in rhythm to the soft song she whispered in the boy's ear. Jacob laid his head on her shoulder, his eyes meeting Gideon's. The smile on his perfect face was unmistakable.

Gideon had disappeared while she was changing Jacob. After finding her boots, Lonnie slipped them on in the kitchen. Once outside, she heard Gideon before she found him. She made her way to the barn, where he was clattering about. On the workbench lay countless little branches. Gideon was in the corner, trying to separate two old buckets. With a grunt, he finally pried them loose.

"What's all this?"

Holding the bucket to his chest, he stepped in beside her. "A bit of the future."

"Is that so?" Gently, she touched a thin stick. Then she noticed the gnarled, dried roots. "What kind of trees are these?"

"Apple."

"Your orchard."

"My orchard."

But she sensed that wasn't the way he wanted it. Folding her hands behind her skirt, she leaned back against the work surface, the weathered wood rough against her hands. She watched him work in silence for several moments. Finally she spoke. "Gideon, what's going to happen?"

"What do you mean?"

"With the courthouse. With Cassie."

"Does this mean you like me?"

"You can be so impossible sometimes." She tried to focus on a stray thread in her blouse. "I've been meaning to ask you…"

Pressing a palm against the work surface, he leaned casually on that arm. "Ask me anything."

"It's about Cassie."

Briefly, he closed his eyes. "I promise you I will tell you the truth."

Lonnie moistened her lips. "What happened? You were married to her for months. Yet you never touched her. I believe you...but I just don't understand. If I'm not mistaking, you did care for her once. Very much."

An emotion passed in his eyes. His face sobered and he didn't glance away. "Um..." Turning fully, he leaned both hands against the workbench and stared at his boots. "I just did whatever I could think of. I slept in the rocking chair most nights."

"And...and the others?" Her voice sounded small.

Green eyes found hers. "I kept my distance."

She allowed his words to sink in. "And what did Cassie think of that?"

Hands still pressed to the wood, he lifted one shoulder. "She wasn't too pleased about it. I won't lie to you." His gaze was fierce when he looked at her. "We've come too far for that."

She circled around him, and he leaned back, facing her. "I'm sorry to put this on you," she told him, "but these are questions that are going to need answers at some point. I don't know that I can keep going with these uncertainties."

"And you shouldn't have to." Gideon picked up a pencil and turned it idly. "Let's see, um, Cassie... I spent most of those months trying not to get too close."

"Trying."

"Did...did I say that?"

"You did." She watched his hands. Hands she knew so well. "Does that mean you didn't always...succeed?"

As if lost in thought, he ran his thumb over his mouth. "It means that some instances were better than others."

Her heart dipped. "Meaning?"

He set the pencil down and folded his arms. Still leaning against the workbench, his eyes lifted to the open doorway. She wondered where his thoughts took him.

"Meaning that no, Lonnie, I didn't take Cassie as a wife. But there was a time—near the end—when I thought perhaps I ought to. I thought that I should *try*. That maybe then it would fix what was broken between us."

"And did you? Try?"

He nodded, eyes tight.

She was going to be sick. Lonnie sank onto a crate. "What made you stop?" Her voice sounded strange to her own ears.

"Cassie did." He knelt in front of her. "It didn't go far. Trust me. Cassie didn't let it."

"But you would have. If she would have let you."

This wasn't happening. She wasn't here talking to Gideon about this.

The man who held a place in her life no other did.

Peering into his eyes, all that had passed between them washed over her. She knew his smile. He knew her shape. She'd loved him in the light. And in the dark. She'd whispered him beloved—yet here he was. Breaking her heart.

"I'm so sorry, Lonnie."

A strip of cloth bound her hair, and she tugged it loose, turning it in her hands. "Thank you for being honest with me."

Slowly, he shook his head.

She sensed he had more to say.

"It wasn't as easy to leave her as I thought it would be." He moved to sit beside Lonnie. "I came to care for her in many ways. She wasn't the same person anymore. Neither of us were, I suppose. She'd changed in so many ways."

Lonnie listened, each word a pinprick to her heart. But she valued his honesty and waited for him to say more.

When he spoke, his voice was soft. Distant. "She'd been real sick there for a while. Real sick."

Something surfaced in Lonnie's mind. The memory of Reverend Gardner's words that day in church.

"Scarlet fever," Gideon said.

Lonnie's fingers stilled.

"She fought it for days. Had everyone scared out of their wits. Me included." His eyes found hers. "There was a time, there at the end, that I didn't know if she was going to make it." He shifted his feet, his heavy boot brushing softly against hers. "I also knew that I hadn't done a good job of being her husband. I'd failed at it. Miserably. I kept thinking about how it was too late."

The fondness in his voice threaded through her heart, binding it painfully tight.

He slid his hands together, green eyes so distant that Lonnie could only guess what he saw. Suddenly, he ran a palm down his face as if to wipe away the memories. "She made it through. Cassie's as tough as nails."

"Don't change the subject, Gideon."

Fingers in his hair, he stood. "I'm sorry, Lonnie." He stepped back, then turned. "I just..." He blew out a slow breath. "I'm trying to be honest, and I'm not sure how to say this and *what* to say."

Still sitting, she pressed her shoes together and wrapped a hand around her knees, pinching her skirt tight. "There's no shame in having loved Cassie."

He squinted down at her, heartache carved in and through his expression. Did he sense she was trying not to cry?

"She's your wife." Lonnie rose, and before he could speak, she walked from the barn.

Twenty-Three

"Toby's here!" Elsie called from the hallway.

"Coming!" Lonnie peered at her reflection in the mirror. She fiddled with a loose strand of hair, tucking it into her coiled bun. A glance left and right, and all seemed in place. Leaning closer, she pinched her cheeks and nibbled her lips until they were rosy. In the hallway, Elsie's face brightened.

"My, but you look fine, Lonnie."

Lonnie turned in a slow circle, then made a show of patting the comb she'd stuck in her bun of curls. "Thank you for the loan."

"Consider it yours, my dear. Consider it yours." Elsie pulled her into a hug. "Enjoy this day and tell me all about it when you get home."

"Are you sure you won't come?"

Elsie waved away her words. "The children and I are staying right here. You need an afternoon out. Enjoy the festivities and don't you dare hurry home."

Lonnie hugged her again. "Thank you, Elsie." She turned and, knowing Toby was waiting, all but flew down the stairs and through the kitchen.

Outside, Toby stood beside Gael, as tall and handsome as ever in his new shirt and dark waistcoat. Lonnie's eyes skimmed the width of his broad shoulders, remembering his sweet request. Each stitch by candle-light. He nodded softly and seemed to take her in from head to toe. Fighting a blush, Lonnie smiled. She clutched her skirt and glanced up just as Gideon stepped from the barn. His hair was slicked off to one side, still shiny from his bath.

At the sight of him, she had to remind her feet to carry her down the stairs.

A black tie draped the back of Gideon's neck as if he weren't quite ready to put it on. Even from a distance she could see his face was smooth. Lonnie didn't realize she was staring until he half grinned. Quickly shaking her head, she hoisted her blue skirt away from the snow and stepped toward the wagon.

"Och, Lonnie," Toby said for her ears alone. "If you're not the bonniest lass I've ever seen."

She peered up at him. "Why, thank you, Toby. You look mighty fine yourself."

Gideon came around the wagon and stood just a ways off. Without hesitation, Toby took her hand, carefully helping her onto the seat. Lonnie glanced back to see Gideon climb over the side, his eyes down.

"Where's Jebediah?" Lonnie asked.

"He decided to stay with Elsie and the children." Gideon set his mandolin beside him and pulled up one knee.

"So it's just us then?" Toby asked.

"Just us," she said.

They rode mostly in silence. Lonnie and Toby chatted here and there, but unease flitted through her at having Gideon so near. She had a hard time maintaining conversation and hated how unfair that was to Toby.

He guided the wagon onto McGuire land, and in the distance, Lonnie spotted the large barn and dozens of wagons all around. "This is going to be just lovely," she said.

"Aye." Toby slowed Gael beside a team of horses, and the wagon swayed when he climbed down. Gideon hopped out, and Lonnie turned just as Toby reached for her hand.

"Thank you." Her foot found the wagon wheel, and she was glad most of the snow had melted, for there was a clear path to walk along. She turned to fetch her shawl from the seat.

Standing at the side of the wagon, Gideon fiddled with his tie, chin to chest. From what she could see, he was making a mess of things.

"Do you need help?"

His large fingers tried again, making the matter worse. "Jebediah lent it to me. My mother or Mae always did this," he confessed.

Lonnie moved toward him. "Let me see."

Lifting his chin, Gideon dropped his hands. She untangled the knot he'd attempted and slid one side of the tie down. Looping it around itself, she formed the knot carefully. Eyes straight ahead, Gideon stood as if he were a statue. Her thumbs brushed against his neck as she gently lifted the collar of his shirt. His Adam's apple dipped, and he cleared his throat, stony gaze faltering ever so slightly. Lonnie finished tucking the rest of the tie through. She slid the knot into place and, out of habit, was about to smooth a wrinkle from his shirt when Gideon stepped away and flicked his collar into place.

"Thanks, Lonnie." Striding toward the barn, he spoke without glancing back.

Blinking quickly, Lonnie simply watched him disappear into the crowd. Within moments, Toby was at her side. He brushed his hands together, no doubt having just fed Gael her oats. She didn't loop her arm through his as she once would have. Oh, if she could just know how to behave around the two of them.

Side by side they walked into the massive barn. The doors were decorated with evergreen boughs. Jars of daffodils were scattered about. Someone must have bloomed them indoors for the occasion. Lonnie soaked in the cheery sights and sounds. She looked around for Gideon, but he was nowhere in sight. A twinge of disappointment, and she forced a smile up at Toby.

"Shall we find somewhere to sit?"

"Aye." He waved her forward. "After you."

Spotting an empty bench near the back, she walked that way. There would be enough room for the three of them and then some. Still not seeing Gideon, she slid her shawl off and set the folded fabric beside her to save his place. Toby chatted to a gray-haired woman at his side. Lonnie did her best to join in the conversation, but as soon as she complimented the woman on her hat, the woman's smile faded and she suddenly had something to say to the couple behind her.

Spurned, Lonnie straightened. The cold bench beside her yawned an emptiness that made her feel ill at ease. Toby squeezed her hand a moment, and Lonnie was grateful for his kindness. She heaved in a quick breath, and the ceremony began.

The bride was beautiful. The groom's smile so broad that tears pricked her eyes. But all she could think about was the empty seat beside her and the green-eyed man who'd vanished into the crowd. Lonnie looked from side to side as nonchalantly as she could. When Reverend Gardner asked for the rings, she shifted a bit in her seat and glanced behind her.

Gideon stood against the back wall, half shadowed by the rafters overhead. Arms folded over his chest, he watched the scene with a sober, almost broody expression. His eyes shifted to hers. Heart tripping, Lonnie turned back around. When the crowd burst into applause at the sight of the kissing couple, Lonnie joined in and stood along with the others. A sigh bubbling up inside her, she watched the bride and groom dash back down the aisle, the magic of their night having just begun.

Settling down on a crate in the center of the stage, Gideon rested his mandolin on his knee. Beside him, the banjo player paused to check the tune of his top string. The off note sweetened, and he nodded an approval to himself. "Ready, boys?"

"What's the tempo?" Gideon pressed his mandolin to his chest, the feeling of it the only thing that made sense this night.

"Six-eight." The man adjusted the strap of his banjo. "Can you swing on the back of the beat?"

Gideon nodded. That he could do.

"All right then. Let's start this thing."

As if the floodgates had burst open, the spirited banjo twanged. Feet stomped and hands clapped, and anyone who wasn't keeping time was hurrying for a partner.

Gideon watched Toby walk toward Lonnie. His intentions clear. He dodged around a chatting circle, nearly to her. Gideon frowned. But then a tall, lanky man stepped in front of Lonnie. Senses heightened, Gideon watched closely. He couldn't see Lonnie, but a moment later, the man led her toward the dance crowd. Toby halted and folded his hands behind his back.

Nearly laughing, Gideon tried to focus his attention on the song. He strummed quickly, enjoying this moment. Enjoying the feel of the mandolin vibrating against his chest. Enjoying the fact that there Toby stood.

Empty handed. Gideon grinned to himself and bobbed his head in time with the music. The banjo twanged, and he picked the sweetest notes, tangling them together in a way that lifted the corner of his mouth. They played for several minutes, then in a quick rush of strumming, the song raced to a halt.

The cheer of the crowd was deafening. Gideon glanced down to see a bloom in Lonnie's cheeks as the man leaned toward her and whispered something. She nodded, and with a laugh, the man tipped his hat and was on his way, no doubt in search of his next partner.

Good. Gideon was liking this night after all.

Then the band slowed, a one-two-three that Gideon knew well. The slow waltz drew a different crowd. Sweethearts. Lovers. Gideon stared at Toby, daring him to even move one foot toward Lonnie. But it was she who stepped toward him. Her dark hair caught the lantern light as she peered up at him and spoke. A curl fell loose, taunting Gideon's fingers. Toby smiled and followed Lonnie out onto the dance floor. Gideon swallowed a curse.

He plucked the strings of his mandolin. For no reason other than that he was supposed to. Toby turned Lonnie around, slowly, his hand pressed to the small of her back in such a way that Gideon nearly fumbled the chords. *Get ahold of yourself, man.* He focused on the tempo. Tapping his foot slowly, he played the high notes of the waltz as the fiddle teased out a melody that was filled with yearning. Here he was, setting their feet in motion. Gideon clenched his jaw and kept his eyes on the space between his boots.

When it ended, the crowed clapped politely. He played along for several more songs and was glad when the rest of the musicians stopped for a break. Murmurs ensued when they set aside their instruments. Gideon leaned his mandolin against the crate and rubbed his hands on the tops of his thighs. Toby led Lonnie toward a refreshment table.

Preferring a fist in the gut to joining them, Gideon strode in the opposite direction.

At the dessert table, he grabbed a plate of cake but hadn't the appetite to eat it. Instead, he strode toward the far wall and settled down on a bale of hay. He took a bite of cake and set the rest aside. Settling his forearms on his knees, he watched as a stocky woman took the stage and reached for the fiddle. She took a moment to tune the keys, then pulled the bow long across the strings. Slowly. A romantic tune that beckoned, spurring Gideon's blood. He glanced around for Lonnie. This was his chance.

Someone settled beside him. A girl with pale-blue eyes. "I don't know that we met," she said sweetly.

Perfect. Gideon fought back a surge of irritation and forced a cordial nod.

"Lydia McGuire."

He didn't have time for this. "Gideon," he blurted. But then her last name pulled something to the front of his mind, and he allowed a second glance at her face. No doubt a sister of the groom.

"I saw you playing."

He nodded.

"Do you dance as well?"

He rubbed his hands together and watched Toby turn Lonnie, their smiles so perfectly matched he thought he was going to be sick. "Depends." His chance was gone.

"On who's asking?" she finished for him.

He glanced at her, feeling a twinge of guilt for his rudeness. He ought to be somewhat polite. "I'm sorry. I'm afraid my dancing days are over."

"But you would dance with her." She pointed to where Toby and Lonnie had moved to the edge of the crowd. Where Gideon was staring.

"Well…she's…" It was a story he wasn't about to tell. "Never mind." How could he hope to dance with Lonnie but snub someone else? He stood and smoothed his tie. "Would you do me the honor?" he asked without feeling, grateful the song was half over. But perhaps she didn't know that.

Her face brightened, and she rose, nearly reaching for his arm. Quickly, he strode toward the twirling crowd, and a glance over his shoulder confirmed that she was right behind. Turning, he faced her and held out a hand. She slid hers inside his palm and smiled in a way that sent his heart into his stomach.

This wasn't what he wanted.

He wanted Lonnie. He wanted his freedom. He caught the faint scent of moonshine when the girl moved closer. Head spinning, his boots felt shackled to the floor, but somehow he turned. Bringing her with him. She stepped closer than he liked, and he moved back a bit. She only followed. Clearing his throat, Gideon stared past her at the blur of people. He stayed in the same spot, leading them in a slow circle.

She spoke, breaking the settled silence, but he wasn't listening. Then remembering that he was *trying* to be a gentleman—trying and utterly failing—he looked down at her. He couldn't remember what she'd said. "I'm sorry?"

"You're not from around here?"

"Sort of. I've recently moved back."

"Ah. I didn't think we'd met. I would have remembered."

Not much to say to that, so he kept silent. He glanced around for sight of Lonnie, but the crowd was too thick. Pressing them closer. He looked down at his dance partner. Or was that her doing? She blinked her pale eyes too prettily, and her fingers found the base of his hair.

He realized that being a gentleman in this moment was beyond the call of duty.

He released her, relieved that the song was ending. A twirl of her dark hair around her finger, and she seemed to size him up. "Thank you for the dance." She stepped toward the massive entryway. A glance over her shoulder and a sly smile, she disappeared into the dusky light of evening.

Two years ago, he would have followed her like a cat to cream.

But he shoved his hands in his pockets and wished with all his might to be out of this place. Some quiet corner where he could just sit and talk with Lonnie. If Jacob were there, the dream would be perfect.

He wanted to go home. He wanted his son. First thing was to get out of here. He turned and nearly plowed straight into Lonnie. She gasped, and he caught her by the arm, then quickly stepped back. "Sorry, Lonnie. I didn't know you were standing there."

She lifted one foot as if to rub her toes. "That's all right. I shouldn't have snuck up on you like that." She winked, and he knew she was teasing.

He soaked in the sight of her, and his melancholy scattered. Hand pressed to his chest, he swallowed hard. "Would—would you like to dance?"

"Love to." Her brown eyes twinkled, sending his heart soaring toward the rafters.

Her small hand slid in the crook of his arm, and he wove them through the crowd, their feet moving as one. Finally, he turned and took her in his arms. *Not too close,* he reminded himself. He held her as he would a sister. He'd have to remind himself of that a hundred times if he wanted to get through the next few minutes.

"Have you had a nice time tonight?" she asked, her voice so sweet and genuine that he nearly tightened his grip on her waist. Instead, he expanded his chest, opening his arms so there was a wider breadth between them.

"This moment." The words slipped out awkwardly, and he wanted to kick himself for not making any sense. She blushed and watched her feet as if to remember the steps.

Her hand slid over his shoulder, fingers tracing his back ever so softly. He wondered if it was intentional. If she realized what she was doing. Or if it was merely a habit from their past. Clearing his throat, he rolled his shoulder, loosening her grip. Praying she wouldn't notice or take offense. For if she only knew what he was fighting back.

"Where is your reverend?" he blurted, needing a change of subject. And quick.

"He's not *my* reverend. And he went to prepare the wagon. I was feeling tired, and..." Those doe eyes looked up at him. "I came to find you, actually."

"And you found me." He couldn't help but let a smile through.

It must have been contagious for she smiled too. "I found you." Her thumb circled the back of his hand.

Gideon gently pressed her away just the slightest.

"Gid!"

Gideon looked back to see Gus stride toward him.

"There you are!"

Their dance stopped. He released her.

Breathless, Gus pulled an envelope from his chest pocket. "I saw Lonnie and was about to give this to her, but I'll just as soon give it to ya meself."

"Thanks." Gideon took the crisp envelope and, turning it over, read the tidy script. The return address.

Stuart.

Twenty-Four

The wagon jostled as Gideon broke the seal on his letter. With a glance at Lonnie, he pulled out the sheet of paper, grateful for the last bit of golden sunlight on the horizon. He squinted at the dark ink and struggled to make out the words. His hand shook so bad, he had to press the paper against his thigh and try again.

He studied the scribble of a signature at the bottom. *Judge Monroe, March 3, 1902.*

The ink blurred in the evening haze, and Gideon forced it closer to his face. The words jumped out. A fiery slap.

...have been unable to locate Cassie Allan.

Gideon swallowed hard.

...the ruling hangs in the balance. Without her official affidavit, I'm afraid my hands are tied.

Heart picking up pace, Gideon breathed harder with each following word.

It would be wise to prepare yourself...

He looked at Lonnie, her shape so perfect against the sunset. Her shoulder pressed to Toby's.

...for an alternate outcome of what you desire.

He was going to be sick. Warring with the urge to crumple the letter in his fist, Gideon forced himself to fold it and slide it back in the envelope. His chest heaved. He'd read it again with better light.

He needed to be sure his eyes weren't deceiving him. But he knew they were not. The words were as he'd read them.

Prepare himself? To lose Lonnie? Again.

There was no preparation in the world that would be sufficient. He'd already lost her once. He wasn't about to do it again. Gideon wanted to break something. Anything. Leaning toward her, Toby spoke low and soft. Hands fisted, Gideon glared at the man's back, a heat in his spirit rising as a flood.

The wagon stopped, and Gideon glanced around, realizing they were home. Heart hammering in his chest, he struggled to his knees, then climbed down. He was shaking so fiercely he had to grip the side of the wagon.

He scarcely heard Toby speak. "I'll walk you up, Lonnie."

"Thank you." Her voice sounded distant through the ringing in his ears.

Toby helped her from the wagon, his hands about her waist.

How easy to break his fingers.

Reaching the top of the porch, Toby spoke something to her and turned to go. Lonnie's hand on the reverend's arm halted him. Gideon wished he could hear her words, for the lantern light that poured through the kitchen window lit her face in such a way that even in the dark, he couldn't miss the tenderness there. It was a question she spoke—of that he had no doubt, if not in the way Toby hesitated to respond, then in the earnestness with which she watched him.

At his words, she lowered her face, but Toby's hand was beneath her chin, tilting it toward him.

This wasn't happening.

Gideon turned away. Finally, he heard Toby step back down the stairs. He glanced up. A little wave in his direction, and Lonnie slipped inside. Gideon straightened. Blood surged hot through him.

Toby moved toward the wagon.

"She doesn't need you as much as you think she does," Gideon said coolly.

Stilling, Toby looked at him. "Aye. I ken that. She's a strong one, Lonnie."

"So why are you still here?"

The man seemed to choose his words with care. "I want to be her friend."

"No. You're in love with her."

Toby stared at him a moment. "And what of it?" He lifted his chin. "I willna stand in your way, but from what I understand, you already have a wife."

Gideon stepped toward him.

"And I...don't."

Gideon nearly shoved him. "Don't you even come near her." He circled Toby. "Don't even think about it."

Eyes hard, Toby didn't move. He slid off his hat and turned it in his hand, finally tossing it in the back of the wagon as if he knew what was coming. "I'm afraid that's not your decision."

Well. It should be. But everything was wrong.

"I'm not going to take Lonnie from you."

"Oh. You're so holy."

"Do you even listen?" His feet firmly planted, Toby shook his head. "I dinna say I was a saint. But if you start accusing me of breaking some kind of law, you ought to look a wee bit closer to home."

Bursting forward, Gideon grabbed Toby by the collar and shoved him back. Toby yanked his shirt free, then planted his feet.

Gideon shoved him again; every ounce of his strength seemed to belt through his arms. Toby's back smacked the side of the wagon, the old wood groaning under the force. Toby turned slightly just as Gideon's fist pounded into the box bed, missing him.

Pain shot hot through Gideon's arm.

Toby glared at him. "That's enough, Gid—" A hook to the face silenced him. Toby doubled over and shook his head. Blood dripped from his nose. Another shake and he blinked quickly. Toby gasped and straightened, eyes dark.

"Hit me." Gideon kicked him, slamming him harder against the wagon box. "Come on!" Gael reared and bolted, the wagon speeding away.

Toby turned and socked him in the jaw. "You idiot!"

Pain burned through Gideon's skull. Fire blurring his vision, he rammed every ounce of his strength into Toby, sending the man barreling into the porch railing. The wood cracked. He shot a fist into Toby's ribs.

Once. Twice.

Then Toby's knee in his gut made him double over. Toby moved away. Gideon saw stars as he struggled to breathe. The man was an ox.

The door flew open, crashing against the wall. Jebediah stormed out, shotgun in hand.

Lonnie flew onto the porch. She seemed to take in the scene, and in a moment, she was down the steps and at Toby's side. She glared at Gideon. *Of course.*

"What's goin' on?" Jebediah demanded.

Gideon stumbled to his feet, and Toby pressed the back of his hand to his nose. Blood dripped down his wrist.

Standing in his nightshirt and bare feet, Jebediah broke open the gun, clicked a shell into the chamber, and using one arm, pointed it toward Gideon. His gray eyes snapped. "I should throw you right outta here."

"Jebediah," Toby began, "I'm equally at fault." He wiped his hand on the hem of his shirt.

"Then you git too."

Jebediah flicked his gun toward the fence, driving home his message. "You're just two…pig-headed stallions," he growled. "Don't you set one foot inside my house." The gun shifted to Toby then back at Gideon. "Neither one of you. Not ever again." He lowered his gun and released the hammer. "Nearly punchin' holes through some person's wagon…" He glared at Gideon. "I hope you *broke* your hand."

Gideon rubbed his sore knuckles. This night couldn't get any worse.

"Now. I'm going to go upstairs and get dressed. And then we're gonna talk. If either one of you kills the other while I'm gone, I'll shoot the one still standing."

Twenty-Five

The first stars glittered in the evening sky as Lonnie peered through the screen door. Gideon and Toby sat on the top step of the porch, a broomstick apart. Neither spoke. Gideon's head hung between his shoulders, and with his elbows on his knees, he locked his fingers together. Toby sat in the same manner. With a bowl of warm water and a pair of damp rags tucked in the crook of her arm, Lonnie stepped out. She held Elsie's medic basket in her other hand. The men turned. After shifting her load around, Lonnie threw a wet rag at Gideon's chest, and when it slapped against his shirt, she hoped it was cold.

Sitting between them, she turned toward Toby. She motioned for him to straighten, and with her hand on his shoulder, he did. Gently, she placed her palm just below his ribs, where Gideon's boot had left mud on the fabric. He flinched.

"Sorry." She pressed again.

He winced and lifted his chin, eyes distant. "He didn't break them." His voice was low.

"Good." She shifted to a lower step. She peered briefly to where Gael was tied up near the barn. Toby had spent the last ten minutes trying to coax the horse from a stand of trees.

The rag was warm when she wrung it out. Toby took it and wiped his face. She looked at the drops of blood that stained the top of his shirt.

Gideon rose and walked into the yard a few paces, his back to them. He pulled the envelope from his pocket, studied it a moment, then slid it back in. She'd forgotten to ask him who it was from. Right now, she was too angry to care.

Toby ran the rag beneath his nose, and a muscle flexed in his jaw. She wanted to ask him if he was all right but, with Gideon watching them, doubted Toby would want her to. After another minute, Gideon turned and walked toward the barn.

"Something set him off," Toby said softly.

"How do you know?"

He rubbed his ribs. "I just know."

"Doesn't mean it's right."

"No. It doesn't. Then again…I wasn't either." He glanced down at his hands as Jebediah stepped out onto the porch. "If Reverend Gardner gets wind that I punched him…"

With a soft smile, Lonnie took the rag from him. "We'll try and keep it between us." She rose so Jebediah could move into her place.

"I'd appreciate that." Toby nodded a thank-you as she turned to go.

Chisel in hand, Gideon worked it through the soft spruce, savoring how this work made sense. It always made sense. And with the letter from Stuart folded up beside the lantern, Gideon needed something that made sense. Something he could control in some small way. He heard Jebediah before he saw him. After stepping into the dim barn, the older man pulled the door closed behind him.

"Figured I'd find you here." Jebediah pulled a stool beside him and sat. He rested his thick fists on the workbench. "Just finished talking to Toby. He's gone now, but he'll be back tomorrow." Jebediah held out a hand. "Don't make that face. Let me finish."

Gideon set his chisel aside.

Closing his eyes, Jebediah held his hands in front of him. "This has got to stop."

"I agree," Gideon said softly. The sooner Toby left, the better.

Jebediah straightened and crossed his arms over his chest. "What do you two think you're doing? Do you really believe that beatin' each other to a pulp is gonna make Lonnie want either of you? She's better off on her own than with the likes of either of you." He shook his head.

Eyes on the wall across from them, Gideon slowly lifted his head.

Jebediah turned in his stool and kicked Gideon's boot. "Are you even listening?"

"I'm listening." Gideon glanced at the letter from Stuart. Grabbing it, he held it out for Jebediah.

The older man took the letter. Gideon watched the lantern light flicker as he read.

"I'm so sorry, son."

"Me too."

"All the more reason for Toby to stick around, I'd say."

"Don't say that, Jeb."

"I'm sorry, but somebody's got to. You ain't exactly in a position to take care of Lonnie. It's not fair to her for you to run the reverend off... just 'cause of your pride."

Hands pressed together, Gideon felt the tendons in his wrist straining. Slowly, he nodded. "I don't know what to do." Tonight he'd chosen the wrong path. And it had hurt her. It was as Jebediah said. All because of his pride.

"Lonnie's seen too much trouble in her life to have more from the two of you."

Shame burned through him. Gideon dipped his head in a nod.

"I have a solution. Toby's already agreed to it."

Shifting his feet, Gideon looked at his friend and waited.

Steel-gray eyes found his. "If you're going to plant an apple orchard, you'll need help. We both know that, and I'm *willing* to lend you hand. Was lookin' forward to it, truthfully. But I'm not going to."

Heat rose up Gideon's neck.

"Toby's gonna be your helper."

"I don't think so."

Tapping his fingertips on the work surface, Jebediah shrugged one shoulder. "Fine. Then tomorrow you'll move off my farm."

"Jebediah—"

"If you don't want to work with Toby, fine. I'll find another use for that land—other than an orchard. And you can find yourself somewhere else to live while you wait to hear back from the courthouse."

Head dipped in a nod, Gideon stared at the space between his boots. It suddenly felt like a very long time ago that he'd looked at Lonnie's pa and pleaded for the man not to make him marry her. Hoping there was some way he could slip out of the situation unscathed. Leave Lonnie in someone else's hands, for he certainly hadn't wanted to be burdened by Joel Sawyer's oldest girl. No matter how much he'd thought he needed her after a quart of moonshine had warmed him through.

The image of Toby gently cupping her cheek had somehow embedded itself in his mind. In that moment by the wagon, he knew, without a shadow of a doubt, that he and the reverend were nothing alike.

Gideon's eyes shifted to the letter. Jebediah must have noticed.

"This is tough news, son. I'll give ya that." He turned the envelope over in his leathery hands. He studied the return address a moment.

Elbows on the workbench, Gideon lowered his head in his hands.

"This what started all this?"

"Among other things. I'm not proud of it, Jeb." He tossed his head toward the house. "I wish I hadn't lost it." He glanced at his friend. "For Lonnie's sake."

Something flickered in Jebediah's expression. "And Toby? He's the one you were beatin' on. You sorry for him?"

Gideon didn't like his answer, so he said nothing. The truth hung thick enough in the silence.

"Well, then." Jebediah pounded a fist gently on Gideon's knee. "I'll leave you to get some sleep." He shoved the door open. Then hesitated. The wind tousled his gray hair as he stood several moments without speaking. Finally, he stepped back and squeezed Gideon's shoulder as a father would a son.

Twenty-Six

Gideon sat up and rubbed his eyes with his palms. He pulled straw from his hair and, after combing fingers through it a few times, figured it wasn't helping. He shook his blanket and folded it off to the side. Other than a crate with the kerosene lantern, his books and pipe, and a few other odds and ends, the stall was empty. That's if he didn't count the lingering scent of animals.

His shirt hung over the railing, dry and crisp. After knocking on the back door, he'd asked Lonnie for a bar of soap the night before. Without so much as a word, she'd practically flung it at him. With a scrub in the bucket last night, he'd done his best to wash Toby's blood out. If only washing away his guilt was as easy. Tugging the wrinkled shirt over his head, his hand still hurt. He folded back his cuffs and, ignoring the suspenders on the top of his pack, didn't bother to tuck his shirttails in. He needed to fix the Bennetts' porch railing, but he didn't want to start pounding on the house while everyone was rising and trying to have breakfast. He'd do it this evening.

Making mental notes of what supplies he still needed, Gideon moved tools to the clearing. The morning sun had cleared the horizon as he tugged Sugar's lead rope from the barn. The old mule plodded along, and

Gideon knew better than to try and hurry her. It hadn't snowed in days and days, and here in the clearing, almost every patch had melted away.

Hitching Jebediah's old plow to Sugar's back, Gideon flicked the reins, and she slowly marched forward. The plow's blade cut through soil softened by warmer days and melting snow. Gideon leaned back, enjoying the satisfying feeling of breaking ground. When the plow stopped suddenly, he bumped into the handle, then knelt to see that it had snagged on a root. Using his hands, he probed the soil, trying to gauge the root's depth.

He'd set his tools against a nearby tree. After grabbing a shovel, he tried to work the root out. The blade shot free, spraying clumps of dirt into his face.

He grunted.

Startled, Sugar marched forward without him. Gideon jogged after her and, in a few long strides, wrapped his hand around her harness. He smoothed her scruffy neck. "Sorry, girl." He brought her back around to where he was working. "Easy. You just stay right there."

After running the back of his wrist over his forehead, he bent and dug at the root. Another spray of dirt shot up.

Sugar lunged forward, breaking into a trot. Gideon went after her. He dug his heels in the dirt when his hand caught the harness. "What are you doing?" he asked in as soothing a voice as he could manage. He brought her back, commanded her to stay, and went in search of the root. He found it when it snagged his boot and he tripped. He caught himself against the dirt with his hands. Standing, Gideon picked up his shovel and flung it towards the wood. A low growl rose in his throat.

"Stay." He motioned to Sugar when she leaned forward.

"Your technique could use a wee bit o' work." Standing not ten paces away, Toby lifted his chest and slid his hands into a pair of work gloves.

Gideon stared at him. Slamming his mouth shut, he marched toward his shovel, snatched it up, and leaned it against the tree. Beside it sat his ax, and he lugged it forward. Toby stepped back. In one swoop, Gideon flung the ax over his head and down on the root, which split beneath the sharp blade. Bending, he threw the root aside. Without giving Toby a second glance, he exchanged his ax for the shovel and, after thrusting the blade through the soil, worked the rest of the root loose.

Without speaking, Toby took hold of a second shovel, and other than the sound of their blades breaking ground, they worked in silence.

The March sun beat down, bringing perspiration to their brows. Gideon slapped the reins against Sugar's thick coat, and she picked up her feet, nearly a quarter of the plot tilled. Gideon glanced back as Toby unearthed a thick chunk of root. It clomped on top of a nearby pile when he tossed it.

Gideon spoke only when necessary, as did Toby. Gideon tried not to pay attention to the flesh beneath Toby's eyes that was tinted blue. He kept his grip on the plow. Toby followed behind, moving the largest rocks and sticks out of the way. A line of sweat appeared on the reverend's shirt between his shoulder blades, and Gideon knew he should switch jobs. He mulled over the thought for several minutes before finally offering.

"I'm fine." Toby straightened. "I'm happy just to follow you." He knelt and freed a rock from the soil, then tossed it toward the tree line.

Gideon clicked his tongue, urging Sugar onward. His arms jerked forward with the motion, grip tight. When his sore hand ached, the knuckles tinted with a greenish bruise, he shook it out gently. After lowering a large rock, Toby winced. Gideon pretended not to notice.

And he pretended not to notice each time Toby glanced at the house. Which was more often than need be. Lonnie emerged only once, both of them stopping their work when she did. She offered a small wave, ducked into the chicken coop, then walked back to the house without looking their way again.

Toby and Gideon exchanged sharp looks before turning their attention back to their work, as if each man silently dared the other to let his gaze linger. The sun made its slow arc, rising up one side of the sky and, when it could go no higher, beginning its descent.

The screen door slammed, and Gideon looked up to see Elsie emerge. A basket hung on her arm. Skirt clutched in one hand, she plodded toward them.

Her words were breathless. "Sweet tea and sandwiches." Her bun of gray hair bobbed when she lowered the basket to a stump. Gideon and Toby stopped their work. After unhitching Sugar from the plow, Gideon led the tired mule to some shade for a break.

They crowded around her, and Elsie handed them each a damp rag. Gideon wiped the grit from his hands. After studying their faces, she arched an eyebrow. "Where you expecting someone else? someone younger, perhaps?" Her smile was genuine as she pulled out two glass jars of golden-brown tea and a pair of sandwiches. "Don't worry. You don't hurt my feelings. Eat up." She handed them each a napkin-wrapped sandwich.

Gideon nodded his gratitude. The bread was warm in his hand, the yeasty scent thick and rich. "Thank you, Elsie." He tucked the jar in the crook of his elbow and sat on a nearby stump. Propping a foot up on a fallen log, he used his thigh as a table.

"Aye, thank you, Elsie," Toby said.

"Looks like you boys have been hard at work." She glanced around the field.

With his mouth full, Gideon nodded. He took a moment to swallow. "We have. But we haven't even started clearing away the trees." He pulled a pickle from his sandwich and popped it into his mouth, then licked the tangy taste from his thumb.

"Well, I'd say the two of you got a lot accomplished this morning." She glanced at each man, a knowing glint in her eye. Instinctively, Gideon slid his injured hand from view, though he knew there wasn't much about last night that Elsie didn't already know.

With half his sandwich left, Toby leaned against a tree and crossed one ankle over the other. "This is good, Elsie." He took another bite and chewed in silence. "Thank you."

Elsie flashed them a smile as she strode away.

Gideon started on his second half, his fingers stiffening in the cold.

"Why an orchard?" Toby asked.

Gideon pretended not to hear him. After a few moments of being watched, Gideon sensed the man would wait for the answer. Fine, then. "It's something I've thought of doing for a while now."

The Mason jar flashed in the sun when Toby downed the last of his tea. He set the jar on his knee. Waiting.

What was this? "You know, on second thought, it's not really your concern."

"Fine. Fair enough."

Fair enough. It was none of Toby's business. None of his business what Gideon did with his life. His family. Gideon picked up a massive root and hurled it toward the pile. An orchard? Because it's all he had. For Lonnie and Jacob. All he had to give them.

To leave to them. For everything he read in Judge Monroe's words suggested that his chance to be with them was slimmer than either of them had imagined. Because Cassie was gone. And the judge was having a mighty hard time finding her.

In his side vision, Gideon saw Toby stand.

This was killing him. Slowly, surely, killing him. An orchard? Because he needed to know that they would be all right. That they would be cared for. Even when he could not. Everything rising back up inside him, Gideon tamped it down, forcing his anger to scatter. He couldn't go there again.

Gideon motioned to Toby's face, the flesh flanking his nose badly bruised. "I'm sorry I did that."

Toby nodded an acceptance. "And I apologize as well. I'm equally at fault."

It wasn't true, and they both knew it. Rising, Toby grabbed a shovel and got back to work.

The children's spirited laughter filled the air. A sound as old as time.

Sitting on the steps, Lonnie watched Addie play with Jacob in the yard. Lonnie slid to the side when Gideon walked over with a box of tools. Jebediah was just a few steps behind.

She remembered Elsie's words as Gideon set the box beside her.

"He was worth loving."

Yes, he was. But in moments like this, everything she knew and loved about him seemed buried under the weight of his actions. She knew what a broken heart felt like—and the sadness she felt this morning was born of the same seed.

"Am I in your way?" she asked softly.

"No. Not at all."

Eyes down, Gideon shuffled through the box, then moved to the banister and fingered the broken wood. He softly shook his head. Lonnie watched him crouch down and study the damage, wondering if he was recalling all he'd done.

Finally, he looked at her. "I'm so sorry, Lonnie. I shouldn't have done this. I have no excuses."

No. He didn't.

He moved back to the box and pulled out a saw. Addie picked up Jacob and carried him over to the little wagon that sat on the side of the barn. Saw in hand, Gideon worked it slowly against the broken banister. Jebediah went into the house, leaving the door ajar.

"You have every right to be mad at me."

"I'm not mad at you. Not anymore," she said.

He looked at her.

"I'm sad for you."

The saw idle in his hands, he rolled his shoulder. Finally, he nodded. The splintered wood shook as he cut it free. The broken piece fell at his boots, and he picked it up. She wondered what he saw. If he saw the pain he'd inflicted on Toby.

A muscle flexed in his jaw.

Lonnie slid her hands into her apron pockets. He sat beside her, the piece of wood still in his hands.

"What are you going to do?" she finally asked.

"Carve a new piece."

She smiled softly. "I know that, Gid. I mean about Toby."

Thumb tracing along the fresh cut, Gideon stared at the broken spindle. Jebediah stepped back out, and they leaned away so he could plod down the stairs.

Turning the wood in his hands, Gideon watched the older man pick through the box of tools. "There's something that I need to tell you." Gideon's words were near her ear. "I should get back to work, though." Rising, he reached for his saw, then looked back at Lonnie. "We'll talk. As soon as you have a quiet moment to spare."

Twenty-Seven

With no moon shining in through the inky black window, Lonnie sat on the edge of the sill. The room around her was dim save a single candle burning on the nightstand. Addie and Jacob were fast asleep; Jebediah and Elsie, long since turned in. Lonnie had thought about going to bed herself, but her nightgown lay idle in her lap.

For sleep was hard to find.

She'd tarried as long as she could, scrubbing her face at the washstand until her cheeks were pink. She unplaited her hair only to run a brush through it more times than necessary. She thought of Gideon. She thought of Toby. Her thoughts as tangled as a web, she finally sat, knowing that there would be no unraveling them tonight.

A glance into the dark night, and she could picture Gideon in the barn. Was he cold? Was he comfortable? She longed to sit and talk as they once had. But those days were gone. Lonnie fiddled with the sleeve of her nightgown, finally setting it aside, her thoughts anywhere but in this room.

With a sigh, she let her head rest against the window. The glass against her back was so cold, Lonnie found herself rising. She moved toward the bed. After a moment's hesitation, she tugged off the top blanket, folded it quickly, and stepped from the bedroom. The hallway was dark. Not wanting to disturb Jebediah or Elsie, she tiptoed down the stairs in a series of creaks and groans from the floorboards.

Nearly breathless, she grabbed the lantern from the kitchen and lit it. She almost stopped to think about what she was doing, but for the first time in her life, she didn't want to. What she wanted was to see Gideon. And for too many months, she'd been denied that. The thought of him so near all but pushed her toward the door. Her shawl was on its peg, and she threw it over her shoulders before slipping out into the night, the air grabbing her in its icy hands. She shivered.

With quick feet, she hurried to the barn, not liking the dark or how alone it made her feel. Her unbound hair whipped as she nearly ran across the yard. Her hand found the barn-door latch, and she hesitated briefly. What was she doing? Barging in on Gideon like this. Unexpected. A part of her felt it was wrong, but with the blanket pressed to her chest and an unnamed desire thudding beneath it, she pulled the door open.

A soft glow met her, and she spotted Gideon immediately. Sitting cross legged on a blanket, he held a book in his lap. His head shot up when the door opened. Chest heaving, Lonnie blushed beneath the shift in his face. A surprise—an intensity that nearly took her breath away.

"Lonnie."

"I-I brought you a blanket."

"Thank you." His book closed and he rose. He still wore his boots, but his wrinkled shirt hung in untucked folds around his waist.

Standing in the entryway, she was unsure of what to do. "I...I..." She glanced around nervously. "H-here." The blanket unfolded when she thrust it toward him.

Kneeling, Gideon gathered it up. His green eyes glanced up at her, an impish grin on his face. "Developed a stutter, have we?"

Lonnie pursed her lips. Heat rose from her toes to her ears. He stood to his full height, shadowing her. The lantern all but shook in her hand. Her other caught the tangles her hair had become, collecting them best she could.

"I'm sorry about last night," he said.

She could tell he meant it.

"I should never have done that to Toby. It was uncalled for. I truly am sorry. I won't do it again. You have my word."

"Thank you."

Raising the blanket ever so slightly, he gave her a soft nod. His voice was tender. "You didn't have to do this."

"It's a cold night."

He nodded, still standing close. Much too close.

Her heart was jumping in her chest, demanding her attention. Lonnie pressed a palm there. Gideon took the lantern from her and turned it off, his own burning brightly from the near stall. Feeling more a fool with each passing moment, she glanced around. The animals were bedded down or eying her sleepily. The air felt still, quiet. "You're reading," she said dumbly.

He smiled. "I do that from time to time."

Straw crinkled underfoot as she stepped forward. In one blink, she took in his makeshift home. The narrow stall. The fresh, golden straw. A plaid blanket spread over his bedroll, his things scattered around. He knelt, picked up the book, and set it on his jacket.

"Would you like to sit?" he asked.

She opened her mouth to speak. Then closed it.

"Don't start stuttering again. It's just to sit." His grin disarmed her. "See." He reached for a crate. "I'll sit here." He straddled it. "Like this. And you"—he gestured toward the soft plaid folds—"can sit there." With a broad hand, he motioned to the space between. "Perfectly innocent."

It was impossible to fight her smile, so she didn't. It felt good. This being here. With him. Smoothing her dress beneath her, she sat and pulled her feet in. Her palm slid up the buttons of her boots to the top of her ankles. She pressed her other hand into the humble cot. Smoothing the wool, she was glad he was somewhat comfortable here in the barn.

The side of his mouth quirked up. "Are you asking me to sit by you, Lonnie?" He made a *tsk* sound, then winked.

Picking up his book, she fought the urge to throw it at him. "You hush." Her smile deepened. "Or I'm gonna leave." But she didn't want to. She wasn't sure what to make of that.

Straightening, his expression sobered. But his eyes were bright. "I'll be good." He leaned forward and rested his forearms on his knees.

The book in hand, she read the title page. "James Fenimore Cooper." Her eyes flicked to his face. "I confess, I'm surprised."

He chuckled. "I *can* read, Lonnie. I just choose not to—almost all the time." He nodded toward the book in her hand. "Mrs. Jemson gave it to me. It helps pass the time. I have no idea what he's talking about, though. Probably because I skip the big words." He grinned, and she could tell he was teasing.

Lonnie drew in a deep breath, holding it. Savoring the warmth she felt sitting here with Gideon. Her shawl slipped from her shoulder, and she pulled it back into place. "Maybe I will borrow it when you're done." *Do you really want to talk books, Lonnie?* No. She didn't. But it felt so safe. She tucked a strand of hair behind her ear.

She studied the page he'd been reading, but the words didn't register. Not with him watching her. Or his pillow nestled against her hip. It struck her hard that she shouldn't be here. Not alone with him. Not when she felt afresh just how much she cared for him, leaving nothing but memories in its wake. Memories she'd locked away.

And for good reason.

Perhaps this wasn't a good idea. Her nerves suddenly akilter, she ran her fingers through her hair, thinking that if she focused on unraveling the tangles, her heart wouldn't pound so.

From the corner of her eye, she watched his heel bounce, slowly at first. Then quicker. Lonnie glanced up. His face had grown so serious, she felt her jaw drop a little. He ran his palms down his thighs. Something had shifted. Was he nervous? Senses heightened, she adjusted her ankles, still crossed. She really shouldn't be here. The guilt that had pricked her conscience pounded now. He was too close, and his company felt too right.

"I should go," she blurted. She rose and his gaze followed.

When she stepped from the stall, he made no move to stop her. He sat on his crate. Keeping his distance. Finally, he looked at her. A yearning had flooded his eyes, all humor gone. "Good night, Lonnie." His tone was reined in. Fighting something. His pain hit her, and Lonnie realized her mistake. She shouldn't have come here.

Guilt pierced her, and Lonnie stepped closer to the door. She grabbed her lantern, realizing it was out. Hesitating, she nearly stepped into the dark, but Gideon voiced her name. She halted, her chin to her chest.

"I have a match," he said, his tone a brick wall in front of his heart.

"Thank you," she said softly.

He rose, shuffled among his things, and stepped toward her. "Here." He took the lantern and set it on the ground between them. Kneeling, he struck a match and, with a turn of the knob, lit the wick. He stood and passed her the lantern. She gripped the handle, but he didn't release it. They stood there, fingers touching, neither of them moving. Her heart raced.

Braving a glance up, she watched his eyes rove her face.

"I should go," she said again. But before she could move, his hand found the base of her neck. His grip was gentle, and he leaned forward. His lips nearly brushed hers, and Lonnie tensed. He froze. Their foreheads touched. His eyes squinted closed so tight she sensed the battle within him. He turned his head to the side and let out a breath. Releasing her, he moved back.

"Sorry." His throat worked. Turning, he stepped away from her. "I'm so sorry." His voice was so distant, she sensed he wasn't speaking to her.

But to Cassie. As was right. Tears stung her eyes.

Fingers interlocked, he pressed them to the back of his neck. He glanced around the room quickly, finally looking back at her, expression torn. "You need to leave now."

His face was so urgent, she nearly tripped over her feet reaching for the door.

He groaned. "Lonnie. Wait." Frustration ran thick in his voice, and she took a few breaths before turning. "There's something you need to know. I'm sorry I didn't tell you sooner. I just haven't had the chance."

She stood, waiting.

"I heard from the judge, Lonnie. The letter. That Gus had."

Drawing in a slow breath, she held it.

"It's not good. It's not good." He pressed a thumb to his bottom lip. "They can't find her, and without her signature on that form"—he swallowed—"there's nothing to be done."

Ever so slowly, Lonnie lifted her head. Nothing to be done. So this was it. She looked at him. His eyes searched hers. "There's no hope," she breathed.

His expression softened. "A little…maybe? Cassie wanted this. It sounds as if she's moved on. But if she can't be found…"

Lonnie wanted to ram her fists against his chest for coming back to her like this. Coming back to her when he wasn't hers. But she simply stood there, searching for the piece of hope he mentioned. Was it there? hidden among all the ashes? She took a step back and then another, the draft that sifted beneath the barn door cooling her ankles.

"Good night, Lonnie."

She slipped past the door and, without glancing back, hurried across the yard.

Twenty-Eight

S *wish...crack!* Wood splintered, and even as the first flakes of snow
began to fall, Gideon loosened his ax from the dead fir tree. He pulled
it back and brought it around with all the force in his arms and back. The
blade spliced deeper into the cut; chips flew. The breeze of a rising storm
stirred his coat. The air that had once been alight with the breath of spring
was now faded to a bitter gray. Winter had one last fight in it. Gideon fell
in rhythm with the blows, his breath a series of gasps and grunts, moving
around the stout tree, until the sound of popping wood announced the
tree's doom. He'd worked in the field nearly every hour for the last few
days, and as the weather steadily grew colder, so did his hope of breaking
any more ground.

He moved around the thick trunk and made fresh cuts, dictating
where he wanted it to land. The dead, rotting tree swayed. Stepping back,
he watched as it gave one final attempt to remain upright, then the lifeless
wood crashed to the ground in a spray of brittle needles and rotted bark.

The wind shifted, sending snow pelting against his neck and down his
collar. Gideon lifted the flap of fabric, blocking the cold from his ears as
best he could. He tapped his ax against the ground. It was frozen now, and

there was no use in trying to plow. Toby was not due to come by today. Even if the man's absence meant more work for him, he welcomed it.

Gideon shook his head and his hand at the same time. He hadn't stepped foot in the house in three days. It was his own fault. Because of his own stupidity, he'd scarcely seen Lonnie, and he certainly had not seen his son. He glanced toward the house, wishing it did not have to be this way. Banished to the barn each cold night, he lay awake in the dark, knowing that although he had returned and his family was mere steps away, his life remained half-lived. Gideon fixed his grip on the handle of his ax and started on the next tree. Wood splintered. He pulled the blade back with a satisfied grunt.

Work was his only relief. The only thing to free his frustrations. When the tree fell he stumbled back, panting. Gideon yanked his hat off, then ran his sleeve over his face and down his neck. He gripped the ax, exhausted with trying to shake off the pain. As the afternoon passed, two more trees plunged to their frozen graves. He pulled his gloves off, and his sweaty palms were grateful for the frigid air. Although sweat still dampened the shoulders of his shirt, he grabbed his jacket from a nearby branch. He shook off snowy powder before putting it on.

Countless white flakes danced in the breeze as Gideon worked. He stood still and quiet as the forest dimmed, and when he could make out the first glow of candlelight from the kitchen window, he trekked toward the house with no idea what he was doing. No idea what he would say.

He simply needed to hold his son.

Climbing the steps slowly, Gideon listened for voices. He moved to the window. Dishes gleamed in the soft glimmer of candlelight. He pressed his face closer to the glass. He knew everyone was inside, but the kitchen appeared empty. Then Lonnie bustled in, apron neatly covering her plaid skirt. Gideon stepped back. He tried to quiet his breathing as if she could hear it. He watched her sink to one knee, open the black iron door, and pull a golden loaf of cornbread from the oven.

She pressed the top of the bread with her finger and, seemingly satisfied, stuck her finger against her lips. He suddenly forgot how to breathe. The pan rattled against the stovetop. She reached for a knife, apron strings swaying.

He heard Addie call out. Lonnie set down the knife and vanished into the parlor. Gideon's hand hesitated. Then, with a quick breath, he knocked. No one came. Gideon cleared his throat and knocked a second time, louder, his sore knuckles complaining. Lonnie returned, her gaze on the window—searching. He squared his shoulders.

She opened the door slowly.

"Evenin'." He nodded.

"Evenin'."

Jebediah's voice came through the parlor. "Is that Gideon?"

Lonnie's gaze roved his face before answering. "Yes."

"Don't let him in."

A sad, sweet smile softened her mouth, and she pressed her cheek to the door. "I won't." When she looked up at Gideon, he cleared his throat.

"I…uh…was wondering if I could see Jacob for a minute."

Surprise passed over her face, and she quickly nodded. "Of course. I'll fetch him." She glanced briefly out into the falling snow before turning.

Brushing his hands against the sides of his pants, Gideon was suddenly aware of his ragged appearance. He checked the buttons of his coat and straightened his collar. A glance in the window confirmed that his hair stuck out at odd angles. He thought of his hat where he'd left it. Passing a hand over his jaw reminded him that he hadn't shaved since Friday. With the door still open, the warmth from the stove urged him forward. But he remained where he stood.

When Lonnie returned, Jacob sat contentedly in her grasp with more sweaters on than Gideon thought possible. The boy grinned and Gideon's heart soared. Lonnie closed the door behind her. She sank onto the top step and set Jacob in her lap. Gideon sat close beside her, not liking the idea of them being cold.

Lonnie lifted Jacob onto his lap, and the boy rested his head against Gideon's shoulder. Gideon's chest lifted in a slow, contented breath. His heart overflowing, he watched their fingers entwine. Jacob's small, pudgy hands played a soundless game with his large, callused fingers. Distracting him from the words he knew needed to be said.

"Will you do me a favor, Lonnie?"

She peered up at him.

He wasn't sure how to say this. "I just need to ask you to promise me something." He crossed his feet, then motioned with his head toward the barn. "Please don't visit me again."

Expression sober, she nodded. "I promise I won't."

He sensed her regret.

"I'm so sorry that I did. I didn't think clearly, and I should have. It was inconsiderate of me. It wasn't fair to you. And it wasn't fair to Cassie."

Cassie. He blew out a slow sigh, chasing it with another. "I haven't done a lot right in my life, Lonnie. It seems odd to start now, this way, but I need to do this right. I can't live with any more regret." He ran his palm over Jacob's head.

"What will you do?" she finally asked. "If nothing changes. Will you return to her?"

He hadn't really thought about it. He told Lonnie as much.

"There's time enough for that, I suppose. You'll know more. Hopefully soon?"

Yes, he would. May that day be a long time coming. But it was coming. Whether he wanted it to or not.

Lonnie sat quietly, her shoulder warm and soft against his. He kept silent. Words would just muddle the moment. At least his would. With no moon to be seen, her form hid beneath the blue quilt of shadows, and in perfect silence, Gideon held his son and listened to the whisper of falling snow.

Twenty-Nine

Wood clanged against metal when Toby stuffed another log into the fire. The stove, though too small to bake in, kept the tiny shanty warm in the winter. The door creaked closed. Shaking his scorched fingers, he checked his pot of water that was near a boil. Then he went to the porch where the rabbit he'd shot draped limp on the clothesline where he'd left it. Grabbing it from the scratchy twine, he strode down to the creek. Perched on a frosty rock, he cleaned his knife in the swift, icy current. He worked slowly. Quietly. And in the end, did his best to remove the skin in one piece. It would never pass for a sellable pelt. More capable men would have done a better job.

Men like Gideon.

Toby rinsed his hands. His knees were stiff when he stood, and his near-frozen fingers complained for warmth. Finally back inside, he pieced apart the rabbit and set it to boil in the pot along with a carrot and an onion from the vegetable basket. A kind neighbor had brought by a loaf of bread and a quart of milk. With the food passing hands, they'd thanked him for helping repair their fence. He knew Reverend Gardner saw it as unconventional, but he couldn't see a need not met...and just pass it by. Through his sweat, firewood piles grew, fences were repaired, and any-

thing else needing to get done was done. Yet it didn't satisfy. Nothing satisfied anymore.

Using a charred spoon that was more appropriate for kindling than
his supper, Toby stirred the broth. Exhausted, he ran his hand over his
neck. As much as he enjoyed the work, he wished it were his home, his
family he labored for.

With his supper stewing, Toby pulled off his boots and sat on his
neatly made bed. He made it daily. Though there was no one there to
complain if he didn't. Resting his palms on the edge of the faded quilt, he
glanced around the uneven walls of the shanty. It wasn't much larger than
a wood crib. He had to duck to get through the doorway. The walls shook
in the winter winds, leaked in the rain, and provided little more than shade
in the hot summer months. He slid his forearms to his knees and stared at
the floor. This was no place for a bride. Toby clenched his hands together,
the veins in his wrists bulging. What was he thinking when he asked Lonnie to marry him? He had nothing to offer her. He was just a foolish Scotsman with no home and no family. Nothing to offer a woman. Besides
that, he could see who she loved.

And it wasn't him.

The realization pierced him deeper each time he saw her with Gideon.
It's as it should be, he told himself. For the hundredth time, it seemed. Toby
reached for the small Bible under his pillow. It fell open, and using his
thumb, he turned the thin pages to his favorite passage. "But they that wait
upon the LORD shall renew their strength; they shall mount up with wings
as eagles; they shall run, and not be weary; and they shall walk, and not
faint."

To run and not be weary. Toby lowered the Bible, cradling it in one
hand. He wanted that kind of strength. And looking back, he knew there
was a time in his life when he felt it.

Gideon had changed everything.

If only the man had moved on. Stayed out of Lonnie's life. Toby closed
his eyes, ashamed at the desire, when deep within him he knew that
Gideon was the right man for Lonnie. As it should be. *Forgive me, Lord.*
His heart whispered each word slowly, deliberately. The need sank all the
way into his core. *Forgive me.*

The outcome shouldn't change him. It shouldn't allow this bitterness
to take root. Toby hung his head.

He wondered if it was enough. Enough to simply find peace again. To
simply stop loving her when all he wanted to do was spend the rest of his
life doing just that. He blinked up at the walls of his home and tried to
keep his thoughts from roaming to what could have been.

Lonnie loved Gideon. Of that much he was certain. Though she tried
to hide it, she did not hide it well. He saw it in the way she watched him.
The way she spoke his name. They had once been one. Toby ran his hands
down his face. His anger rose afresh. Bouncing his heel, he blew out a
controlled breath. Forcing the anger away. There was nothing he could do
to change that. Gideon was Jacob's father. No matter how hard he tried,
Toby would never be more than a substitute. Though he would have given
it his all.

That made it impossible to give up. Until the day Gideon was free to
ask for her hand, he would be there as her friend. If nothing more, so be it.
But he was in too deep to walk away. He would not give up hope and, ul-
timately, would pray that she would find the happiness she deserved.
Wherever it might be. Turning the Bible in his hand, Toby closed it and
set it aside.

Whatever it might be. Because God called him—reverend or not—to
love others. Even his enemies. Toby pinched the bridge of his nose, uncertain if he could do this. For he'd never had an enemy in his life. Until now.

Thirty

The two-handled saw pumped back and forth, neither man slowing. Gideon glared at Toby across the fallen trunk. Veins bulging, their arms moved in a blur. Gideon's shoulders burned, but he did not slow. Sawdust sputtered from the cut like sweat from a man, and when the crosscut saw stuck on Toby's pullback, Gideon shoved it forward with all his might. Toby fumbled the handle. Setting his jaw, Toby found his grip, and the saw sliced downward through the wood, quicker than before.

Gideon's breath puffed in short grunts. Fire pulsed through his arms, igniting every nerve and muscle. He struggled to keep his grip locked around the sweaty handle. Toby gritted his teeth, eyes glued to the enormous blade as sharp metal teeth devoured cedar. Gideon felt the end near. Toby's eyebrows lifted as if their thoughts were the same. Suddenly the blade cut free, the fallen tree breaking in two.

They stumbled back, the saw forgotten between them.

Toby doubled over and, with his palms to his thighs, dropped to a crouch, still panting. He rested an elbow on his knee and lowered his slick forehead into his hand.

Chest heaving, Gideon rubbed his shoulder against his temple. The fabric was wet when he pulled away. "I take it you've done that a time or two." It was an understatement. Very much so.

"How many more trees to come down?"

"Changing the subject?"

"I didna change the subject. You did."

At the surprise edge in Toby's voice, Gideon let the matter fall. He moved five paces down the log, then set the blade into the wood. "This is the last one." Spring had arrived, and he needed to get his trees in the ground quickly. He could finish clearing the rest of the land after that. He gripped the handle of the saw and waited for Toby to do the same.

Toby rose and dabbed at his face with his shirt. He clamped his broad hands around the handle. The blade sliced forward. Slower this time. As if both men had agreed to a momentary truce. They worked through most of the morning, and as much as he longed for one of Elsie's cold sandwiches, Gideon forced himself to stay in the field. He had thirty-three holes to dig in the next few days, and spring wasn't going to wait on him.

"You go on up." Gideon tossed his head toward the house. "Don't skip dinner over this. You've earned a break."

"I'm fine." Toby matched him stride for stride as Gideon went to fetch the wooden stakes he'd cut the night before by lantern light.

"Suit yourself." He didn't want the man doing him any favors. But there Toby was. At his side. The realization irked him to no end. "I'm serious." Gideon halted and turned. "Don't you have anything better to do? Don't you have a friend or someone you can go…pray for?"

Toby half grinned. "No. Not at the moment."

Gideon handed him a pair of stakes. "Follow me then."

Using the rows he had disced, he mapped out where the trees would stand. Bending, Gideon tapped a stake into the ground. The earth was warm and soft. He glanced up to where Toby was walking. "No." When the man turned, Gideon motioned him closer one row. "There."

Toby pounded the stake into place and, eying where Gideon moved

next, followed until they stood in the same row again, far enough apart
for the trees to grow broad and wide. "Here?" Toby asked.

"That's the spot."

Kneeling, Gideon pounded his own stake in. They worked without
speaking much. The screen door slammed, and Gideon turned to see Lonnie walking to the chicken coop, Jacob waddling along beside her, his
small hand tucked inside hers. Gideon turned back to see Toby watching
them, the man's face holding an expression that made Gideon nauseous.

The last stake was in Gideon's hand, and he threw it at him. It clat-
tered against Toby's shoulder, snapping him back to attention. "I'm standing *right* here," Gideon said, hands held out. The man was unbelievable.

Palms up peaceably, Toby turned back to work.

"Good grief. I can't wait until this orchard is done." Gideon glanced
at the reverend. "You do realize you won't be needed around here anymore." Gideon grabbed up his hammer and jacket and strode toward the
barn. He grumbled an invitation for Toby to follow. He needed to show
him a few things before tomorrow.

"Does that mean you've heard from the courthouse?"

Gideon yanked open the barn door. "That's none of your business."
He propped the door open, and Toby followed him inside.

"As ye wish." Toby arched an eyebrow.

Fine. He had no secrets. Gideon ducked into his stall and pulled out
the letter. He handed it to Toby. "If you're so bloomin' curious."

Toby held it in his hand, making no move to open it.

Back in the stall, Gideon grabbed his pipe and pouch of tobacco. A
thumb full of tobacco, and he stuffed it inside. Slipping the pipe between
his lips, he reached for a match, his hands unsteady. Then he used the pipe
to point toward the letter. "Read it."

Slowly, Toby turned it over and pulled out the letter.

Watching him, Gideon struck the match and lit his pipe. The sweet scent of tobacco calmed him. He shook out the match. Toby folded the letter back in half. "That clear enough?" Gideon asked.

"Aye. Clear enough." His eyes were bright.

Now that that was out of the way… Gideon moved to the workbench, where he'd spread the trees out by variety. Tonight, he'd soak them so they'd be ready to plant. He took a steadying breath before speaking. "Be careful of the roots," he mumbled around his pipe. "They're brittle."

"Aye. I can see that."

"All right, Mr. Observant. What next?"

"Are you always this way? Or is it just with me?"

Gideon pulled the pipe from his lips. "Pretty much just you." Especially in this moment. He tried not to think of the letter. Or what it said.

The hope it must have given Toby.

"I don't expect you to like me, but I'm going to see this through. I want to help you. Maybe it doesn't seem that way. Maybe you think I'm just here for Lonnie. But I want to help you."

"I don't need your help. And I certainly don't want it."

"That's fine. I still made a promise to Jebediah."

Gideon couldn't argue with that. "Just don't think it makes you welcome."

Brown eyes hard, Toby stared at him a moment. "What time would you like me to come back tomorrow?"

Crossing his arms, Gideon leaned against the workbench. "I'll start at sunrise. Come whenever you want."

"Sunrise. I'll be here." Toby turned and was gone.

Another draw on his pipe and Gideon beat it against the back of his hand before tossing it on a shelf. Knowing supper would soon be ready, he strode up to the house. Settling down on the porch steps, he waited for

MY HOPE IS *Found* 209

Lonnie or Elsie to appear with a plate as they usually did. But when the door opened, Lonnie slipped out empty handed. She crouched beside him, her skirt brushing his hand.

"Would you like to come inside?" Her eyes were bright.

"Are you serious?"

"I asked Jebediah...just this once. I thought it would be nice for you to tuck Jacob in." She winked. "For Jacob's sake, of course."

A half smile formed. "For Jacob's sake. Jebediah said I could?"

"He did." She motioned for him to follow her into the house. "He even said you might as well join us for supper." Her expression was warm. "Just this once, of course."

"Just this once." He grinned.

Sitting beside Lonnie, Gideon ate his supper but was too distracted by her face in the candlelight to truly taste his food. And when Elsie reached for his empty plate, he offered to help get Jacob ready for bed.

After wiping Jacob's cheeks clean with her napkin, Lonnie lifted him from his chair and into Gideon's hands. He pressed Jacob to his chest and carried the boy up the stairs. He sat him on the bed as Lonnie directed. She followed behind, a pitcher of warm water in her hand. She filled the washbasin and looked on as Gideon gently tugged Jacob's sweater over his head.

Lonnie pushed his filthy clothes aside. "Tomorrow's wash day." A strand of hair fell in front of her face. She brushed it away.

Gideon forgot what he was supposed to be doing.

She dipped a clean rag in the basin and lifted it. Water trickled into the bowl and dripped down her arm. Several drops hit the floor.

Knowing he shouldn't be in the room, Gideon swallowed.

Not with Lonnie. Not when they were alone.

She slid the rag under Jacob's chin. Gideon knelt in front of his son, trying to focus on the task at hand. He tickled the bottoms of Jacob's bare feet, and Lonnie smoothed her rag over his laughing belly. When Jacob was wiped clean, she draped his nightshirt over his head. She stepped back as Gideon wiggled the boy's arms through, finally pushing each button into place.

Gideon lifted Jacob from the bed and turned as Lonnie tugged the quilt back from the low cradle. Gideon lowered his son, and as if on cue, the boy flipped onto his tummy and buried his cheek into the feather pillow.

Their fingers touched as they each pulled his quilt higher.

Lonnie drew her hand away and offered Gideon a soft, sad smile.

"Mind if I sit with him for a while?"

"He'd like that." She rose, and the folds of her skirt fell around her ankles in perfect silence. She blew out one of the two candles before slipping soundlessly out the door.

Turning his attention to his son, Gideon ran his thumb along Jacob's limp arm, pausing at the dimple in his soft elbow. He smoothed his hand over his son's small back and felt his steady breathing beneath his palm. The tiny chest rose and fell with a sigh. Gideon leaned his weight on the cradle and, resting his head on his arm, watched Jacob sleep. After several more minutes Gideon rose, went down the stairs, and with a good-night for Jebediah and Elsie, gathered up his folded shirt Lonnie had set out for him. He spoke his thanks, and she offered him a soft nod, then he walked back to the barn.

Inside, he sank on his blanket and, resting the shirt at his side, lowered his head to the makeshift bed. He flicked at a piece of straw, tearing it in two before tossing the pieces aside. Exhausted, Gideon knew there was nothing left to do but try to get some sleep. He could have an early start tomorrow. Get some work done before Toby showed up.

Folding his arms in front of him, he rolled over on his side and faced the pile of white folds. Gideon rose to his elbow and lifted the shirt to his face. He inhaled the sweet scent of soap. *Lonnie.* He sat up and, setting the shirt in his lap, unfolded it until he felt the rough, raised bump of her perfect stitches. Yearning flooded him, and he forced himself to set the shirt aside, reaching instead for the pair of books on his makeshift nightstand. He started to open the novel, thinking to maybe get a few more pages read before his eyelids grew heavy, but instead he set the Bible in his lap and opened it to nowhere in particular.

It fell open to a storm. A group of fishermen in a boat during a tempest. Gideon could feel the wind. Feel the rain. He read about Peter, how he could be so confident and sure in his faith one moment, following the Lord onto the water, only to start sinking a moment later because of his lack of faith the next. Baffled, Gideon ran fingertips across his forehead.

Then his hand stilled, for in a way, the story hit closer to home than he liked.

He read the words again. "Wherefore didst thou doubt?"

"Easier said than done." Cheek resting against his fist, Gideon muttered to himself, "So what should he have done?" He shook his head, wishing he knew the answer. Toby would know. He probably had a whole sermon on it. Gideon closed the small black book and tossed it beside him in the straw. He glanced around his stall a moment.

Reaching back over his shoulder, he tugged his work shirt over his head and threw it aside. He slid the clean shirt on. Lonnie's essence surrounded him. Not bothering to button it, he crossed his arms over his chest and lay back on the straw. With his eyes closed, he tried to imagine what life would be like without Toby McKee.

Thirty-One

Lonnie pressed the wide, flat basket to her hip. Her skirts dragged in the mud, moistening the already dirty hem of her work dress. She fumbled with the frosty gate latch. Though puddles still covered the farm and a cluster of clouds hung overhead, the sound of birdsong reminded her that the first buds of spring were not far behind. The garden was all but empty, but soon seeds would be scattered about, poked through the warm soil. Lonnie picked her way to the far corner, where the hearty swiss chard grew against the pickets.

Morning's frost was still etched over the lanky green leaves, and she plucked the largest ones and laid them in her basket. When she had gathered enough to fill Elsie's pot, she propped the basket on her hip and hurried across the yard.

When she glanced across the freshly plowed field, her steps slowed. Gideon and Toby, shovels in hand, each worked a few paces away from the other. Neither one looked up from his work, so Lonnie simply took in the sight. The threads of her heart pulling toward the nearest man in countless ways, toward the farther in so many others. A droplet of rain struck her arm. She glanced at the darkening sky, and knowing she hadn't the time to give another moment to her yearnings, Lonnie clutched her dark skirt and scurried into the house.

Elsie looked up from her steaming pot and dumped a board full of diced potatoes into the boiling water, sending droplets over the edge, where they sizzled and hissed on the hot iron. "We'll add the chard last."

"I'll get it ready for you." Lonnie set the basket aside, then carefully rinsed each leaf.

Addie slid down from her chair, abandoning a slate scrawled with tiny letters. "Can I help you?"

"Of course. Finish up your lesson, and you can fetch your apron." Lonnie laid the damp chard on the cutting board. "Is Jacob still sleeping?" she asked Elsie.

"I checked on him a few minutes ago, and he didn't look like he'd be wakin' anytime soon." Elsie rolled the dark leaves into a tight bundle and made quick, thin slices with her large knife. Holding the board over the pot, Elsie scraped the blade across, and the chard tumbled into the bubbling soup.

Lonnie didn't realize she'd glanced out the window again until Elsie spoke. Several droplets of rain struck the glass.

"I can make a soup all by myself, Lonnie." Elsie winked. "You go on out. Get yourself out of the house. Go see what those boys are up to." Elsie motioned out the window. "That man sure as shootin' ain't plantin' that for Jebediah or me."

Lonnie understood the weight of her words. The future lived in every step of Gideon's boots across that land. It breathed with every turn of the soil. It was the future he was planting, even though he might never be a part of it. That kind of love humbled her, carrying her out the door and into the growing mist.

Draping her shawl about her shoulders, she glanced up at the gray sky. Hurrying on, she spotted Toby. Alone. He stabbed a shovel into the earth, pounded it with his boot, and tossed the dark soil aside. He glanced up when she approached.

"A bonnie sight ye are, lass."

Realizing her hair had come unraveled, Lonnie drew it together and twisted it out of her face.

The top of his shirt was damp from the droplets of rain falling. "What brings you out this fine day?"

She laughed. "I came to see what you two are up to." She surveyed all the trees that had been planted, counting nearly thirty. "This is incredible!" The words slipped out breathless.

"Aye." Toby glanced around, his face filled with pride, and Lonnie knew he was as good a friend as Gideon could ever have. Gideon didn't see it that way—and she couldn't say she blamed him for it—but standing there, watching Toby take in their surroundings with joy in his dark eyes, Lonnie knew he was the best of men.

"It's almost over," she said.

A hint of sorrow in his expression, he nodded. He wouldn't be around as often, and they both knew it. "I'll miss seeing you."

"And I will too. But surely, we'll cross paths often."

He swiped at the moisture across his forehead and glanced past her.

Lonnie turned to see Gideon striding toward them.

Toby's voice drew her back. "Aye. And I intend to marry you, lass. If this other fella can't."

His words sent a jolt to her heart for more reasons than one, producing a smile. She couldn't help it around Toby. He was honest and kind and one of the dearest friends she had. And he loved her. It was ever so clear.

And you, Lonnie?

Toby moved his shovel aside and stabbed it into the moist earth. His damp shirt clung to his shoulders. She couldn't begin to count the ways she cared for him. Lifting her shawl, Lonnie lowered it over her hair. Gideon was nearing.

"I willna see you as often as I'd like." He wiggled the blade farther in, his broad hand lingering on the handle, idly. "Reverend Gardner's informed me that he's going to be returning to Rocky Knob for good."

"But that means…" She felt Gideon walk up behind them.

"That means I'll take over the church here." Toby's eyes moved from Lonnie's to Gideon's.

"Oh, Toby. That's wonderful!"

"Thank you. It's a responsibility that I feel most great." He finished the hole and moved to the bucket where the trees were soaking. "I hope that I can fill the role half as well as Reverend Gardner."

Without speaking, Gideon moved past them and grabbed his shovel. With only two trees remaining in the bucket, Lonnie could only guess it would be the final hole to be dug.

She brushed damp tendrils away from the side of her face, thankful the rain was scarcely a sprinkle. "So you will be much busier. So many things for the head reverend to do."

Stilling his work, Gideon studied Toby with a sober expression. A thousand burdens seemed to hang heavy in those green eyes.

Toby gently lifted a spindly tree out. Water dripped from the roots. "Aye. And I'll be even more so this summer, helping Reverend Gardner pack up his belongings. And then I'll have the privilege of moving into the cottage." He set the young tree in its home with care.

Without moving, without speaking, Gideon simply watched.

"And say good-bye to the shanty," Lonnie said.

"Och! I won't miss another winter in that place."

"What is the cottage like?"

Toby glanced at Gideon as if wishing he'd held his tongue.

"There's a proper barn for Gael and even a buggy. She won't know what to do with herself." He winked at Lonnie and reached for his shovel, and she knew he wasn't disclosing half the details of the fine home. "There's a wee garden and an icehouse, but most of the provisions come through the church." He scratched his head. "When Reverend Gardner told me all this, I wasn't sure what to say, and frankly"—he softly shook his head—"I'm still a bit overwhelmed by it all." Bending, Toby pressed dark earth over the roots.

Gideon turned and glanced around the farm. Taking in the barn, Jebediah's fine house. Something lived in his expression that Lonnie couldn't read, but she felt a pang in her heart at watching him. As if noticing, his face changed. "Lonnie." He motioned with his head toward the last remaining tree. "Would you like to do the honors?"

She walked toward him, not caring how damp her shawl had become. His wet hair curled around his ears when he smiled down on her.

"What do I do?"

Grabbing his shovel, he broke through the soil. "I'll get it started for you." He moved several mounds of dirt, then handed Lonnie the shovel. His eyes were bright. "Keep going."

And she did. After a minute, he offered to help. "Like this," he said softly, shaping the hole so that the base of the tree would sit higher and the roots could filter lower. "Now." He motioned with his hand for her to bring the last tree.

Water spilled from the roots as she lifted it from the bucket. "Just set it in?"

He nodded, watching her. "Perfect." Kneeling, Gideon started to fill in the dirt. Lonnie crouched at his side. Their hands moved in quiet tandem as they buried the tender roots.

It was then she realized that Toby was gone. Lonnie glanced around, her stomach plunging at having not said good-bye. But then she spotted him, at the far edge of the clearing. He led Gael from the barn. He lifted his hat from his head and arced it down in farewell.

Slowly, Lonnie waved back.

Thirty-Two

Lonnie lifted the smooth wooden box from the cupboard beneath the washstand and clutched it under her arm as she strode down the stairs. The evening light cast a warm glow through the house. Shadows hid her shoes as she hurried past the parlor and into the kitchen. Gideon had knocked on the door only minutes ago, asking if she would fetch the shaving kit for him.

He sat on the back porch, watching the rain fall. He ran his hand along the bristles of his jaw. Finally, he glanced her way, rose, and brushed at his pants. Then his eyes fell to the box. "Thank you."

"Elsie said you'd asked for it." She moved to the washstand and peeked inside. "I'll get some water on the stove."

Without looking at her, he pressed the lid open with a *creak*. "Elsie already did." He pulled out a leather pouch. After loosening the ties, he pinched the handle of the straight razor inside, pulling it free.

"You'll need towels. I'll go get some," Lonnie blurted, needing an excuse to leave.

Gideon half grinned, and his eyes fell to a stack of small towels already on the washstand. He rolled one of his shirtsleeves up past his elbow and started on the other.

She pursed her lips. "Elsie thought of everything."

"She did." Finally smiling at her, he made no attempt to hide that he sensed her distress. "You can go on inside." He set the pouch down. Staring into the small mirror hanging in front of him, he ran fingertips over his chin. "Or sit." He flicked his head toward the steps. "Stay with me." His eyes found hers in the mirror.

"All right."

He pressed the top button of his shirt free, then the one below it, finally folding the fabric away from his neck. He secured one end of the strop to a hook on the side of the house. The sinewy muscles of his forearms tightened as he pulled the other end taut. He ran the blade up and down on the leather strip in quick rhythm, flipping the razor with practiced precision each time. Lonnie looked on, silenced by the simple motion. Gideon caught her watching him.

"Oh, the water," she blurted. Inside, she nearly burned her palm on the kettle handle and, with a shake of her head, grabbed a hot pad. She was worse than a schoolgirl. She returned with the steaming kettle and filled the washbasin. Her hand stung, and she blew on it.

"Do you need some salve?" His eyes smiled, everything about him warm, familiar. She shook her head. The supplies in the shaving box rattled as he shifted through it. "Thanks again for fetching this." He smeared a finger full of glycerin soap into the enamel shaving bowl. Using the boar-bristle brush, he whipped it into a white froth. He wet his face, dampening the scruff, and smeared soap in a circular motion along his jaw.

"Reverend Gardner's making his announcement tomorrow at church. About him moving and Toby taking over."

"And are you going?"

"Don't really have a way of getting there." As she spoke, Lonnie stared at the darkening sky, the colors of charcoal and ice. She moved to light the lantern on the washstand as he worked the blade up his throat.

Stepping back, Gideon snapped his fingers. "Darn. It sounded like a heap of fun."

She settled down on the top step. "It's not about having fun, Gideon."

"You're right. I'm sorry. That's not what I meant."

Lonnie pulled loose the strip of cloth that bound her braid. With slow fingers, she unraveled it. "Then why don't you just start saying what you mean?"

Gideon's eyes shifted to the mirror and then down to his boots. He tapped the razor against the edge of the basin. "He's a good man, Toby." He wiped the last of the cream from his face. "I mean it. He's a real good man. If I can't... If I'm not able to..." He swallowed hard and tipped his head to the side as if fighting something. "If I'm not able to take care of you and Jacob, I can't think of a better man to..."

Watching his face, she knew what the confession cost him.

He turned the handle in his fingers and shook his head. Mischief crept into his expression. "Then again, you could just become a nun."

A laugh slipped out. "Gideon!"

"Just saying what I think...per the lady's request." He winked.

"You're impossible."

Humor fading, he sat on the step beside her and folded his hands together. "I hope that day doesn't come, Lonnie. But if it does..." His eyes darkened. "I might not have as much of a fighting chance as I had once hoped. I won't ask you *not* to marry him. That's not my place."

Lonnie circled her fingers around her wrist.

"Just tell me the truth." He bounced his heel for a few moments. "Are you resigned to marry him or not?"

"I...I don't know."

He chuckled darkly. "Yes, you do. He's either the man you want to spend the rest of your life with. Or he's not." He pushed a shirt button into place, then another. "What's for supper?"

She blinked. "Food? You're thinking about food all of a sudden?"

Hands pressed together, he spoke without looking at her. "No. But you're pale, Lonnie."

Was she truly? Lonnie fiddled with the hem of her apron.

"I figured you could use a change of subject. Should I talk about the weather instead?" He flashed her a lopsided grin.

"Rabbit stew. No, I don't want to talk about the weather. And as for Toby..."

She had his attention now.

"I don't want to lead him on unfairly. Whatever I decide, I want to do it soon. For his sake. And for yours."

"Is there a decision to be made?" She sensed he hoped it would be an easy one.

"Honestly? I don't know how to answer that question."

"Come on, Lonnie. You can do better than that."

"I'm serious. And I've given it a lot of thought. But it's not an answer that I have for you. Not now."

"What are you waiting for?"

Reaching down, she squeezed his hand. "The same thing you are."

Lonnie heard Elsie call for her. Gideon's head lifted at the sound of her name, but he said nothing more. Lonnie hesitated a moment, wondering. "I should set the table." When she stepped back, she nearly tripped over the ash bucket.

Back inside, she pressed her hand to her heart. Elsie looked at her, forehead wrinkling.

"Are you okay?"

Lonnie bobbed her head. "Yes." But it felt like a lie.

And when she sat at the table as everyone enjoyed the meal, she watched Elsie carry a single bowl and spoon through the dark doorway. The woman returned empty handed. Just before the door closed, Lonnie peered into the night but could no more make out the form of the man who sat alone on the steps than she could make sense of all that might happen.

Thirty-Three

G ideon walked between two rows of trees, his boots sinking in the freshly tilled soil. Wind spilled over the woods, pressing through the farm, whipping at his coat. He watched the clouds roll over the land, dark with moisture. Heavy. Powerful. Their shadows danced in waves over the grass. A silent prayer lifted from his heart each time he knelt beside a young tree. Each time, he felt the roots and patted soil into place where need be.

In the yard, just a holler away, Lonnie pulled sheets from the clothesline, Jacob waddling around at her feet. Hearing a horse in the distance, Gideon lifted his head. Toby just didn't know how to stay away, did he?

But this rider was moving fast. Too fast.

Gideon stood and watched until the horse galloped into view. The thin rider who lifted a black hat in salute wasn't Toby. The horse's hooves pounded through the mud, spraying a dark splatter when it slammed to a stop in front of the house. Wiping his dirty hands on a rag in his back pocket, Gideon strode toward him.

"Can I help you?" he called.

"I'm looking for a Gideon O'Riley."

His walk turned to a run. "That's me." Gideon met the man halfway, and a letter was crammed into his hand.

"What is this?" He glanced over as Lonnie hurried toward them.

"It's from the courthouse. On urgent business," the rider said.

His eyes on Lonnie's muddy hem, Gideon couldn't bring himself to think beyond the pounding of his heart. Then she was beside him, speaking his name. Jarring him into action. Gideon ripped the envelope open, the letter nearly slipping from his hands in his haste. He read quickly, but the words jumbled in his mind, and he had to begin again.

I bid you to return at once…

Gideon read the line once more. And then the next. The paper began to tremble.

Most urgent…

"Gideon." Lonnie touched his arm. "What does it say?"

He looked at her. "I need to go to Stuart. I need to go now." A quick thank-you to the rider, and he started toward the barn.

"What's happened?" Lonnie called.

As if of their own accord, his feet carried him back to her. What was he thinking? "I'm sorry, Lonnie." He could scarcely put two thoughts together. He handed her the letter, knowing it would do a better job than he would in this moment. "Cassie's there."

Her eyes widened. She quickly scanned the page. Color drained from her face, and then she handed it back.

"Cassie's there, Lonnie. But I have to hurry." He wanted to pull her close, have her nearness be the only piece of normal he could grasp in this moment. But his mind whirled with too many outcomes to do anything other than force himself to step away. "I have to go, Lonnie," he said, his tone urgent even to his own ears. "I'll be back. No matter what, I'll be back." Even if it were to say good-bye, he needed her to know that.

Ducking into his stall, he looked around, his hands moving faster than his mind. In his haste, he knocked the books from his crate. The tie

Jebediah had lent him was still where he'd left it, and Gideon rolled it around his hand before stuffing it in his pack. He tried to think if he was forgetting anything, then with a jolt, he grabbed his tin can of money. What few bills and coins he had, he crammed into his pocket. Gideon hurried out into the graying light and jogged across the yard.

Lonnie had moved to the shelter of the porch. Waiting. Jacob in her arms. The road called to him. Only because his freedom called to him. But seeing her standing there, her shawl whipping around the pair of them, Gideon moved toward her in a few long strides. For one brief moment, he allowed himself to pull them close. His lips grazed the top of her head, and before he could forget himself, he slid his hand behind Jacob's head and held them as tight as he could. As tight as he dared. Slamming his eyes closed, he sent up a prayer that this would end well.

Oh, God, that this could end well.

And just as quick, he pulled away. Forced himself down the steps. Toward Stuart.

The wagon jostled, and Gideon gripped the side of the wagon bed. Feet dangling over the edge, he rested his hands on his knees and lifted his eyes to the sky. The air was still bright, the sun holding its ground.

"'Bout half a mile more to Stuart," the man called over his shoulder.

"Thank you." Gideon leaned back on a sack of grain. He'd walked all that was left of the day before and come sunrise had walked several hours before the wagon had passed by, ushering him toward Stuart more quickly than he'd expected.

He'd sensed that the man was the quiet type, and it was just as well, for his mind was whirring with too many outcomes to hold a proper conversation. He savored the quiet, rehearsing over and over in his mind what the judge might do and say. His thoughts held him captive until the first sounds of town drew his attention back to the road. They'd passed the blacksmith's and were ambling slowly beyond the locksmith's, the wooden sign that hung overhead creaking in the wind.

"This is where I stop."

Gideon jumped down and grabbed his pack. "Thank you for the ride. I *really* appreciate it."

"My pleasure. Was headin' this way anyway. Happy to help, son."

With a tip of his hat, Gideon turned in a circle, trying to get his bearings. Then he spotted a sign for Main Street. Quickly heading that way, he saw the courthouse in the distance. It took all his self-control not to run down the street and up the steps. Walking as fast as he could, Gideon threw decorum to the wind and jogged toward the massive brick building, stormed up the steps, and pressed past the doors, amazed to find them unlocked. Breathless, he stopped short. The entryway was dim, vacant. He glanced around at the hollow corridors.

"Hello?" His chest heaved.

A dark bun popped up from behind the desk. "Oh!" Mrs. Peterson said, a hand pressed to her heart in surprise. "I didn't know anyone was there." She pulled papers into her lap that must have fallen, for they were scattered behind her desk.

Gideon moved to help her. "Is Judge Monroe here?"

"I'm afraid he's gone home for the day. I should be out of here myself, but I had some things to finish up. I thought I'd locked the door."

The papers collected, Gideon straightened and stepped back, feeling more than a mite guilty for barging in on her like this.

"But"—she tapped the page edges against the floor, straightening them—"I have something for you. I'm glad you're here. The judge sent a circuit rider out yesterday." She struggled to stand, and Gideon quickly helped her. "Thank you." Her wrinkled hands brushed dust from her skirt. "I didn't know he would find you so fast. It's providential," she said with a shake of her head, handing him a small crease of paper. "This is from Miss Allan."

Gideon took it.

"Come back tomorrow, Mr. O'Riley." She pulled a beaded purse from the back of her chair, then picked up a cloak. "Judge Monroe will be eager to speak to the both of you." Her eyes sparkled, filling Gideon with a flood of happiness.

Was this really happening? "Yes ma'am. I'll be here."

"Good, good." With a ring of heavy keys in her hand, she moved toward the door. Gideon followed. Together they stepped out into the darkening evening, and she tugged the heavy door closed with a hollow *thud*. A jingle of the keys, and the lock clicked into place.

"Miss Allan told me she would be at the ordinary. The one just at the end of the road, owned by the Smiths."

"Thank you, ma'am." Gideon tipped his hat. With a friendly smile, she started down the steps, no doubt toward home.

Surrounded by the strange town, Gideon stood a moment and forced himself to take a few deep breaths. He opened Cassie's note, the words no different than the message Mrs. Peterson had spoken aloud. He started toward the ordinary. Reaching the yellow two-story house, he was unsure if he was supposed to knock or walk in. He chose to tap his knuckles against the red door. After a moment, the door opened, and a stout woman with silver hair peered up at him.

"Evening, sir." Her Irish accent reminded him of his grandmother's. Thick and mossy. "Are ye looking for lodgings?"

"Mrs. Smith? I'm looking for a Miss Cassie Allan."

"And who be askin'?"

Gideon hitched his pack higher up on his shoulder. "I'm—"

The woman arched an eyebrow, and he could see why this was the best ordinary in town. She wasn't about to let just anybody in. "I'm her... husband."

She sized him up from his boots to his hat. "I'll be seein' about that, young man. Just you wait there on the bench. I'll be just a moment, laddie."

The door closed in his face.

Gideon shifted his feet. Shoulders aching, he set his pack on the bench, nearly knocking over a pot of lacy flowers. His heart pounded at the thought of seeing Cassie. He tried not to glance in the window, but the glow of a fire in the parlor drew his attention. The smell of something sweet baking hung in the air.

He saw the woman return. Her boot heels clicking stormily across the hardwood floor. "The laddie down here says he's your husband." The glass muffled her voice.

A second trailed it. "The *laddie?*"

Cassie.

He moved away from the window and quickly straightened his coat collar.

In a gust the door opened, and suddenly Cassie was before him. "Gideon!" Her eyes widened. "It's you!" A tenderness in her expression made him remember all that had passed between them. She flung her arms around his neck, hugging tight. Her scent so flowery it made his head spin, Gideon finally loosened her grip.

"You're the one who's been hard to find."

"So the lad *is* your husband?"

Cassie's smile was mischievous. She propped a hand on her hip as she studied Gideon. "Husband, you say?"

He shifted his feet again.

A sparkle in her blue eyes, she made a show of whispering to the woman. "If I were you, I wouldn't let him in."

"That was me instinct as well. I'm sorry, Mr...."

"O'Riley."

"You'll just have to find alternate lodgings."

Of course. "Thanks, Cassie," he said flatly.

Her shawl draped over her arm, Cassie stepped onto the porch. "We do have some unfinished business to attend to, though." She slid her hand through the crook of his elbow and motioned for them to walk down Main Street. "Shall we?"

At the bottom of the steps, Gideon remembered his pack. "I left my stuff behind."

"Mrs. Smith will see that it's taken care of. She doesn't permit stealing."

He laughed. "And why do I *not* want to know how you already know that?"

She winked. "Her bark is worse than her bite."

"I can see that. And thanks a lot. Now where am I supposed to stay?"

"The hotel?" By her tone, she knew how much it cost.

"I thought they'd have more than one room."

"They do." She patted his forearm and nodded toward a passing couple. "But others might not know that." Her voice was soft and near. "You're one day from freedom, Gideon. Even a simple little rumor can wreak havoc. It's better this way."

She was right. He gave her arm a little squeeze, then released her when they passed another couple. "And what does tomorrow hold?" He stopped walking, and she turned to face him, her heart-shaped face so peaceful that part of him wondered if she was the same person he'd met all those years ago.

Her blue eyes blinked up at him. "You won't be able to call me your wife."

His expression must have changed, for she tilted her head to the side. "Gideon, did you think I wouldn't come?"

"I didn't know what to think. We couldn't find you. What happened?"

She twirled a strand of molasses-hued hair around her finger. Ever so playfully.

He smiled. The old Cassie wasn't buried too deep after all.

"It's a long story," she finally said, propping a hand on her hip. "And I'm *very* hungry."

He tipped his head toward the hotel. "C'mon. I'll buy you dinner, and you can tell me this long story."

Thirty-Four

L eaning back in his chair, sweet tea in hand, Gideon watched Cassie over the rim of his glass. She studied the menu as if she'd never read a word of English. Finally the waitress returned for their order. For the second time.

Cassie pointed to the menu. "I'll have the chicken potpie." She closed it and hurried to add, "Please."

Gideon couldn't help but smile, and when the waitress looked at him, he simply asked for the same.

"So many choices. I thought I'd never decide," she said.

"That makes two of us."

Unfolding her napkin, she slid it in her lap. She wore a white blouse with a lace collar that made her look mighty pretty. Her dark hair was done up stylishly.

Nearly all the tables in the hotel restaurant were full, and Gideon was glad to be near the wall where it was a bit quieter. The elderly couple seated behind Cassie chatted happily. Pearl earrings danced against the woman's neck each time she laughed. The man with her was dressed in the same fashion as Reverend Gardner.

"So tell me, Cassie, what happened?"

"I went to Roanoke. There's a hospital there, and they needed nurses. Still working on the training part."

"You're going to be a nurse."

"Don't look so shocked." She gently kicked his shin under the table. "I'm doing quite well."

"That's wonderful." He straightened in his chair and, leaning forward, clasped his hands on the table. "And are you happy, Cassie?"

She nodded, her smile wide. "For the first time in my life, I really am."

He studied her to see if she meant it. But she kicked him again.

"Stop staring at me like that. I ain't lyin' to you. Trust me. If I didn't want to go through with this tomorrow, I wouldn't be here."

And he believed her.

A sip of tea and she wrinkled her nose at the taste. "I got a letter from my ma—it had *another* letter from the judge enclosed, along with something else I was supposed to sign and bring back. I hurried here as quick as I could. I went to the courthouse and spoke to the judge—"

"You spoke to him?" Gideon tried not to sound concerned.

"Yesterday morning, when I arrived." She leaned back when the waitress returned with two plates. Steam rose from the one in front of Gideon. The tall, slender waitress then lit the candle in the center of the table, casting Cassie's face in a soft glow.

"Thank you." Cassie reached for his hand. "Shall we?"

He took it and bowed his head. He spoke a soft prayer, feeling so much more gratitude than he could fit into those brief words. When he finished, Cassie turned her fork in her hand.

"Where was I?"

"The judge."

"Oh yes. I spoke with him yesterday, and he said that there were a few loose ends we needed to tie up, and it would be best if you were here for it.

That's when he sent the circuit rider. He told him to hurry." Her smile was soft. "And I can see that he did." Her fork gently pierced the pastry and ducked it into the cream sauce.

Suddenly realizing he hadn't eaten since dawn, Gideon took a bite of his own.

"What was it like going home?"

"Reverend Harris!" a man bellowed.

Gideon shifted slightly in his chair as another couple gathered around the table behind Cassie.

"Jimmy!" The man in the black coat stood. His bald head caught the candlelight, and his silver beard brushed his coat. "It's good to see ya!" Their voices softened as they all took their seats, and just as Gideon turned his attention back to his food, he better glimpsed the woman at the reverend's side. The one with the pearl earrings. Seeing a ring on her pale hand, he assumed she was the reverend's wife. She smiled cheerily at the other couple, white hair piled high into a fashionable bun. Her dress was fine— like it had never spent a day on a farm.

He thought of Lonnie when he'd left her, hands rosy from laundry. Feet weary from the never-ending work. He loved every bit of her for it. She would never complain, but life would take sides whether he wanted it to or not.

What he wouldn't give to have comforts to offer her.

The woman with the pearl earrings laughed and rested her cheek on her husband's shoulder. Gideon swallowed hard.

"Cat got your tongue?" he heard Cassie ask.

The woman unfolded her napkin and caught his gaze. Her kind smile in his direction was so soft, it took him a moment to realize he was staring.

Shaken back to the moment, Gideon quickly looked down at his plate.

"Did you hear me?" Cassie asked.

"Sorry." Gideon ran a hand over the back of his neck. "What was it you asked?"

"About coming home. I bet everyone was surprised to see you."

"That they were." He sipped his tea, if only to draw moisture to his suddenly parched throat.

"And Jacob. Tell me about him."

"He's grown." Gideon's heart swelled at the thought of his son. "He's a good lad. I missed him terribly. More so when I saw him again—so much time seemed to have passed."

Cassie's eyes glistened. "I'm so glad you are back in his life."

"Thank you, Cassie." It was a debt he didn't know how to repay.

"And Lonnie?"

Gideon sipped his tea. "You don't have to ask, Cassie."

"I want to."

He could tell she meant it. "Um…Lonnie." He blew out a quick breath. "Let's just say that trouble has a way of following me, it seems."

Cassie's eyebrows shot up.

"Lonnie was engaged. Is still. Sorta." At Cassie's surprised expression, he continued. "It's been the last thing in the world I wanted to come back to…"

"But life works that way sometimes," she finished for him.

He nodded, feeling a soft smile surface. "Does that…" He searched for the words and began again. "Cassie, does that change how you feel about tomorrow?"

She pressed her fingertips to her lips, thoughtfully. With mischief in her eyes, she studied him intently.

Gideon felt his face warm.

"You're blushing, Gideon O'Riley."

He chuckled.

Letting his curiosity wonder a few moments longer, Cassie finally spoke. "No. It doesn't. I'm not saying that this isn't bittersweet, but this is as it should be."

He squeezed her hand.

"So what now?" she asked.

"I'm not sure." His eyes shifted to the woman who smiled up at her reverend husband. Gideon cleared his throat. "Not sure." Though he was no longer hungry, he took a bite of his supper and then another. Cassie did the same. They chatted here and there until their plates were clean. Gideon slid several coins onto the table, and when Cassie snapped open her reticule, he held up a hand.

"Please. Let me."

The candle had burned down to a stub. She pushed her chair back and reached for her shawl. "We ought to get back before it gets too late. The judge asked me to return to the courthouse by nine in the morning."

"Nine o'clock. I'll walk you over."

"And where will you be staying?"

His hand on the small of her back, he led them through the restaurant and out into the night. "I have my own special place."

They strode across the street in silence. A thousand stars winked in the black spans overhead. The temperature must have dropped, for Cassie shivered and pulled her shawl tighter. Gideon felt none of it. He wasn't sure how his feet carried him to the yellow house, but before he knew it, he was bidding her good night.

"Until tomorrow," he said, picking up his pack.

"Until tomorrow."

"Sleep good, Cassie."

In one quick motion, she rose on her tiptoes and kissed him on the cheek. "And you too, Gideon."

Gideon sat in the lobby at Cassie's side. Hat in hand, he leaned forward and rested his forearms on his knees. A repeated *thunk* sounded somewhere nearby, and he realized he'd been bouncing his foot against the bench.

"Are you all right?" she whispered.

Too nervous to speak, he simply nodded. Two minutes to nine.

Cassie patted her hair that was done up in a puffy bun. She snapped open her reticule, searching for something. A moment later, it snapped closed. Gideon glanced around. The thunking started again. A trio of men stood against the far wall talking softly, and he felt Mrs. Peterson watching him over her spectacles. Unable to sit a moment longer, Gideon stood and started to pace. He hadn't taken but three steps when the judge's door opened and the older man waved them in. Gideon turned and nearly crashed into Cassie when she rose. He gripped her arms to keep from knocking her back.

"I'm so sorry."

She squeezed his wrist. "Take a deep breath. It's going to be all right."

Moistening his lips, he swallowed. "I don't know how to thank you for this, Cassie. I don't deserve it."

"Then think of it for Jacob." A sorrow filled her eyes as her gaze shifted against his. He wondered if this was harder for her than she was letting on. She squeezed his wrist again. Her words were whispered but bold. "Think of it for Jacob. The boy needs his papa." Quickly, she kissed his hand, gripping it tight.

His chest expanded so fiercely, it hurt. "Thank you."

Her hand still clasped around his, she motioned toward the open door. "Come on. The judge is waiting."

Thirty-Five

With Jacob's small hand holding tight to her fingers, Lonnie let him walk part of the way home from Gus's. They'd spent the morning visiting the goats, and she'd savored every quiet moment of it. They'd had a joyous time, especially with her little nanny she'd named Anne. The morning passed quickly, and Lonnie was ever so glad.

For she was trying very hard not to think of Gideon and what was happening.

She stopped walking when Jacob bent to pluck a piece of grass from between his little shoes. He slid it in his mouth, and Lonnie pulled it out before swinging him up into her arms. She gave him a tight hug. "You don't have to eat everything, my son!"

He kicked his feet and laughed.

"Like the carrot that was supposed to be for the goats." She patted his belly, clad in his warm wool sweater. "You're just like your papa. Always hungry."

Gideon.

And there went that idea.

She blew a lock of hair from Jacob's forehead, glad they'd reached home. The cool breeze tickled her arms and stirred her hair. A cup of tea would be just the thing to chase away the chills from this early spring day.

The kitchen door was ajar, Elsie no doubt inviting in the sweet air. At chatter coming from the parlor, Lonnie carried Jacob through the kitchen and spotted Addie playing with her doll in the center of the rug. Elsie sat on the sofa, mending in hand. She looked up and smiled when Lonnie walked in.

"How was your morning?"

"Lovely, thank you." Lonnie settled Jacob down on the rug. She sat a few minutes, and when Jacob ran a fist over his eyes, Lonnie pointed to the nearby book. "Why don't I read you two a story?" Lonnie tucked her legs beneath her and pulled Jacob close. Within moments, Addie snuggled up against her side, the picture book in her small hands. Sliding an arm around her sister, Lonnie called a thanks to Elsie, who rose to make tea. The fire crackled in the hearth.

"Which story should we read?"

"I like the one about Robin Hood!" Addie called with glee.

"Is that so?"

"Yes. He's so brave and so good...even though he's kind of naughty."

Laughing, Lonnie squeezed her sister tighter. "That about puts it right. Well then..." She turned to the story, nearly passing it, but Addie was quick to help her find the right place. "Shall we begin?"

Addie nodded quickly, her dark curls dancing against Lonnie's shoulder.

Lonnie read where she could, making sure to stop whenever Addie had a question or Jacob tried to turn the page, so eager he was to move on to a new activity. When he tried to tear a piece from the book, Lonnie lifted him from her lap and set him on the floor, where he toddled to his basket of blocks. Her lap free, she patted her skirts for Addie to sit down. Elsie bustled in with two cups of tea and settled back on the sofa.

Lonnie read, stopping only when Addie leaned her head against her shoulder with a contented sigh. Peering down, Lonnie saw that she had fallen asleep. She set the book aside, happy to just hold Addie and watch Jacob play. Anything to keep from thinking of Gideon. Yet still she wondered if he'd made it to the courthouse all right.

And if Cassie would be there.

Had the judge decided? Lonnie glanced toward the window, yearning for answers, but all the while knowing the wondering and worry would drive her mad. She took another sip of her tea and was glad when Elsie spoke.

"I hope Gideon made it there safely."

"I do too."

Jacob rubbed little fists against his eyes again, and Elsie bent to pick him up, cradling his sleepy head against her shoulder. When his dark lashes fluttered, Lonnie knew he was moments from drifting off.

With her hands clasped around Addie, her fingertip played a slow circle over the skin where Gideon's tin ring had once lain. She imagined it in the box in her dresser drawer. The metal cold. Remembered the tears that had spilled down her cheeks as she'd tugged it from her hand and pressed it away. Pushing it from her life forever.

Or so she had thought.

"You're quieter than usual," Elsie said, holding a sleeping Jacob.

After reaching for her teacup, Lonnie glanced at Elsie over the rim. "Am I?"

"You have much on your mind, I'd say."

Leaning against the sofa, Lonnie closed her eyes. "Gideon promised to come back no matter what."

"Would it be to say good-bye?" Elsie's words held a power that Lonnie wasn't ready to face, but she knew the wisdom she felt there.

And it was best to prepare her heart. For any outcome.

Feeling Elsie watching her, Lonnie nodded. "Possibly. But"—she glanced up—"oh, Elsie, I hope not."

"And so we shall watch the road." She kissed the top of Lonnie's head. "For him to come home."

Walking backward, Gideon casually held out a hand when a wagon approached. The sun was warm on his shoulders, but winter's chill still clung to the breeze. Ever so eager to get home, he smiled to himself. When the wagon neared, the driver tugged on the reins, slowing the horses.

"Afternoon, there," the man said.

"Afternoon."

"Where ya headed?"

"Fancy Gap."

"Hop on in, and I can take you as far as the fork."

"That'd be great, thank you." Gideon shoved his pack across the narrow wagon bed, the backboard missing. Long since gone, he thought, seeing the splintered wood and rusted hinges that hung haphazardly at odd angles. With a flex of his arms, he lifted himself into the wagon and sat.

The driver flicked the reins once. The wagon jolted forward.

They hadn't gone but a half mile down the road when the driver turned in his seat. He couldn't have been more than a year or two older than Gideon. His black, wiry beard was trimmed close to his face.

Gideon pulled off his hat and set it beside him.

"Recognize you from someplace."

The cuff of his pants leg was turned up, and Gideon straightened it. "Yeah?"

"You're that fella who played at the wedding." His voice fell to a mutter. "The one who kept taking all the pretty girls."

Twisting his mouth to the side, Gideon wasn't sure how to respond.

The man turned back around. Content to just enjoy the quiet, Gideon folded his arms over his chest and tilted his face to the sun.

"So tell me." The man's words pulled him back. "And be honest, now…" He glanced over his shoulder again. "Is what they say true?"

Gideon squinted at him and forced himself to sound interested. "What do *they* say?"

"That you went to jail."

"No," he indulged in a chuckle. "I didn't go to jail."

"I heard you've been in a heap of trouble."

Kicking his feet out, Gideon crossed his ankles. "I've had my fair share." And he wasn't proud of it. Maybe walking would be a better idea. He glanced at the road. A few hours until he got home by wagon. He wouldn't make it today any other way.

And he wanted Lonnie.

The man spoke over his shoulder. "I heard that little lady you were dancing with is a mighty good time." His eyebrows bobbed.

Something cool puddled in Gideon's chest. He'd only danced with two. "Which one?"

"The brown-eyed one. The *pretty* one. She's got them two young uns. Not a papa in sight." He flashed Gideon a sickening smile when he turned to speak over his shoulder. "Now that's my kinda girl, if you know what I mean. Too bad I couldn't get her to dance with me."

A numbness took over him. Gideon blinked once. Twice. Something within him burned to drag the man down from his wagon seat, but he sat, frozen in place. Scared of what he would do.

"They say she's tried to patch things up real nice-like. What, stayin' with that rich family and all." The man pulled his hat off and ran a hand through dark hair, his other hand grasping the reins. The wagon lumbered on at a slow, steady pace.

He'd rather walk. Gideon reached for his pack.

"But folks have their own opinions about that little girl and boy."

Gideon froze. Jacob. It took him a moment to fit the rest of the accusations together. Took him a moment to find any words. "Addie?"

"Don't know her name. Just know she looks like her mama. Them same big brown eyes."

The man's words fell into place, landing with a hollow *thud* in the pit of Gideon's stomach. He grabbed the strap of his pack. "You don't know anything about them. She's not the girl's mother." Sick, Gideon yanked, but his pack was stuck. "And she was married when she had that baby."

"To who?"

Gideon freed his pack from the wagon bed. "Me."

Glancing back briefly, the man studied him a moment, a jealous light flickering through his beady eyes.

"So watch what you say from here on out."

"If you say so." His tone said otherwise. "All in all, it might be better for them young uns."

His self-control waning, Gideon forced himself to jump down from the wagon before he did something he regretted.

"What with her gettin' hitched to the reverend and all."

Gideon's feet barely caught him.

"The preacher's good Christian name'll smooth things over for those little uns. Give them a right bright future despite it all."

Gideon turned and walked away.

"Where ya goin'?"

By the sound of the wagon, the man drove off, a muttered curse trailing him on the breeze.

Vision blurring and pulse hot, Gideon forced himself to keep walking.

Thirty-Six

The sun was nearing the horizon when Gideon recognized the edge of the Bennett farm. His feet ached, and his back was sore from walking, but he quickened his pace, allowing the joy that had been sleeping for far too long to stretch out inside him. He tugged on his hair, unable to fight a smile. The house came into view. Glancing around, he searched for Lonnie.

And in an instant he saw her. She straightened and lifted a hand, shielding her eyes.

Dropping his pack, Gideon strode forward. The farm blurring. Everything blurring. The reverend's wife fading. The driver's words fading.

Everything but Lonnie.

His legs carried him to her. Those doe eyes seemed to widen with every step. A basket in the crook of her arm, her brown hair, unbound and free. Cheeks pale but a blush blooming with each step he took.

Then his hands were cupping her face. The skin so soft. So perfect. "It's settled," he whispered. And his lips found hers.

Everything else was gone.

All save the pounding of his heart and the feel of his fingers in her hair. He kissed her soundly. Not caring if he should or shouldn't. He was free. And she could be his. Forever. She kissed him back. Her hands rose to clutch the sides of his coat, pulling him closer. Filling his heart to overflowing.

Something told him to pull away. A reason he didn't want to acknowledge, and every doubt that he was the better man for her formed a knot in his chest—and in the moment. He winced hard against it, gripping the small of her back as if to hang on. Losing the battle, he forced himself away. Breathless. Her eyes fluttered open.

Lonnie peered up at him. Her expression one of wonder. He ran his thumb against her cheek, the feel of her skin like home to him. She smiled.

Forget the reasons.

He stepped closer. And kissed her again—the thousand kisses he'd yearned to give her pouring into that single moment. He breathed deep. His heart in his hands, he whispered her name. And she whispered his. So this was what happiness felt like. This was what it meant to be whole again. To be home. He pulled her closer, tighter.

"Gideon!" she screeched. And he realized they were falling.

He caught her fall best he could, but even then, she hit the grass in a mound of skirts. He landed beside her, trying not to crush her any more than he'd apparently been doing. He turned to apologize, but she was already laughing. Bending his knee up, he rested his arm atop and covered his face with his hand.

"I'm so sorry, Lonnie. I didn't mean to get that enthusiastic." He took in a deep breath. "I forgot myself for a moment."

He could tell she was trying to speak, but her shoulders were shaking too hard.

"I didn't mean to knock you down." His words only made her laugh harder.

Finally catching her breath, she brushed her hands together. "Well, if you're gonna do something, you might as well do it right."

"That's not quite how that was supposed to go."

Leaning toward him, she kissed the tip of his nose and then his forehead.

His eyes nearly slid closed, all humor melting away.

"It was perfect." Her eyes searched his, so warm and brown, he knew she meant every word.

"I never thought this moment would come." Really? That was the best he could say? Gideon rolled his eyes and hoped she didn't notice what an idiot he was.

She glanced toward the house and pointed. Jacob was at the window, patting his small hands against the glass. Holding him, Elsie waved. Addie jumped up and down.

Gideon helped Lonnie to her feet. "I sure hope they didn't see that." He steadied her.

"So I never got the chance to ask...what happened?" She smiled up at him.

He pulled a piece of grass from her hair. "Cassie was there. Everything's finally settled. It's over."

Tears flooded her eyes. "Oh, Gideon." She reached for him again.

But this time, he remained where he was, the man's words taunting him. *"The preacher's good Christian name'll smooth things over for those little uns."*

Swallowing hard, he glanced past Lonnie to the little faces in the window. Jacob. Addie.

"Give them a right bright future despite it all."

They had shame on their names. Because of all he had done.

And Lonnie. She was peering up at him, her face shining with joy.

Did she know the rumors that followed her? His sweet, sweet Lonnie. She didn't deserve it. Not one bit of it. Yet it was her life. All because of him.

She may have a piece of paper from Reverend Gardner, proving her marriage to Gideon when Jacob came along. But the folks around these parts didn't know that. And they didn't care. He could marry her this minute, but the damage had already been done. The weight of it all avalanched around him. Ripping open his hopes. His dreams. Could he give them up?

Could he live for others? And not for himself?

"Gideon. What's wrong?"

Realizing he'd been standing there without speaking, Gideon looked down on her. "There are some things we need to talk about."

Her eyes rounded with worry.

"Don't worry. I'm not married." He took her hand in his, not ready to let go. "But, hey, there's time enough for that." He squeezed her hand. "I'm starving." He was stalling and he knew it.

"You and your stomach."

"No, really. I'm starving. That must be why I fell down."

Throwing her head back, she laughed.

Lifting her hand, he kissed it. Lingering. His eyes slid closed for the briefest of moments. Every desire inside him battling.

Thirty-Seven

G ideon awoke to a dark sky. The evening had been magical. With his family all around him, he told them of all that had happened while he was in Stuart. Lonnie listened, her eyes shining. He allowed himself the hours of happiness, unwilling to think of what the future could hold. *Should* hold.

But when his head hit the pillow later, his fears found him. Haunting him.

Unable to lie still, he led Sugar from the barn. The mule's coat flinched in the sunless glow of early morning. He patted her thick neck. He knew they could both have slept another hour. Waited for the sun to warm the land. But Gideon had no reason to wait. His bed on the hard barn floor left him too cold to get comfortable, and the troubles of mind made sleep impossible to catch.

The mule stood still as he lugged the singletree from the barn, and the metal rod was cold to his bare hands. Gideon attached the heavy choker chain with its large hook meant to pull logs behind muscular Belgians. Sugar blinked at him as if knowing as much. Gideon patted her brown coat.

"I know, girl. Don't worry. We'll take it easy." He scratched her between the ears.

Metal chains clanged as he led her toward the far field. The first rays of light crested a black wall of trees. "Few more days and this will all be done."

And then what will you do?

Gideon shrugged off the thought. He'd come out here to work. Not to think. There was time enough to find his way down the road he didn't know. At least that's what he kept telling himself. He led Sugar to a pile of felled trees waiting to be moved to the chopping block. He and Toby had cut the larger logs into manageable pieces since the old mule would have to skid alone. Kneeling beside the nearest log, Gideon wrapped the heavy choker chain around the dense maple and secured it with the steel hook. Sugar stepped sideways, and he took hold of her reins.

"Easy now," he said softly and gave the leather straps a gentle tap against her hide. She leaned into the load, and the log slid toward the farmyard. Gideon let his pace mimic the animal's. There was no need to rush her. She could only move so many logs before her legs wearied.

The quick *thud* of trotting hooves turned his head.

Toby rode toward him, crossed the clearing, and after dismounting, led Gael to a knoll where she dropped her head and nosed the bracken littering the forest floor. "Mornin'," Toby called as he pulled a pair of work gloves from his back pocket.

With a shake of his head, Gideon watched the man approach. "You do know you don't need to be here, right? Orchard's done."

"Then what are you doing?"

"Cleaning up the mess."

"And so I'm here."

Gideon gave a soft flick of the reins. Sugar strode forward. "So what does Reverend Gardner think of your new occupation as a farmer?"

After falling in step, Toby squinted sideways at him. "He thought it was rather int'resting."

"Interesting?"

Toby took his time pulling on his gloves. "Truth be told, he started laughing when I told him how it all came about."

Gideon glanced at him, the man he'd once hated. This morning, it felt strangely hard. "And then?"

"He told me to make sure and get my other duties finished first. Which I assured him I would." He fiddled with his shirt cuff, tucking it inside the leather. He sensed there was something else Toby wanted to say.

"Does he know about Lonnie?"

"Aye. That he does."

"And?"

"And then he told me, 'Good luck. If I know anything about Gideon O'Riley, you're gonna need it.'"

Gideon chuckled. "I'd say he's a smart man." When Sugar slowed, he flicked the reins, and she leaned into her load again.

"What would you like me to do?" Sugar neared the chopping block, and he slowed her.

"Gael ever pulled one of these? Or is she just known for standing around looking pretty?"

"I think she could manage." He turned, hesitating, and was about to speak when Gideon tipped his head toward the barn.

"Stuff's in there." He wasn't ready for this. Gideon yanked the hook loose. The freed log sank where it lay. "Do you know how to use it?" he blurted.

Toby strode toward the barn. "I think I can figure it out."

After turning the mule, Gideon led her to the clearing. He secured another log with the chain. Toby returned empty handed, grabbed Gael's harness, and began to lead her back to the barn. The other singletree was too heavy to carry. He should have said as much. A flick of the reins and Sugar walked forward, her steps slightly slower than before. He reached the chopping block just as Toby was lowering a harness onto Gael's back.

The Scotsman spoke. "I haven't seen Lonnie in a few days. I could wait and ask her. But I'll just as soon ask you now."

Bending, Gideon freed the log from the hooks. He straightened and looked at Toby.

"What's happened?"

Gideon ran his sleeve over his forehead. Stalling. A month ago, he would have enjoyed this moment. But not now. Not with Toby looking at him so. "It's done and settled," he finally blurted. "Cassie and I are no longer married." He watched Toby's face carefully for some sign of irritation. Some reaction. Ducking his head, the man simply nodded slowly. Gideon knew Toby would never ask Lonnie to marry him now.

But there was no sweetness in this victory.

He needed to know. Needed to understand the man's motives. "Do you love her?"

Toby turned Gael. "I wouldna say it matters."

"I'm still asking." He didn't care if he was pushing. He needed to know what Toby was made of.

Toby blinked at him for several heartbeats. "Aye. Verra much. What's gotten into you?"

Gideon let the matter fall.

They worked without speaking, and though Toby worked as quickly as ever, he was silent, almost broody. Gideon had no words. They'd moved nearly two dozen logs before Lonnie crossed the clearing, a basket on her arm. Using a rag, Gideon wiped Sugar's bit and slid off her harness before

MY HOPE IS *Found*   253

giving her coat a quick rubdown. The mule wandered toward the knoll for a much-needed break.

"Good afternoon." She set the basket down, and her eyes drifted from man to man.

Hands gripped to the back of his neck, Toby turned and walked away.

Lonnie's eyes flooded with sadness.

Gideon moved to her side. "I told him," he said softly.

"And?" Her gaze followed the reverend, a sweet fondness living in the brown depths.

"He won't—" Gideon shook his head. "He won't marry you, Lonnie. Said it wouldn't be right."

"I need to talk to him." She watched Toby walk away, and he wondered what it was she would say to him.

"Do you want to marry him, Lonnie?"

As if from the power of his question, her head tipped to the side, surprise filling her face.

"Because… Do you know the life you could have with him?" His heart pounded.

"Gideon."

He slammed his eyes close. "I'm being serious. I know what he says about you and me…how we're supposed to be together and how it wouldn't be right any other way. But is that enough? Is that enough for you to give everything up?" He motioned toward Toby. "The life he can give you, what he can give the children. All he could be for them. Do you want to give that up just for what was…between us?" His voice broke. He pressed a hand to his chest. "Is this really enough for you?"

She motioned between them. "This isn't just about what was. It's about what *is*. Oh, Gideon…" She glanced back to Toby, a broken heart in her expression. Tears pooled in her eyes.

He tipped her chin and locked gazes with her. "Lonnie. It's because of what *is*..." When her chin trembled, he pulled away, overcome with her nearness. Her sweetness. A glance up and he groaned at the sight of Sugar lumbering at the far edge of the clearing.

"I should go get the mule before she walks to the next state." Gideon started after Sugar, who had slowly lumbered across the farm. Reaching up, he tugged on his hair and wished with all his might that he didn't have to feel so torn.

Thirty-Eight

Two stumps remained to be unearthed. Ax in hand, Gideon planted his feet in front of the larger one. Steel struck wood as he pounded the blade against the roots. He worked until a trickle of sweat formed between his shoulder blades. He kept a steady tempo, taking care with his aim. For he had a great ability to mess things up.

Not just for him. For others involved. He thought of Lonnie. He thought of Jacob. Little Addie. And he didn't know what to do. Didn't know what was right. Bending, he yanked the root free. If only the answer could be pulled to the surface as easily.

Lonnie was the only good thing about him. The only thing that was pure and right and deserving. Without her, he was nothing. And that frightened him. Frightened him at the thought of losing her. Worse was the realization that he could burden her by simply staying in her life. He'd hated his rotten existence—until he'd met Lonnie. The girl with the big brown eyes. The girl who had trusted him to walk her home. But he wasn't worthy of the trust; he'd kissed her in a way he had no right to.

Gideon ran a hand over his face. Wishing he hadn't been that man. The man who let his lusts rule him. He'd have taken her innocence that night if she'd let him. There were few things he cared about back then, save himself and what he wanted. Gideon glanced around him. Was all that lived inside him in this moment any different? He knew what it was to be addicted. Knew how to hold on to something with everything inside him. All for his own satisfaction. How many times did he tell himself that his love for Lonnie was different?

How many times?

Gideon picked up the ax handle, smooth from years of wood oil and sweat. Out of habit, he glanced over his shoulder, but Toby had left a few hours back. The man had been quiet, somber. Gideon couldn't blame him. Not for one moment. He grunted as he brought the blade down, making a splice through the moist, sinewy fibers and, after countless strikes, stepped back for a breath. He shifted his stance, adjusted his grip on the ax, and after three more blows, the masticated root fell loose.

With the choker chain wrapped around the jagged stump, he urged Sugar on, the sounds of popping roots and falling soil filling the quiet clearing. When she finished, sides heaving, Gideon pulled half an apple from his pocket. "That's a good girl." He patted her hide and loosened the chain before leading her back where she could rest as he started on the second stump.

By sunset, he heard someone approach and, when he turned, saw Lonnie striding toward the clearing, Jacob on her hip. Gideon smeared his palm against his chest, though it was useless in rubbing away the ache he suddenly felt. Her eyes were serious. Sad.

He hoped and prayed for the strength to do this.

She stilled beside him. "Amazing." Her gaze drifted over the new trees planted in neat rows.

He leaned back on one leg and tugged his gloves off. "Thank you. Of course...I had help."

She glanced at him, a knowing look in her eyes.

Wishing he hadn't brought that up—not just yet—he pulled Jacob from her grasp and nuzzled the boy's neck until Jacob giggled.

Her shoulders rose as she let out a sigh. "Shall we sit?" Jacob dove toward her, and Gideon lowered their son into her arms. The boy's wiggling continued, and Lonnie set him down. He wandered toward the nearest stump and patted a chubby hand against the rough bark.

"Is he…" she began.

Gideon nodded. "He's safe." But he stepped toward the boy, and Lonnie followed.

Sinking down, Gideon leaned against the stump, and Lonnie surprised him by doing the same. She tucked her plaid skirts beneath her before sitting in the dirt. They watched Jacob in silence. The boy gathered sticks and chewed on each one before adding them to a little pile at his side. The sky grayed, and the hazy shadows that swallowed up the land sent a chill through Gideon's damp clothes. Although he knew where his jacket lay, he had no intention of moving from this spot. Her shoulder was too warm beside his. This moment, too right.

And he was about to mess everything up. He might as well place her hand inside Toby's. Was he ready for this? Gideon squeezed his shoulder. He spoke before he could change his mind. "There's something I need to tell you, Lonnie." He picked up a twig and snapped it. "I'd rather not…but it just doesn't feel right not to. No more secrets, right?"

A smile was in her voice. "No more secrets." She leaned back, settling in, and smelled as sweet as ever with hints of soap clinging to her damp apron.

"Lonnie, I don't know how to say this, but I'd rather you hear it from me than some stranger." He pressed his fists to his knees. "It's been made known to me that there are some folks who don't believe right. About you.

And the children." When she didn't speak, he continued. "Because you're not married. Because I wasn't around."

Her face was sad. "I know."

"You do?"

"Toby told me."

Toby. He flexed his hand, then tucked it against his stomach. "Are you all right?"

She nodded thoughtfully. "People will think what they want, I s'pose. There's not much I can do about it now."

But there was. Did she not see that? "You're just fine with it? You're just fine with what they say about you and Jacob? about Addie?"

Jacob started to fuss.

"Addie?"

"That she's *yours.*"

"Mine?" The word slipped out small. Lonnie's mouth opened, then closed.

The man's words still haunting him, the pain in her face all but sealed his decision. *"The preacher's good Christian name'll smooth things over for those little uns."*

Her eyes searched the ground. "But that would mean—"

"Yes. It's not good, Lonnie. Not for you or them."

"Give them a right bright future despite it all."

The name McKee held a goodness that he could never hope to have. O'Riley—only shame. Trouble. Gideon clenched his fists. Jacob's whimpers growing louder, he rose and picked up his son. Lonnie followed a step behind.

She seemed lost in thought, so Gideon allowed her the quiet as they walked back to the house. They strode into the kitchen, and at Lonnie's bidding, Gideon nestled the baby into his highchair, fumbling with the leather strap. Lonnie's eyes were sad as she buttered a piece of bread for him. Gideon moved to speak to her, sliding his hand to the back of her neck, the skin so soft his head spun. He was glad when Addie bounded into the kitchen, followed by Jebediah and Elsie. Gideon stepped away.

"Look what's happened!" Addie held up a wooden pull toy, a small horse that had seen better days. "His little wheel fell off." Her bottom lip stuck out.

Hungry for the distraction, Gideon knelt and took it gently from her. "Let's see here." He took the wheel and slid it into place. "This little peg snapped off." Using his pinkie, he showed her just where it had broken. "See that?"

Addie nodded.

"After supper, I can make a new peg. Would you like to watch?"

Her dark curls bobbed when she nodded.

"You can be my helper." He tousled her hair and her dimples appeared. "Why don't I set it on the desk, where it'll be safe until then?" He stepped into the parlor and returned just as quick.

Addie hopped into her seat as Jebediah unfolded his napkin. Gideon pulled out his own chair, and Lonnie sat with a sigh, slowly unfolding her napkin. When she'd smoothed it across her lap, Jebediah blessed the food. Lonnie spooned food onto Jacob's tray without speaking. In the flicker of candlelight, Elsie and Jebediah exchanged glances.

"Tell us about your trees," Elsie blurted.

"My trees." Gideon straightened and collected his thoughts. "My trees are good."

She slapped her napkin in his direction. "You know what I mean."

"Yeah," Jebediah lifted his cup. "How has it all gone?"

Gideon gripped the breadbasket when it came his way and pulled out a piece before passing the lot to Lonnie. Accepting it, she seemed to take care that their fingers didn't touch.

"Really well." His voice faltered. "They're all in the ground in time, and now I'll just watch them closely and keep them watered. Hope we don't have any late storms." He ran his hands along his thighs, not really wanting to talk about his trees.

Elsie patted his arm. "Such a blessing. To think, we'll have an orchard right out our back door. No more climbin' up to Apple Hill."

"All the cider and pie you could ever make. But it'll take a few years to get there."

"It'll all happen in due time," Elsie added.

"That it will."

Jebediah's mustache lifted. "Do I sense…calm and patience? What happened to you?"

Gideon chuckled. "Is that an insult?"

"Not in the slightest."

After breaking his bread in half, Gideon offered it to Lonnie, motioning with his head toward their son. She slid the bread onto the boy's tray, and Jacob dropped a green bean to reach for it, sending a chorus of laughter around the table.

Lonnie shook her head, but a soft smile parted her pretty mouth.

"Well." Gideon leaned back in his chair. "I guess there's no point in worrying."

"So you've realized that it's better just to wait on the Lord, huh?" Jebediah asked.

When Lonnie reached for the butter, her arm brushing his, he cleared his throat.

"Let's say I'm working on it." Gideon poked food around his plate. "Sometimes better than others."

When supper was over, Addie hopped up and ran into the parlor, returning with the toy and a toothy grin. The way Addie reached for his hand, holding it tight, made Gideon thankful for the distraction.

"I'm ready to be your helper, Mr. Gideon."

He squeezed her hand. "Then off we go." They walked through the kitchen and out into the night. In the barn, he lit the lantern. She sat on the workbench, watching closely as he whittled a new peg. She talked the whole time about everything under the sun, from the goats to Jacob to the little garden Elsie was going to let her plant.

Gideon looked at her—brown eyes just like her sister's—and soaked in her happiness. When he nicked his finger with his chisel, he thought she was going to cry. She jumped to her feet and, standing right there in the middle of his workbench, took up his finger in her little apron. She bundled it tight, her sweet face drawn in worry.

His finger was no pain compared to the ache in his heart.

He wanted to rewind time. Rip that man down from his wagon. Tell him what it meant to love someone and to be loved. He wanted to stanch the rumors. Snuff out each flame with his bare hands. But he could no more do that than he could hold the river back. Looking into Addie's chestnut eyes, he wished with all his might that he could.

Thirty-Nine

With the sun peeking through the clouds just so and the echo of birdsong coming from the forest, Lonnie's heart felt light as she lowered the corners of her apron, dropping a pile of thyme onto the cutting board. She'd found a small, rickety table in the barn, and it had taken most of her strength to drag it to the right spot. Through the open barn doors, she could see Gideon at the workbench, Addie at his side. The pull toy and an array of tools were sprawled between them. Though he'd fixed the wheel the night before, he'd offered to help her paint it.

With a shake of her head, Lonnie smiled and turned back to her work. Earlier that morning, she'd knelt in Elsie's garden, gathering sprigs of the hearty thyme. Lonnie worked the large kitchen knife through the fragrant herb. The only thing that made sense in this moment was sitting right in front of her.

Grabbing the pan she'd prepared, Lonnie strode to her lye barrel and, after pouring rainwater through, set the pan to catch the drips. Her patchwork skirt brushed the mud, and she hoisted it above her knees, black stockings poking out. Gideon jogged toward the well. The morning sun glinted golden on his shoulders. Filling a bucket, he hurried back to the barn.

Lonnie stood and shielded her eyes. "Everything all right?"

"Oh yeah!" His voice was a bit higher than usual. "We may or may not have knocked over the can of paint." He disappeared into the barn, and Lonnie heard Addie laugh.

Her heart near to bursting, she carefully carried the lye mixture back to her work space. She added fat, stirred it slowly, and mulled over what oil she might add for fragrance. Small bottles of lavender, rosemary, and peppermint stood at attention, and she reached for the lavender oil, certain it would make a nice accompaniment to the thyme. Gus had returned from his last trip to town with the oils wrapped in parcel paper and a message from another shop owner that if Lonnie's soap was as fine as the neighbors had made it out to be, he'd order three dozen bars or more. The corner of Lonnie's mouth turned up in a smile.

As the fat melted, she rushed into the kitchen for her soap molds. In the low cupboard, she pulled out a trio of old pans and hurried back into the sunshine and her soap mixture that desperately needed to be stirred. Working an old spoon through it, she waited for the trace, the telltale sign that the soap was ready to pour. Her spoon hit the table, and with a flick of her wrist, she sprinkled in specks of thyme. The familiar motions—the busy dance of this work—filled her with contentment.

At the sound of hooves, she glanced up. Toby rode into the yard, his black coat flapping open. She forced herself to keep her hands steady as she filled the first pan. Nearing, he dismounted. His gaze as earnest and as kind as she'd ever known. The last drops of soap mixture dripped into the third pan, and she set the pot aside.

"Afternoon," he said when he neared.

She peered up into the face she'd come to know so well. "It's good to see you, Toby." She meant it with all her heart.

"And you." He smiled and a dimple dented each cheek. He stood a moment watching her. "Oh, wait." He opened the saddlebag and pulled out a wilted bouquet. "Och, these looked better a quarter of an hour ago." He held them gently in his oversized hands, the sight touching her heart. He handed them to Lonnie. "It's to say sorry for walking away the other day. I was just…"

And she knew. Lonnie smelled the flowers. "You have nothing to be sorry about. If you only knew the gentleman that you are."

He ran a hand through his hair, expression humble.

"A bit of water, and they'll perk right up. I'm nearly done here, and then we can walk up to the house." She peered up at him. "I'd love to sit and talk. There's so much to say. I can put on some tea."

"I canna stay long. I just came to say good-bye."

"Good-bye?"

He chuckled. "For a few days. I'm going to take some money to the church up in Richland Knob. A large group has been meeting in a barn for years, and we're putting in some funds to help them break ground on a small building."

Gently setting the flowers at her side, Lonnie tapped the pan, letting bubbles rise to the surface of the soap mixture, her mind no longer on the task. "That's wonderful. How long are you going to be gone?"

"Just a few days."

Addie bounded into the yard. "Reverend McKee!" she squealed and hopped over a puddle, then another, her path zigzagging to find them. Barreling past him, she buried herself in Lonnie's skirt, then poked a grin around just for him. "I'm ever so glad you're here. I want to show you my horsy! Mr. Gideon fixed it for me, right quick. He even let me use his hammer." Tongue sticking out the side of her mouth, she mimicked a pounding motion. "And I only squished his finger twice!"

Lonnie's eyes widened, and Addie bounded back the way she'd come.

"I think perhaps he has a new admirer." Toby winked at Lonnie, but his eyes were sad. In a motion that caught her by surprise, he reached out and brushed his thumb over her cheek. A farewell—she could feel it.

And she knew he wasn't really talking about Addie.

Toby glanced past her, and following his gaze, Lonnie saw Gideon leaning against the doorway of the barn, wiping paint from his hands with a rag.

A tip of his hat and Toby stepped back. "I need to speak to him. I will see you soon," he promised. His eyes found Lonnie's. "Good-bye."

Gideon watched as Toby walked toward him. The man nodded cordially, and Gideon returned the nod. He stepped into the barn. Toby followed. Picking his chisel up, Gideon looked around for something to keep his hands busy. His fields called to him. Sweat called to him. But this would just have to do. He pulled down a kitchen stool he'd started for Elsie and worked the chisel through the soft wood.

"I see you got the rest of the field cleared."

"Suppose I could have waited." Eyes on his work, the shavings fell.

"But you didn't." Toby's voice held admiration.

"Yeah, well, I'm sorta new to this patience thing." Gideon pressed the chisel in deeper—wounding. He forced himself to take a deep breath.

"At least you're trying."

Gideon tossed the chisel aside before he lost a finger.

"I don't know how you're doing it." Toby watched him.

Gideon let out a heavy breath. The man was the epitome of patience.

"You've been home for days, Gideon." Toby glanced at the house. "And still…" He shook his head. "If it were me, I'd have married Lonnie by now."

"Are you waiting for me to put you out of your misery?"

Toby said nothing.

"Lonnie needs to choose. It's the best way, and we both know it." He'd watched the exchange between them. The tender way Toby reached for her. The tender way she responded.

Gideon grabbed a piece of sandpaper, but it felt insufficient. He needed a hammer. An ax. He wanted to crush the wood in his hands, not make something out of it. Forcing himself to cradle the sandpaper gently, he fought the urge to give up.

"I'll be gone for a few days. Heading up to Richland Knob. I have a deliv'ry for the church there."

"Well…try not to get eaten by a bear while you're gone."

"I'll do my best." Toby scratched the back of his head, then glanced at the sun that was rising higher. Jebediah was walking toward them. "I need to be going. I have a few things to see to before I leave."

Gideon watched his greatest rival walk from the barn. His greatest fear mounted the dark mare and, with a click of his heels, disappeared from view. If only life were that simple.

Forty

G ael lumbered along slowly, and as much as Toby knew he should tap his heels, urge her on quicker, he no longer cared that he was running late. There wasn't much about this day that made him in a hurry to be anywhere. For no matter where he went, troubles of mind would follow.

The air was aglow. Lit with an early evening sun that glinted on the wildflowers that traced the edge of the road. Hedging the path in beauty when everything inside Toby was anything but. He was about to lose all he held dear. Nay...he'd already lost it the moment Gideon had stepped back into their lives.

Lonnie loved Gideon. Of that he had no doubt. And someday soon, Gideon would make her his bride. His wife. The thought gnawed at Toby's heart, though it was nothing other than what must be. What *should* be. For Gideon had already made Lonnie his wife a long time ago, and that bond was not easily severed, no matter how much Toby had wished it were so. *It must be.* But he loathed the thought.

Deep down in every dark corner of his heart, he hated it. Realizing his jaw was clenched, Toby forced himself to relax.

That kind of thinking couldn't live. It couldn't thrive inside him. Not if he were to truly walk in the Lord's will. Even so, he couldn't linger and watch it all unfold before him. To simply close his eyes—pretend it wasn't happening—was beyond him. He wasn't strong enough to stand by as their lives went on together. Wasn't strong enough to stand in the church where they would give themselves to one another again. He pulled his hat off and set it on the saddle.

No. It was time to begin again.

For days—nay, weeks—he hadn't known how he would step out of Lonnie's life. Didn't know how he would bid farewell to Jacob. To Addie. But the time had come. One last farewell, and he would start a new life down a new path.

He'd already told Reverend Gardner. The head position would have to go to someone else. He couldn't stay here. Though it killed him to think of not watching those children grow up. Killed him to think of not growing old with Lonnie. Never bringing her home as his bride.

He tightened his grip on the reins. "Git on up!" That life was dead, and the less he thought about what may have been, the better. He'd go mad otherwise.

As the smoke from his chimney faded into memory, Toby's thumb grazed the metal of the shotgun that balanced on the saddle in front of him. He had no intention of using it, but Reverend Gardner had insisted. The older man had looked him square in the eye as he handed him the double-barrel.

"I won't send a man off with that much money in his pocket unarmed."

Even as he remembered the reverend's words, Toby patted his coat pocket, the lump beneath his hand enough to help raise the new building. Gael flicked her head, and Toby patted her dark neck. "Easy, girl."

A glance to the left showed the sun flickering like a candle between two peaks as clouds feathered across a purple sky, and he prepared himself for what was sure to be a cold evening. He shrugged deeper into his coat, glad there was another hour before dark. He'd arranged lodgings for nightfall, but he was behind in his course and wouldn't make it until much later than planned.

His saddle creaked when he turned. Toby glanced around at familiar, spindly trees. Gael plodded along. Her steps sure. A pace that would get them to Richland Knob by the following evening. He settled into the saddle for the hours ahead. Trying to find pleasure in the silence and solitude. To be content to simply remember all he owed thanks for. An abundance of blessings that he had taken for granted much too often.

His life had seemed to stretch out for miles and miles, the path clear, the future bright. But now it seemed to swallow itself in doubt. Disbelief. And he no longer sensed what was around the corner. A few days ago, he'd been certain it no longer included Lonnie, and he tried not to give the words Gideon had spoken to him any weight.

"Lonnie needs to choose. It's the best way, and we both know it."

Wasn't the choice already made? Yet he sensed doubt in every step that Gideon took. What was the man afraid of? Toby rubbed a hand over his face. Surely she wouldn't choose anyone but him. It made no sense. Who was Toby compared to Gideon? The man knew everything about her. He'd been there from the beginning. He was Jacob's father. Toby's heart tightened with yearning. He wanted to kick himself for letting his thoughts wander back to what ought never to be.

Lifting his face to the horizon, where the first star appeared in a graying sky, he asked the Lord to fill the weary spaces of his spirit. Prayed for that comfort to fill him. The wholeness that he'd been yearning for. The surrender he'd been fighting against.

With Addie at her elbow, Lonnie scrubbed the last plate and shook off droplets of water. She handed it to her sister, who had a damp towel at the ready. Elsie ran a broom over the floorboards, sweeping dust and flour toward the door, where the tuning of Gideon's mandolin filtered in from the cool evening. Clearly eager to finish, Addie stacked the last of the plates and hopped down from her stool.

"May I be done?" she asked, tugging on the strings of her apron.

"Yes, and thank you for your help. Why don't you run on upstairs and get into your nightgown?"

"Might I go outside?"

"It's getting late. Why don't you climb into bed, and I'll leave the window open a bit so you can listen as you fall asleep."

Addie scurried into the parlor, small feet padding up the stairs. Lonnie peeked into the parlor to see that Jebediah had rocked Jacob to sleep. After placing a trio of cups in the high cupboard, she wiped the table with a damp rag. Her hand traced the wood in rhythm with Gideon's playing. The song was slow. Sweet. And wholly peaceful. A hymn she'd never heard him play before. Lonnie felt her feet carry her to the doorway, where a sprinkle of stars blinked down from a darkening sky.

In the fading light, Gideon sat against the porch railing, feet stretched out along the top step. His boots were unlaced, one over the other. Leaning against the jamb, Lonnie crossed her ankles and watched him. The familiar hymn seemed to fill her, and she hummed along. When the last notes faded, Gideon looked at her.

"Not quite sure where that came from." His face was pensive.

"'It Is Well with My Soul.' When did you learn it?"

A shrug of his shoulder, and he ducked his head, feigning interest with the cuff of his pants. He bent the folds of denim with his thick fingers, then looked up at her. "Just picked it up. S'pose I heard it at church a time or two, and it just sort of came back to me. What was it called again?"

She repeated the title, and when he nodded thoughtfully, she added, "Yet you know it so well."

His head pressed against the banister, and he turned to look out over the moonlit farm. "It doesn't take much for me to know a song." He seemed to wrestle with something. "The chords and the notes is what I'm trying to say." He tapped the side of his head. "I hear them once, and they just sort of stay, I reckon." When he glanced at her, his gaze was intense. Serious. And she could see that he was struggling with something. Greatly.

"You don't seem proud of that." She shifted. Wanting so very much to draw nearer.

"Is there a reason to be?" he asked. "To be good at something just because you can't help it?" Head to the banister, he blinked up at the stars. "This"—he played a few beautiful notes, then let his hand fall away— "won't get me anywhere. It's the *meaning* of a song that's harder for me to grasp." He sifted a hand through his hair. "It's the meaning of just about anything."

She understood what he meant. "It's one of my favorites," she said softly.

"Is it?" He looked back at her.

"Oh." She uncrossed her ankles. "I promised Addie I'd tuck her in." Lonnie straightened to go. "I'll be right back. Please don't leave."

The glimmer of his eyes searched hers. "I won't."

After a nod, Lonnie slipped away. In the parlor, she lifted Jacob from Jebediah's arms and left the gray-haired man to snooze. Elsie glanced up from her knitting and winked. In the bedroom, Lonnie tucked Jacob into his cradle. She moved to the bed and tugged the quilt higher up Addie's shoulders. The little girl's eyelids were heavy, hands tucked beneath her round cheek. Moonlight spilled across the floor.

"Sleep good, little one. I love you." Lonnie kissed her curls.

"Love you too," Addie said softly, and her eyelids fell closed.

Lonnie tiptoed back downstairs and stepped out into the night. The air was cool. Draping her shawl about her shoulders, she stepped over Gideon's legs and sank onto the step below him. Mandolin clutched to his chest, he picked a soft song. A variation of what he'd been playing, but it melted into different melodies, always returning, drawing richer. Perfectly Gideon.

Lonnie sighed, letting the day wash through her. Savoring the cleansing of what filled the night air. Aware of how close she was sitting to Gideon, she glanced up, glad the moon lit his face just enough to catch the sweet pensiveness in his expression.

"You look like you're trying to solve the world's problems," she said.

"Do I?" He smiled and his brow unfolded. "I was thinking of that hymn. I don't really know the words. But even what I do know doesn't make sense."

Lonnie rested her hand on the step beside her. "Tell me."

His gazed filtered over the horizon. "All right. Let's see… How about just the title? 'It Is Well with My Soul.'" He swallowed. "What does that mean?"

Letting out a sigh, Lonnie pulled her feet in. She took her time arranging the folds of her skirt. All the while, she felt Gideon's gaze on her. "What do you think it means?"

"I knew you were going to say that." He chuckled.

"No you didn't." But she felt at home, realizing how well he knew her. And how well she knew him. She wrapped her hands around her ankles.

"Let's see," he finally said. "I think it's talking about peace." He smoothed a hand over his unshaven jaw. "But how? How can someone just up and say that? It seems so simple…but it doesn't feel that way." Gideon set his mandolin aside with slow movements. Finally, he looked at Lonnie.

She nodded slowly, soaking in his words—his heart. Praying with all her might that she could find the words.

"What do *you* think it means?"

"Me?" She let out a heavy sigh. "I think it means just that. A peace. The feeling of resting in God's goodness. In His comfort. That come what may, it is still well."

Her words seemed to tip his chin up. He thought a moment, his gaze distant. Face shadowed. Lonnie studied the familiar lines, from his knotted brow to his wondering expression.

"I think you said it better than I did." He winked and ducked his head. Then just as quickly, his face sobered. "I'm not sure what to make of it all, Lonnie." His voice was so soft, she had to strain to listen. He looked up at her. "I'm just not sure."

Reaching out, Lonnie squeezed his hand, fighting the urge to lace her fingers within his as she once had. "There's nothing wrong with that. Nothing at all. I think sometimes the Lord wants us to wonder. To ask. To share our uncertainties. He wants to give us those answers. Keep thinking. Keep wondering, Gideon." She squeezed his hand again, the feel of it so rough and perfect in hers. Though she didn't want to, she released it. "Keep listening to His voice. And I will do the same."

Toby's head snapped up. Had he fallen asleep? A glance to each side of the road, and he was unsure of his surroundings. He peered up at the moon, satisfied that it was in the right spot. At least he hadn't veered off track.

Straightening, he wiped the weariness from his eyes, wishing his lodgings were just around the bend, all the while knowing he had another hour or two to go. He hoped the family wouldn't mind his late arrival.

At a sound, he glanced over his shoulder but saw nothing other than darkness. He wrapped his hand around cold steel when the sound started again. Footsteps on the bracken. He turned Gael slightly and glanced around. Yet in an instant, her head veered back, and she let out a frightened whinny. Toby gripped the reins when she sidestepped. The black outline of a man stood in the path.

As if floodgates had been opened, blood raced through Toby's veins. For one heartbeat, he considered ramming his boots into the horse's side and blowing past the man, but when moonlight glinted off the barrel of a rifle, Toby steadied his mount. "Easy."

"Stop right there," the man said, his voice muffled. As he spoke, three more emerged from the woods—each man's head covered in a burlap sack with slits for eyes and a mouth.

Mouth dry, Toby pulled his fingers away from the shotgun. He lifted his hands. He and Reverend Gardner had told very few people about his departure. Few folk would have known when he was transporting the money. Unease settled in the pit of Toby's stomach.

Gritty words growled from behind the burlap. "Get down from your horse."

"You don't want to do this," Toby said, surprised by the steadiness of his own voice.

"You don't know what we want."

The men circled closer.

Pick up the gun. He could do it. And then what? Take as many lives as he could? And they would take his. He'd stand before his Maker, flanked by the men he killed, and God would send them on their way. *Depart from Me. I never knew you.*

The man lifted his rifle—aiming.

Toby stared at the faceless man, knowing it was not his job to deal out death. "You don't want to do this."

One of the men flicked his head, and before Toby could react, a pair of men yanked him off his mount. Gael kicked her hind legs. A man tried to grip her reins, but she bolted. Her hooves thundered away into silence. Angry hands shoved Toby to his knees. Wet cold seeped through the knees of his pants.

"Empty his pockets," ordered a muffled voice.

"I have nothing." Toby blinked into the burlap face. Colorless eyes glinted through the slits.

"We'll see about that."

Hands tore at his pockets, and Toby gritted his teeth, knowing the money would be discovered. His pants pockets were turned inside out. Grimy fingers yanked at the folds of his coat.

"I have nothing!" He struck the nearest hand, smacking it away. He scrambled to his feet and stumbled back.

"Get 'im!"

His gun was in the path, near enough to grab. Toby fumbled the end of the barrel and turned, smacking the man behind him in the head. The man fell back, and ignoring the trigger, Toby gripped the gun with both hands and drove it into the nearest gut. The faceless man doubled over with a groan of agony. Toby kicked him.

A fist struck the side of his head, and Toby fell to his knees as a sharp pain clawed its way through his temple. He blinked. His vision blurred. Greedy fingers tore at his coat. Toby felt the money pouch slide from its hiding place. *Get up.* He shook his head, but the world tilted on its side. *The money.* Blinking furiously, Toby rose to his feet. He lunged toward the nearest man and saw the pouch in his hand only a moment before ramming his own shoulder into the thick chest. Air hissed from the man's lungs, and Toby didn't stop until he had slammed him against a tree. Cold chills ate through Toby's nerves as his head pulsed with pain.

"Somebody get 'im. Stop 'im!"

Toby's shoulders burned as his arms were forced behind his back. He stared at the burlap-covered face before him. A pair of nameless eyes behind the black slits.

"Don't do this," he struggled to say.

"Enough with this," a muffled voice said. "What kind of preacher puts up a fight? I don't want him on our trail."

Toby heard the ring of steel being unsheathed and gritted his teeth as the burn of a blade pierced his side. He cried out. The blade was yanked free. He fell forward, catching himself with his hands. His eyes watered. Arms shook. Head still thrumming, his vision went black.

The leader spoke. Fainter this time as if from a great distance. "Quick. Get him off the road."

The words fogged in Toby's mind. The world darkened.

He gasped for breath, fire in his flesh. Hands gripped his arms, pulled them over his head, and dragged him into blackness.

Forty-One

Arm draped over his face, Gideon let the dreams wash over him. Out of him. He saw his family. Every piece of them so beautiful, he flexed his hands as if to grip them tighter. A sweetness worth hanging on to. Would that he simply trust God in this unseen plan.

Then all that could be began to fade.

He needed to wake up. Get to the fields. But he didn't want to let this go. The images faded and he sat up, slowly, groggy. Shaking the clouds from his mind, he shoved his blankets off and pushed himself to a stand. The morning was going to be a cold one. He stuffed his knit cap over his hair, tugging it low. He grabbed his jacket, then threw it on and pulled on his boots. A quick yank of the laces, and he strode out into the early dawn. The sun was yet to rise, but a gray glow on the horizon beckoned him forward. Perhaps he'd get a bit done before breakfast. Shivering, he longed for a hot cup of coffee by the fire.

Hands stuffed in his pockets, he strode toward his fields. Then froze. Gael stood in the center of the field. No more than a dark outline in the budding dawn. She dipped her head toward the ground, then lifted it. Circled in dim haze, Gideon strode closer. Black-walnut eyes blinked at him. Her reins hung loose. Fully saddled. Heart threaded with alarm,

Gideon slowed his steps so as not to frighten her. She lifted a hoof, placing it back, uncertain.

"Easy, girl." After a few more feet, he crouched, catching the end of the reins. Gael's breath blew white before her face. She shook her mane, and Gideon slid his hand up her neck, comforting. It took only a few breaths for him to take in the saddle and bags. A lift of the flap and he saw they were filled. He quick-glanced around for any signs of her master. Kneeling, Gideon saw a gash low on her leg, just above the fetlock. It wasn't deep, but it would need some tending as soon as he could. "Come on, girl." He needed to get her in the barn to keep her from using the leg, but for the moment he led her toward the house, where he tied her up at the porch. As quickly and quietly as he could, he went inside and rapped his knuckles on Jebediah's door. The gray-haired man appeared a few moments later.

"It's Toby. Gael's here. Saddled and everything. No rider."

Eyes widening, Jebediah nodded. "I'll get dressed. Be there in two minutes." He shut the door.

Gideon turned at the sound of Lonnie's door opening. At the sight of her nightgown, he dropped his eyes.

"What's happening?" she asked.

"I'm not sure. But something's not quite right."

"It's Toby?"

Gaze still down, Gideon nodded. "Gael's here but no rider."

She drew in a shaky breath, and he was glad he couldn't see her face. He didn't want to know the whispers of her heart. Not when it came to the Scotsman. "I'm sure it's fine, Lonnie." He took a step back, finally forcing his eyes to meet hers. "I'm sure everything's fine."

All that was good and lovely flooded her eyes.

Torn, Gideon stepped away.

A feather-light mist fell, and the air nipped through his coat as Gideon stomped forward. In the rising dawn, he saw Toby's shanty in the distance. Jebediah walked at his side, gun in hand. Nearing the tiny house, Gideon slowed. The windows were dark. His boots beat against the steps, and he peeked in the window. Nothing. He banged on the door, unsure of what he expected. The reverend sleeping while Gael trotted over the country-side, fully saddled? Or worse. The door shook under his fist when he banged again. Jebediah strode around the small building, returning with a puzzled expression.

"There." Jebediah pointed to where Gael's tracks had pocked the trail toward Richland Knob. "He said he was going yesterday. Had something to deliver."

Gideon glanced around, unease filling him. He pounded again.

If Toby were home, he'd answer. That much Gideon knew. Lunging off the steps, he knelt beside the trail and fingered a deep hoofprint. Very fresh. Only a few things separated a man from his horse. "Something's not right."

Jebediah crouched beside him. "No. It's not."

Straightening, Gideon stared up the path. The mist continued to fall. He let out a heavy breath in a white cloud. "Let's follow."

Forty-Two

J ebediah panted at his side as they scaled another hill. The path dropped
and dipped out of sight as if chasing the sun. The light hit Gideon's
face. "How you doin'?" he asked Jebediah.

"Just fine." But worry threaded Jebediah's gray eyes.

That made two of them. Gideon could hear himself. Breathing like
an ox. Rifle in hand, he gulped, trying to steady his heart. Trying to shove
off all the possibilities that struck him. Not liking what they did to his
mind, his conscience. One after the other. "Did Toby tell you what he had
on him? what he had to deliver?" he asked, trying to change the course of
his thinking.

"No." Jebediah shook his head.

"Good." That meant he'd kept it to himself. Wise man.

Jebediah's feet stilled, and he tilted his head to the side. His eyebrows
tugged together.

"What is that?" Gideon's boots slammed to a halt. The ground was a
mess. The road they had been following had been pristine, save Gael's
hoofprints in the soft soil. But it all stopped here in a tumult of mud,
stirred into patches of old snow that lined the shaded areas. Jebediah knelt,
Gideon close at his side.

Jebediah brushed against a pink patch of snow, then another. "That's blood." The older man's voice was throaty.

Gideon glanced around. The woods swallowed up both sides of the road. Boot prints disappeared through the trees to the left. And to the right. It made no sense.

"You go that way." Gideon tossed his head to where the woods looked flat and motioned himself toward the steeper side. "I'll go this way."

Gideon stepped into the shadows of the trees and stood as quietly as he could manage. He flexed his hand around his rifle. He listened until he couldn't hear Jebediah anymore. Silence. Even so, he kept to the shadows as he continued on, pausing every so often to listen for telltale signs of other life. A creek roared in the distance, not far off. He walked a minute more, keeping an eye on the signs around him. A broken tree branch, the wood still green and fragrant as if it had just snapped. The prints in the soft soil made by more than one man. Then the forest yawned, pulling him into a clearing that dipped to the rushing creek. His boots scuffled to a halt, and Gideon froze.

A crushed hat. Lifting it, Gideon popped the center out and turned it in his hands. The reverend's hat. The unsettled feeling that had been chasing him suddenly caught up in a rush of heat. Gideon's heart thundered.

He turned in a quick circle. Gloves cupped to the sides of his mouth, he called Toby's name, then it struck him that he might not be alone. He ducked beneath bramble, sharp branches snagging at his coat like angry fingers. He fell to his knees and crawled free. Sitting back, he spotted the water. The angry froth rose and fell over rocks, pulling whatever landed on its surface into a frigid grave. Gideon stood slowly. His eyes searched every shadow for danger. For life.

Gideon squinted. A huddled form lay at the water's edge. He tried to make out what he was seeing and realized the white foam rushed around the legs of a man.

Gideon ran down the slope. His boots skidded to a stop where the man lay, and he tugged on his limp shoulder, turning him over. But he already knew.

Toby. The reverend's face was ashen. Using both hands, Gideon gripped his head and shook it.

"Toby!"

He pressed his ear to the Scotsman's chest and held his breath. The water was too loud. Biting back a curse, he quickly shook his head and pressed his ear to Toby's chest again. There. The faint beat of a heart. Gideon gripped Toby's thick wrists and pulled with all his might. Toby's body inched up the bank. With a grunt, Gideon pulled again.

Light pierced through distant trees, nearly blinding him. With one final heave, he pulled the reverend out of the water. The creek roared in his ears. Kneeling, Gideon searched for a wound, yanking Toby's soaked coat free. His fingers fumbled the man's abdomen, then his side, finally finding the gash. Gideon pulled back his bloody hand. Toby was dying.

Toby. Was dying.

The only other man Lonnie loved—was dying. Gideon's hands shook harder. Then his whole body. The land lightened. Warming as the sun cleared the treetops. But half-soaked, his teeth chattered. Lowering his head to Toby's chest, he heard a heart fighting. Blood stained the ground, turning it darker. Gideon's pulse pounded away the seconds. A ticking clock.

His blood-stained hands hung limp at his sides.

Everything he'd hated about Toby came rushing back to him. The reverend's love for Lonnie and that he was a better man. Their dance. Her smile. Gideon's fists fighting for what he could never win. Regret.

Quips and apple trees and Jacob and Addie and sun. Countless hours. Wise words and handshakes.

His friend.

"No," Gideon said softly. And with that word, everything he knew to be true and good flooded his mind. He cringed. Felt his face twist in agony. "No!" Gideon growled.

He yanked at a shred of fabric on Toby's shirt and ripped it free. He crammed it into a bundle and stuffed it against the gash, using all his strength to keep the life from pooling out of the man, even as he lifted a prayer for a miracle. "Jebediah!" he shouted.

Lonnie loved this man.

"Oh, God," Gideon groaned. "Forgive me." He pressed harder, knowing he had to make up for lost time. *Forgive me.*

He held the cloth to the wound with one hand and ripped more fabric with his other, using his teeth to tear the cloth strip free. He wrapped it around the reverend's ribs, rolled the man to his side and slid the strip beneath his back. Gideon yanked the makeshift bandage tight, knowing it would cost Toby's life if he didn't. He knotted the fabric, pulling it as hard as he could. A slow groan came from the man's throat. When the bandage was secure, Gideon rose to his knees. "Jebediah!" he called again.

Doubt struck him. His own weakness assaulted him.

Gritting his teeth, Gideon crouched beside Toby and, with the cry of a madman, heaved the reverend onto his shoulder. He struggled to stand, tired legs threatening to buckle. Clenching his jaw, he took one step forward. Then another. And another. Light warmed the air, bringing with it the promise of hope. Gideon carried Toby—branches crashing against them—as far as he could. But the Scotsman was bigger than he was. Gideon walked on, his heart pulsing from the exertion, then in despair, he lowered Toby back to the ground. Gideon stumbled beside him. Exhausted. Toby groaned.

Yanking off his own coat, Gideon spread it over Toby's chest. He shouted for Jebediah. Finally he heard the man coming. Gideon had carried the reverend for less than half a mile, but his strength was gone. Blood seeped through the bandage, and he pressed his hand against it as hard as he could, veins bulging in his arms.

The sun's rays hit Gideon's shoulders, warming him through the thin fabric of his shirt. His hands were turning numb, cuffs stained in the reverend's blood. Still he held them to the wound with everything he had. *Forgive me.* He hung his head, knowing there was nothing more he could do. He was too weak. He was just a man.

And he wasn't even a good man. A good man wouldn't have hesitated.

Pressing his eyes closed, Gideon did the only thing he could think of. He prayed. Something he knew he wasn't very good at.

He hoped God would look past that. He knew the God who brought Jacob safely into this world, the One who made the whole earth, didn't fit into a box. No matter how many times he had tried to put Him there. *Forgive me.* The one plea pounded through him.

Jebediah broke through the bracken, starting in the opposite direction.

"Here!" Gideon shouted.

Turning, Jebediah hurried toward them.

"Get help!"

Glancing around for the briefest of moments, Jebediah seemed to decide on a direction and strode off as quickly as Gideon had ever seen him move.

Toby groaned and turned his head to the side. His eyes opened, glazed. He blinked into the light as if seeing nothing before his eyes slid closed. His lips moved, forming a single name. "Lonnie."

Gideon swallowed. "She's safe."

Toby's chest heaved as he struggled for a breath. "Lonnie."

"Yes, Lonnie." Gideon nodded, feeling hot tears sting the backs of his eyes. He grimaced but bit back the burn of jealousy. That jealousy—that man he once was—could be no more. Not for one more day. As the minutes passed, Gideon held Toby's wound with all his strength. How he wished he could do more. The reverend deserved more. Yet Gideon was all he had.

At the sound of a harness jingling, Gideon's head shot up. "Here!" he shouted, hoping Jebediah had found someone. The sound came from a distance, and he called again, louder this time. He held his breath and listened as the driver called back. Within moments, the creaking of wood crested over the hillside and a pair of gray horses pulled a wagon into sight.

"Whoa!" With a tug on the reins, the wagon slowed to a halt. The driver jumped down, followed by Jebediah.

Gideon rose and gripped Toby's shoulder. He glanced up at the driver. "Can you get us out of here?"

The man moved to Toby's other side. "Where to?" He slid his hands beneath the reverend's back.

"My farm's a few miles up the road," Jebediah said, crouching.

They heaved Toby into the back of the wagon, startling a pair of collies. Gideon climbed in next, followed by Jebediah. The driver ran around and climbed onto the seat. The wagon jolted forward, and Gideon gripped the side. Then, shifting over, he applied pressure to the wound. Knowing that Toby would be dead in minutes if he were left to bleed, Gideon pressed with all his might.

Forty-Three

I s he alive?" The driver turned and peered down over his shoulder. His mouth drew into a straight line. Facing back to the road, he flicked the reins harder.

The wagon jostled, throwing Gideon's hands deeper against the wound. Toby let out a low groan, the veins in his neck bulging.

Gideon pulled back slightly, knowing the reverend was in the worst kind of pain. "Barely." Gideon's hands, sticky with blood, had lost all feeling, and he used his shoulder to wipe a bead of sweat from his temple. The two collies lay at Toby's side. One dog rested its head on its paws. The other had his snout nuzzled against Toby's arm.

Jebediah held his gun close, steely eyes searching the woods. "We should be there in a few minutes," he called to the driver.

Nodding, Gideon glanced at the balding man on the seat. "Thank you for your help. He'd be a dead man if you hadn't come along."

The driver shook his head. "He'd be a dead man if you two weren't keeping him alive." He slapped the reins. "I'll drop you off, then fetch the doctor."

"Farm's comin' up!" Jebediah called. The horses sped forward as fast as the muddy road allowed.

Gideon straightened. He peered at the road ahead, knowing he'd see the house soon, and even before the wagon stilled in the yard, he shouted for Lonnie and Elsie. As if the sheer urgency in his voice had pulled her forward, the screen door flung open, and Lonnie darted into the yard, her unbound hair spiraling behind her. She reached the wagon and her eyes widened.

Gideon helped her clamber into the bed.

"Toby!" She crawled to his side. Her hands gripped his shoulders, and she shook him, her thin arms barely moving the large man.

"He's alive," Gideon hurried to say. He lifted his palm, revealing the bloody gash in Toby's side. Lonnie's hand flew to her mouth.

She bent over and pressed her face to Toby's neck, her arms still wrapped around him. Hair scattered across the reverend's chest, her shoulders shook with sobs.

She called his name countless times.

Gritting his teeth, Gideon kept his hands pressed to the wound. It was pointless to try to comfort her. He simply sat there. Doing everything in his power to keep the man she held alive. It was the only thing he could do. And for the first time in a long time, he truly loved her enough to do just that.

Flames licked the back of his throat, and he glanced away, unable to witness the anguish in her face. Then, realizing this was his fate, he turned back. He had to be brave. It was time to grow up and face the truth. Even if he had to watch it unfold before him.

Lonnie pressed her lips to Toby's forehead and closed her eyes. A tear fell.

No matter how much it hurt.

Elsie stepped onto the back porch and, after filling the washbasin with hot water, stood beside Gideon without speaking.

He plunged his hands into the steaming water. As he scrubbed, it tinted red.

"How is he?" he asked without looking up.

"Doc's with him. I don't know what's gonna happen." Elsie folded her arms in front of her. "He's in a bad way."

Gideon nearly asked her if a few moments—the time it takes a man to hesitate—would have made a difference. "Is Lonnie with him?"

Elsie didn't answer.

Gideon scrubbed at the blood on his forearms until his skin stung. Water sloshed over the side of the basin as he plunged his hands back in, soaking his boots. "Where is he?"

"In Lonnie's room. I'll fetch you a clean shirt and anything else you'll need. I just set more water to boil for the doc, but I wanted to come check on you a moment."

Looking down, Gideon saw for the first time the stain of Toby's blood over his right shoulder. "Thanks."

Pressing her fingertips to her mouth, Elsie looked up at him. Her eyes glistened with unshed tears. "I'm just so glad you were there. That you found him. If no one had been there to bring him home…"

Home.

"Gid…" A tear slid to her cheek, and she brushed it away. "The doc asked me… He's gonna want to know how…" She glanced at the porch floor. "What I'm trying to say is, he'll need to know what…"

"It wasn't me, Elsie." Gideon stared at his boots and felt his eyebrows tug together. He couldn't blame the woman for needing the truth. "Believe me." He shook his head. "It wasn't me," he said again darkly.

A cool hand touched his arm. "I know, dear." Elsie patted the cuff of his shirt, clearly not caring that blood tainted it. "I never would have thought it for a moment." Her eyes tightened, driving home the sincerity of her words. "But most folks around here know what's been goin' on. The doc included."

Gideon glanced up and, seeing the honesty in her face, knew she truly believed him.

"He just needs to know *what* happened." She tugged a towel from the crook of her arm and handed it to him.

"I don't know." After drying his hands, Gideon draped the towel beside the basin and started on the top button of his shirt.

Elsie's forehead crinkled.

"I just found him that way. Lying at the edge of the creek. I honestly thought he was dead at first."

She took his shirt, and Gideon tugged his suspenders up over his thermal undershirt. It was just as stained, but there wasn't much he could do about it in this moment.

Squeezing his hand, her eyes were wide. "But he's not."

"Not yet." Few men would survive losing that much blood.

He didn't mean to be pessimistic. But he'd seen the Scotsman. Felt the weight of his body as he carried him. There had hardly been any life left in the man. Gideon yanked the basin from the wash table and tossed the water into the yard.

Elsie's face saddened. "No. But we will hope and pray for the best."

Drying his thumb on his pants, Gideon nodded. He could still hear Lonnie's sobs as she held the reverend. Pray, he would. But he'd lost his hope.

Forty-Four

Taking each stair as soundlessly as he could, Gideon turned the corner to the bedroom and stood just outside. With her head pressed to the back of the rocker, Lonnie's eyes were fixed on Toby's face. A sleeping Jacob nestled in the folds of her apron, his round chin pressed against his little sweater. The sun streaming through the window glinted on the plaits of Lonnie's braid. Gold. Honey.

Using his knuckles, Gideon rapped softly on the doorjamb and stepped into the room.

Lonnie's mouth parted.

With quiet movements, Gideon held a finger to his lips, then moved a chair to the other side of the bed and sat facing her. He glanced at Toby. The man's face told a story of pain. Gideon gritted his teeth. Feeling Lonnie's eyes on him, the back of Gideon's throat burned. He'd tried to divide his heart before—tried to separate Lonnie from all that was in and through him. Could he do it this time? Truly do it? *God, I don't know the answer.* Might as well start off with honesty.

It was beyond him how to take the next steps alone if that was what was required of him. He didn't know how to find that kind of strength, but he knew where it lived. And it was in that moment that everything he knew he needed flooded him. Would God be enough? For him? Gideon folded his hands, and his knees pressed into his forearms.

He stared down at Toby. The man's lips were still swollen and cracked, and a bruise had formed on his right cheekbone. But his chest slowly rose and fell. It was then that Gideon realized Toby was going to live.

He blinked as the truth set in. Finally, he spoke. "He said your name."

"What?"

He lifted his gaze to a pair of brown eyes that he knew better than his own two hands. "Toby. When I found him. It was the only thing he said." His throat closed around the words.

"Oh." She looked at Toby and her face softened.

The ache in Gideon's heart pressed against his chest as if to break it in two.

Lonnie fingered Jacob's small hand. Her lashes blinked furiously. "I just don't know why this happened. Who would do this to him?"

Shifting his feet, Gideon stared at the battered face and wondered the answer himself. "He'll probably be able to tell you everything when he wakes."

Her chin trembled. "You think he's going to be all right?"

Gideon nodded once. "He will." The ache pressed harder.

"How do you know?"

The urgency in her voice pulled his eyes back to hers. Her face was so innocent, so desperately hopeful, that Gideon couldn't look away. From the corner of his eye, he saw Toby's chest slowly rise and fall. Toby would live. A man did not let go of life easily when there was a woman like Lonnie waiting for him. The man would fight with everything he had. Gideon was certain of it. Toby's eyelids fluttered but did not open.

"He'll live." Gideon looked at Lonnie, but it was as if she hadn't heard him.

She simply stared at the man on the bed. Gideon watched her, not caring if she caught him. Her face was a blank slate. He would have given every dime to his name if it would buy him her thoughts. But she simply watched Toby sleep. Staring into the face of the man who could give her a happy life. A peaceful life. And Gideon finally knew he couldn't blame Toby if he fought for that. If Toby loved Lonnie half as much as he did, then Toby would find a way to marry her.

He would live. Toby was strong. He would fight.

Gideon stood and, sliding the chair back into place, stepped from the room. Toby needed his rest and so did Lonnie.

He strode down the stairs and stopped at the sight of Jebediah sitting at the bottom.

Jebediah spoke first. "He's a tough one. Toby."

"That he is."

"And what about you, Gideon?" the man asked soberly.

Exhausted, Gideon sank down on the steps beside him.

"What about you?" Jebediah whispered again. "Always trying to solve the world's problems."

Fingers pressed together, Gideon stared at the wood between their boots.

"I see those wheels of yours spinning. Ever since you came home from the courthouse."

Unable to lift his eyes from a knot in the oak, Gideon nodded slowly. "I don't know what to do, Jeb." When the man waited for him to say more, Gideon searched for the words. "I forced myself into her life the first time. I don't want to make that same mistake again." He glanced at his friend. "What if—all this time—I've been doing just that? In trying to get her back...without stopping to think that maybe I shouldn't. Maybe she could have a better life"—he felt Jebediah's gaze on him—"with someone else."

A tug on his beard, and Jebediah lifted his shoulders and let them fall as if under the weight of his thoughts. "A man can change, Gideon. I see it in you each and every day. You're not the man I met on the hillside. The one I wanted to fill full of buckshot."

Gideon interlocked his fingers, knowing the air was full of wisdom whenever he was near Jebediah.

"But there's a thing or two you haven't figured out yet about life. You can't solve all of Lonnie's problems. I know you want to. And I don't blame you for trying. But there's gonna come a time when you're just gonna have to give her up to the Lord."

Sliding his fingers in his hair, Gideon lowered his head. His voice muffled against his forearm. "How do I do that?"

"You realize that Toby can't solve her problems either. No one can. Granted, that ain't meant to diminish the role we can play in one another's lives, what we're called to do." His expression turned soft. "Sort of like Elsie 'n' me bringing home a scraggly, useless mountain man. And his sweet wife. I sure as shootin' didn't want you steppin' one rotten foot inside my house that day I found you. But God had a different plan. You listen to *His* will…and nothing else."

"How do I know what that is?" The words slipped out so quiet, he hoped Jebediah heard.

"You start by getting to know Him."

Sleep wasn't his to be had. Gideon paced the floor. The moon had made its arc in the sky and would soon fish the sun from sleepy waters. Whether his head hit the pillow or not. Slowly, Gideon ran his hands together and, with the barn door open, looked toward the house. Every window was black. A color he felt in and through him.

He'd never felt so empty in his life. Never had he felt so alone.

Knowing every inch of the barn by memory, Gideon closed his eyes, and even as hay crackled beneath his boots, his pacing slowed to a halt. He felt a cold breeze in his face and knew he stood in the doorway. Glancing up at the star-studded sky, he stepped forward, letting the cold air swallow him up. He shivered, but he didn't care.

Earlier, as he stood in the parlor, he'd watched Lonnie slowly move about. He needn't hear her prayers to know what she longed for. He'd seen it in her face as she dragged two quilts from the cupboard beneath the stairs and began dressing the makeshift bed Elsie had helped her create on the parlor floor. It wasn't long after she'd folded back the tattered quilts that she had called for Addie and Jacob to lie down. A soft smile was on Lonnie's lips, and Gideon knew his words had filled her with hope. Or perhaps it had nothing to do with him.

Perhaps? Gideon shook his head. No, he was certain. Lonnie drew her faith from another place. The same place Jebediah and Elsie did.

One Gideon understood little about.

He wanted that kind of faith. The kind of faith that assured him that no matter what happened in life, he would always have peace. The doorjamb was rough beneath his palm as he leaned against it. He knew where peace like that could be found. He'd always been aware. But he had no idea how to begin. He didn't even know what to say. "How do I know?" he whispered.

Did he even deserve to ask?

Gideon tugged the door closed, blocking out the cold. He didn't deserve forgiveness. He'd stolen Lonnie when she hadn't been his to steal. Then he betrayed her just weeks after he'd betrayed Cassie. He'd orchestrated every desire of his heart into being without ever weighing the consequences. He'd stomped on people's feelings. Their hopes. Their dreams.

And for what?

His own happiness. That was the only thing he'd ever cared about. A lump rose in his throat, and feeling his walls crumbling, Gideon no longer cared to fight it back. He didn't want this burden anymore. He didn't want this guilt. Not because he deserved happiness. But because he wanted peace. The peace others had. The peace he'd always seen but never grasped.

The peace he knew came free—if he were to just ask.

He wanted it. With his whole heart, he wanted it.

"How do I know?" he whispered again, his voice strained to his own ears.

Hands trembling, he pressed them to his sides. Every sin he'd ever committed rose like a black disease inside him—taunting—punishing. Overwhelmed, Gideon turned. A heat flushed through him. He wanted to be free of this. To be free of himself.

"How do I know?" he shouted. Snatching up a tin can, he hurled it at the wall. It clanged to the ground, where it spun out of sight.

Leaning against the workbench, he pushed his palms against the coarse boards. His breath came in quick gasps. Eyes wide, he felt them focus for the first time in his life. *God, how do I know?*

A voice spoke to his heart. *I'm enough.*

Gideon nodded, knowing it to be true. But he'd never let himself feel it before.

He'd always been chasing his happiness. Always been consumed with his own pride. His own fate. And he'd never been satisfied.

But God had never made a single choice for him. Gideon had always been allowed to choose.

Gideon hung his head. He'd made every decision in his life. Made every mistake. He was a man and he'd chosen freely. Never once had he looked to himself. Instead, he'd always blamed the world. Blamed fate.

Blamed God.

I'm sorry. Crouching, Gideon pressed his forehead to his arm. *I'm so sorry. Please forgive me.* Covering his face with his hands, he felt his shoulders shake with sobs, and he didn't fight them back. He didn't even try. He was too tired of trying. Too weary of pretending to be strong. There was nothing strong about him. Not on his own.

And he heard it. In the still small place of his heart, he heard the most beautiful words in the strongest of voices.

You're forgiven. It's forgotten.

He drew in a deep breath and felt a cleansing wash through him. A cleansing he didn't deserve, but he felt it all the same. So pure and so right. For the first time in his life, he felt peace. The kind he knew would never come until he'd asked for forgiveness. Really asked. Breathing came easier, and Gideon blinked into the dim light of the barn. The day was soon to dawn.

And he didn't feel like the same man. He sank onto his bedroll, the scent of fresh straw inviting him to lie down. Even so, he couldn't sleep.

Gideon stared up at the thick boards of the roof. This peace didn't win him Lonnie, but he was done fighting. He was done blaming. And he knew, without a shadow of a doubt, that she would be happy. Because she always had—and always would—follow God's will. Gideon pressed his eyes closed and felt a surge of comfort that he would no longer bear this burden alone.

No longer bear for her what wasn't his to bear.

For the first time in his life, he didn't feel alone. If it took him the rest of his days, he would learn how to hang on to that.

He would let her go. And if it was God's will…she would come find him.

Forty-Five

Strolling into the kitchen, Lonnie set an armful of kindling on top of the woodbox. Addie and Jacob giggled in the parlor, and she peered in just as Addie's head popped up.

"Where did Elsie go?" Lonnie asked.

"She went upstairs. She said she would be right back."

"What are you two doing?" Lonnie stepped closer.

"It's a surprise!" Addie's cheeks flushed pink, and she thrust something behind her back.

Lonnie arched an eyebrow. "A surprise? For who?"

"Reverend McKee," Addie whispered.

"Oh." Lonnie straightened. She studied her sister. "It might be a while until he—"

"No. He's awake." Addie rose onto her knees. "Elsie heard him a few minutes ago, and she ran up there."

"Really?" Lonnie peered up at the ceiling.

Addie's curls bobbed. "Yep. I heard Elsie talking to him just a moment ago. That's when I decided to make him a surprise. But you can't see what it is."

Lonnie stepped toward the stairs. With one hand on the banister, she listened. Elsie's soft murmurs floated down. Then Toby's voice, so faint Lonnie scarcely heard it. She pressed a hand to her heart. The back door closed, and boots stomped through the kitchen. Lonnie turned. Gideon rounded the corner. He seemed to take a moment to read her expression, and Lonnie wondered what he saw there.

"What's the matter?" He stepped closer.

"Toby."

Gideon's eyes lifted. He seemed to hold his breath for several moments. He moved closer and rested a hand on the railing. He spoke without looking at her. "So the old boy woke up, huh?" He smiled. "Well, that's good news." One side of his mouth genuinely quirked up. He studied her a moment. "Everything all right?"

Oh. She was staring.

He chuckled.

Addie giggled from the other side of the room. Slowly, Lonnie nodded, her gaze still pinned to his.

Gideon glanced up the stairs. "How's he doing? Did he say what happened?"

"I haven't seen him yet."

"Oh. Well, when you do, let me know." He stepped back, knocking into a chair, and he stumbled to the side.

"I will. Gid, wait—"

He looked at her.

"Are you okay?"

He nodded, and to her surprise, his face looked relaxed. "I'm pretty good, actually." He thrust his hands in his pockets.

She squinted at him, wanting to say more, but the words weren't coming. "That's…that's good. Real good."

He chuckled. "Why are you looking at me like I'm crazy?"

"I'm just…confused."

"Confused."

She nodded, knowing full well she must look a fool. "You…you saved his life. You saved Toby's life."

Gideon shook his head. "I just happened to be in the right place at the right time. He would have done the same for me."

"Thank you, Gideon."

He blinked slowly. "You're welcome." His eyes were fiercely green. "I'm sorry it took me so long." Glancing away a moment, he rubbed a hand up his arm. "What I did, Lonnie…it wasn't heroic." When she started to speak, he held up a hand. "Let me get this out."

Addie crawled to the sewing basket and pulled it back to the blanket where she and Jacob huddled together.

"I love you," Gideon finally said. "But I don't want you to suffer anymore." His thumb grazed her chin, turning her to face him. "I want you to be happy. If it's Toby…"

She wanted to turn her cheek into the cradle of his hand.

"If it's Toby"—he swallowed visibly—"allow yourself to have peace."

Tears flooded her eyes. He'd done everything he could to return to her, and here he was, uncertain that she would choose him. The words he needed to hear, the words that flooded her heart, bubbled up inside her.

"Promise me that, all right?"

"Gideon."

The door opened upstairs. He kissed her forehead. Elsie carried a tray down the stairs, and Addie hopped up.

"Can we visit Toby now?" the little girl asked.

"For a few minutes," Elsie said.

"Come on, Jacob!" Addie said, reaching for his hand.

Lonnie forced her eyes away from Gideon's. "Wait, Addie. Let me go with you. We need to be quiet." She looked up at Gideon apologetically.

His smile was knowing, a muted tenderness.

Her heart filled with an emotion she couldn't name at the sight of his expression. One of humbleness. One of peace.

Lonnie sat in the chair beside Toby and watched as two puppets danced at the edge of the footboard. A sock goose chased a sock chicken, and Toby's mouth lifted in a strained smile.

She leaned toward his ear. "Is this too much for you?" she whispered.

His fingertips grazed hers on the quilt, and he offered a slight shake of his head. Earlier that afternoon, Lonnie had ushered Addie in for a few brief moments, then they'd left Toby to sleep for several more hours. When he'd woken, he'd taken a few sips of broth at Elsie's urging and, at the sight of Addie poking her head around the door, had graciously welcomed her in.

Lonnie drew in a slow breath. "She practiced this all morning," she whispered and felt Toby's gaze flick to her face.

"She's…doing a good job." His voice was strained. Hand still resting beside hers, he moved it back into his lap.

Brown curls popped up from their hiding place, and Addie scowled at them. "You are not supposed to be talking during the performance."

Lonnie fell silent but had a hard time focusing on the puppet show, and when Toby cleared his throat, she knew she wasn't the only one.

The goose and the chicken embraced, and Toby let out a wheezy chuckle. Alarmed, Lonnie touched his arm, but after a subtle shake of his

head, she leaned back in her chair. Addie's puppets jigged through an en-
core, and Lonnie found herself laughing when they sashayed off into an
imaginary sunset.

Lonnie clapped her hands for both of them. Addie rose and, with her
puppets dangling at her sides, performed a bow. She scampered to the
corner of the room, where she tugged off the duck and goose, setting them
on the windowsill before making several costume changes.

Leaning closer to Toby, Lonnie spoke. "I bumped into Gideon
downstairs..."

Toby licked his lips. "Was he happy"—his voice rasped and he swallowed—"to learn that I didn't die?"

Lonnie glanced at him but saw that he was teasing. "He...was." She
fell silent, fingering the lace edge of her apron. "Um, there's something you
should know."

With a grimace, Toby shifted his head on the pillow, facing her.

"Gid... He, uh..." Her finger traced the floral pattern. Her eyes
moved to Toby's face. "He brought you back."

"What do you mean?"

His voice was so strained, she feared this was too much for him. "You
were bleeding. I think he carried you a ways, but then a wagon... I mean
a farmer stopped and..."

"Gideon. Carried me?" The words slipped out airy, weak.

"Toby, he's the one who found you. He found you. And he brought
you back."

Realization dawned in Toby's eyes. His head sank deeper into the
pillow.

Lonnie turned to her sister. "Addie, will you excuse us for just a
moment?"

Addie's face fell, but she nodded and moved toward the door.

"I'll call you back in a few minutes, and you can say a good-night for the evening."

Addie vanished down the hall.

Lonnie turned back to Toby. "Do you remember what happened?"

His chest lifted as he sighed. He stared at the far wall, blinking slowly, and Lonnie wondered what pain passed inside his mind.

"You don't have to tell me if you don't want to."

"No." He grimaced when he shifted his shoulders. "It's fine." Without looking at her, he told her what he remembered, his words slow in coming, patchy. In her mind she saw the faceless men. Heard their voices. And although she saw the bruises and cuts on his face, the gash on the side of his forehead, he mentioned nothing of pain.

She could only wonder what memories he was sparing her.

"I'm so sorry." She touched the edge of the bed.

"Don't be." His Adam's apple bobbed. "I've lived to tell the tale." He let out a weak chuckle and, with a wince, moved his hand toward his side. His voice was nearly inaudible. "That was good of him." His eyes shifted to the window, hand still pressed to the bandage that hid beneath his shirt.

Lonnie knew he was speaking of Gideon. "I think it's what any man would do."

Toby glanced at her, and she could tell that he disagreed. "Under the circumstances, Lonnie, it's what few men would do."

Forty-Six

Wax dripped from the ivory candle in the center of the table, puddling around the base of the copper holder. An icy rain pattered against the window, but the fire roaring in the stove kept the kitchen snug.

"Thank you, Elsie." Gideon held his tin mug steady as she filled it with dark brew. He smeared butter on his biscuit, then tore off a piece and handed it to his son. Candlelight danced on curls the color of gingerbread, and Gideon couldn't resist tousling the little boy's hair, the strands silk between his fingers.

Elsie ladled stew into each bowl, then moved her heavy dutch oven back to the stove, where it clanged into place. Lonnie asked for the milk. Gideon grabbed the jug and gently plucked the tin cup from her hand.

"Can he hold this on his own?" he asked as he splashed milk into the small cup.

"Not really. But he will want to anyway." Her mouth lifted in a half smile.

"Sounds like he's taking after someone."

Her eyes sparkled. "I'd say you're right."

Gideon gave the cup to Jacob and watched as milk dribbled down

Jacob's chin and onto his shirt. His lips smacked, and lowering the cup, his smile was covered in cream.

"Well, he did fairly well." Using his napkin, Gideon wiped his son's shirt. "Was that good?"

Jacob kicked his feet and held out his empty cup, eyes bright and wide.

Lonnie laughed. Gideon watched her. His hand itched to hold hers. He all but sat on it, forcing himself to look at his plate. Slowly, Gideon shook his head to toss off the dregs of sorrow. He reached for his coffee, knowing one way or another, he'd have to accept what their future held. He straightened in his chair and sipped the bitter brew.

A sticky hand landed on his arm, and Gideon looked over at Jacob. He fingered the boy's small wrist, and staring at his son, *knew* he had to accept it. He had to.

Leaving just wasn't an option.

He would witness Jacob growing up. Even if from afar. When his throat constricted, Gideon took another sip, but it didn't wash away his ache. He stared at his plate. He had to push through this. *God, I don't even know how to begin. Show me how to do this.*

Candlelight danced across Lonnie's glass as she took a drink, and he remembered the peace he'd longed for and knew how it felt to finally be filled with it. He wanted more. Needed more. Yet he had one last thing to do. One last burden to shed.

"Has Toby eaten?" Gideon blurted. When he felt every eye turn toward him, he set his napkin on the table.

Elsie's lips moved as if to speak but no words came. She tilted her head to the side. "He wasn't hungry. I figured I would check on him after we eat and see if he's got any appetite."

Without speaking, Gideon stood and grabbed a biscuit from beneath the cloth. At the stove, he ladled steaming stew into a dish. Without bothering to grab a tray or napkin, as Elsie would have, he marched into the parlor and up the stairs, the silence in the kitchen a clear indicator that he was being watched.

Toby heard a soft knock and looked up from the Bible in his lap. Gideon stepped into the doorway, his expression a mix of uncertainty and determination. Toby motioned him forward. Grabbing a chair, Gideon set it beside the bed and shoved the bowl of stew onto the nightstand. He sat and lowered his head in his hands.

Stunned, Toby closed the Bible.

Gideon's voice came muffled as he spoke, the words strained, broken.

Toby listened to words of apology. Words he hadn't known were due. His eyebrows lifted, but he waited, letting the man share his piece, knowing full well the urgency he himself felt. The need to do the same.

Gideon fell silent. He glanced up, and his watery gaze fixed on the darkening window. "I'm so sorry," he said one last time.

Turning the black book in his hands, Toby stared down at the leather binding, worn and frayed from years of use. He was unsure how to begin. He searched for the words he needed to say, but before he could find them, Gideon continued.

Rain pelted the window.

At Gideon's revelation, awe filtered through him.

A smile lit Gideon's face, and he leaned back in his chair. "God and I have a bit more of an understanding now, I think. I thought I would tell you. I figured those kinds of things make preachers happy."

Toby couldn't help but grin. "They make us verra happy." His voice came out strained, and he stifled a cough.

Gideon had finally found what he was searching for, what Toby had been praying for. No doubt what Lonnie had been praying for. Toby leaned against the headboard, his heart and mind full of wonder. "I'm amazed, Gideon."

Crossing his arms over his chest, Gideon settled back in his seat. "So you didn't think it was possible, huh?" His tone was teasing.

Toby shook his head, the Bible still heavy in his palm. "No. I knew it was possible. I'm just… You were always…"

Gideon leaned forward, his voice urgent. Eyes alive. "It was always right there. So close yet so far. I just never knew how to take that final step."

"Have you told Lonnie? She'll be thrilled."

"Not yet. I don't know… It would just feel like words." He scratched his head.

"You're a good man, Gideon." Shifting to the side, Toby tried to push the Bible onto the nightstand. His wound burned and he grimaced. Gideon took hold of the book and slid it into place. Leaning back, Toby rubbed the scruff of his jaw. He had an apology of his own. One that went beyond anything Gideon had ever done to him. "Gid…there's, uh, something I should tell you."

"You're leaving." Gideon's eyes widened, but his mouth broke into a smile, clearly teasing.

Toby's side burned when he wheezed out a laugh, but he couldn't help it. "I *am* going home t'morrow." When the words came out strained, he winced and swallowed. "So that's a start in the right direction, I s'pose." And for an instant, he thought of Lonnie, but remembering what still needed to be said, he sobered. "Gid. The other night. On the road."

Gideon leaned onto his forearms.

Gulping, Toby searched for the words. "I listened to their voices, the men." He glanced at the open doorway, his voice lowering. "I didna tell Lonnie all of this, just parts. But…I couldn't see who they were. They were covered." He motioned the shape of the sacks out with his hands. "Their faces were hidden."

Gideon shook his head, his disgust evident. "I'm sorry—"

"Gid…" Toby lifted his hand. He deserved no apology. No pity. "I listened to their voices, wond'ring if"—he swallowed, the truth acidic in his mouth—"if you were among them."

A slow emotion dawned in Gideon's face. Finally, he leaned back.

Unable to watch the hurt he saw there, Toby stared down at his hands. "There were few people I'd told about the trip. The money. And, well…" He blew out his cheeks.

After drawing in a slow breath, Gideon spoke. "And what conclusion did you come to?" The words came out quiet.

"That you're a better man. A better friend than I deserve."

Leaning forward, Gideon shook his head slowly.

Finally, Toby cleared his throat. "I don't deserve to ask for your forgiveness—"

"It's forgotten." Gideon's eyes searched the floorboards at his feet, then he lifted his face. He shook his head again. "Toby, it's forgotten."

Forty-Seven

With Jacob on her hip, Lonnie strode forward and, after setting her son down, dumped the bucket's contents into the mucky pen. As the young hog nuzzled at the pile of potato peels and carrot tops, she looked to the wagon tracks that led into the edge of the forest where Toby had disappeared earlier that morning.

Standing by the side of the wagon, she'd watched him climb into the back, his face hard as stone—concealing pain. She had squeezed his hand, and after speaking to the driver, Toby lifted a wave to them all. The wagon lurched forward, and he clutched the side, his jaw clenching for a moment before he forced a weak smile.

She'd been doubtful of his leaving. Voicing her concern to Elsie as they watched him go. Elsie had reminded her that he would be well taken care of. That there wasn't a woman on this mountainside that wouldn't be bringing him a meal or looking in on him. Lonnie tried to rest easy in the memory of her words, as her hem brushed along young spring flowers, damp with the constant dew. The rain that had started a few days before had finally drizzled out, but a soft fog lingered. Fiddling with the scrap of flannel that held her braid together, Lonnie walked slowly across the yard,

Jacob waddling beside her. In the distance, she heard Gideon in the clearing. Lonnie reached for Jacob's hand, deciding.

"Shall we go see your papa?" she whispered in her son's ear.

Gideon did not look up as she came toward him, and it wasn't until her skirts had brushed past a dozen freshly planted trees that he saw her. He tipped his hat and rested his wrist on the end of the garden hoe.

"Your trees are budding. That's good," she said.

He tilted his head from side to side. "It is. I'll have to watch them carefully. There may be a shift in the weather yet, but they'll be all right. At least I won't have to worry about losing any apple blossoms to a cold snap. Another few years before they're ready to produce." He paused long enough to tap the hoe against a weed between them. "A few years before they get their feet under them."

"You've learned so much about all this."

"Did it sound that way?" He winked. After cutting free another weed, he rolled his shoulder. Another roll and he stretched his neck to the side.

When Jacob tugged on her apron, she picked him up, eyes still on Gideon's movement. "I bet you're gettin' a little tired of sleeping in the barn."

He tilted his head to the side again. "It grows on you after a while."

She doubted it. A hard ground. Prickly hay and the smell of animals.

Gideon rested the handle of the hoe against his chest and rolled his sleeves past his forearms. "I'm trying to focus on the positives." He poked a mound of dark earth around. "Three hot meals a day. A place that's out of the rain. Out of the snow." He bent and tossed a weed to the side. Kneeling, he pulled another free. "And I get to be near my family. My son." He pushed dirt into the hole. "And you."

Lonnie nibbled on the tip of her thumb, his words touching her.

"Those are good reasons." When Jacob squirmed, she set him down. He wobbled to the nearest tree and patted it.

"They're the only reasons I have." Standing, Gideon looked at her. "There's no other place for me. But"—he hurried to add—"I'll keep my distance, of course. If you end up deciding..." He looked toward the road, and she could tell he wanted to drop the matter.

He would stay. No matter what she decided, he would stay. She studied him in silence. His hair curled around his ears, damp from the fog. Did he not know? The decision had already been made. Lonnie stuffed her hands in the pockets of Gideon's coat and searched for the right words to begin. Jacob picked up two handfuls of dirt before sprinkling the soil onto his pants.

Gideon watched him a moment. "He's growing up so fast."

"He really is."

"I've already missed so much of his life." Gideon kicked at a clump of dirt. "I don't want to miss any more." His eyes bore into hers.

"I don't either." Her heart quickened.

"So you won't mind?" The words nearly trembled on his lips.

"Mind?"

He poked at the ground with the end of the hoe, his eyes still on her. "If I...stick around."

"Stick around?"

"Yeah. It'd mean the world to me to watch this little boy grow up." His work stilled and his face sobered. "I promise I'll deal with the consequences. I just want to make sure it's all right with you."

"All right with me?"

His mouth quirked up in a smile. "Lonnie, stop repeating everything I say. It's making me nervous." His cheeks colored. Something that rarely happened.

She clasped her hands in front of her. "I'm sorry. I'm just…confused. The thought of you leaving, that you would even consider it. Gid…I don't want you to go." She swallowed a rising lump in her throat. "This is your *home*." Her voice cracked on the last word at the doubt and torment he was surrounded by. Wishing she hadn't failed him so in expressing her heart.

His eyebrows lifted, his face losing every line of concern. "My home." She nodded.

Gideon yanked off his gloves, tossing them aside. He hesitated a moment, then reached for her hand. His fingers were warm around hers. Another hesitation, and then he sank to one knee.

Lonnie let out a soft gasp.

His damp shirt clung to his shoulders. "I love you, Lonnie Sawyer. And this is what I want. It's all I've ever wanted." His thumb circled the back of her hand. "But I want what's best for you. What's best for Jacob." Gideon glanced at their son, his face peaceful.

Moving closer, Lonnie grazed her fingertips against the side of his hair.

Gideon gulped, his nerves showing. "And if that's not me, then so be it." He shook his head. "I've spent too much time seeking my own happiness. My own satisfaction. I want what's best for you." His lips grazed the back of her hand, and green eyes lifted to her face. "I want you to be safe. I want you to be loved." He shifted forward. His grip tightened on her hand. "I would love to be the man to spend the rest of his life doing that. But if not…" He released her. "I've made so many mistakes in the past. I'm sorry. For everything."

Lonnie's chin trembled. Gideon rose.

"But most of all…I'm sorry for never being the husband you deserved. Or the father Jacob needed. Yes, I was gone. The sins of my past pulled me away from you, but when I was here, when I had you both in my arms, I tried to be enough on my own strength. And that's where I failed. Above all else, that is my biggest regret."

She blinked, trying to keep her tears at bay.

"I'm willing to fight, Lonnie. Not for your heart, because I couldn't want it any more than I do in this moment, but I'm willing to fight back the man I was and let the man you need come forward. And I can't do that without God." He pulled her head against his chest, and his scent surrounded her. Cedar. Earth. "I'm done trying."

She nodded, her hair shifting beneath his palm. Hot tears dripped onto her cheeks, and she found herself clutching his sleeve.

"Please don't say anything just now. I want you to have the time you need."

She didn't want to let go.

Then he chuckled, the heavenly sound rumbling against her ear. "One of us should probably be watching our son."

Lonnie lifted her head to see Jacob standing up to his knees in a small hole. The boy waved his arms and bounced up and down before tipping to the side, a helpless bundle of sweaters.

Releasing her, Gideon stepped toward the boy. "Do you want to be planted too?" He tossed Jacob in the air. The boy squealed, and Gideon caught him with broad hands.

Lonnie's heart was so full, she thought it would burst. Turning, Gideon glanced at her. His smile was wide, his eyes tender, and she knew. He was waiting for her. Ever so patiently. But more than that, he had found his peace. The peace that comes only from God.

"I'm going to go visit Toby later," she said.

Hoisting Jacob up on his shoulders, Gideon's eyes never left her face. "And?"

She started away.

"Where are you going?"

She turned. "You asked me not to say anything." But something must have shown in her face for his own bloomed into wonder. He smiled.

"I'll be back in a little while."

"And people say I'm difficult."

Laughing, Lonnie walked away, but her light heart quickly floated down into reality at what was to come. Her joy was bittersweet. By hour's end, she would see Toby. He loved her so very much, and in countless ways, she loved him too. She searched for the words as she walked to the house, praying they would be sufficient. Praying for God's strength, His grace. And most of all, praying for Toby.

Forty-Eight

Gideon held the nail steady. The steel was cold between his stiff fingers, and with two quick blows, he pounded it into the post. "See? That's how you do it."

The sun glinted in warm patches on Jacob's hair, and Gideon tousled the boy's curls. Leaning against a post, Jacob sat with the can of nails between his legs. He pulled out another one.

"Thank you." Gideon pounded it into place, then sank back on his heels. He wiggled the mended post, pleased that it did not sway. "Do you want to help me fix another one?"

Jacob held out a handful of nails.

"I'll take that as a yes." After grabbing the can and his hammer, Gideon used his free arm to hold his son to his chest. They strode to a shaded patch where the sun was yet to melt the last traces of snow. He set Jacob on a flat rock. Kneeling, his arm brushed Jacob's knee, and Gideon shifted the post deeper into the ground. He felt a small hand on his shoulder.

It took only a few minutes to finish the fence. "Now I need to go check on Gael, and I'd love for you to be my helper."

Jacob blinked large green eyes up at him.

"But something tells me that your ma will have wanted you to go down for a nap." He hoisted his son off the rock. "But when you wake up, we'll spend the evening together." He kissed Jacob's cheek, suddenly overwhelmed by all that could transpire.

He thought of Lonnie, speaking to Toby. Almost this very moment. Gideon closed his eyes, content to simply stand and hold his son. Both desperate for this hour to end and desperate to dig deeper into that well that only God could fill. To find peace. No matter what happened.

With slow steps, Lonnie climbed the stairs to the porch of Toby's shanty. She smoothed the collar of her best dress, then pressed a hand to her stomach. The pearl-like buttons grazed her palm, unease flitting about beneath them. It didn't matter what she looked like. It just hadn't felt right coming here in her work dress and stained apron. Not for what she was about to say and all that had passed between them. Fingers tingling, Lonnie knocked. She forced herself to take several slow, steady breaths.

It was no use, for when Toby called her in, she struggled to turn the knob. The hour she'd had to prepare her words suddenly felt inadequate. Lonnie opened the door, just enough to peek inside, and seeing that he was in bed, she hesitated. He wore a shirt, but the top buttons were undone, the cuffs hanging loosely around his thick wrists.

"Dinna worry, lass. Half the ladies from the church have already vis'ted today. Your coming in would hardly be a scandal."

She stepped in and closed the door. "How are you feeling?"

"I think I'll mend." His voice was stronger. He motioned to a chair beside his bed. "I'm glad you're here. You're a sight for sore eyes."

Tucking her skirts beneath her, Lonnie perched on the edge of the hard chair.

Lowering his head, Toby fiddled with a thread in the quilt. His eyes worked back and forth as if the words he searched for were written there. The words she'd rehearsed scattered as fireflies. When his shoulders rose and fell in a sigh, her heart broke afresh.

Toby.

"Yer the only woman to come today without soup or bread in hand." His Scots thickened, and she sensed his distress. "Ye haven't come to fluff me pillow, lass, or tidy up the place." He looked at her. "Ye've come for a verra different reason, haven't ye?"

She took his hand and bent forward. Her lips pressed to his rough, warm skin, and she closed her eyes. Releasing him, she looked up to see that the expression in his handsome face was one of torment.

Lonnie clutched her trembling fingers in her lap. "Are you managing all right?"

"I am." He squared his shoulders, but his eyes were sad.

A warm fire crackled in the hearth, and she slid off her shawl. The wind shifted, bringing with it the smell of smoke from the chimney. Toby rested his hand atop his abdomen. He stared past her for several moments. His Adam's apple bobbed, and Lonnie noticed that his jaw was freshly shaven. Smooth.

He glanced at her. "It's so good to see you."

"It's good to see you too." Her eyes stung.

"Dinna cry, Lonnie."

She realized a tear was sliding down her cheek. She quickly brushed it away.

His eyes roamed her face. Moistening his lips, he reached for her hand. Lonnie let him take it.

"I dinna want you to be sad." His thumb turned a circle on her wrist.

"Let me make this easy on you." He held her hand with such tenderness, another tear slipped, and she quickly wiped it away.

Toby drew in a slow breath. "I'm leaving." He loosened his grip. "I've spoken with Reverend Gardner, and there's a position available at another church. I intend to take it."

"You are?"

"Yes." His face was agonized. "I have to leave, Lonnie." He swallowed. "This isna my place. Not anymore."

She wanted to argue with him, but that would be so unfair. How could she expect him to be here—as her friend and no more?

"I'll miss you terribly."

He struggled to sit up farther, and Lonnie hurried to help him.

"I got it," he said, his voice strained.

When his pillow slid down, she raised it back up. The muscles worked in his back. He let out a quick breath, and she could only guess the kind of pain he was in. "Sit down, Lonnie." Distress hung thick in his voice, his words so intense, she did as he pleaded.

He took a few measured breaths before speaking. "You'll stay where you are, lass."

She nodded, the words slipping to her tongue. "I'm going to miss you."

"And I'll miss you. More than I ought to say. But I know that you will be happy." He looked at her. "This is for the best." Hair damp, he pushed it back. "I can see that you love him, and I'm glad."

Her fingertips brushed his sleeve. "I don't know what to say."

"Then simply say that you love him."

Fists pressed to her knees, she couldn't look away from his face. "I do." She studied all that lived in his eyes—a fire, dying. "And I love you too. I want you to know that. It was very real for me."

A soft smile surfaced. "Then I willna feel too bad." Finally, he glanced around at the walls of his shanty. "God makes all things new." The distance in his voice drew nearer. Bolder. "Even what may seem impossible."

A new tear threatened to fall.

"I should have stepped away long ago. But I was just too selfish to let you go."

No. Her chin trembled. There was nothing selfish about Toby McKee.

His eyes were large and wide as he studied her. Staring back at him, she remembered his face the day he'd knelt near the woodpile, asking for her hand. The joy—mixed with fear—she had seen there.

"Dinna be sad." He covered her hand in his as if they were the best of friends. How she wished some things didn't have to change. But if she truly loved Toby, she would let him go. His voice was urgent. "Jacob has his father. And you…you need Gideon. I know it to be true. I've always known it. I just hoped…" His eyes glistened. "There is a part of me that always hoped I might win your heart. But it was never mine to win."

Oh, Toby.

"So I just prayed." He let out an exhausted laugh, and dimples dented his cheeks, making her heart soar. "I can't tell you how many times my prayers contradicted themselves."

Lonnie searched his face.

"Some days I prayed it would be me. Other times I prayed that Gideon would find what he was looking for. That he would find peace." He glanced at her, mischief in his eyes. "At times, I wanted to pray him right off a cliff."

Tears gave way to laughter and she sniffed.

Toby chuckled and pressed a hand to his side. When he pulled his hand away, his shirt was spotted in red.

"You're bleeding!"

He half smiled. "Dinna worry. It comes and goes."

"And your bandage?"

"Mrs. Krause will be here in a little while to change it. She's been coming by twice a day."

"Is there anything I can do?" Lonnie glanced around and, spotting a basket of bandages, rose. "I can change your bandage."

"No." His voice was so urgent, she froze. "Thank you, but I'd prefer to wait for Mrs. Krause." His eyes on her held desperation. "Please, Lonnie."

He was letting her go. Trying to, at least, as she had been doing with him. A bittersweetness. Lonnie sat back in her chair, determined not to make it any harder.

"I'll mend." Sweat glistened along his temples.

"May I open the window for you?"

Another dimple appeared. "Aye. The window would be perfectly harmless."

She smiled when he did. Across the room, it took her a moment to shimmy the glass up, and when she did, the cool air stirred his shirt. His eyes slid closed, chest rising and falling in a slow sigh.

"Is that helping?"

His throat worked. "Aye. Better. Thank you."

She prayed it would be so. She prayed God would mend him completely. Heal him of all his wounds. With his eyes closed so, she thought perhaps he might drift off. Ever so gently, Lonnie straightened his blankets. She brushed a lock of his damp hair away from his forehead.

"I'm not asleep, Lonnie."

She snapped her hand back, and his face bloomed into a smile. His dark lashes fluttered open, but she could see that he was more tired than he let on. "I should have asked you, how is Gael? I was told Jebediah put her up in the barn. I can't thank you enough."

"Gideon's been taking care of her."

"Gideon?"

She nodded softly. "He's taken real good care of her. He wants you to know he'll bring her by whenever you're ready."

Toby's eyes shifted to the window. "Have him bring her today, if he doesn't mind."

"Are you sure?"

"I'm leaving t'morrow. As long as Gael doesn't mind being pulled behind a wagon."

"Oh, Toby—"

He gave her a look that silenced her.

"You're in pain." It wasn't a question.

"I'll be fine. Really." He waited for her to nod, as if needing to know she believed him. "On all accounts." He motioned for her to sit back down. "God has a plan for your life and for mine. I'm not afraid of what the future holds. I do hate that it doesn't include you. But…it will give me something to work on."

Her chest burned.

Toby's eyes sparkled. "I'll find myself a wife someday."

Lonnie sniffed, tears stinging the back of her throat. "You will."

His dimples deepened. "A woman who has absolutely no idea who Gideon O'Riley is."

Pressing her cheek to her shoulder, Lonnie smiled. A bittersweet joy.

Toby chuckled. "And one who wants a houseful o' kids and makes stovies and Tantallon cakes."

Despite herself, she laughed. "I have no idea what that is."

"See?" Reaching out, his thumb brushed against her chin. "That should have tipped me off from the start." Dark eyes warm, he pulled his hand away.

should have tipped me off from the start." Dark eyes warm, he pulled his hand away.

"Easy, girl." Gideon caught hold of Gael's halter and led her from the barn. Lonnie had come home not an hour ago, asking him to bring Gael around to Toby's house. It was the least he could do. The very least. He'd spent the last hour brushing the mare's coat until it shone, and now she stepped lightly into the sunshine as if eager to see her master.

Gideon clicked his tongue, and with Gael's lead rope in hand, they settled into an easy walk toward Toby's place. The ground underfoot was soft and damp, the trees dark with moisture. The air hung heavy with the scent of the forest after a rain. Gideon loosened his grip on Gael's rope. She would head home whether he led her or not. Some things just happened.

Like the way he'd found his way back to Lonnie. Never had he fully believed that his path—so tangled and thorny—would eventually bring him to her. He didn't deserve God's grace, yet still, he felt it spilling about him like sunshine. Gideon shook his head. He knew he could never repay the depth of this gift, but he was determined to spend the rest of his life showing his thanks.

The trail narrowed, and Gideon brushed against a spruce branch, the needles bright with new growth. Gael plodded along behind him as if this was the only place in the world she wanted to be. Going home. They walked through sun. Shadow. And before Gideon knew it, he was stepping into the small clearing that held Toby's shanty. He wondered if he should make his presence known or see that Gael was put away first. He opted to lead her toward the corral that filled most of the clearing. When she was settled, head bowed to the young grass, Gideon strode up to the shanty.

He knocked gently, then knowing the reverend would be slow moving about, called through the door.

"It's Gideon. I've brought Gael back." He listened. Waiting.

The door opened and Toby stood—not quite as tall as usual. One hand was pressed to his side, and he seemed to favor it.

"You shouldn't be up," Gideon said.

"I've had three different women tell me that today. Don't you start as well."

"Fair enough."

"Come on in." Toby moved to a chair beside the fireplace and slowly lowered himself. His face was a mask, but Gideon could tell he was in pain. Of more than one kind.

Dressed in pants and an unbuttoned shirt, Toby slowly leaned back and kicked one leg out. His entire abdomen was wrapped in rows of white bandages. He looked up at Gideon, a resolve deep in his eyes. Gideon searched for words.

"I vis'ted with Lonnie earlier." He motioned for Gideon to sit at the small table. "I suppose she spoke with you."

Gideon sat. "She did. Said you were leaving tomorrow. I brought Gael." He motioned with his thumb out the door.

"That was good of you. Thank you for looking after her. Thank you for finding her."

Gideon lowered his head in a single nod.

"Would you like some coffee?" Toby stared out the window as he spoke.

"Thank you, no. Can I get you some? Anything?"

"I'm fine, thanks."

They sat without speaking. Hands clasped together, Gideon leaned forward and worked slow circles with his thumbs.

Finally, Toby spoke. "Take care of her?"

"I will." Gideon looked up at him. "I will."

"And Jacob. Addie." His eyes flooded with moisture.

Throat tight, Gideon coughed into his fist. "I will." The words were hard to form, but the promise ran deep. Mighty deep.

Toby nodded slowly, his gaze out the window. A coming sunset warmed the trees on the horizon.

"You're a good man, Gideon."

Gideon knew how dearly the words cost him. He didn't deserve this kindness. Not after all Toby was losing. Not after all Gideon had done to him. "I'm sorry." It was all he could say.

"Me too." Toby pressed a hand to his side and shifted in his seat. A single wince and he masked over the rest. "But that doesn't mean this isna the right thing."

Shifting his feet, Gideon looked at the reverend. "And where will you go?"

Toby spoke without looking at him. "There's a church up in Roanoke that could use my help. I'll head there t'morrow."

"A fresh start?"

"A fresh start." Toby mumbled something about the authorities following a lead…and not wanting to stick around for it. He shifted again. Face twisting for the briefest of moments, he let out a quick sigh. His neck was glistening when he settled. "It's for the best. I'm ready to begin again." Toby's eyes roamed the small room, finally landing on Gideon. "I won't lie. This is going to be the hardest thing I've ever done."

His throat tight, Gideon could only nod. He wanted to say he was sorry again, but the words were so inadequate. If he hadn't come home, Lonnie would no doubt have been Toby's bride by now. A flood of emotions hit him. Glancing through the window, he saw an older woman coming toward the shanty, a basket on her arm.

"Looks like Mrs. Krause is here."

"She's come to help me pack the last of my things. I'll head off in the morning, doctor's orders. He arranged for his son-in-law to drive me."

Gideon stood. "I won't stay in your way." He looked down on Toby. "Roanoke. That's quite a change."

"There's a hospital there that might come in handy." He stared into the fire. "Maybe convalescing won't be so bad after all."

Gideon couldn't help but smile. "Watch out for those nurses. There's one in particular who can be a handful."

Looking back at him, Toby's eyes brightened at the challenge. "I'll be on the lookout."

Mrs. Krause called out.

Gideon slid his hat on and stepped toward the door. "I better be off." Then just as quickly, he moved back to where Toby stood and extended a hand. "Thank you. For more than I can say." They shook hands, their grip nothing like the first time they'd met.

"So you're not going to try and break my hand this time," Toby said.

"Trying to change my ways."

Toby smiled thoughtfully. Mrs. Krause knocked before entering. The sun was sinking. The light dimmed. A quick greeting to the neighbor woman, and Gideon stepped back. Expanding his chest, Toby lifted a hand in farewell.

Gideon backed away and, turning, strode from the shanty. From the clearing.

From one of the few real friends he'd ever had.

Toward the only home he ever wanted. He tried to focus on the path ahead of him. And prayed he'd always remember the path that had led him here.

Forty-Nine

T his one is red." Lonnie pointed to the checker on the far side of the board, and Jacob touched it with his small finger. "And this one," she said, pointing to another, "is black. No, don't put it in your mouth." She took the piece from him and set it back down. "You don't have to taste *everything.*"

The back door closed, and wood clanged into the box in the kitchen. Elsie poked her head into the parlor. "Good morning."

"Good morning." Lonnie rose to her knees, dumping a clattering pile of checkers from her skirt. "Have you seen Gideon? He never came in last night."

Elsie moved to the window and tied the curtains back. "He left early this morning." She swiped at a cobweb.

Lonnie's heart lurched. "Left?"

Amusement warmed the older woman's round face. "Sap's done running. He went to gather the buckets. He said he'd be home in time for dinner."

Her feet as restless as her heart, Lonnie glanced out the window. She felt Elsie watching her.

"Did you need him for something?"

"Very much so."

Elsie's face brightened. "He's in the maple grove."

Lonnie's heart skittered. She glanced back at the children, knowing the mess they'd made in the parlor would take a while to tidy. And dinner ought to be started soon.

"Go." Elsie waved at her. "I will watch them."

Dropping to her knees, Lonnie picked up a handful of wooden pieces, stacking them as quickly as she could. "Are you sure?"

The older woman laughed and pointed toward the kitchen. "Go!"

"Thank you!" Lonnie tossed the checkers on the sofa and planted a kiss on Elsie's round cheek as she scurried by. She snatched her coat from its peg even as she flung the door open. "I'll be back," she called over her shoulder.

Elsie's delight rang clear in her laughter. Lonnie slammed the door behind her and thundered down the steps, running toward the woods. To the spot where the maples grew. Her heart near to bursting.

Gideon stepped closer to the maple tree and set the iron pry bar in place. The notched end of the curved metal rod fit right on top of the spile, and with a flex of his arms, he popped the spile free. It fell to the ground, and Gideon tossed it in a bucket with a dozen others and moved to the next. A few dozen more to go.

"I don't want to startle you," a sweet voice said.

The corner of his mouth lifted, and he turned to see Lonnie step closer. He let his gaze wander the length of her. "Couldn't startle a blind man."

"Are you saying I walk...loud?"

She drew closer, and Gideon peered down into a pair of chestnut-colored eyes. "I'm saying I could hear you from a mile away."

Her mouth twisted to the side, and he knew she was trying to fight a smile. How he wished she wouldn't. He loved nothing more than to make her smile.

"I've been looking for you."

His heart was so full he could hardly get the words out. "And you found me."

She stood mighty close. "Do you need any help?"

He glanced around at his tools, suddenly a jumble of nerves. "If you'd like." He handed her a bucket of spiles. "You can follow me."

Stepping up to another tree, he carefully loosened the spile. "You're wearing my coat again." He moistened his lips, hoping he sounded smoother than he felt. "You do that a lot."

With the bucket in front of her feet, Lonnie slid her fingers inside the worn pockets. "I'm sort of attached to this one."

"It suits you." His heart raced. Their fingers touched when he handed her the spile. His nerves colliding into one another, all he could do was move on to the next tree. He heard her follow. Swallowing hard, he searched for what he yearned to say.

Bucket in hand, she watched as he freed another metal spout. It took all his strength to keep from looking directly at her. With her fingertips, she smoothed a strand of hair away from her cheek. His coat stretched taut as he bent to lean the pry bar against the tree. "Lonnie..." His voice was so weak, he winced. *Come on, man.*

Rising inside him was all that had passed between them—the moment she became his wife. And made him a papa. Gave him her heart. Just as he was realizing how his own had been slipping away piece by piece, growing more whole on the other side.

The tip of her braid brushed the ground beside his boot when she bent to lift the bucket of metal spouts. Crouching, Gideon caught hold of the bucket handle, pinning it to the ground. Lonnie straightened. He slammed his eyes shut, doing everything he could to muster his courage. Finally, he stood. He opened his eyes and found himself looking down on her bowed head. He touched her chin, lifting her face.

"Why didn't you tell me what happened yesterday?" he asked.

"I didn't have a chance," she said softly. "You were gone."

He pulled his hand back. "And now?" His heart galloped.

"Now?"

"What would you tell me now?" He watched her worry a thread between her fingers. As if of their own accord, his hands slid to the sides of her face. "Lonnie, what would you tell me now?"

"I'd say you're an incredibly patient man, Gideon O'Riley."

He let out a low chuckle. "I've been called many things in my life. 'Patient' was never one of them."

"Then I'd say it's time."

He kissed her hair as softly as he could manage.

She tilted her head back and peered up at him. Her face full of joy.

He leaned closer and kissed the tip of her freckled nose, his tools forgotten at his feet. "I love you."

She rose to her tiptoes and laced a hand behind his neck.

He searched her face, waiting, fighting back a battle he was certain that showed. If not for the way her eyes drank from his face, then for the way her smile formed as she took in his expression. She sank back down, the curve in her mouth slipping away just as quick. Fear bolted through him. His heart wrestled with what he saw in her eyes—a hundred emotions and words he couldn't begin to pin down. Heart hammering, he searched for something more to say, but nothing came. Too much filled him, and he had no words for what lived in the span of his chest.

Then she leaned her forehead against that very space, so softly, without warning, that he drew in a rough breath. Her hands slid to his shoulders. Holding, clinging. As if to never let go. Was she crying?

Stupid man, he couldn't move. Couldn't think. Nothing beyond her name, which he finally spoke.

"And I love you," she whispered.

Jarring the breath from him. She looked up, her eyes so moist two tears slipped and fell when she blinked. He ran his thumbs gently over their trails, once. And then again. Her smile returning, she turned her cheek into his palm and closed her eyes. Stepping back, legs shaking, more nervous than he'd ever been in his life, he lowered himself to one knee. Her eyes widened. His heart beat so loud he was certain she would hear. Taking her hands in his, he marveled at the sensation and sent a plea heavenward that this was what his future held.

"Lonnie Sawyer..." His heart was in his throat.

She tilted her head to the side, eyes glossy.

"Will you do me the honor of becoming my wife?"

Another tear slid down her cheek.

Gideon forced himself to breathe. And then again. And again. Finally, Lonnie nodded, her face a sunrise.

He kissed both of her hands. "So that's a yes?" Without releasing her, he rose.

She nodded again. "Yes." Her face tilted toward his in sweet invitation.

Suddenly, something struck him. A fear. An awareness of how brokenly human he still was. Holding the sides of her face, he ran a thumb over her lips. "I want to kiss you, Lonnie." Gideon gulped, suddenly realizing how alone they were. Her smile softened, making the battle he fought that much harder. "But I..." His throat worked to swallow. The last time he'd kissed her had been in front of the Bennetts' house. Making a mess of things. But now... "It's just you and me...here. Alone. And if you knew how much I love you...how much I..." The words weren't coming. Pulling her closer, he kissed her hair. "May I kiss you Lonnie, as my wife?"

Her chin trembled.

He needed witnesses. A whole heap of them, for his yearning for her had only deepened with time. "I fear I oughtn't do it any other way." The admission humbled him. He prayed she wouldn't think less of him. Releasing her, he forced his feet back. "You deserve nothing less, and I want to give you the best I can, and I wish I'd done it sooner."

Though she was still crying, joy flooded her face.

"Will you walk with me, Lonnie? To find a preacher?" He knew mischief crept into his expression when she choked out a little laugh.

Sniffing, she wiped her cheeks with her apron, then reached for his hand, pulling herself close, wrapping her other hand around her arm as if she meant to never let go. At her nudge, they took the first steps from the maple grove. Walking through the speckled light, Gideon looked down, unable to tell where he ended and she began.

With Jacob pressed to his chest and Lonnie's hand wrapped securely in his, Gideon led the way to Reverend Gardner's house, determined to knock the door down if necessary. They'd delivered the news to the Bennetts, and even as Jebediah slapped him on the back, Elsie pulled her apron over her face and sobbed. Addie had jumped up and down, giggling. Jacob let out a joyful squeal, though Gideon knew he had no idea what was going on.

Now, as they walked to Reverend Gardner's house, a midday sun shone bright all around them. The air fragrant with spring blossoms. The walk took most of the morning, but not once did Lonnie's hand slide from his. And by the time Jacob fell asleep—the boy's soft cheek pressed to Gideon's shoulder—the reverend's house came into view.

Lonnie rapped on the door with a gentle hand, and after flashing his wife-to-be a grin, Gideon pounded on the wood, nearly shaking it from the frame.

She blushed at his eagerness.

"Coming!" An irritated voice called from inside.

The door burst open. The reverend's eyebrows lifted, and with short, stubby fingers, he pulled the napkin from his shirt and brushed crumbs from his pants.

"I hope we're not interrupting," Lonnie began.

"I was just finishing up my dinner." Reverend Gardner glanced from one face to the other, finally landing back on Gideon. "May I help you?" He wiped his mouth with his napkin.

"We'd like to get married," Gideon said, squeezing Lonnie's hand.

"Married?" The reverend nearly choked.

Gideon let out a slow breath, his nerves a mess. "I know what you're thinking, sir." He held up a hand. "But believe me when I say I am a free man to be married." He took the envelope from his pocket and handed it over. "And as far as I know"—he glanced down at Lonnie, who smiled up at him—"as crazy as it seems, this lady here *will* have me."

Taking the envelope, Reverend Gardner began to open it. Jebediah stepped forward, and Gideon felt a reassuring hand squeeze his shoulder.

"He's free to marry. I am witness to that."

"So am I," Elsie added.

Grateful, Gideon glanced at them. His family.

Even as he shook his head, Reverend Gardner's eyes skimmed the words. Then with a nod of approval, he ushered them into his house, motioning toward the sitting room. "In there."

The fire crackled in the hearth. A white cat lifted its head as the parade of intruders passed by the sofa, and stretching out its paws, the bundle of fur rolled onto her back as if the guests had nothing better to do than rub her belly.

"Your dinner's getting cold, dear." A gray-haired woman stepped out of the kitchen, and then her face filled with surprise.

"Maura, these folks have come to be married." The reverend tossed his napkin onto the mantel and made quick work of straightening his collar. "Will you please draw up the license?" He cast Gideon a curious glance. "You're certain you have no other wives?"

With a chuckle, Gideon lifted his hands, palms up. "I promise."

After a moment of silent study, Reverend Gardner shook his head. "I believe you." He set Judge Monroe's letter on the mantel, then glanced at Lonnie and back to Gideon. Despite his sober demeanor, he nearly smiled. "I've never married the same people twice before."

Gideon took hold of Lonnie's hand, not liking the way his felt without it.

The reverend motioned for them to stand in front of the fireplace, and after his wife brought him a large Bible, he turned to face his unexpected guests. He cleared his throat and began with the words he'd spoken to Lonnie and Gideon on that cold morning they'd stood inside his church, her hand trembling inside his.

Gideon stood as close to Lonnie as he could, glancing away only long enough to peek at Jacob, who rested in Elsie's arms. His small cheek was pressed to the woman's shoulder. Black lashes brushed his pale skin in slumber. Gideon glanced back at Lonnie, who watched him with a curious expression.

After closing his Bible, Reverend Gardner clutched it in one hand. "Do you have a ring?"

Gideon grimaced. He had nothing to offer her. Slowly he shook his head.

All was silent except for a clatter coming from Reverend Gardener's kitchen. Lonnie pulled a folded handkerchief from inside her sleeve. "I do." She carefully unwrapped the bundle and held the offering out to Gideon.

Gideon took the ring between his broad fingers, studying it. His face was pained, and Lonnie could almost hear the breaking of his heart.

"What's the matter?" She touched his sleeve.

"This isn't a good ring." His eyebrows pulled together, and she knew his memories had drifted to a time when he was a different man. "This... I..." He shook his head again.

Lonnie took hold of his hand, closing his fingers around the tin he'd offered her all that time ago in Rocky Knob, the day she'd vowed to become the wife of a man she hardly knew. "It's a perfect ring. I would never want another."

Gideon's chest heaved, and Lonnie's thumb grazed his skin.

"Do you believe me?"

Glancing up, his eyes glistened with unshed tears. "You're a better woman than I deserve."

She shook her head and held out her hand.

With determination brightening his eyes, Gideon slid the cold tin to the tip of her finger. "Are you sure?" he breathed.

Lonnie nodded. She'd never been more certain of anything in her life, and when Gideon slid the ring onto her finger, the tin warming between their hands, the last pieces of her broken heart pulled together.

"I now pronounce you husband and wife. You may—" Reverend Gardner arched an eyebrow and bent toward the kitchen entryway. "For heaven's sake, wife. What is that knocking about in there?"

Mrs. Gardner poked her head out of the kitchen, bowl in the crook of her arm, whisk working in quick motion. "I'm beating egg whites to a *froth* like the recipe says." Her cheeks reddened. "Can't have a wedding without a cake."

Reverend Gardner chuckled. "And we can't have a ceremony without a 'kiss yer bride.' "

"Yes, dear." Her whisk stilled and she stood at attention.

From the corner of the room, Addie giggled.

With a shake of his head, Reverend Gardner grinned and turned back to Gideon. "Mr. O'Riley"—his eyes sparkled—"you may now kiss your bride."

AUTHOR'S NOTE

There was a time near the completion of this book that as a storyteller—and more simply as a person—it was beyond my ability to put the words on paper. I had been trying to walk outside the storm. Skirting around the heart-aching places this book would take me. That was when I knew it was time to simply trust God to see me through to the other side. For in our weakness, He is strong. And I felt ever so weak. So I opened my hands and let go of everything I had thought this story would be.

I searched my heart. Every piece of it. Felt along the scars from life and loss, the healing remnants. It was there I allowed myself to tell a journey of the mire sin can pull us into, and the healing that can be found in His will. In those days and hours, I finished *My Hope Is Found.*

My constant prayer is that these stories will bless and encourage you. I pray that they will point to the Cross—the redemptive love of Christ. The One who died for our sins. Though we were so, so undeserving of that kind of sacrifice. The ultimate act of love.

There is no love story sweeter than that of Christ and His church. It's a dance—a pursuit. I think this is why I write romance. It's a beautiful reflection of that ultimate love. The never-ending story of a hero, holding out his hand to the one he loves. A story of sacrifice. And in the Cadence of Grace series, a story of how a sinner can change, and hope can be found.

Gideon's journey back to Lonnie took some twists and turns that led me to the city of Stuart. The courthouse, completed in the early 1800s, was the hub for legal happenings in Patrick County, Virginia, in 1902. John and Sallie Moore were a prominent family in Stuart at the time, with John Moore serving as judge of the county court for a number of years. In wanting to respectfully honor Judge Moore and his family, I created the fictional character of Judge Monroe. *The History of Patrick County* states that upon his retirement, Judge Moore engaged in orcharding.

One of the greatest joys of being an author is connecting with readers. I am so thankful to all of you who have been a part of the Cadence of Grace series. The way you've embraced Lonnie and Gideon's story blesses me to no end. If you'd like to keep in touch, you can find me at www .joannebischof.com. While there, if you would like to drop me a note, please do! It's always such a joy to hear from you.

READERS GUIDE

1. What does the title *My Hope is Found* signify to you? In what way does the theme of hope run through the story?

2. As Lonnie strives to move on from Gideon, what strengths do you see in her? After all she's been through with her father, and then with Gideon, what do you think she yearns for? If you could encourage her early on in the story, what would you say?

3. Cassie's decision to let Gideon go is a difficult one. Do you think peace may be on the horizon for her? Will her time with Gideon play a role in how she lives out the rest of her life? If so, in what ways?

4. Twice, Tal welcomes Gideon into his home and onto his farm. Each time, Gideon has been in a place of wandering and searching. Why do you think Tal treats Gideon with this kindness? How does the man and his family affect Gideon's life?

5. One of Toby's great strengths is his ability to love through difficult circumstances. This is both a gift and a burden for him. It allows Toby to minister to people but also brings him heartache as he lives out the sacrifices of Christlike love. What role does Toby's selflessness play in Lonnie's spiritual journey? What role does it play in Gideon's? How would the story have been different without this element?

6. Knowing that he may not always be in Lonnie and Jacob's lives, Gideon desires to leave them something of worth—the orchard. What does this symbolize about his love for them? In what ways has this love changed and grown since we first saw Gideon in *Be Still My Soul*?

7. When Lonnie learns that there are rumors surrounding her and the children who have no present father, she is hurt but manages to

turn the other cheek and recognize the gossip for what it is—empty words. In 1902 Appalachia, what could this mean for her future or her place in society? Do you think the rumors hurt Lonnie more than she let on?

8. Gideon looks to Toby as an example of a godly man, something he feels he can never become. At the same time, Toby looks to Gideon as a capable man for carving out a life in the Appalachian hills. Each man sees himself differently than his rival does. What does this say about them? Is this a tendency we humans have?

9. Near the end of the story, Jebediah tells Gideon that he needs to learn to entrust Lonnie to God. In what ways does this conflict with Gideon's personality? What steps does he take toward trusting God with the outcome? At what time in your life have you had to rely on the Lord in this way?

10. Toby is willing to risk his heart for Lonnie's love. What does this cost him in the end? Why is Toby willing to put his heart on the line? Lonnie learns to care for Toby in a way she never anticipated. As his friend, what does it cost her to break Toby's heart?

11. In chapter 38, Gideon realizes that "he knew what it was to be addicted. Knew how to hold on to something with everything inside him." He fears that his love for Lonnie—this deep need for her—is no different than his other desires in the past. In what ways is he correct? In what ways is his love for Lonnie very different?

12. Lonnie's life has always paralleled the hymn "His Eye Is on the Sparrow." How have you seen this reflected in her journey?

13. The theme for *My Hope is Found* is "My brethren, count it all joy when you fall into various trials, knowing that the testing of your faith produces patience" (James 1: 2–3). In what ways did you see this verse unfold?

ACKNOWLEDGMENTS

"Thanks" never seems enough to the team at WaterBrook Multnomah for all you do. You've given these stories wings and have been there for each step of this amazing process. I will be forever grateful. A very special thank-you to my editor, Shannon Marchese, for knowing that somewhere inside of me is always the *deeper* story. You know just how to ask for it. Thank you.

Three years ago I sent MacGregor Literary a note and wondered if it would get an answer. Thank you, Sandra Bishop, for being that answer and for seeing something in this series worth trying for.

To my parents, for a life of love, for being baby-sitters extraordinaire, and for always providing chocolate whenever the going got tough. I'm so thankful for you. And to sweet friends who make this journey not a lonely one, thank you for the hugs and the smiles and the happy tears.

A special thanks to the Patrick County Historical Society for providing invaluable knowledge on the cities of Stuart, Fancy Gap, and Rocky Knob. Also to Pat Ross and William Luebke for going the extra mile in answering my questions.

To my little family: You make life happy and messy and perfect. I adore you.

And to the God who makes all things new: Thank You for filling my heart so that I can find the words. May each one sift through Your fingers so that each story will be for Your glory.

About the Author

Christy Award finalist and author of *Be Still My Soul* and *Though My Heart Is Torn*, Joanne Bischof lives in the mountains of Southern California with her first sweetheart and their homeschooled children. When she's not weaving Appalachian romance, she's blogging about faith, writing, and the adventures of country living that bring her stories to life.